We were being invaded and it was impossible.

I know it happens all the time on Earth. We studied history and I've read and watched movies about invasions and wars and countries fighting each other. Dad was in the military, before he got his degree and came to the Moon. He said there was hardly ever a time when some place on Earth wasn't at war with some other place.

But we were on the Moon. There were only twenty adults and five of us kids, The adults were all scientists, and none of them military.

Mom said it was a chance at a new beginning, a clean break with the old Earth rivalries. That with infinite space there would be less war.

My first hint that something was wrong came when I was exercising in the centrifuge room. Okay, it wasn't a room exactly. The entire place we live in is a vast cavern, a tube really, created by lava flow. We had the type of centrifuges where you lay on your back and are centrifuged to get your muscles used to Earth gravity. I—Robert Anson MacDonald—was the first baby born on the Moon, so I was used to being spun to simulate higher gravity.

In the centrifuge, I used to go into my head and design space ships. In six months, I was going to go to Earth to study aerospace engineering. I'd gone through most of what I could learn long-distance. So, I was lying there and designing a space ship. Which I think is why I was the only one to hear the shots.

The first one sounded odd, and I thought it was just some lab equipment malfunctioning.

Then there was another one, and this time I was sure it was a shot.

—Sarah A. Hoyt and Jeff Greason
"Home Front"

BAEN BOOKS EDITED BY HANK DAVIS

The Human Edge by Gordon R. Dickson
The Best of Gordon R. Dickson
We the Underpeople by Cordwainer Smith
When the People Fell by Cordwainer Smith

The Technic Civilization Saga
The Van Rijn Method by Poul Anderson
David Falkayn: Star Trader by Poul Anderson
Rise of the Terran Empire by Poul Anderson
Young Flandry by Poul Anderson
Captain Flandry: Defender of the Terran Empire
by Poul Anderson
Sir Dominic Flandry: The Last Knight of Terra
by Poul Anderson
Flandry's Legacy by Poul Anderson

The Best of the Bolos: Their Finest Hour
Created by Keith Laumer

A Cosmic Christmas
A Cosmic Christmas 2 You
In Space No One Can Hear You Scream
The Baen Big Book of Monsters
As Time Goes By
Future Wars . . . and Other Punchlines
Worst Contact
Things from Outer Space
If This Goes Wrong . . .
Space Pioneers with Christopher Ruocchio
Overruled! with Christopher Ruocchio (forthcoming)
Time Troopers
with Christopher Ruocchio (forthcoming)

To purchase these and all Baen Book titles in e-book format,
please go to www.baen.com

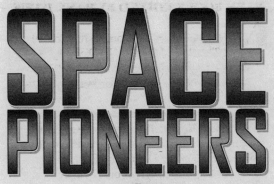

SPACE PIONEERS

edited by
HANK DAVIS
and
CHRISTOPHER RUOCCHIO

BAEN

SPACE PIONEERS

A Baen Books Original

Baen Publishing Enterprises
P.O. Box 1403
Riverdale, NY 10471
www.baen.com

ISBN 13: 978-1-4814-8360-5

Cover art by Bob Eggleton

First Baen printing, November 2018

Distributed by Simon & Schuster
1230 Avenue of the Americas
New York, NY 10020

Printed in the United States of America

10 9 8 7 6 5 4 3 2 1

CONTENTS

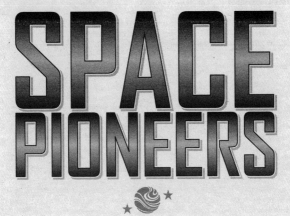

WILL THE SPACE OCEAN HAVE GEMS?

by Hank Davis

LET'S GET COLUMBUS out of the way first. But don't worry, he'll be back for a curtain call.

Two things: first, Columbus did not decide, against the prevailing thinking of his day, that the Earth was round and go off in three little ships to find a new route to Asia. (Speaking of which, is there still anyone who thinks that Columbus set off to discover America, or even a new land? In the seventh grade, I actually had a social studies teacher write that on the blackboard and had to correct her–but then she was fresh out of college, this was her first teaching job, and she realized I was right and took it well [in spite of my being a snotty little brat back then], which was a relief since she was certainly the prettiest teacher in the school at the time. Ah, puberty.)

In fact, the Greeks, as usual, were there first. At least as early as the sixth century, B.C., the spherical shape of the world had supporters, and the notion was considered proven fact by the third century, B.C. Plato and his star pupil Aristotle considered the spherical world in the "well, of course" category. (However they were quite sure that the Earth was the center of the "universe" and the Moon, planets, and "fixed" stars all revolved around it. Can't win 'em all. . . .)

The second thing about Columbus is that he was very, very lucky that he was ever heard from again. Like most people back then, he was sure the world was round, but he had somehow gotten a prepostrous figure for its circumference, thinking it was far smaller than was the reality, and if there hadn't been a continent unknown to Europeans, between him and Asia, he would never have reached land before his supplies of food and drinking water were exhausted. Keep that in mind the next time you hear someone complaining about America being named after Amerigo Vespucci when it should have been named Columbia instead. (Nevertheless, it certainly is the gem of the ocean.) Vespucci concluded, correctly, that the land he had reached was a new, unknown continent while Columbus continued to insist that he had reached Asia. And unlike Columbus, Vespucci was working from a far superior figure for the circumference of the world that was only fifty miles off. Finally, Vespucci did reach the Americas, as they would later be named, while Columbus, on his first trip, only reached the Bahamas. Sorry, Chris baby, but you *were* a dope, as someone once put it in a different context.

Of course, I haven't noticed a national holiday named Vespucci Day . . .

Okay, the long-suffering reader may say, so an explorer's

life (or pioneer's life—I'll be using the terms somewhat interchangeably, so sue me!) is not always a success story, and as space exploration of the Solar System continues, hopefully not always by robot probes, and reaches beyond (keeping in mind that the Solar System is a *lot* bigger and more complicated than we used to think), maybe history, or a garbled version thereof, may be unfair to real achievers. Got it—but can we get on to *space* pioneers now?

Well, one more point: before you can go somewhere, you have to know that there's somewhere to go.

So far, I have referred to "the world," but haven't called it a planet. That's because the word *planet* comes from a Greek word (yes, we're back to the Greeks; s'matter, you got something against gyro sandwiches?) for "wanderer," and Mercury, Venus, Mars, Jupiter, Saturn— the planets visible to the naked eye—were called that because they *moved*, unlike the "fixed" stars which slowly moved in a mass across the sky with the seasons, but did not change location in the sky with respect to each other. They, the planets, all five of them that the Greeks could see, *did* change location. Some of those wanderers would even come to a halt in the sky, then go backwards from their previous motion. This is easily explained if you know that the Earth is itself a planet/wanderer, going around the sun with the rest of the planets, in the same direction but at different speeds, and the Earth, like a faster race horse, overtakes the slower outer planets so that an observer will think they slow down, then go into reverse gear. With the exception of Aristarchus (and maybe a few now-forgotten disciples of his), who argued that the Earth went around the sun, the Greeks bet on all the "fixed" stars being attached to a gigantic crystal sphere around the (spherical but stationary) Earth, while each planet was on a different, separate crystal sphere, each rotating differently from the others and, yes, sometimes stopping, then reversing course.

Since the Greeks came up with this idea, they were doomed to never come up with a pulp like *Planet Stories*, pardon me, *Wanderer Stories*. Win some, lose some. How can you travel to the Moon if it's attached to a crystal sphere, let alone take a trip to the planets, which must be even farther away because they sometimes are seen to go behind the Moon, and so their crystal spheres must be outside of the Moon's sphere. Besides, the opinion seems to have been divided on whether those lights in the sky are named after gods, or actually *are* gods. If a Pegasus knock-off were available, maybe he could be ridden to the moon (they had no idea that the space above the Earh was not filled with air), but remember what happened when Bellerophon (not to be confused with a wrecked starship in *Forbidden Planet*) tried to drop in on Mt. Olympus and say, "Hey, Zeus, baby, what's shakin'?" Those gods can be touchy about trespassers on their home turf, and the heavens might be a worse test case than was buzzing Olympus.

Do I hear objections? (I don't, of course, but it's a useful rhetorical fiction.) Why all this ancient history, and, even worse, ancient mythology? The Greek gods never existed, and we can reach the planets and even the stars using time dilation at relativistic speeds, or generation ships, if nothing better is available.

Maybe . . . but, on the other hand, are you *certain*

there are no gods, or at least godlike beings out there? If Sir Arthur C. Clarke's famous quip that "any sufficiently advanced technology is indistinguishable from magic" is true, then won't any sufficiently advanced extraterrestrials be indistinguishable from gods? Suppose they're touchy about the savages (or worse, the monkeys, or even mice) dropping in on them uninvited.

As for that technology . . . if the speed of light is indeed an absolute limit, with no way to dodge or detour around it, traveling close to that speed to take advantage of time dilation might still be unworkable. Back in the sixties, a card-carrying scientist wrote an essay in a book on interstellar communication, which he thought demonstrated that the propulsion required to travel close to lightspeed required technology that was not only beyond anything we might build, ever, it was impossible by the mathematics of the thing. The essay was quoted at length in a review in *Scientific American* of the book it appeared in. The magazine's reviewer cited the article with an unholy glee, writing that "this will send the idea of the starship back to the cereal box, where it belongs." (And this was back when *Scientific Amerikan*, pardon me, *American*, was worth reading, a situation that ended several years ago!) Other writers with comparable credentials have attacked the premises and reasoning of that article, but even so, we can't assume that time dilation will give us the stars.

And there have been arguments why a generation ship of less than planetoid size would soon become unlivable, aside from the gene pool of the crew being too small to prevent genetic deterioration; and if the ship *were* planetoid size, the reaction mass to propel it would be beyond anything we can imagine.

In other words, we don't have a Pegasus to fly us up to the crystal spheres, and suppose the planet or star or the Moon is on the other side of that crystal sphere. And what if it's some sort of magic fire (cue Wagner; I don't care if it's anachronistic) and there's nothing to land on. And suppose the aliens, I mean the gods, don't want you there?

Columbus (I *told* you he'd be back) didn't know there was a continent in his way to Asia, and also operated with a conception of the size of the Earth that was way off. How do you know we aren't way off now?

We've known about the speed of light and relativistic effects for barely more than a century. Do we know the whole story? What do you mean the Earth goes around the Sun? Next, you'll be saying the Earth is flat and we're way beyond that old nonsense now!

Suppose I concede that we can never reach the stars, except maybe by a robot probe that will still be working somehow centuries after it was sent out at a pathetically sublight velocity. Supposed I concede that, as some spoilsports have argued, all stories about starflight are fantasy masquerading as science fiction?

Even if it's true. Fantasy is fun ("Hey, Conan, get your broadsword and run outside and chase off that dragon before he takes a bite out of the starship's hyperdrive unit.") In fact, I don't concede anything of the kind, but so what? Stories of apace exploration and pioneering are jolly good fun, and even if we're limited to starships of the mind, I say, keep 'em coming, and with the fascinatingly strange aliens be handy.

While we're waiting and hoping for real starships, there's a bunch of terrific stories right here, following this introduction. Not all are set in interstellar space and some even tell how the space age began—in a way that didn't happen. But that doesn't matter because they're still good stories.

Back in the 1950s, Gnome Press issued a series of sf anthologies, each of which purported to give a loose future history, in spite of the stories all having been written independently by different writers. It didn't always work, but in any case, that's not what I'm trying to do in *Space Pioneers*. This theme is deep in the very heart of science fiction, from Jules Verne and Cyrano de Bergerac to whatever *Star Trek* spinoff is on the telly this week, and I could easily have assembled another collection of as many good stories. (Buy this book, helping it to sell out, and maybe Baen will let me do just that. And I promise not to give you another history lesson.)

And while we're riding in our paper starships, maybe some new breakthrough in physics, or mathematics. or even sewing machines (read Fredric Brown's *What Mad Universe* and you'll get it) will mean that we can go to the stars after all. We can take along a stack of recent issues of *Scientific American* for ballast. Or maybe give them to aliens we meet, though that might start the first interstellar war. But consider Magellan, who was killed by unfriendly natives while attempting to circumnavigate the globe, and though the voyage was finished (successfully) by his second in command, he's still famous (can you name his second in command?), and has the Straits of

THIRD STAGE

by Poul Anderson

This tale of men and their machines challenging the space frontier, by one of the very best SF writers of the 20th Century, amazingly (and it did appear in the February, 1962 Amazing Stories) has, until now, never been reprinted in an anthology or collection, as far as I have been able to determine, (it did reappear in an offshoot magazine of Amazing, *but that impermanent curtain call was over four decades ago) and it's a pleasure to bring it back to entertain new readers three generations later. But did I say* entertain? *Of course, it does that . . . but watch out for the gut-punch of an ending. . . .*

NOT LONG AFTER SUNSET, a storm far out to sea veered in a direction the Weather Bureau computers had called improbable. By midnight there was rain over Cape Canaveral and Buckler, roused from his bed, said the shot

11

would likely have to be postponed. But the rain soon slacked off and technical crews beneath the arc lights could find no harm done their bird. At dawn there was only an overcast sky, beneath which a muggy breeze came sighing through the gantries and across the field. The final decision, whether to abort or go ahead, was left to the men who must actually ride the rocket. "Why on earth shouldn't we take her?" Swanberg shrugged. "Or off earth, for that matter." Holt nodded, a quick jerky movement: "Yeah, think a fifty million women who might have to watch Enis Preston today, if we aren't on the TV."

When Swanberg noticed a passing thought, he seldom let it go in a hurry. He was a large, squinting, tow-headed man with a friendly slow voice. As they left the briefing room and started toward the rocket, he went back to Holt's remark. "Do you really think this flight is such a big production, Jim?"

"Sure." His companion made a wide gesture at buildings, machines, and bare concrete. "Didn't you know? We're clean-limbed American boys bound forth to Ride Out the Lethal Space Storms."

"But, uh, it isn't that interesting. Just a routine orbital flight. Not as if we were the first men around the moon, or even the first Americans—"

"But we are the first men of any stripe, chum, to head into the Van Allen belt and stay a while. Haven't you watched TV-*Time?* Don't you know how far the new radiation screen puts us ahead of those Russian nogoodniks?" Holt shifted his helmet to the other arm. "No, I guess you're uninformed, Bill. All you ever did was help develop the gadget. Probably spent your spare time with a book or some such anachronism. Downright subversive, I calls you."

Swanberg chuckled. He didn't like rapid-fire New York accents; the taut, status-scrabbling, publicity-wise types who infested the space project got on his nerves; but he made an exception for Holt. "Really, though," he said, "I don't get the reason for the ballyhoo. This hop is nothing but the last test of a long series. If the news services want something significant to report, why don't they do a piece on . . . oh, the ion feedback work, or—"

Holt spat. "You misunderstand, Bill. You think the news programs are to enlighten the people. Actually, they're to sell cigarets."

"Bitter today, aren't you?"

"Me? Christ, no. What have I got to be bitter about? A laugh a minute, every time I lift up mine eyes unto the hills, whence cometh the video transmission. You're the soured old gaffer, not me."

"Could be." Swanberg sighed. He made no secret of wanting to go back to Idaho, where he spent every vacation as it was, tramping the mountains and the forests. But how do you get a job remotely comparable—in interest and importance; to hell with pay—that far from anyplace? When he looked at the rocket where it stood waiting, tower high, iceberg massive, but with speed and grace, *upwardness*, built into every flowing line, he forgot climate and office politics and his dreary little tract house and the desperate gaiety of Laura's farewell. There was only the bird, about to fly.

★ ★ ★

Holt, brisk even in the blue spacesuit, reached the pad first. He gave his helmet to one of the technicians, who slipped it over his head and made it fast. All the techs were enlisted men this morning. Swanberg noticed. Though civilians like Holt and himself had been infiltrating the project in ever greater numbers since the organizational shakeup of '63, the Pentagon was fighting a valiant rearguard action. At that, he'd rather have generals breathing down his neck than the reporters who'd invaded his privacy during the past few days. Swanberg was by nature an obliging soul, but after while he began to resent being told what pose to assume on his own patio. . . . The helmet went on him too. He stared through clear polydene at a last-minute bustle which had become muffled and vague in his ears.

"How's that, sir?" asked a voice in the 'phone. "Comfortable?"

"Fine." Swanberg went almost absent-mindedly through the check routines. Not until he was rising in the cage with Holt, seeing the rocket's clifflike immensity slide past him, monster first stage, lanceolate second stage, and the capsule in the nose which would carry him around the world and through the radiation zone and back, not until then did he fully realize that the talking and planning and trying and failing and starting over again were likewise past, that today he personally was going up.

He'd done so before, of course, nowhere near as often as Holt, the test pilot, but several times, in connection with trying out some electronic development in which he had had a part. Not even a night along the upper Kootenai was as beautiful as the night above this gray heaven. He had envied the *voyageurs* who first saw the loneliness of the high West, until he became one of today's *voyageurs*—if only his journeys could be oftener! He pulled his mind back to practicalities, squeezed through the capsule airlock after Holt and strapped himself into his adjoining seat. Though the Aeolus three-stager was by now the most reliable workhorse in the whole American space program, there would be a dull couple of hours to go through, checking and testing, before blastoff.

He threw a glance at Holt. The pilot's dark sharp features were misted. Sweat? Swanberg felt a slight shock. When he listened closely, he detected a note of shrillness in Holt's responses on the intercom. But Holt couldn't be scared; he wouldn't do this, time after time after time, if he was scared; why, merely thinking of his responsibilities, his own wife and kids, would—high-strung, that was it. Of course. Swanberg tried to relax and concentrate on his own job.

"Stage Two dropped on schedule. A-OK," said the voice from above. There was no need; telemetered instruments had registered the fact clearly enough in the control blockhouse. But Tom Zellman was glad of the words. They were a much-needed dramatic touch. Blastoff had been great, as always, vapor clouds and immense boneshaking roar and sudden, accelerating climb of the giant. But since then there had been little to see down here. He had had his cameramen pan in on the faces of the ground crew—visible through a thick glass panel between their work space and the TV booth—until he felt his audience was sick of it. His roving reporters elsewhere on the base had gotten nothing interesting from the scientists. The interviews amounted to a bunch of young crewcuts and old Herr Doktors saying yes, we sent men on the final test of the radiation screen, but not to check on the screen itself; our unmanned shots gave us enough such data; only because man is the one instrument whose observations are not limited to those for which someone designed him. What kind of show was that? Especially when the Dodgers-White Sox game would soon start on another network.

Zellman signaled for the view to cut back to him. He beamed and said resonantly: "A-OK. Everything's fine up there, Laura Swanberg, Jane Holt, and all your kids. Everything's fine, Mr. and Mrs. America." He deepened his tone. "Cold thousands of miles above the green fields of their native land, two young men are entering the deadly radiation current which boils eternally around our planet. Trusting their lives to an invisible shield of pulsed magnetic energies—and to God," he remembered to add, "they are going to circle the globe for ten lonely hours. If they succeed . . . if they come home again unharmed to their loved ones . . . then the way is open for Americans to explore the Solar System, unafraid of those lethal blasts from the sun which—" He saw the Number Two cameraman holding his nose and barely suppressed a scowl. That smart aleck would hear from Tom Zellman after this was over "—which have so long limited the time and places our ships could venture beyond the atmosphere." Well, maybe the corn syrup was getting too thick at that. Zellman flipped a switch and projected a still pic onto a screen for transmission.

It was a cutaway view of a standard Aeolus third stage. Because a good deal of the innards had still been secret when the drawing was made, the artist had relied considerably on his imagination. Joe Blow wouldn't know the difference anyway. The capsule was shown blasting with its spin jets as well as the main rocket motor. Actually, Zellman supposed, those small swiveling nozzles were only to aim it in the right direction. The real thrust would come from the stern jet. And would hardly be used at the present time. Maybe a bit of push here and there, to get Stage Three into precisely the correct orbit. But generally speaking, Stage Two did that job. The main task of the Stage Three motor was to bring the capsule down again—to brake orbital velocity until the ship spiraled into atmosphere and its parachute could take over.

However, the clip was a good dramatic pic. Zellman left his desk and pointed at the two human figures. "That's Jimmy Holt piloting the spaceship. The ground crew is standing alertly by, ready to take over if he needs help. A giant computer clicks madly," (or does it whirr, or flash lights, or what?) "digesting the information sent down by radio instruments. Powerful remote-control impulses are sent back, guiding, helping. But in the last analysis, the pilot controls the ship. How do you like that, Pete and Hughie? That's your dad there, riding that rocket like a cowboy rides a bronco. Next to him Billy Swanberg peers at the radiation shield meters. If the screen should fail— but no, little Julie, that isn't going to happen. Your father is going to come back to you, safe and sound—"

"Preparing to assume final orbit," said the dry voice. There went a hissing and crackling undertone of static.

"That was Jimmy Holt," explained Zellman. "Jimmy Holt, preparing for the last delicate touch of jets that will throw him into the heart of the densest Van Allen belt." He glanced at the clock. The damn capsule ought to be stabilized or whatever you called it in another few minutes. Then he could turn the program over to Harry while he got lunch. He'd missed breakfast and his belly was growling. Good Lord! Suppose the sound mikes picked that up?

The idea worried him so much that for a while, a whole thirty or forty seconds, the fact didn't register on him, what it meant, Holt speaking again: "The main jet doesn't respond. The goddam thing won't fire. What's gone wrong?"

The vision scope showed Earth like a globe of itself, so enormous against blackness that Holt's eyes joined his middle ear canals in making weightlessness appear to be a meteor's fall. Any minute now, any second, they'd *hit* the ground and spatter . . . He shook off the illusion. *Stop that, you schnook. You've been orbital often enough to know better. I wish to God we were headed down. No, we're stuck in the sky like Mohammed's coffin. Like half a dozen other dead guys in capsules that never returned, still whirling around the world. I wonder if we'll see one of 'em.*

He pulled his gaze from the scope. Bill Swanberg could sit for hours mooning over how pretty Earth was. Holt had other business on hand. He'd long ago stopped getting any kicks from the scenery. (Oh, no denying it had beauty, the vast round ball, softly blue, banded with white clouds, blazoned with green and dusky continents . . .

crowned by uncountably many stars, guarded by the Horned Goddess herself . . . but the cabin here wasn't big enough to swing a kitten, it clicked and whickered, ventilators blew continuous gusts in your face, the air stank of oil and man, and you really had no time to look at anything but the meters.) He had never been glamor-struck by the spaceships anyhow. When routine psychophysical exams showed he had a natural aptitude for piloting, he'd snapped at the offer from Canaveral, because that was an even quicker route to executive rank than the engineering in which he had trained. A pilot who knew his way around people and watched his chances could step into some very fat jobs after a few years.

If he lived that long, of course.

Holt glanced at Swanberg. Unhelmeted, the electronics man's broad freckled face glittered with sweat. Little droplets broke off and floated in the air currents. But he proceeded doggedly with his instrumental checks. From time to time he told Base his results, in a perfectly cool tone. Bill was a good joe, Holt thought. The phrase struck him funny. He started to laugh but stopped himself in time.

"That's about everything," Swanberg finished.

"You're getting near our horizon," said the man down at Canaveral. Static hissed and sputtered around his words. "I think we can figure out what your trouble is, though, before you're gone from line of sight."

"Hope so," Swanberg drawled. "Hate to wait out another half-orbit or thereabouts, wondering whether it's gremlins or trolls." He hesitated. "Standing by, then," he said. "Over and out." He cut off the transmitter.

★ ★ ★

Traveling eastward at miles per second, the capsule was once again over the night side. Earth's disc had become a crescent, its darkness edged with sunlight and tinged by moonlight. Had the tracking stations in that hemisphere been prepared, continuous contact would have been maintained. But they weren't. No one had expected this to be anything but a milk run.

"How's the rad screen holding out?" Holt asked, to drown the machinery noises. His throat felt caught between cold fingers.

"Fine," Swanberg said. "Hardly an electron more is getting through than 'ud get through half an Earth atmosphere."

Suddenly his calm was intolerable. Holt pounded the control panel with his fist, softly and repeatedly. His thin body rebounded in the harness. "What's gone wrong?" he groaned. "Why won't the main jet fire?" In a rush of resentment: "Goddam Rube Goldberg monstrosity. Five million things to go haywire. Why can't they design 'em simple and right?"

"They're working on it," said Swanberg. "But a spaceship has a lot of separate functions to perform, you know. You and I are Rube Goldberg monstrosities too. It doesn't take much to make us stop functioning—one blood clot can do it."

"Yeah, yeah. I guess so." Holt tensed his tongue to spit, but recalled where he was. "So much for that God guff," he said. "I can't believe in a God who's that lousy an engineer."

"I daresay a molecule of fuel could make a similar

objection as it burns," Swanberg answered. "No religion worth a hoot ever promised us happiness. We do get a fighting chance, though. Does a man really want more?"

"This one does," Holt said. "I want to get back where I belong."

"Sure," Swanberg said. "Don't misunderstand me, Jim." A grin stretched his mouth, less a smile than a baring of teeth. "I'm scared worse than you are."

"Wanna bet?"

Silence closed in again. Holt tried frantically to think of something to say that wouldn't sound too stupid. Speculation on what the trouble with the rocket was . . . but that was being computed, not guessed at, down on Base, where they had not only the data Swanberg sent but information telemetered from the entire ship . . . Continue the God argument? No, he and Bill had left their sophomore years behind them . . . . Sentimental reminiscences about wives and kids? Cannonballs! Laura and Janie—oh, Janie gal—

"Canaveral to Aeolus. Canaveral to Aeolus."

The voice was dim, wavering across the scale, nearly drowned in hoots and squeals and buzzes. So fierce was the ionic current beyond this hull that a tight, hard-driven FM beam could barely get though. But Swanberg leaped in his chair to switch on the transmitter. Holt beat him to it.

"Do you receive me, Aeolus? Cana—"

"Aeolus to Canaveral," Holt rattled through a mouth full of cotton and pepper. "We read you. What's the word?"

The voice dropped formalities. It shook. "We've identified your trouble. I'm afraid—the—your main discharge valve is stuck. Probably a thin seal of ice, due to condensation last night when the air was so damp. A, a little water vapor in that cranny—you know?—normally the rocket exhaust would flush it out, but in this case—"

"Get to the point!" Holt screamed, for the voice was fading away every second. "What do we do?"

"Can't cut out the safety circuits and blow the valve open with a minimal jet," came the remnant of answer. "Ordinarily you could, but—" Static sheeted.

"I know that," Swanberg barked. "The rad screen's in the same hookup, to save weight. We'd fry. I helped install the blinking thing, you! What *can* we do?"

A gulp: "Someone . . . got to go out the airlock . . . crawl around behind, into the tube, bust the ice loose by hand—one of you—" Then there was only the seething.

Holt stared at a meter face for an indefinite while. Eventually, he glanced at Swanberg. The big man was finishing a slide rule calculation.

"I suppose you know the magnetic deflection effect drops off on a steep inverse square curve," Swanberg said without tone. "If a guy went outside here in the middle of the Van Allen, even hugging the hull, he'd get a lethal dose in something like ten minutes. How long would he need to free the valve and get back inside?"

"Half an hour, at least," Holt heard himself answer. "It's a clumsy business, working in free space."

They fell silent again.

Tom Zellman looked straight into the pickup. As soon as the news arrived, he had ducked out to change his sports shirt—although it was his trademark—for a dark suit and sincere tie. Now he spoke in measured cadence.

"You have just seen an interview with General Buckler, commander of Cape Canaveral Base, the man on whose shoulders has fallen the agonizing responsibility of choosing who shall live and who shall die," he said. "General Buckler did not, of course, have time to explain the situation in detail." (General Buckler, in point of fact, had retreated so far into his military shell that getting a dozen words from him had been like milking a constipated cow. Hysterical reaction; this kind of publicity could crumple a career. But Zellman would cover for him; such IOU's were always collectible later.) "So let me try, Mr. and Mrs. America. You want to know what faces your boys out there. Savage cold, blazing heat, whizzing meteorites, weightlessness, raw vacuum . . . and now the deadly, blasting radiation of the charged particle zone in which they are trapped.

"Because one valve has stuck, the main jet on their capsule won't fire. The side jets are only for steering. Their small separate motors can't burn long enough to bring the capsule down out of orbit. It won't be hard to get that vital part unstuck. Half an hour or less, and the third stage rocket is free to come home again. But—that half-hour must be spent outside the hull. The force screen that protects Billy and Jimmy from the radiation *inside* the cabin cannot protect the man who goes out. He will get such a searing blast through his spacesuit that no medical science can save him. In a few days he will be dead. But his comrade," (oops!) "his friend will come down to Earth unharmed." Zellman dropped into the upper bass register. "Greater love hath no man than this, that he lay down his life for his friend."

The teleboard behind the cameras had been forming words for some seconds. Zellman crooked a finger beneath his desk. A boy came running and handed him a sheet of paper. Zellman unfolded it and spent thirty seconds letting emotions play across his face. Then he lowered the paper—carefully, so the audience couldn't see it was blank—and raised the pitch and speed of his delivery.

"Flash! Three more tracking stations have locked onto the capsule. This means that continuous two-way contact can be maintained. Billy and Jimmy can't see us, but our voices, our prayers, can come to them. By special arrangement, this network will have the honor of preparing the unofficial messages they can now receive. Do you hear me, Jimmy and Billy? You are not alone. One hundred and ninety million of your fellow Americans are with you, fighting, suffering, praying with you." The teleboard wrote: STANDING BY WITH JANIE STILL CAN'T GET LAURIE. "But you don't want to hear me talk," Zellman said, venturing a gallant smile. "We have contacted Jimmy's wife, Janie Holt, and his four children, Pete, Hughie, Susie, and little Gail. The engineer is signaling me that we can go on the air, Jimmy, direct from your own home to you. Do you hear me?" Faintly, scratchily, as if it were a midge caught somewhere inside the blackness of a telephone receiver, there came: "Holt speaking. I read you." The engineer scowled and twiddled knobs in his cage. The sound wasn't going onto the TV frequencies very well. But his assistant nodded, and a monitor unit came to life beside Zellman's desk. The visual transmission across the country would be split-screen, one side showing himself in the blockhouse TV booth on Base, the other side showing the scene in the monitor: Holt's family in their house downtown.

Jane Holt was small and dark like her husband. The plain black dress showed her figure to advantage, and the makeup man had done a good job on her and the kids. They were well posed too, the boys on either side of her chair, the girl at her knee and the baby in her arms.

"Hello, Janie," said Zellman with his Undertaker's Special smile.

"Hello . . . Tom." He wished she wouldn't speak quite so thinly.

"In a minute, Janie, we'll put you through to your Jimmy. But first, wouldn't you like to say a word to the rest of your family? Your family and his—the great, warm, wonderful family of America, hanging on the edge of their television screens, hoping, loving, and praying. Their hearts are with you at this moment. Believe me, they are; I know those wonderful people so well. Just a word, Janie?"

Whoever had set up the idiot board behind the camera in her place knew his job; her eyes seemed to look straight from the screen, into the viewer's. There hadn't been time to rehearse her, so her delivery was rather mechanical—

"—Thank you so much, each and every one of you. I, I know how much Jimmy thanks you too—"

—but on the whole, Zellman thought, she was effective. Harry had always been able to whip out a fast script with zing in it.

The teleboard said: STILL CAN'T GET LAURIE STOP

DOORS LOCKED AND CURTAINS DRAWN STOP DOESN'T ANSWER PHONE STOP HODGKINS AND BURR CAMPING ON HER PORCH WITH OTHER NETWORKS MEN AND REPORTERS.

"—God's will be done. But oh, we do hope Jimmy comes back safe!"

Having finished, Jane sat at a loss. Her kids stared woodenly into the camera, and the baby started to cry. Zellman said hastily, "Thank you, Janet. Have you been in touch with Laurie Swanberg yet? You know her well, don't you?"

"Yes. No, I mean, I haven't heard from her. I . . . I tried to phone . . . we ought to be together, oughtn't we? . . . but—" Jane drew a deep breath and flung out: "She's probably off by herself, with her *two* children."

"I'll switch you over to your husband now," Zellman said before a crisis was precipitated.

"Jimmybuck," Jane said like a sleepwalker.

"Hi, kid," said the voice torn by static.

"How . . . how are you?"

"Okay so far. Sweating out the Old Man's decision."

"Jimmy—come back. Tell your daddy to come back." Hughie began to blubber. "We need you so."

"Hey, wait—" Holt's response was lost in the crackling.

"Jimmybuck, I love you," Jane said. She began to cry, too.

"Same here, kid. All youse kids. But—" The static chose that exact moment to let up, so the harshness came through. "This is no place to say it, huh? We'll do whatever the Old Man tells us, Bill and me. So long, darling."

"*Jimmy!*" she called, once and again. Only the static

answered. Until Swanberg said, recognizable as himself: "I think we better cut off transmission for a while."

"Is that you, Billy?" Zellman asked.

"This is Swanberg, yes."

"Billy, we've been trying as hard as we can to get your Laurie for you, but—"

"Aeolus to Canaveral," Swanberg said. "Over and out." There was a distinct snick. The static went off the air.

That bastard!

Zellman turned to Jane in the screen. She was weeping, quite prettily. But beyond a certain point in affairs like this, you risked a public squawk. "I think we had best leave you for a while, Janie," he said, sweet and low. "Not alone, of course. You will never be alone again; our hearts will always be with you."

She whirled on him and screamed: "I've played your game! Why not? It might get him back. And we've got four children and she only has two!"

Luckily, Zellman and the camera crews had seen that coming, and had a delay circuit to help them. None of her outburst went onto the air.

The teleboard said: BILLY'S MOTHER CONTACTED IN TWIN FALLS AND CONSENTS TO INTERVIEW BUT NO SCRIPT. Zellman signaled "Stand by" and his order was phoned to Idaho. Better space the tear-jerking scenes further apart. He switched to outside views of the Holt and Swanberg houses, with his own commentary. The state police were breaking up the traffic jams.

Whoa! Laurie herself came out on the porch. She swatted three reporters aside and yelled for a cop and got him to chase everybody off her grounds. There was no chance for closeups; her door slammed again before a telecamera could arrive. But even from a distance—what a scene, what a scene!

Of course, she wasn't doing her husband's chances any good. Buckler wasn't dumb enough to sentence the more popular man to death . . . Trouble was, though, Swanberg was a big, good-looking, outdoors type and not just any slob rocketeer, but a co-inventor of the rad screen. Popularity . . .

The teleboard awoke. Zellman surged from his chair. He almost didn't find words, this was so big. He actually did forget to signal for a sheet of paper.

"Flash! Here's the word from Base headquarters. General Buckler has issued an announcement. Quote: 'Not only are Mr. Holt and Mr. Swanberg both valuable members of our project and citizens of our community, they are both civilians. As such, they lie beyond my authority to give more than normal orders, and this is not a normal situation. I have therefore sent a special request to the President that he decide which of them should perform the task in question. A reply is expected shortly.'

"Unquote. That was General Buckler's decision: to let the President of the United States choose, in the name of all America. While we wait, anxiously and prayerfully, here is a word from—"

Falling and falling, Swanberg thought. And now the silence had begun to press inward. Still he heard click, buzz, whirr, whuff; lately he had been hearing the blup-blup of his heartbeat. (Maybe that was because it had gotten irregular, sometimes skipping so that he jerked in his harness and tried not to gasp.) Yet the silence grew.

Imagination, he understood irritably. Silence wasn't a thing, it was an absence of sound, just as the void was an absence of matter. His sensation of black nothing eating in toward the core of himself was purely subjective, based on no more than . . . well, reality. The universe was in fact a trillion light-years of emptiness wherein a few sand grains were lost.

*No, now you're thinking like Jim. Size hasn't got anything to do with importance. Vacuum and gamma radiation are real, sure. But so's the sunlight on a mountain lake, and Laura, and—*He shook his weary head and turned to Holt. The pilot had tuned radio reception so far down that they could hear only a murmur; but he was alert for anything important. "What's being sent us now?" Swanberg asked.

Holt put his ear close to the receiver. "The Reverend Norbert Victor Poole, author of the best-selling book *The Strength in Confident Living*, will deliver us a message of hope shortly. And the Emperor of Abyssinia has added his official best wishes to those of other governments."

"Yeah," Swanberg mumbled.

Presently: "If they don't get off their dead ends and reach a decision soon, we'll have to toss a coin."

"Can't toss a coin in free-fall, even if we had one," Holt said. "Gotta match fingers. You know, odd or even number of fingers spread at the same time. If you match me, you win, otherwise I do. Unless you'd rather it was the other way around."

Swanberg checked the odds. "Makes no difference."

"Maybe we should'a done it that way in the first place," Holt said. "Instead of asking Base for orders. But I just automatically figured—or didn't I have the nerve? Better this way. Let an outsider give the word, backed by public opinion if not by law, and the unlucky one has got to go, period. But if we matched, and I lost . . . dunno what I'd do."

"Scared?" Swanberg asked, forcing a smile.

"Christ, yes. Worse every minute. Why don't those sods *decide?*"

"Would you like to make a choice like that . . . for somebody else?"

"I'd get it over with. I would! Judas, Bill, you aren't human, sitting there so quiet and—Why won't Laura talk to you?"

"With a planetful of morons listening in?" Swanberg snapped. "We know what we're thinking right now, she and I. It's nobody else's business."

"Hey!" He saw Holt stiffen in the spacesuit. The pilot reached a fist toward him. "Do you mean Janie—What're you getting at? Spit it out!"

"Sorry. I'm awfully sorry," Swanberg exclaimed in dismay. "I didn't mean anything. Honest. Your arrangements are your own affair. She's got to do what she thinks is right."

Holt unclenched his fist. The hand drifted limply between them. "I'm sorry too," he muttered. "I blew my top. She did embarrass the hell out of me." Suddenly he laughed. "What are we doing, being embarrassed? One of us is going to die in an hour or so."

"No, he'll take several days to die, on Earth,"

Swanberg said, stolidly, since that was his best defense against panic. "They'll send him wherever he asks." He paused. "They might even let him alone."

"Fat chance," Holt said.

Swanberg fumbled for words. "If . . . if you're the loser, Jim . . . I'll see to it that your family—"

"Oh, they'll be left well off, moneywise," Holt said. "Yours too, I suppose. Bill—"

"Yes?"

"Are you scared like I am?"

"Worse, probably."

"Thanks for saying so, anyhow. It's this sitting and waiting. I'd almost rather go out and do the job now, myself!" Holt started. "Hey, isn't that a call from Base?" He turned the receiver to full volume. The mellow baritone rolled forth:

"—Oh, my brave brothers, be happy, be confident. There is no death. God is waiting to call you home."

Swanberg reached out a long arm and switched on the transmitter. "Aeolus to Earth," he said, loud and clear. "Horse manure." He switched off again and Holt turned the receiver back down.

The President of the United States left his desk and went to a window. Outside, the White House lawn stretched dazzling green—*What a beautiful planet we have,* he thought. *Why do men go away from her to die?*—until it ended at the fence. Beyond, sidewalk and street were packed solid. The police had stopped trying to make the crowd move on. It wasn't physically possible. The latest word was that one man had had a fatal heart attack and one women of less than average stature had suffocated out there. Not that the crowd was disorderly. The President thought he had never seen one more quiet.

"Death watch," he said aloud.

"Sir?" asked his press secretary. They were alone together.

"Nothing. You know," said the President, "it's funny how a person keeps thinking of irrelevancies at a time like this. Anything to postpone the main issue. I keep wondering whether Buckler pulled me such a scurvy trick that I ought to have him transferred to the Aleutians . . . or did the only right and honorable thing under the circumstances."

"He could have told Holt and Swanberg to make their own decision," said the press secretary.

"No. That would have been shifting the burden onto them. And they have enough to bear." The President sighed. "There isn't any basis for decision. I've spent an hour with their dossiers. Both are fine, decent, outstanding citizens. Both have dependents who'd be cruelly hurt."

"Holt has two more kids than Swanberg does, Mr. President."

"That cuts very little ice with me. Especially remembering that Holt has no close kin alive, while Swanberg's got a mother and two sisters."

"Last time I had Tom Zellman on the phone, down at Canaveral, he said calls coming in to his station were running about five to three in favor of Holt. Of Holt getting back whole, I mean."

"No doubt," said the President dryly. "Swanberg and his wife have been less politic, shall we say. However, I feel reasonably sure that his backers tend to be more intellectual, somewhat wealthier, and with more influence per capital. Three bankers and college presidents versus five housewives and mail clerks. Beg pardon, I mean five homemakers and junior executives. What sort of odds will that amount to by the time the next election rolls around? Pretty even, I'd guess."

The secretary made no answer, but the President filled one in for him and went on: "Bitter? Of course I am. Bitter at how this whole affair has been mishandled, and bitter, with quite a little self-pity, at becoming the goat. The one who has to say, 'He shall live and you must die.' I never wanted to play God."

"You'll have to, Mr. President."

"Uh-huh. Right now. I've prepared two statements here, one for Holt and one for Swanberg, explaining the reasons why he should be the survivor. They are good, sound, carefully chosen and shrewdly phrased reasons, if I do say so myself."

"And—?" The secretary stepped close.

"Lend me a quarter, Bob."

Wordlessly, the coin changed hands. "Heads, Holt," the President said. "Tails, Swanberg." He tossed. The coin caught a shaft of sunlight and glittered. He didn't catch it. It went on the rug. Both men knelt to look.

"Heads," said the secretary in a whisper.

The President nodded. He got slowly to his feet, like an aging man, and tore the paper with Swanberg's qualifications into shreds. The other he handed to the secretary. "Give this to the press as my considered reasons for picking Holt," he said. "Then clear my calendar. I'll call Buckler myself—I've got that much guts left—but I can't see anyone else today. Nobody."

"Canaveral to Aeolus. Canaveral to Aeolus. Are you there? Come in, Aeolus."

Abruptly, Holt knew what the mumble was—two or three syllables leaped out into his understanding—and he turned the volume high with darkness rising ragged before his eyes.

"Aeolus to Canaveral," said Swanberg across the roar in Holt's ears. "We read you. Come in, Canaveral."

How could Bill sit there like a stone toad and talk? Holt wondered for a moment if his own heart was going to explode.

"(Got them for you, sir.) Hello, Aeolus. This is General Buckler. How are you doing?"

"Okay," said Swanberg. Fighting his pulse rate down toward something reasonable, Holt saw that every trace of color had left the electronician's face. Yet he spoke with machine precision.

"But we'll have to begin deceleration soon or our air supply will get dangerously low."

"That's understood, Swanberg . . . Bill . . . that is you, isn't it? Yes. We, uh, we've heard from the President. Five minutes ago."

"What?" asked Swanberg without inflection. Holt clenched his fists until the nails scored the palms.

"I'm sorry, Bill," Buckler got out.

Swanberg didn't move a muscle, but the ventilation stirred the yellow hair on his head.

"The President's message is as follows," Buckler said.

"'My decision has been impossibly difficult, for both William Swanberg and James Holt are men whose loss will be felt as grievously by their country as by their own loved ones. However, since a decision must be made, in view of the fact that he has more children and that possibly he will make less pilot error in returning the capsule to Earth if he knows he is to live, I recommend that Mr. Holt remain within the cabin. To Mr. Swanberg and his family I can only extend my deepest sympathy and my assurance that none of us will ever forget his service.'"

"Thanks," Swanberg said. "We'll get right to work."

"W-w-we're trying to contact your wife," said Buckler.

"No!" Swanberg exclaimed. "Not that. Leave her alone, you hear me?" He snapped off the transmitter with such violence that he almost broke the switch.

I'm going to live, it shouted in Holt. *I'm going to live.* Then he met Swanberg's eyes.

They regarded each other a long time. "What can I say, Bill?" Holt managed in the end. He could barely form the words; his tongue felt like a lump of wood.

"Nothing. It's okay, Jim. No hard feelings." Swanberg was quite gray, but he extended his hand.

"Damnation, I wish—I almost wish—"

"It's okay, I tell you." Swanberg left his hand out, untaken, for Holt hadn't seen it. "The President's a good man. Wasn't easy for him either."

"N-no. I wish he'd left out that 'loved ones' cornball, though."

"Me too. Well, no sense wasting time. Shake," Swanberg reminded him.

They clasped hands. Both felt cold.

"Hello, Billy, and you too, Jimmy," roared the receiver. "This is Tom Zellman down at Base. By special arrangement, at this most solemn moment, the Boys' Choir of the New York cathedral of your church, Billy, is preparing to sing the hymns chosen by your mother in Twin Falls. We will be bringing you her own voice as soon as we can. Meanwhile, the Reverend Norbert Victor Poole—"

"Oh, no!" Holt breathed.

"Hello, Jimmy," said the rich baritone. "Yes, you, Jimmy. I am talking to you. For you have a role even more difficult than Billy. He is making the supreme sacrifice and then going to his so fully deserved eternal reward. But you must live. You must use the life your friend is giving you, confidently, inspiringly, so that the youth of America—"

Holt turned him off.

"You'll have to switch back on," Swanberg sighed. "To get return instructions. But I daresay they'll skip the organ music then." His lips tightened. "Help me on with my helmet, will you? I've got to get outside. Before Mother— hurry up, will you?"

Holt sat very still. *I don't have to dance at their show*, he thought. *I haven't got strings tied on me. Yet.* It was as if someone else entered him. "Wait a minute," he said, speaking fast so that he wouldn't get time to interrupt himself for the fear was thick in his chest. "Ease off. I've got some say in this, too."

"You?" Swanberg's tone hurt. Maybe he didn't mean the way he spoke, but—

"Yeah," Holt chattered. "I've been here with you a good many hours now, listening to 'em below passing the buck, like a mucking three-stage rocket, Buckler to the President, and meanwhile using us to sell underarm grease. Using Janie, as far as that goes. I wish she'd had Laura's backbone."

"Hell," muttered Swanberg, flushing the least bit, "that's only a matter of—uh—"

"Lemme finish, damn you! We started this nightmare, you and me, passing the buck ourselves. Now it's come back to us. Or ought to, at least. We're the third stage. What the hell am I saying? Mainly, I guess, we don't have to go along with this farce. The President knows that. Think his words over. He didn't order, he recommended. He hasn't got power to give orders. As long as this bucket is aloft, only the captain can give orders that stick, and I'm the captain."

"What are you getting at?" Swanberg's big hands reached as if to seize Holt and shake him, but withdrew again, an inch at a time. The ship mumbled, tumbling through endlessness.

"We don't have to go along with them," Holt yelled. "I've had it, I tell you. Up to here. Shut up, I'm the captain. Listen. I'm not trying to be any hero, but—I don't know. Maybe I'm afraid you'd come back every night . . . I'll take full responsibility, when we reach Base. You don't have to fear any consequences. Buckler, the President, and now me. I'm the third stage and I've cut loose and I'm going home under my own power!"

He recognized the hope that flickered so wildly across the other man's face, and a part of him shrieked with anger at the foolishness of the other part and none of him understood very well what this was about. But having gone this far, he couldn't retreat. And it was worth it— maybe completely worth it, maybe only almost worth it—to know, for however long he might live, that he was a free man.

"What do you mean?" Swanberg sagged in his harness.

"We're going to do this right," Holt answered. He put one hand behind his back. "Odd or even. Match me."

BECALMED IN HELL

by Larry Niven

Early in his promising career as a new writer of hard sf (and the promises have been more than kept), Larry Niven wrote this story of the first two men on Venus, though, since this was Venus as the latest planetary probes had shown it to be, so "on" needs some clarification. And one of the "men" is more than a bit out of the ordinary, too. This was a sequel to his first published story, "The Coldest Place," and the advance shown in writing skill and depth of characterization in less than a year (1964, 1965) is enough to make most beginning writers consider a career in computer programming.

I COULD FEEL THE HEAT hovering outside. In the cabin it was bright and dry and cool, almost too cool, like a modern office building in the dead of the summer. Beyond the two small windows it was as black as it ever

39

gets in the solar system, and hot enough to melt lead, at a pressure equivalent to three hundred feet beneath the ocean.

"There goes a fish," I said, just to break the monotony.

"So how's it cooked?"

"Can't tell. It seems to be leaving a trail of breadcrumbs. Fried? Imagine that, Eric! A fried jellyfish."

Eric sighed noisily. "Do I have to?"

"You have to. Only way you'll see anything worthwhile in this—this—" Soup? Fog? Boiling maple syrup?

"Searing black calm."

"Right."

"Someone dreamed up that phrase when I was a kid, just after the news of the Mariner II probe. An eternal searing black calm, hot as a kiln, under an atmosphere thick enough to keep any light or any breath of wind from ever reaching the surface."

I shivered. "What's the outside temperature now?"

"You'd rather not know. You've always had too much imagination, Howie."

"I can take it, Doc."

"Six hundred and twelve degrees."

"I can't take it, Doc!"

This was Venus, Planet of Love, favorite of the science-fiction writers of three decades ago. Our ship hung below the Earth-to-Venus hydrogen fuel tank, twenty miles up and all but motionless in the syrupy air. The tank, nearly empty now, made an excellent blimp. It would keep us aloft as long as the internal pressure matched the external. That was Eric's job, to regulate the tank's pressure by regulating the temperature of the hydrogen gas. We had collected air samples after each ten mile drop from three hundred miles on down, and temperature readings for shorter intervals, and we had dropped the small probe. The data we had gotten from the surface merely confirmed in detail our previous knowledge of the hottest world in the solar system.

"Temperature just went up to six-thirteen," said Eric. "Look, are you through bitching?"

"For the moment."

"Good. Strap down. We're taking off."

"Oh frabjous day!" I started untangling the crash webbing over my couch.

"We've done everything we came to do. Haven't we?"

"Am I arguing? Look, I'm strapped down."

"Yeah."

I knew why he was reluctant to leave. I felt a touch of it myself. We'd spent four months getting to Venus in order to spend a week circling her and less than two days in her upper atmosphere, and it seemed a terrible waste of time.

But he was taking too long. "What's the trouble, Eric?"

"You'd rather not know."

He meant it. His voice was a mechanical, inhuman monotone: he wasn't making the extra effort to get human expression out of his "prosthetic" vocal apparatus. Only a severe shock would affect him that way.

"I can take it," I said.

"Okay. I can't feel anything in the ramjet controls. Feels like I've just had a spinal anesthetic."

The cold in the cabin drained into me, all of it. "See if you can send motor impulses the other way. You

could run the rams by guess-and-hope even if you can't
feel them."

"Okay." One split second later, "They don't. Nothing
happens. Good thinking though."

I tried to think of something to say while I untied
myself from the couch. What came out was, "It's been a
pleasure knowing you, Eric. I've liked being half of this
team, and I still do."

"Get maudlin later. Right now, start checking my
attachments. Carefully."

I swallowed my comments and went to open the
access door in the cabin's forward wall. The floor swayed
ever so gently beneath my feet.

Beyond the four-foot-square access door was Eric.
Eric's central nervous system, with the brain perched at the
top and the spinal cord coiled in a loose spiral to fit more
compactly into the transparent glass-and-sponge-plastic
housing. Hundreds of wires from all over the ship led to
the glass walls, where they were joined to selected nerves
which spread like an electrical network from the central
coil of nervous tissue and fatty protective membrane.

Space leaves no cripples; and don't call Eric a cripple,
because he doesn't like it. In a way, he's the ideal
spaceman. His life-support system weighs only half of
what mine does, and takes up a twelfth as much room.
But his other prosthetic aids take up most of the ship. The
ramjets were hooked into the last pair of nerve trunks, the
nerves which once moved his legs, and dozens of finer
nerves in those trunks sensed and regulated fuel feed, ram
temperature, differential acceleration, intake aperture
dilation, and spark pulse.

These connections were intact. I checked them four different ways without finding the slightest reason why they shouldn't be working.

"Test the others," said Eric.

It took a good two hours to check every trunk nerve connection. They were all solid. The blood pump was chugging along, and the fluid was rich enough, which killed the idea that the ram nerves might have "gone to sleep" from lack of nutrients or oxygen. Since the lab is one of his prosthetic aids, I let Eric analyze his own blood sugar, hoping that the "liver" had goofed and was producing some other form of sugar. The conclusions were appalling. There was nothing wrong with Eric—inside the cabin.

"Eric, you're healthier than I am."

"I could tell. You looked worried, son, and I don't blame you. Now you'll have to go outside."

"I know. Let's dig out the suit."

It was in the emergency tools locker, the Venus suit that was never supposed to be used. NASA had designed it for use at Venusian ground level. Then they had refused to okay the ship below twenty miles until they knew more about the planet. The suit was a segmented armor job. I had watched it being tested in the heat-and-pressure box at Cal Tech, and I knew that the joints stopped moving after five hours, and wouldn't start again until they had been cooled. Now I opened the locker and pulled the suit out by the shoulders and held it in front of me. It seemed to be staring back.

"You still can't feel anything in the ramjets?"

"Not a twinge."

I started to put on the suit, piece by piece like

medieval armor. Then I thought of something else. "We're twenty miles up. Are you going to ask me to do a balancing act on the hull?"

"No! Wouldn't think of it. We'll just have to go down."

The lift from the blimp tank was supposed to be constant until takeoff. When the time came Eric could get extra lift by heating the hydrogen to higher pressure, then cracking a valve to let the excess out. Of course, he'd have to be very careful that the pressure was higher in the tank, or we'd get Venusian air coming in, and the ship would fall instead of rising. Naturally, that would be disastrous.

So Eric lowered the tank temperature and cracked the valve, and down we went.

"Of course there's a catch," said Eric.

"I know."

"The ship stood the pressure twenty miles up. At ground level it'll be six times that."

"I know."

We fell fast, with the cabin tilted forward by the drag on our tailfins. The temperature rose gradually. The pressure went up fast. I sat at the window and saw nothing, nothing but black, but I sat there anyway and waited for the window to crack. NASA had refused to okay the ship below twenty miles . . .

Eric said, "The blimp tank's okay, and so's the ship, I think. But will the cabin stand up to it?"

"I wouldn't know."

"Ten miles."

Five hundred miles above us, unreachable, was the atomic ion engine that was to take us home. We couldn't get to it on the chemical rocket alone. The rocket was for use after the air became too thin for the ramjets.

"Four miles. Have to crack the valve again."

The ship dropped.

"I can see ground," said Eric.

I couldn't. Eric caught me straining my eyes and said, "Forget it. I'm using deep infrared, and getting no detail."

"No vast, misty swamps with weird, terrifying monsters and man-eating plants?"

"All I see is hot, bare dirt."

But we were almost down, and there were no cracks in the cabin wall. My neck and shoulder muscles loosened. I turned away from the window. Hours had passed while we dropped through the poisoned, thickening air. I already had most of my suit on. Now I screwed on my helmet and three-finger gantlets.

"Strap down," said Eric. I did.

We bumped gently. The ship tilted a little, swayed back, bumped again. And again, with my teeth rattling and my armor-plated body rolling against the crash webbing. "Damn," Eric muttered. I heard the hiss from above. Eric said, "I don't know how we'll get back up."

Neither did I. The ship bumped hard and stayed down, and I got up and went to the airlock.

"Good luck," said Eric. "Don't stay out too long." I waved at his cabin camera. The outside temperature was seven hundred and thirty.

The outer door opened. My suit refrigerating unit set up a complaining whine. With an empty bucket in each hand, and with my headlamp blazing a way through the black murk, I stepped out onto the right wing.

My suit creaked and settled under the pressure, and I stood on the wing and waited for it to stop. It was almost like being under water. My headlamp beam went out thick enough to be solid, penetrating no more than a hundred feet. The air couldn't have been that opaque, no matter how dense. It must have been full of dust, or tiny droplets of some fluid.

The wing ran back like a knife-edged running board, widening toward the tail until it spread into a tailfin. The two tailfins met back of the fuselage. At the tailfin tip was the ram, a big sculptured cylinder with an atomic engine inside. It wouldn't be hot because it hadn't been used yet, but I had my counter anyway.

I fastened a line to the wing and slid to the ground. As long as we were *here* . . . The ground turned out to be a dry, reddish dirt, crumbly, and so porous that it was almost spongy. Lava etched by chemicals? Almost anything would be corrosive at this pressure and temperature. I scooped one pailful from the surface and another from underneath the first, then climbed up the line and left the buckets on the wing.

The wing was terribly slippery. I had to wear magnetic sandals to stay on. I walked up and back along the two-hundred-foot length of the ship, making a casual inspection. Neither wing nor fuselage showed damage. Why not? If a meteor or something had cut Eric's contact with his sensors in the rams, there should have been evidence of a break in the surface.

Then, almost suddenly, I realized that there was an alternative.

It was too vague a suspicion to put into words yet, and

I still had to finish the inspection. Telling Eric would be very difficult if I was right.

Four inspection panels were set into the wing, well protected from the reentry heat. One was halfway back on the fuselage, below the lower edge of the blimp tank, which was molded to the fuselage in such a way that from the front the ship looked like a dolphin. Two more were in the trailing edge of the tailfin, and the fourth was in the ram itself. All opened, with powered screwdriver on recessed screws, on junctions of the ship's electrical system.

There was nothing out of place under any of the panels. By making and breaking contacts and getting Eric's reactions, I found that his sensation ended somewhere between the second and third inspection panels. It was the same story on the left wing. No external damage, nothing wrong at the junctions. I climbed back to ground and walked slowly beneath the length of each wing, my headlamp tilted up. No damage underneath.

I collected my buckets and went back inside.

"A bone to pick?" Eric was puzzled. "Isn't this a strange time to start an argument? Save it for space. We'll have four months with nothing else to do."

"This can't wait. First of all, did you notice anything I didn't?" He'd been watching everything I saw and did through the peeper in my helmet.

"No. I'd have yelled."

"Okay. Now get this. The break in your circuits isn't inside, because you get sensation up to the second wing inspection panels. It isn't outside because there's no evidence of damage, not even corrosion spots. That leaves only one place for the flaw."

"Go on."

"We also have the puzzle of why you're paralyzed in both rams. Why should they both go wrong at the same time? There's only one place in the ship where the circuits join."

"What? Oh, yes, I see. They join through me."

"Now let's assume for the moment that you're the piece with the flaw in it. You're not a piece of machinery, Eric. If something's wrong with you it isn't medical. That was the first thing we covered. But it could be psychological."

"It's nice to know you think I'm human. So I've slipped a cam, have I?"

"Slightly. I think you've got a case of what used to be called trigger anesthesia. A soldier who kills too often sometimes finds that his right index finger or even his whole hand has gone numb, as if it were no longer a part of him. Your comment about not being a machine is important, Eric. I think that's the whole problem. You've never really believed that any part of the ship is a part of *you*. That's intelligent, because it's true. Every time the ship is redesigned you get a new set of parts, and it's right to avoid thinking of a change of model as a series of amputations."

I'd been rehearsing this speech, trying to put it so that Eric would have no choice but to believe me. Now I know that it must have sounded phony. "But now you've gone too far. Subconsciously, you've stopped believing that the rams can *feel* like a part of you, which they were designed to do. So you've persuaded yourself that you don't feel anything."

With my prepared speech done, and nothing left to say, I stopped talking and waited for the explosion.

"You make good sense," said Eric.

I was staggered. "You agree?"

"I didn't say that. You spin an elegant theory, but I want time to think about it. What do we do if it's true?"

"Why . . . I don't know. You'll just have to cure yourself."

"Okay. Now here's *my* idea. I propose that you thought up this theory to relieve yourself of a responsibility for getting us home alive. It puts the whole problem in my lap, metaphorically speaking."

"Oh, for—"

"Shut up. I haven't said you're wrong. That would be an ad hominem argument. We need time to think about this."

It was lights-out, four hours later, before Eric would return to the subject.

"Howie, do me a favor. Assume for a while that something mechanical is causing all our trouble. I'll assume it's psychosomatic."

"Seems reasonable."

"It is reasonable. What can you do if I've gone psychosomatic? What can I do if it's mechanical? I can't go around inspecting myself. We'd each better stick to what we know."

"It's a deal." I turned him off for the night and went to bed.

But not to sleep.

With the lights off it was just like outside. I turned them back on. It wouldn't wake Eric. Eric never sleeps normally, since his blood doesn't accumulate fatigue poisons, and he'd go mad from being awake all the time if he didn't have a Russian sleep-inducer plate near his cortex. The ship could implode without waking Eric when his sleep inducer's on. But I felt foolish being afraid of the dark.

While the dark stayed outside it was all right.

But it wouldn't stay there. It had invaded my partner's mind. Because his chemical checks guard him against chemical insanities like schizophrenia, we'd assumed he was permanently sane. But how could any prosthetic device protect him from his own imagination, his own misplaced common sense?

I couldn't keep my bargain. I knew I was right. But what could I do about it?

Hindsight is wonderful. I could see exactly what our mistake had been, Eric's and mine and the hundreds of men who had built his life support after the crash. There was nothing left of Eric then except the intact central nervous system, and no glands except the pituitary. "We'll regulate his blood composition," they said, "and he'll always be cool, calm, and collected. No panic reactions from Eric!"

I know a girl whose father had an accident when he was forty-five or so. He was out with his brother, the girl's uncle, on a fishing trip. They were blind drunk when they started home, and the guy was riding on the hood while the brother drove.

Then the brother made a sudden stop. Our hero left two important glands on the hood ornament.

The only change in his sex life was that his wife stopped worrying about late pregnancy. His *habits* were developed.

Eric doesn't need adrenal glands to be afraid of death. His emotional patterns were fixed long before the day he tried to land a moonship without radar. He'd grab any excuse to believe that I'd fixed whatever was wrong with the ram connections.

But he was counting on me to do it.

The atmosphere leaned on the windows. Not wanting to, I reached out to touch the quartz with my fingertips. I couldn't feel the pressure. But it was there, inexorable as the tide smashing a rock into sand grains. How long would the cabin hold it back?

If some broken part were holding us here, how could I have missed finding it? Perhaps it had left no break in the surface of either wing. But how?

That was the angle.

Two cigarettes later, I got up to get the sample buckets. They were empty, the alien dirt safely stored away. I filled them with water and put them in the cooler, set the cooler for forty degrees absolute, then turned off the lights and went to bed.

The morning was blacker than the inside of a smoker's lungs. What Venus really needs, I decided, philosophizing on my back, is to lose ninety-nine percent of her air. That would give her a bit more than half as much air as Earth, which would lower the greenhouse effect enough to make the temperature livable. Drop Venus' gravity to near zero for a few weeks and the work would do itself.

The whole damn universe is waiting for us to discover antigravity.

"Morning," said Eric. "Thought of anything?"

"Yes." I rolled out of bed. "Now don't bug me with questions. I'll explain everything as I go."

"No breakfast?"

"Not yet."

Piece by piece, I put my suit on, just like one of King Arthur's gentlemen, and went for the buckets only after the gantlets were on. The ice, in the cold section, was in the chilly neighborhood of absolute zero. "This is two buckets of ordinary ice," I said, holding them up. "Now let me out."

"I should keep you here till you talk," Eric groused. But the doors opened and I went out onto the wing. I started talking while I unscrewed the number two right panel.

"Eric, think a moment about the tests they run on a manned ship before they'll let a man walk into the life system. They test every part separately and in conjunction with other parts. Yet if something isn't working, either it's damaged or it wasn't tested right. Right?"

"Reasonable." He wasn't giving away anything.

"Well, nothing caused any damage. Not only is there no break in the ship's skin, but no coincidence could have made both rams go haywire at the same time. So something wasn't tested right."

I had the panel off. In the buckets the ice boiled gently where it touched the surfaces of the glass buckets. The blue ice cakes had cracked under their own internal pressure. I dumped one bucket into the maze of wiring and contacts and relays, and the ice shattered, giving me room to close the panel.

"So I thought of something last night, something that wasn't tested. Every part of the ship must have been in the heat-and-pressure box, exposed to artificial Venus conditions, but the ship as a whole, a unit, couldn't have been. It's too big." I'd circled around to the left wing and was opening the number three panel in the trailing edge. My remaining ice was half water and half small chips; I sloshed these in and fastened the panel. "What cut your circuits must have been the heat or the pressure or both. I can't help the pressure, but I'm cooling these relays with ice. Let me know which ram gets its sensation back first, and we'll know which inspection panel is the right one."

"Howie, has it occurred to you what the cold water might do to those hot metals?"

"It could crack them. Then you'd lose all control over the ramjets, which is what's wrong right now."

"Uh, your point, partner. But I still can't feel anything."

I went back to the airlock with my empty buckets swinging, wondering if they'd get hot enough to melt. They might have, but I wasn't out that long. I had my suit off and was refilling the buckets when Eric said, "I can feel the right ram."

"How extensive? Full control?"

"No. I can't feel the temperature. Oh, here it comes. We're all set, Howie."

My sigh of relief was sincere.

I put the buckets in the freezer again. We'd certainly want to take off with the relays cold. The water had been chilling for perhaps twenty minutes when Eric reported, "Sensation's going."

"What?"

"Sensation's going. No temperature, and I'm losing fuel feed control. It doesn't stay cold long enough."

"Ouch! Now what?"

"I hate to tell you. I'd almost rather let you figure it out for yourself."

I had. "We go as high as we can on the blimp tank, then I go out on the wing with a bucket of ice in each hand—"

We had to raise the blimp tank temperature to almost eight hundred degrees to get pressure, but from then on we went up in good shape. To sixteen miles. It took three hours.

"That's as high as we go," said Eric. "You ready?"

I went to get the ice. Eric could see me, he didn't need an answer. He opened the airlock for me.

Fear I might have felt, or panic, or determination or self-sacrifice—but there was nothing. I went out feeling like a used zombie.

My magnets were on full. It felt like I was walking through shallow tar. The air was thick, though not as heavy as it had been down there. I followed my headlamp to the number two panel, opened it, poured ice in, and threw the bucket high and far. The ice was in one cake. I couldn't close the panel. I left it open and hurried around to the other wing. The second bucket was filled with exploded chips; I sloshed them in and locked the number two left panel and came back with both hands free. It still looked like limbo in all directions, except where the headlamp cut a tunnel through the darkness, and—my feet were getting hot. I closed the right panel on boiling water and sidled back along the hull into the airlock.

"Come in and strap down," said Eric. "Hurry!"

"Gotta get my suit off." My hands had started to shake from reaction. I couldn't work the clamps.

"No you don't. If we start right now we may get home. Leave the suit on and come in."

I did. As I pulled my webbing shut, the rams roared. The ship shuddered a little, then pushed forward as we dropped from under the blimp tank. Pressure mounted as the rams reached operating speed. Eric was giving it all he had. It would have been uncomfortable even without the metal suit around me. With the suit on it was torture. My couch was afire from the suit, but I couldn't get breath to say so. We were going almost straight up.

We had gone twenty minutes when the ship jerked like a galvanized frog. "Ram's out," Eric said calmly. "I'll use the other." Another lurch as we dropped the dead one. The ship flew on like a wounded penguin, but still accelerating.

One minute . . . two . . .

The other ram quit. It was as if we'd run into molasses. Eric blew off the ram and the pressure eased. I could talk.

"Eric."

"What?"

"Got any marshmallows?"

"*What?* Oh, I see. Is your suit tight?"

"Sure."

"Live with it. We'll flush the smoke out later. I'm going to coast above some of this stuff, but when I use the rocket it'll be savage. No mercy."

"Will we make it?"

"I think so. It'll be close."

The relief came first, icy cold. Then the anger. "No more inexplicable numbnesses?" I asked.

"No. Why?"

"If any come up you'll be sure and tell me, won't you?"

"Are you getting at something?"

"Skip it." I wasn't angry anymore.

"I'll be damned if I do. You know perfectly well it was mechanical trouble, you fool. You fixed it yourself!"

"No. I convinced you I must have fixed it. You needed to believe the rams *should* be working again. I gave you a miracle cure, Eric. I just hope I don't have to keep dreaming up new placebos for you all the way home."

"You thought that, but you went out on the wing sixteen miles up?" Eric's machinery snorted. "You've got guts where you need brains, Shorty."

I didn't answer.

"Five thousand says the trouble was mechanical. We let the mechanics decide after we land."

"You're on."

"Here comes the rocket. Two, one—"

It came, pushing me down into my metal suit. Sooty flames licked past my ears, writing black on the green metal ceiling, but the rosy mist before my eyes was not fire.

The man with the thick glasses spread a diagram of

the Venus ship and jabbed a stubby finger at the trailing edge of the wing. "Right around here," he said. "The pressure from outside compressed the wiring channel a little, just enough so there was no room for the wire to bend. It had to act as if it were rigid, see? Then when the heat expanded the metal these contacts pushed past each other."

"I suppose it's the same design on both wings?"

He gave me a queer look. "Well, naturally."

I left my check for five thousand dollars in a pile of Eric's mail and hopped a plane for Brasilia. How he found me I'll never know, but the telegram arrived this morning.

HOWIE COME HOME ALL IS FORGIVEN
DONOVANS BRAIN

I guess I'll have to.

DELILAH AND
THE SPACE-RIGGER

by Robert A. Heinlein

Here's one of Heinlein's classic Future History yarns, a tale of building the first space station, complicated by what much later would be called a male chauvinist who's butting heads with one of Heinlein's determined and competent heroines. Speaking of male chauvinists, in some demented quarters of sf scholarship, Heinlein has been dismissed as a contemptible MCP. After reading this story, you may wonder why that absurd accusation was ever made. . . .

Sure, we had trouble building Space Station One—but the trouble was people. Not that building a station twenty-two thousand three hundred miles out in space is a breeze. It was an engineering feat bigger than the Panama

Canal or the Pyramids—or even the Susquehanna Power Pile. But "Tiny" Larsen built her—and a job Tiny tackles gets built.

I first saw Tiny playing guard on a semi-pro team, working his way through Oppenheimer Tech. He worked summers for me thereafter till he graduated. He stayed in construction and eventually I went to work for him.

Tiny wouldn't touch a job unless he was satisfied with the engineering. The Station had jobs designed into it that called for six-armed monkeys instead of grown men in spacesuits. Tiny spotted such boners; not a ton of material went into the sky until the specs and drawings suited him.

But it was people that gave us the headaches. We had a sprinkling of married men, but the rest were wild lads, attracted by high pay and adventure. Some were busted spacemen. Some were specialists, like electricians and instrument men. About half were deep-sea divers, used to working in pressure suits. There were sandhogs and riggers and welders and shipfitters and two circus acrobats.

We fired four of them for being drunk on the job; Tiny had to break one stiff's arm before he would stay fired. What worried us was where did they get it? Turned out a shipfitter had rigged a heatless still, using the vacuum around us. He was making vodka from potatoes swiped from the commissary. I hated to let him go, but he was too smart.

Since we were falling free in a twenty-four-hour circular orbit, with everything weightless and floating, you'd think that shooting craps was impossible. But a radioman named Peters figured a dodge to substitute steel dice and a magnetic field. He also eliminated the element of chance, so we fired him.

We planned to ship him back in the next supply ship, the R.S. *Half Moon*. I was in Tiny's office when she blasted to match our orbit. Tiny swam to the view port. "Send for Peters, Dad," he said, "and give him the old heave ho. Who's his relief?"

"Party named G. Brooks McNye," I told him.

A line came snaking over from the ship. Tiny said, "I don't believe she's matched." He buzzed the radio shack for the ship's motion relative to the Station. The answer didn't please him and he told them to call the *Half Moon*. Tiny waited until the TV screen showed the rocket ship's CO. "Good morning, Captain. Why have you placed a line on us?"

"For cargo, naturally. Get your hopheads over here. I want to blast off before we enter the shadow." The Station spent about an hour and a quarter each day passing through Earth's shadow; we worked two eleven-hour shifts and slapped the dark period, to avoid rigging lights and heating suits.

Tiny shook his head. "Not until you've matched course and speed with us."

"I *am* matched!"

"Not to specification, by my instruments."

"Have a heart, Tiny! I'm short on maneuvering fuel. If I juggle this entire ship to make a mine few lousy tons of cargo, I'll be so late I'll have to put down on a secondary field. I may even have to make a dead stick landing." In those days all ships had wings.

"Look, Captain," Tiny said sharply, "the only purpose of your lift was to match orbits for those same few lousy tons. I don't care if you land in Little America on a pogo stick. The first load here was placed with loving care in the proper orbit and I'm making every other load match. Get that covered wagon into the groove."

"Very well, Superintendent!" Captain Shields said stiffly.

"Don't be sore, Don," Tiny said softly. "By the way, you've got a passenger for me?"

"Oh, yes, so I have!" Shields' face broke out in a grin."

"Well, keep him aboard until we until we unload. Maybe we can beat the shadow yet."

"Fine, fine! After all, why should I add to your troubles?" The skipper switched off, leaving my boss looking puzzled.

We didn't have time to wonder at his words. Shields whipped his ship around on gyros, blasted a second or two, and put her dead in space with us pronto—and used very little fuel, despite his bellyaching. I grabbed every man we could spare and managed to get the cargo clear before we swung into Earth's shadow. Weightlessness is an unbelievable advantage in handling freight; we gutted the *Half Moon*—by hand, mind you—in fifty-four minutes.

The stuff was oxygen tanks, loaded, and aluminum mirrors to shield them, panels of outer skin—sandwich stuff of titanium alloy sheet with foamed glass filling—and cases of jato units to spin the living quarters. Once it was all out and snapped to our cargo line, I sent the men back by the same line—the same line—I won't let a man work outside without a line no matter how space happy he figures he is. Then I told Shields to send over the passenger and cast off.

This little guy came out the ship's air lock, and hooked on to the ship's line. Handling himself like he was used to space, he set his feet and dived, straight along the stretched line, his snap hook running free. I hurried back and motioned him to follow me. Tiny, the new man, and I reached the air locks together.

Besides the usual cargo lock we had three G.E. Kwikloks. A Kwiklok is an Iron Maiden without spikes; it fits a man in a suit, leaving just a few pints of air to scavenge, and cycles automatically. A big time saver in changing shifts. I passed through the middle-sized one; Tiny, of course, used the big one. Without hesitation, the new man pulled himself into the small one.

We went into Tiny's office. Tiny strapped down, and pushed his helmet back. "Well, McNye," he said. "Glad to have you with us."

The new radio tech opened his helmet. I heard a low, pleasant voice answer, "Thank you."

I stared and didn't say anything. From where I was, I could see that the radio tech was wearing a hair ribbon.

I thought Tiny would explode. He didn't need to see the hair ribbon; with the helmet up it was clear that the new "man" was as female as Venus de Milo. Tiny sputtered, then he was unstrapped and diving for the view port. "Dad!" he yelled. "Get the radio shack. Stop that ship!"

But the *Half Moon* was already a ball of fire in the

distance. Tiny looked dazed. "Dad," he said, "who else knows about this?"

"Nobody, so far as I know."

He thought a bit. "We've got to keep her out of sight. That's it—we keep her locked up and out of sight until the next ship matches in." He didn't look at her.

"What in the world are you talking about?" McNye's voice was higher and no longer pleasant.

Tiny glared. "You, that's what. What are you—a stowaway?"

"Don't be silly! I'm G.B. McNye, electronics engineer. Don't you have my papers?"

Tiny turned to me. "Dad, this is your fault. How in Chr—pardon me, Miss. How did you let them send you a woman? Didn't you even read the advance report on her?"

"Me?" I said. "Now see here, you big squarehead! Those forms don't show sex; the Fair Employment Commission won't allow it except where it's pertinent to the job."

"You're telling *me* it's not pertinent to the job *here?*"

"Not by job classification it ain't. There's lots of female radio and radar men, back Earthside."

"This isn't Earthside." He had something. He was thinking of those two-legged wolves swarming over the job outside. And G.B. McNye was pretty. Maybe eight months of no women at all affected my judgment, but she would pass.

"I've even heard of female rocket pilots," I added, for spite.

"I don't care if you've heard of female archangels; I'll have no women here!"

"Just a minute!" If I was riled, *she* was plain sore. "You're the construction superintendent, are you not?"

"Yes," Tiny admitted.

"Very well, then, how do *you* know what sex I am?"

"Are you trying to deny that you are a woman?"

"Hardly! I'm proud of it. But officially you don't know what sex G. Brooks McNye is. That's why I use 'G' instead of Gloria. I don't ask favors."

Tiny grunted. "You won't get any. I don't know how you sneaked in, but get this, McNye, or Gloria, or whatever—you're fired. You go back on the next ship. Meanwhile, we'll try to keep the men from knowing we've got a woman aboard."

I could see her count ten. "May I speak," she said finally, "or does your Captain Bligh act extend to that, too?"

"Say your say."

"I didn't sneak in. I am on the permanent staff of the Station, Chief Communications Engineer. I took this vacancy myself to get to know the equipment while it was being installed. I'll live here eventually; I see no reason not to start now."

Tiny waved it away. "There'll be men and women both here—someday. Even kids. Right now it's stag and it'll stay that way."

"We'll see. Anyhow, you can't fire me; radio personnel don't work for you." She had a point; communicators and some other specialists were lent to the contractors, Five Companies, Incorporated, by Harriman Enterprises.

Tiny snorted. "Maybe I can't fire you; I can send you home. 'Requisitioned personnel must be satisfactory to the contractor.'—meaning me. Paragraph Seven, clause M; I wrote that clause myself."

"Then you know that if requisitioned personnel are refused without cause, the contractor bears the replacement cost."

"I'll risk paying your fare home, but I won't have you here."

"You are most unreasonable!"

"Perhaps, but I'll decide what's good for the job. I'd rather have a dope peddler than have a woman sniffing around my boys!"

She gasped. Tiny knew he had said too much; he added, "Sorry, Miss, but that's it. You'll stay under cover until I can get rid of you."

Before she could speak I cut in. "Tiny—look behind you!" Staring in the port was one of the riggers, his eyes bugged out. Three or four more floated up and joined him.

Then Tiny zoomed up to the port and they scattered like minnows. He scared them almost out of their suits; I thought he was going to shove his fists through the quartz.

He came back looking whipped. "Miss," he said, pointing, "wait in my room." When she was gone he added, "Dad, what'll we do?"

I said, "I thought you had made up your mind, Tiny."

"I have," he answered peevishly. "Ask the Chief Inspector to come in, will you?"

That showed how far gone he was. The inspection gang belonged to Harriman Enterprises, not to us, and Tiny rated them mere nuisances. Besides, Tiny was an Oppenheimer graduate; Dalrymple was from M.I.T.

He came in, brash and cheerful. "Good morning, Superintendent. Morning, Mr. Witherspoon. What can I do for you?"

Glumly, Tiny told the story. Dalrymple looked smug. "She's right, old man. You can send her back and even specify a male relief, but I can hardly endorse 'for proper cause' now, can I?"

"Damnation, Dalrymple, we can't have a woman around here!"

"A moot point. Not covered by contract, y'know."

"If your office hadn't sent us a crooked gambler as her predecessor, I wouldn't be in this jam!"

"There, there! Remember the old blood pressure. Suppose we leave the endorsement open and arbitrate the cost. That's fair, eh?"

"I suppose so. Thanks."

"Not at all. But consider this: when you rushed Peters off before interviewing the newcomer, you cut yourself down to one operator. Hammond can't stand watch twenty-four hours a day."

"He can sleep in the shack. The alarm will wake him."

"I can't accept that. The home office and ships' frequencies must be guarded at all times. Harriman Enterprises has supplied a qualified operator; I am afraid you must use her for the time being."

Tiny will always cooperate with the inevitable; he said quietly, "Dad, she'll take first shift. Better put the married men on that shift."

Then he called her in. "Go to the radio shack and start makee-learnee, so that Hammond can go off watch soon. Mind what he tells you. He's a good man."

"I know," she said briskly. "I trained him."

Tiny bit his lip. The C.I. said, "The Superintendent doesn't bother with trivia—I'm Robert Dalrymple, Chief Inspector. He probably didn't introduce his assistant either—Mr. Witherspoon."

"Call me Dad," I said.

She smiled and said, "Howdy, Dad." I felt warm clear through. She went on to Dalrymple, "Odd that we haven't met before."

Tiny butted in. "McNye, you'll sleep in my room—"

She raised her eyebrows; he went on angrily, "Oh, I'll get my stuff out—at once. And get this: keep the door locked, off shift."

"You're darn tootin' I will!"

Tiny blushed.

I was too busy to see much of Miss Gloria. There was cargo to stow, the new tanks to install and shield. That left the most worrisome task of all: putting spin on the living quarters. Even the optimists didn't expect much interplanetary traffic for some years; nevertheless Harriman Enterprises wanted to get some activities moved in and paying rent against their enormous investment.

I.T.&T. had leased space for a microwave relay station—several million a year from television alone. The Weather Bureau was itching to set up its hemispheric integrating station; Palomar Observatory had a concession (Harriman Enterprises donated that space); the Security Council had some hush-hush project; Fermi Physical Labs and Kettering Institute each had space—a dozen tenants wanted to move in now, or sooner, even if we never completed accommodations for tourists and travelers.

There were time bonuses in it for Five Companies, Incorporated—and their help. So we were in a hurry to get spin on the quarters.

People who have never been out have trouble getting through their heads—at least I had—that there is no feeling of weight, no up and down, in a free orbit in space. There's Earth, round and beautiful, only twenty-odd thousand miles away, close enough to brush your sleeve. You know it's pulling you towards it. Yet you feel no weight, absolutely none. You float.

Floating is fine for some types of work, but when it's time to eat, or play cards, or bathe, it's good to feel weight on your feet. Your dinner stays quiet and you feel more natural.

You've seen pictures of the Station—a huge cylinder, like a bass drum, with ships' nose pockets dimpling its sides. Imagine a snare drum, spinning around inside the bass drum; that's the living quarters, with centrifugal force pinch-hitting for gravity. We could have spun the whole Station but you can't berth a ship against a whirling dervish.

So we built a spinning part for creature comfort and an outer, stationary part for docking, tanks, storerooms, and the like. You pass from one to the other at the hub. When Miss Gloria joined us the inner part was closed in and pressurized, but the rest was a skeleton of girders.

Mighty pretty though, a great network of shiny struts and ties against black sky and stars—titanium alloy 1403, light, strong, and non-corrodible. The Station is flimsy compared with a ship, since it doesn't have to take blast-off stresses. That meant we didn't dare put on spin by violent means—which is where jato units come in.

"Jato"—Jet Assisted Take-Off—rocket units invented to give airplanes a boost. Now we use them wherever a controlled push is needed, say to get a truck out of the mud on a dam job. We mounted four thousand of them around the frame of the living quarters, each one placed just so. They were wired up and ready to fire when Tiny came to me looking worried. "Dad," he said, "let's drop everything and finish compartment D-113."

"Okay," I said. D-113 was in the non-spin part.

"Rig an air lock and stock it with two weeks' supplies."

"That'll change your mass distribution for spin," I suggested.

"I'll refigure it next dark period. Then we'll shift jatos."

When Dalrymple heard about it, he came charging around. It meant a delay in making rental space available. "What's the idea?"

Tiny stared at him. They had been cooler than ordinary lately; Dalrymple had been finding excuses to seek out Miss Gloria. He had to pass through Tiny's office to reach her temporary room, and Tiny had finally told him to get out and stay out. "The idea," Tiny said slowly, "is to have a pup tent in case the house burns."

"What do you mean?"

"Suppose we fire up the jatos and the structure cracks? Want to hang around in a spacesuit until a ship happens by?"

"That's silly. The stresses have been calculated."

"That's what the man said when the bridge fell. We'll do it my way."

Dalrymple stormed off.

Tiny's efforts to keep Gloria fenced up were sort of pitiful. In the first place, the radio tech's biggest job was repairing suit walkie-talkies, done on watch. A rash of such troubles broke out—on her shift. I made some shift transfers and docked a few for costs, too; it's not properly maintenance when a man deliberately busts his aerial.

There were other symptoms. It became stylish to shave. Men started wearing shirts around quarters and bathing increased to where I thought I would have to rig another water still.

Came the shift when D-113 was ready and the jatos readjusted. I don't mind saying I was nervous. All hands were ordered out of the quarters and into suits. They perched around the girders and waited.

Men in spacesuits all look alike; we used numbers and colored armbands. Supervisors had two antennas, one for a gang frequency, one for the supervisors' circuit. With Tiny and me, the second antenna hooked back through the radio shack and to all the gang frequencies—a broadcast.

The supervisors had reported their men clear of the fireworks and I was about to give Tiny the word, when this figure came climbing through the girders, inside the danger zone. No safety line. No armband. One antenna.

Miss Gloria, of course. Tiny hauled her out of the blast zone, and anchored her with his own safety line. I heard his voice, harsh in my helmet: "Who do you think you are? A sidewalk superintendent?"

And her voice: "What do you expect me to do? Go park on a star?"

"I told you to stay away from the job. If you can't obey orders, I'll lock you up."

I reached him, switched off my radio and touched helmets. "Boss! Boss!" I said. "You're broadcasting!"

"Oh—" he says, switches off, and touches helmets with her.

We could still hear her; she didn't switch off. "Why, you big baboon, I came outside because you sent a search party to clear everybody out," and, "How would I know about a safety line rule? You've kept me penned up." And finally. "We'll see!"

I dragged him away and he told the boss electrician to go ahead. Then we forgot the row for we were looking at the prettiest fireworks ever seen, a giant St. Catherine's wheel, rockets blasting all over it. Utterly soundless, out there in space—but beautiful beyond compare.

The blasts died away and there was the living quarters, spinning true as a flywheel—Tiny and I both let out sighs of relief. We all went back inside then to see what weight tasted like.

It tasted funny. I went through the shaft and started down the ladders, feeling myself gain weight as I neared the rim. I felt seasick, like the first time I experienced no weight. I could hardly walk and my calves cramped.

We inspected throughout, then went to the office and sat down. It felt good, just right for comfort, one-third gravity at the rim. Tiny rubbed his chair arms and grinned, "Beats being penned up in D-113."

"Speaking of being penned up," Miss Gloria said, walking in, "may I have a word with you, Mr. Larsen?"

"Uh? Why, certainly. Matter of fact, I wanted to see you. I owe you an apology, Miss McNye. I was—"

"Forget it," she cut in. "You were on edge. But I want to know this: how long are you going to keep up this nonsense of trying to chaperone me?"

He studied her. "Not long. Just till your relief arrives."

"So? Who is the shop steward around here?"

"A shipfitter named McAndrews. But you can't use him. You're a staff member."

"Not in the job I'm filling. I am going to talk to him. You're discriminating against me, and in my off time at that."

"Perhaps, but you will find I have the authority. Legally, I'm a ship's captain, while on this job. A captain in space has wide discriminatory powers."

"Then you should use them with discrimination!"

He grinned. "Isn't that what you just said I was doing?"

We didn't hear from the shop steward, but Miss Gloria started doing as she pleased. She showed up at the movies, next off shift, with Dalrymple. Tiny left in the middle—good show, too; *Lysistrata Goes to Town*, relayed up from New York.

As she was coming back alone he stopped her, having seen to it that I was present. "Umm—Miss McNye . . ."

"Yes?"

"I think you should know, uh, well . . . Chief Inspector Dalrymple is a married man."

"Are you suggesting that my conduct has been improper?"

"No, but—"

"Then mind your own business!" Before he could answer she added, "It might interest you that he told me about your four children."

Tiny sputtered. "Why . . . why, I'm not even married!"

"So? That makes it worse, doesn't it?" She swept out.

Tiny quit trying to keep her in her room, but told her to notify him whenever she left it. It kept him busy riding herd on her. I refrained from suggesting that he get Dalrymple to spell him.

But I was surprised when he told me to put through the order dismissing her. I had been pretty sure he was going to drop it.

"What's the charge?" I asked.

"Insubordination!"

I kept mum. He said, "Well, she won't take orders."

"She does her work okay. You give her orders you wouldn't give to one of the men—and that a man wouldn't take."

"You disagree with my orders?"

"That's not the point. You can't prove the charge, Tiny."

"Well, charge her with being female! I can prove *that*."

I didn't say anything. "Dad," he added wheedlingly, "you know how to write it. 'No personal animus against Miss McNye, but it is felt that as a matter of policy, and so forth and so on.' "

I wrote it and gave it to Hammond privately. Radio techs are sworn to secrecy but it didn't surprise me when I was stopped by O'Connor, one of our best metalsmiths.

"Look, Dad, is it true that the Old Man is getting rid of Brooksie?"

"Brooksie?"

"Brooksie McNye—she says to call her Brooks. Is it true?"

I admitted it, then went on, wondering if I should have lied.

It takes four hours, about, for a ship to lift from Earth. The shift before the *Pole Star* was due, with Miss Gloria's relief, the timekeeper brought me two separation slips. Two men were nothing; we averaged more each ship. An hour later he reached me by supervisors' circuit, and asked me to come to the time office. I was out on the rim, inspecting a weld job; I said no.

"Please, Mr. Witherspoon," he begged, "you've *got* to." When one of the boys doesn't call me "Dad", it means something. I went.

There was a queue like mail call outside his door; I went in and he shut the door on them. He handed me a double handful of separation slips. "What in the great depths of night is this?" I asked.

"There's dozens more I ain't had time to write up yet."

None of the slips had any reason given—just "own choice".

"Look, Jimmie—what goes on here?"

"Can't you dope it out, Dad? Shucks, I'm turning in one, too."

I told him my guess and he admitted it. So I took the slips, called Tiny and told him for the love of Heaven to come to his office.

Tiny chewed his lip considerable. "But, Dad, they

can't strike. It's a non-strike contract with bonds from every union concerned."

"It's no strike, Tiny. You can't stop a man from quitting."

"They'll pay their own fares back, so help me!"

"Guess again. Most of 'em have worked long enough for the free ride."

"We'll have to hire others quick, or we'll miss our date."

"Worse than that, Tiny—we won't finish. By next dark period you won't even have a maintenance crew."

"I've never had a gang of men quit me. I'll talk to them."

"No good, Tiny. You're up against something too strong for you."

"*You're* against me, Dad?"

"I'm never against you, Tiny."

He said, "Dad, you think I'm pig-headed, but I'm *right*. You can't have one woman among several hundred men. It drives 'em nutty."

I didn't say it affected him the same way; I said, "Is that bad?"

"Of course. I can't let the job be ruined to humor one woman."

"Tiny, have you looked at the progress charts lately?"

"I've hardly had time to—what about them?"

I knew why he hadn't had time. "You'll have trouble proving Miss Gloria interfered with the job. We're ahead of schedule."

"We *are?*"

While he was studying the charts, I put an arm around

his shoulder. "Look, son," I said, "sex has been around our planet a long time. Earthside, they never get away from it, yet some pretty big jobs get built anyhow. Maybe we'll just have to learn to live with it here, too. Matter of fact, you had the answer a minute ago."

"I did? I sure didn't know it."

"You said, 'You can't have *one* woman among several hundred men.' Get me?"

"Huh? No, I don't. Wait a minute! Maybe I do."

"Ever tried jiu jitsu? Sometimes you win by relaxing."

"Yes. Yes!"

"When you can't beat 'em, you jine 'em."

He buzzed the radio shack. "Have Hammond relieve you, McNye, and come to my office."

He did it handsomely, stood up and made a speech—he'd been wrong, taken him a long time to see it, hoped there were no hard feelings, etc. He was instructing the home office to see how many jobs could be filled at once with female help.

"Don't forget married couples," I put in mildly, "and better ask for some older women, too."

"I'll do that," Tiny agreed. "Have I missed anything, Dad?"

"Guess not. We'll have to rig quarters, but there's time."

"Okay. I'm telling them to hold the *Pole Star*, Gloria, so they can send us a few this trip."

"That's fine!" She looked really happy.

He chewed his lip. "I've a feeling I've missed something. Hmm—I've got it. Dad, tell them to send up

EXPEDITION

by Fredric Brown

Back when astronauts were an exclusively men-only club, Fredric Brown considered not only some possible outcomes of admitting the superior sex (as Heinlein put it) to the club, but also one particular such outcome of using a gender-blind approach to picking the crew of a Martian expedition. . . .

★🪐★

"THE FIRST MAJOR EXPEDITION to Mars," said the history professor, "the one which followed the preliminary exploration by one-man scout ships and aimed to establish a permanent colony, led to a great number of problems. One of the most perplexing of which was: how many men and how many women should comprise the expedition's personnel of thirty?

"There were three schools of thought on the subject.

"One was that the ship should be comprised of fifteen

men and fifteen women, many of whom would no doubt find one another suitable mates and get the colony off to a fast start.

"The second was that the ship should take twenty-five men and five women—ones who were willing to sign a waiver on monogamous inclinations—on the grounds that five women could easily keep twenty-five men sexually happy and twenty-five men could keep five women even happier.

"The third school of thought was that the expedition should contain thirty men on the grounds that under those circumstances, the men would be able to concentrate on the work at hand much better. And it was argued that since a second ship would follow in approximately a year and could contain mostly women, it would be no hardship for the men to endure celibacy that long. Especially since they were used to it; the two Space Cadet schools, one for men and one for women, rigidly segregated the sexes.

"The Director of Space Travel settled this argument by a simple expedient. He—yes, Miss Ambrose?" A girl in the class had raised her hand.

"Professor, was that expedition the one headed by Captain Maxon? The one they called Mighty Maxon? Could you tell us how he came to have that nickname?"

"I'm coming to that, Miss Ambrose. In lower schools you have been told the story of the expedition, but not the *entire* story; you are now old enough to hear it.

"The Director of Space Travel settled the argument, cut the Gordian knot by announcing that the personnel of the expedition would be chosen by lot, regardless of sex, from the graduating classes of the two space academies.

There is little doubt that he personally favored twenty-five men to five women—because the men's school had approximately five hundred in the graduating class and the women's school had approximately one hundred. By the law of averages the ratio of winners should have been five men to one woman.

"However, the law of averages does not always work out on any one particular series. And it so happened that on this particular drawing, *twenty-nine* women drew winning chances, and only *one* man won.

"There were loud protests from almost everyone except the winners, but the Director stuck to his guns; the drawing had been honest and he refused to change the status of any of the winners. His only concession to appease male egos was to appoint Maxon, the one man, as captain. The ship took off and had a successful voyage.

"And when the second expedition landed, they found the population doubled. Exactly doubled—every woman member of the expedition had a child, and one of them had twins, making a total of exactly thirty infants.

"Yes, Miss Ambrose, I see your hand, but please let me finish. No, there is nothing spectacular about what I have thus far told you. Although many people would think loose morals were involved, it is no great feat for one man, given time, to impregnate twenty-nine women.

"What gave Captain Maxon his nickname is the fact that work on the second ship went much faster than scheduled and the second expedition did not arrive one year later, but only nine months and two days later.

"Does that answer your question, Miss Ambrose?"

NOT YET THE END

by Fredric Brown

Once again, I've picked two stories by Fredric Brown, who, among his many other virtues, was the master of the short-short story, putting high explosive yarns in innocent-looking small packages. We begin with some nonhuman space explorers who have discovered Earth, which would have been bad news for us, except for a slight misunderstanding. . . .

★🌑★

THERE WAS A GREENISH, hellish tinge to the light within the metal cube. It was a light that made the dead-white skin of the creature seated at the controls seem faintly green.

A single, faceted eye, front center in the head, watched the seven dials unwinkingly. Since they had left Xandor that eye had never once wavered from the dials. Sleep was unknown to the race to which Kar-388Y belonged. Mercy, too, was unknown. A single glance at the sharp, cruel features below the faceted eye would have proved that.

The pointers on the fourth and seventh dials came to a stop. That meant the cube itself had stopped in space relative to its immediate objective. Kar reached forward with his upper right arm and threw the stabilizer switch. Then he rose and stretched his cramped muscles.

Kar turned to face his companion in the cube, a being like himself. "We are here," he said. "The first stop, Star Z-5689. It has nine planets, but only the third is habitable. Let us hope we find creatures here who will make suitable slaves for Xandor."

Lal-I6B, who had sat in rigid mobility during the journey, rose and stretched also. "Let us hope so, yes. Then we can return to Xandor and be honored while the fleet comes to get them. But let's not hope too strongly. To meet with success at the first place we stop would be a miracle. We'll probably have to look a thousand places."

Kar shrugged. "Then we'll look a thousand places. With the Lounacs dying off, we must have slaves else our mines must close and our race will die."

He sat down at the controls again and threw a switch that activated a visiplate that would show what was beneath them. He said, "We are above the night side of the third planet. There is a cloud layer below us. I'll use the manuals from here."

He began to press buttons. A few minutes later he said, "Look, Lal, at the visiplate. Regularly spaced lights— a city! The planet *is* inhabited."

Lal had taken his place at the other switchboard, the

fighting controls. Now he too was examining dials. "There is nothing for us to fear. There is not even the vestige of a forcefield around the city. The scientific knowledge of the race is crude. We can wipe the city out with one blast if we are attacked."

"Good," Kar said. "But let me remind you that destruction is not our purpose—yet. We want specimens. If they prove satisfactory and the fleet comes and takes as many thousand slaves as we need, then will be time to destroy not a city but the whole planet so that their civilization will never progress to the point where they'll be able to launch reprisal raids."

Lal adjusted a knob. "All right. I'll put on the megrafield and we'll be invisible to them unless they see far into the ultraviolet, and, from the spectrum of their sun, I doubt that they do."

As the cube descended the light within it changed from green to violet and beyond. It came to a gentle rest. Kar manipulated the mechanism that operated the airlock.

He stepped outside, Lal just behind him. "Look," Kar said, "two bipeds. Two arms, two eyes—not dissimilar to the Lounacs, although smaller. Well, here are our specimens."

He raised his lower left arm, whose three-fingered hand held a thin rod wound with wire. He pointed it first at one of the creatures, then at the other. Nothing visible emanated from the end of the rod, but they both froze instantly into statuelike figures.

"They're not large, Kar," Lai said. "I'll carry one back, you carry the other. We can study them better inside the cube, after we're back in space."

Kar looked about him in the dim light. "All right, two is enough, and one seems to be male and the other female. Let's get going."

A minute later the cube was ascending and as soon as they were well out of the atmosphere, Kar threw the stabilizer switch and joined Lal, who had been starting a study of the specimens during the brief ascent.

"Vivaparous," said Lal. "Five-fingered, with hands suited to reasonably delicate work. But—let's try the most important test, intelligence."

Kar got the paired headsets. He handed one pair to Lal, who put one on his own head, one on the head of one of the specimens. Kar did the same with the other specimen.

After a few minutes, Kar and Lal stared at each other bleakly.

"Seven points below minimum," Kar said. "They could not be trained even for the crudest labor in the mines. Incapable of understanding the simplest instructions. Well, we'll take them back to the Xandor museum."

"Shall I destroy the planet?"

"No," Kar said. "Maybe a million years from now—if our race lasts that long—they'll have evolved enough to become suitable for our purpose. Let us move on to the next star with planets."

The make-up editor of the *Milwaukee Star* was in the composing room, supervising the closing of the local page. Jenkins, the head make-up compositor, was pushing in leads to tighten the second to the last column.

"Room for one more story in the eighth column, Pete,"

he said. "About thirty-six picas. There are two there in the overset that will fit. Which one shall I use?"

The make-up editor glanced at the type in the galleys lying on the stone beside the chase. Long practice enabled him to read the headlines upside down at a glance. "The convention story and the zoo story, huh? Oh, hell, run the convention story. Who cares if the zoo director thinks two monkeys disappeared off Monkey Island last night?"

SUPERWEAPON

by David Drake

*For an explorer, making new discoveries is part of the
territory. Of course, there's no guarantee that one of those
new discoveries might not be Very Bad News . . .*

THE ATTENDANT at the conference room door wasn't
a guard: she was unarmed, and she wore the purple dress
uniform of a full commander in the Navy. Kearney had
thought that the Defense Board might keep the Surveyors
waiting to demonstrate its power, but precisely at 1200
hours Commonwealth City—local—time the commander
opened the door. "The Defense Board is ready for you
now, sirs and madam," she said.

Rosie Rice snorted, but she got up and with Kearney
and Balthus trooped into a room whose two semi-circular
tables faced one another. The clear walls gave an
unobstructed view of the city outside. Five officers in

uniform sat at the more distant table; there were three
empty chairs at the nearer side.

Kearney took the middle chair. Balthus, the Head of
Biology, sat to his left and Rice, Head of Information, took
the right seat and set up her little console on the table.
She ran the hardware for these briefings. Normally
Balthus was the star, describing exotic life forms, but
Kearney was pretty sure that the Defense officials this
time were going to be primarily interested in what Rosie
had to say.

There were no ID tags on either the officers or the
table in front of them, but Rice had made sure the
surveyors had the images, names, and full information
about the folks they'd be meeting today. Topelius, a small
man in the dark green of the army, glared at them and
said, "Quite a gang of scruffs, aren't you? Do you think
this meeting is a joke?"

"The waste of our time certainly isn't a joke," said
Rice. She was short-tempered at the best of times, and
Kearney guessed he could count on the fingers of one
hand how often he remembered her being in a good
mood. "As for you lot, though—"

"Rosie!" Kearney said. "Remember, this is *work*. Do
your job."

The uniforms were already angry. Though Defense
didn't have any formal control over the Survey Section,
it'd be naïve to imagine that, in a bureaucracy as large as
the Commonwealth's, Defense couldn't make life difficult
for individual surveyors if it put its mind to it.

Rice scowled but she shut up. Kearney turned
quickly—he was afraid one of the defense people would

try to fill the silence—and said, "But that's the point, General Topelius: this *is* work for us, so we're in our working outfits."

Rice wore a brown sweater over a checked shirt; Balthus' lab coat was probably cleaner than it looked— many of the stains, though permanent, had been sterilized—but it certainly wasn't clean. Kearney himself had put on a new suit of spacers' slops; they were soft, loose, and comfortable, but he didn't pretend they were strack.

"*Don't* give me that!" snapped Topelius. "I know the Survey Section has uniforms!"

"Central Office does, yes," said Kearney. "Management. But sir, you specified you didn't want Central Office personnel, you wanted the chiefs of the team who actually surveyed the artifact. Real surveyors are almost always in protective gear, so our working clothes are what's comfortable in a hard suit."

"Less uncomfortable," Balthus said. "No way a hard suit is comfortable."

A sky-train was moving across the city in its shimmering tube of ionized atmosphere. It was noticeably lower than the level of the conference room. Kearney wondered just how high in the Defense Tower they were.

A doorman had walked the team on its arrival to a sealed car which shunted them to the elevator. The elevator had brought them up to a waiting room. The attendants who'd put them aboard the vehicles hadn't provided anything but monosyllabic directions, and the commander had remained as silent as the conference room door behind her.

"What I want to know . . . ," said Rice in her usual angry tone. "If Central Office can't talk to you lot and let us get on with our jobs, what bloody use are they?"

Your salary is paid into your account, Kearney thought, *and you draw your rations.*

He didn't say that aloud, because Rice really didn't much care about money or food—and anyway, it wasn't the point of this meeting. To Admiral Blumenthal he said, "Sir, you want to discuss the artifact. We're here to do that."

"What we want to know," said Bowdoin of Operations, "is why Survey Section has been hiding an alien warship from the Ministry of Defense for months!"

"Well, it's more like a year and a half, isn't it?" said Balthus, looking at Kearney with that puzzled expression he got when he was trying to find the precise phrase.

"We didn't know it was a warship until seven months ago when we identified the weapons system," Rice objected.

Her control wands twitched. An image of a prism orbiting the yellow clouds of a gas giant appeared in the air, just above eye level of the seated parties. The body had four rectangular sides and stubby pyramids on both ends.

"Well, we were pretty sure," said Balthus. "There wasn't any room for cargo."

"Suspecting isn't knowing!" Rice said. "We're surveyors, not fortune tellers!"

"What's important . . . ," Kearney said, speaking over his teammates and hoping to shush them before the Board blew its collective gasket. "Is that we weren't hiding anything. We'd been making progress reports through our own chain of command from the beginning. As soon as we were sure that it was a warship, we—the field team—reported that directly to the nearest Ministry of Defense facility."

"Which was a dockyard," Blumenthal said. "A bloody regional dockyard!"

"Well, we'd found a ship," Balthus said. "So we reported it to a dockyard."

He really was as innocent as he sounded. Kearney knew that he'd never have been able to put that fiction across, but Balthus seemed to have done so. Rice, of course, wouldn't have bothered trying.

"You found a ship eleven kilometers long!" Topelius said. "Didn't you think that was special enough to report directly to Commonwealth City?"

"On the long axis," Balthus said, sounding as though the distinction mattered—which of course it did to him. "On the short dimension it's about seven."

Rice adjusted her projector, shrinking down the viewpoint so that the tiny bead of the Survey vessel—which carried a team of ninety-odd comfortably—could be seen floating beside one of the alien vessel's open hatches. "*Much* larger than the *Shield of Justice*," Rice said in a gloating tone.

Kearney hoped his mental wince didn't reach the muscles of his face, but he couldn't swear to that. *Bloody Hell, Rosie, do you want to go straight from here to a prison that doesn't show up in anybody's records?*

Shawm said in a perfectly flat voice, "What do you know about the *Shield of Justice*?"

Shawm was a tall, rangy man with an extremely dark complexion. He wore a khaki Second-Class uniform with no medals or rank indications. He was probably a general, but Kearney wasn't sure that they used familiar ranks in Security.

"Only what's public knowledge in any spaceport in the Commonwealth!" Kearney broke in. "Isn't that right, Doctor Rice? Nothing that big could be truly secret, after all."

He was desperately afraid that Rosie was going to start projecting images of the Commonwealth's supership—a sphere a kilometer in diameter—if he didn't head her off.

Yes, of course the *Shield* was classified as Most Secret—but they were Surveyors, for God's sake! They were trained to learn things, and the alien environments that Surveyors examined as their job were a lot more puzzling than any human riddle could be.

"Yes," said Balthus, blindsiding Kearney. "It's being built on Ferrol and seems to have absorbed half the Defense budget for each of the past ten years. That's figuring the real cost of items listed in the public budget, of course. The costs're remarkably inflated in the published material, but real information is easy to find."

"I think we should leave this subject," said Shawm, after a pause during which Kearney had held his breath.

"Yes," said Kearney. "As I say, we reported the find to a defense facility and got on with our survey. There didn't appear to be any particular urgency about the matter."

"No urgency!" said Blumenthal. "Do you claim you're ignorant of the current political situation?"

"Well sir," Kearney said. "Things are tense between the Commonwealth—"

As he spoke he realized he should have said "us," but he found it very hard to imagine a community between his team and the group at the table opposite.

"—and the Empire of Khorsabad, but—"

"Khorsabad might want to attack before your *Shield of Justice*—" Balthus began.

"Doctor Balthus!" said Kearney. "We were politely asked to avoid that subject!"

Rice said, "Yeah, you've pretty much forced Khorsabad to attack while it still has a chance to win." *It's like having two dogs on long leashes who decided to start running in opposite circles!*

Graz, the stocky woman with the Production portfolio, chuckled like gravel in a chute. "It's too late for Khorsabad now. When the final software checks are done—and that could be any moment!—the *Shield* is done and the Commonwealth's enemies are done."

Hoping to change the subject, to bring it back on track, Kearney said, "But the ship we found couldn't have any contemporary importance. We believe it was in sponge space for thirty thousand years. Only when its fusion bottle depowered completely did it drop into normal space to be found."

"Good God!" said Blumenthal. "This ship is thirty *thousand* years old?"

"Older than that," Kearney said. He was the team's Head of Engineering, as well as being the captain and navigator of the survey vessel. A long time ago he'd been a naval lieutenant, but the Survey Section had been a better fit for him. "That's the probable lifetime of a fusion bottle the size of the one powering the artifact."

Kearney coughed for a pause. "Based on the star charts on the artifact, though," he said, "the real age is probably closer to a half million years. So it didn't occur to us that it had any bearing on present events."

"It's been orbiting a gas giant in the Brotherhood system for as far back as the original catalogue," Balthus said. "It was simply assumed to be a natural satellite until a miner landed on it eighteen months ago and found open hatches. Then we were called in."

"If you have the ship's star charts," said Blumenthal carefully, "then you must have entered the ship's computer?"

Rice nodded and said, "We've accessed portions of the ship's . . . well, I'll call it a computer for want of a better word. Controlling intelligence. We've limited our explorations to discrete sectors of the complex, avoiding any attempt to bring the full system on line."

"Our experts will be able to do that," said Tadeko, Advanced Projects. "We'll want a full report on your operations. You'll arrange for that to be sent over immediately."

He wasn't making a suggestion or even giving an order; he was stating an immutable fact. Tadeko was by far the oldest person in the room. He made Kearney think of a wise old lizard. A poisonous lizard.

"I don't doubt that you'll be able to do that, if you wish to," said Rice, meeting Tadeko's eyes squarely. "And I'll certainly meet with your specialists if you like."

"Look, if this is a warship," said Admiral Blumenthal,

"what sort of weaponry does it have? Because advanced armaments certainly might have bearing on our operations in the near future."

"Not the near future," Kearney said. "Their principle is so different from anything in our arsenal that it took us the better part of a year to realize that we were looking at weapons."

"We had to get into the ship's controlling intelligence to see the connection," Rice said. Without being asked, she brought up images of the alien vessel's interior. The four spherical projectors filled the volume, each connected to the exterior hull by four struts.

"So that you understand the scale . . . ," Rice said. She focused down on one of the bodies lying at the base of a strut, then expanded again to the rank of multi-kilometer spheres filling the huge ship. "Initially we assumed that we were looking at parts of the propulsion system that we didn't understand."

"We've been calling them projectors," said Kearney, "but that's not really correct. They seem to be quantum devices which cause objects to *be* in the center of the target. There's no movement, just a different location."

"Do they throw explosives, then?" Blumenthal said, frowning. "How big are the projectiles?"

Before Kearney could speak, Tadeko looked at his fellow and said, "That's immaterial. The location is already occupied by matter—even in deep space. There would be a total conversion of mass into energy. *Total*. The result would destroy any object of human scale."

Tadeko's voice sounded like scales rasping. Though he hadn't said so, Kearney was sure that he realized that such devices would be just as effective on planets. Unless they were very slow to aim and load, or were very unreliable, four projectors seemed—literally—overkill.

"What's the range, then?" said Graz. She spoke relatively softly. The board members had lost the angry tone and expressions that they'd begun the briefing with.

"It should be infinite," Kearney said. "It's a quantum effect, after all, not Newtonian. Though of course we haven't tried to activate the devices."

"I'd like to go back to where you showed us the scale," said Topelius. "I thought I saw a body. Was that a body?"

Rice obligingly shrank the focus to the dead crewman that she'd used to demonstrate how large the projectors were. The team had left the bodies where they were, pretty much. They'd moved the few who'd been in the way, and Balthus and his team had processed a number when they studied them; but all told, those were only drops in a bucket.

"These individuals run between forty and fifty kilos each," Balthus said with proprietary enthusiasm. "There are two sexes present, but I suspect from imagery in the databases that there was a third sex also—the one that does the actual breeding. Those were much larger; four or five hundred kilos, on my estimate."

"Good God!" Blumenthal repeated. "How many bodies are there?"

"And how did they die?" said Shawm. There was a hint of tension in his voice, quite different from the flat, threatening tone he'd used before.

"Nine hundred and seventy three," said Balthus. He

was noticeably more alert now that the discussion was on his specialty. He'd been used to leading briefings; most Survey reports focused on biology. Engineering and information technology were merely tools that supported the biological studies which determined whether or not a new world was suitable for human settlement. "And as for how they died—"

The close up of the corpse was strikingly ugly, but death generally was. The aliens hadn't worn clothing, but the fine fur that covered their bodies had fallen out over the millennia. It formed delicate halos on the plating beneath the bodies.

The naked corpses—this one was typical—had shrunk as their tendons dried and tightened. There had been no decay in vacuum, but over such a long time the surfaces had sublimed except where the bodies were in relatively restricted volumes.

"—most of them died when the ship depressurized suddenly. There were a few in atmosphere suits at the time. I'll show you those in a moment."

The creatures' faces thrust forward more than humans' did and were generally narrower. Rice's software created images of the creatures as they'd been in life; she now inset those into the central display. With fur in place they were more bestial—and therefore less ugly, because they no longer looked like deformed humans.

"What's the name of the people?" Topelius said. "The race who built it, I mean?"

"We have no idea," said Balthus tartly. "I suppose some day we might be able to understand their spoken language, though I don't see that there's any reason we'd want to. The race doesn't appear to have survived the loss of this warship for very long."

"When this ship vanished, their enemies—another race—made a complete sweep of them," Rice said.

"That race is gone by now also, but much more recently," said Balthus. "They built the lovely crystal structures which I'm sure you've seen."

"We've been calling them the Monkeys," said Kearney. "We had to call them something, and 'the corpses' didn't seem correct. We were more interested in what they'd been doing while they were alive, after all."

"The ship must have had a total systems failure," said Blumenthal. "Was it sabotaged by their enemies, do you suppose?"

"We've been bloody careful on Ferrol," said Graz, "but Khorsabad has been trying really hard to infiltrate the dockyard. We realize it's possible that they've succeeded."

The expression on Shawm's face as he looked at her was that of a diner staring at the half-worm in his salad. "We do *not* realize that," Shawm said. "It is *not* possible that Khorsabad has agents on Ferrol."

Kearney said nothing: this was a fight in somebody else's family. Personally, though, he hadn't been *that* certain about anything since he was thirteen and stopped believing in God.

"It wasn't a systems failure," Kearney said when he was sure that nobody at the Defense table was going to speak again. "And we don't think it was sabotage in the normal sense either."

"Certainly not systems failure," Balthus said. He nodded to Rice, who projected images in sequence showing half a dozen Monkeys in pale green atmosphere suits. The chests of each body had been ripped apart, mostly by mechanical means. The exception had been burned completely through in a hole large enough to pass a man's arm.

"This was done by the ship's maintenance robots," Balthus continued. A turtle-shaped device the size of a bushel basket was in the field of some images, a few with their tri-pincered limbs extended. They looked very much like the machines which did the same job on Commonwealth warships.

"The exception was in one of the ship's boats," Kearney said. "The device closest to him was configured to work on the boats and had a torch."

Rice expanded that image. This time the robot ran on a track in the ceiling and was almost as big as the boat it hung over.

The termini of the robot's arms—the hands—could rotate to bring up any one of multiple tools. Kearney knew from close examination that the one used was an oxygen lance, but he didn't bother volunteering that to the Board. They already looked stunned.

"It *had* to be sabotage," Shawm said. "The enemy took over the central computer and did this."

"I think it was because of the weapons," Rice said. "Aiming, directing, quantum weapons required a unique mechanism. The controlling intelligence had to genuinely *understand* the universe in realtime. This ship—"

She switched to the image with which she'd begun, the prism orbiting the swirling yellow clouds of the planet below.

"—has true machine intelligence. It doesn't mimic consciousness, it acts consciously."

"That's the same thing," Graz said in puzzlement. "For all practical purposes."

"I'd have said that those dead bodies were pretty practical!" Balthus said. Kearney didn't remember hearing him sound snappish before.

"To put it in other words . . . ," Rice said. Her tone made clear the sort of words she was tempted to put it in, but thank goodness she didn't do that. "The ship doesn't mimic the cognition of some large sample of its creators. The ship behaves like an intelligent *ship*."

"Does your ship, your *Shield*," said Balthus, "have a directive to protect itself?"

Graz opened her mouth to reply. Before she could, Shawm broke in with, "Anything to do with such a ship as you postulate would be classified!"

"Well, no matter," said Rice. "I can't imagine that you've created true machine intelligence."

"No warship would have self preservation as its *prime* directive," said Admiral Blumenthal. "That's crazy. No matter what race built it."

"But a truly conscious machine wouldn't be concerned with the priorities of the people who built it," Balthus said. "It would have its own priorities. It's unlikely that attacking a powerful enemy because its builders want it to would be high on the ship's own list."

"Whereas hiding in sponge space as soon as it was activated would prolong the ship's life for, well, thirty thousand years," Rice said. "And its existence for half a million, apparently."

"The ship disposed of the crew as quickly and efficiently as possible," Kearney said. "The crew members would probably have opinions of their own and might damage the ship if they were allowed to run free."

"Good God," said Tadeko. "Good *God*."

He got up and ran for a door. He moved very quickly for a man of his age.

He called something over his shoulder which Kearney heard as, "I have to send a courier!"

Rice looked at the remaining members of the Defense Board. She said, "You don't mean that your undoubtedly clever software engineers *have* managed to create real machine intelligence, do you?"

IN FROM THE COMMONS

by Tony Daniel

Pioneers in the past have undergone hardships, lethal weather conditions, starvation, and (no surprise) death. But the advance of science and technology might lead to going to the stars in comfort and style . . . in more ways than one.

IN THAT SUMMER when the call went out, we were in the mountains fishing up a trout stream that flowed from the cirque lake on Paradise Peak. The sky was carbon blue and the water was very cold on our ankles and calves. There were no clouds. There was no sun that day. Everything was bright and precisely rendered. The call was a sound at first, a metallic tintinnabulation, as from a carillon. Eva looked up, but Gene was playing out his fishing line and Haller was intent on finding a lure that matched the gnats he'd seen swirling in the shadow of the stream's bank. I was sipping tea from an enamel cup.

After the sound came a green flash across the sky. Light travels more slowly than sound in the Time River mountains, of course. Then there was the smell—dandelions, crushed—and then there was the way it felt inside us. It is a strange thing to have sudden knowledge where there was none before—knowledge you neither intuited nor deduced, knowledge that is only and entirely *there*, in an instant. It is not like deja vu or a presaging because it is not knowledge of the past or the future. It is like a sensation that comes from nowhere; it is a finger behind your eyeballs rubbing away a cataract from the backside of your vision.

Gene ceased his casting. Haller put down his hat, which was pricked with lures. I finished sipping my tea, wiped my mouth, and considered what I now knew. We were very far into the continent, into the commons. Traveling back would be an extremely long trip over changing terrain. I always knew that the call would eventually come, but I had not expected it so soon. It was something that was in the back of my mind, but something of which I never spoke. What would have been the point? It either would or would not come.

It had come.

"What do you think it means?" Eva said. She climbed from the stream, water beading and dripping from the wool of her trousers. "Are we there?"

"It'll be a long, hard trek back to find out if we are," Haller said. "We passed through the January Hills over two months ago."

After a moment, Gene began casting his line once again, settling back into his sedate, precise rhythm. His face also settled—back into its usual serenity. It was as if a small stone had been dropped into a pond, and, since it was a pond, there could be no record of the stone's perturbation of the water. That was Gene.

"We're a long way into the commons," I said. "In the cities, we'd have an address and we'd be sought out and asked whether we wanted to leave or not, but we're hidden in the ecology here. It's totally up to us to answer the call."

"It always has been," Gene said, casting, still casting.

"But we aren't trying to hide," said Eva.

"They always expected to lose part of us to the commons," Haller said, "Splitting us up was supposed to help with the problem a bit, but I heard talk of as many as three in ten not coming back."

"We *have* been here a long, long time," said Eva. "Maybe we've forgotten something important. Do we even know how to get back?"

"It isn't a question of that," Gene said, placidly. "We know where we are; Tan has kept a map."

"Yes," I said. "I have kept a good map." The map was always in my back pocket. I could feel it bunched between my rump and the rock on which I sat. It was made on beautybark paper and I worked on it each night with a wild turkey feather stylus filled with ink of liquid moonlight, which I collected from my portable condenser. When we returned to civilization, I had thought to sell my map to finance another trip into the commons. In the cities, such artifacts were highly sought after as interpretative paradigms for sortilege and other means of divination. As any prognosticator knows, the commons are the shadow cast by all of our minds, and vice versa. In the commons, we know what we know, and that is all that there is. So, of course, the interpretation of omens is a precise and useful craft.

"I'm not going, by the way," Gene said. He did not interrupt the rhythm of his casting. "I've been thinking for a long time that I might stay."

"Oh, Gene," Eva said. "Don't decide yet, please." Eva sat down with her legs crossed on a patch of tundra grass near the stream bank. She looked at the back of Gene's head. Each of his hairs was unique and defined in the general brightness. Gene was luminous. He had achieved this long before the rest of us, even though this was the reason we had all traveled into the commons in the first place. Beatification. It was what you did while you waited. When we set out, I had not figured that he would be the first. Haller was quick and clever and Eva had a broad and synthesizing intellect. I had no expectations concerning myself, but I had thought it would happen to one of them first. In retrospect, however, it was clear that Gene was bound for beatification. He was the empiricist who took everything as it came. Over time, he had become a cavern through which all of his surroundings flowed.

"I know what I know," Gene said. "I know where I am, and *here* is where I am."

We were at altitude and so the moon was nearly full every night, since we were so near to it. I had plans to climb Paradise Peak, touch its face, and actually to collect a jar of moonlight ink to take down with me. Now there was no time—not if I were to answer the call and come in from the commons.

That night, Eva unzipped the door flap and crawled into

my tent after midnight. She snuggled up beside me in my sleeping bag and I felt her cool cheek against the scruff of my beard, her chilly arms warming against my chest. She had come in with only a long cotton shirt on and wool socks; a few snow crystals tickled my bare legs where she rubbed her feet against my thighs. "I've been with Haller," she said. "But Gene won't let me touch him."

"What does he say?"

"Nothing much. You know Gene. But I think he is worried about me trying to change his mind."

"I think he's letting you go," I said. "He doesn't want to make up *your* mind for you."

"Yes," Eva said, "that would be a kinder way to look at it."

"It's the best way," I said. "I don't think Gene is being selfish."

"*You're* not going to stay, are you?" She poked my ribs. "Are you, Tan?"

"I don't know yet."

"How could you even think of that. If you don't come, then none of us can. You're the *pilot*!"

"I'm just the surface shine," I said. "Our spokesman to the world. If I don't come, Haller could do the job just as well."

"Haller needs to do the calculating, Tan. He wouldn't have time to do his work."

She unzipped my sleeping bag so she could sit up, then climbed onto my stomach.

"And what about me?" she said. "I'm meant for intimacy, to ease the solitude. Do you want our deepest feelings to go about in the world exposed?"

She undid her cotton blouse and let it fall from her shoulders. Her breasts hung before me like two moons. I touched them and imagined I was touching the moon, as I had wanted to for so long. I wanted to touch the moon, but the call had come and now I would never be able to do that if I answer it.

"You act like you didn't hear the call," she said. "Didn't you hear it, Tan?"

"Oh, I heard it. I have it in me still, just as you do."

"But why is there any question whatsoever about going back?"

She moved back on me and pushed me inside her, where I grew like a melon vine after rain.

"You *want* to go back with me, don't you?" She moved back and forth on me, pushing me deeper.

"Don't ask me that now," I said. "I'll do anything you want *now*."

She laughed and we made love in that way. I came as I suckled Eva's breasts. I was thinking of moonlight and the glamour of the night. For that moment only, I forgot about the call. Then we were lying together, side by side, and I remembered.

In the morning, Gene grilled us a trout he had caught while fishing at sun up. Today there was a blue-green sun, and it was a traveling one, west to east. It cast long morning shadows across the rocky tundra basin where we were camped. We ate the trout on metal plates and it fell apart, scalding and delicious, in our mouths. We drank hot tea and chased it with clear water from the stream.

"I thought of an argument," Haller said. His words were directed at no one in particular, but we all knew he was talking to Gene. "Do you agree that better people have better dogs?"

A ripple of interest passed over Gene's face. He took another bite of his trout.

"Think about it," said Haller. "Good people, on average, choose nicer, smarter dogs. But there is a dog overpopulation problem in the cities. So all the people of good will have their dogs spayed or neutered."

"Yes," said Gene. "I suppose."

"But what that does is take more and more of the good dogs out of the breeding pool, while the bad dogs belonging to bad owners keep multiplying."

"Yep."

"So you end up with a dog population that gets meaner and meaner and dumber and dumber."

"On average," I said.

"Yes," said Haller, "on average."

Gene took a long sip of tea, considered. "The good dogs are dead, but I'm not," he said. "And I'm not a dog. It's *you* who are going somewhere else, you know. I'm just going fishing."

That day, I heard thunder rising from the plains below. People were coming in from the commons down there and the tramp of their feet and the rustle of their clothes was what made the rumble I heard rising from the gray void below us. As soon as the day warmed, the light from the plains would rise and the images coalesce. The sight of the people on the move would bubble up to us.

I took out my map and spent the day studying it.

Haller and Eva took down the tents, all but Gene's, and loaded their packs. Eva was humming a tune, and after a while I recognized it from yesterday as the carillon melody of the call's leading edge.

That night I walked to the stream. I heard a clinking noise and looked downstream. By the light of the moon, I saw Gene. He was standing knee deep in the water. He had a pan from the camp cookset in his hands, and he was panning in the silt of the stream bottom. He raised the pan up, swirled it about, then bent to bring up another plate of sand.

I watched him for a while, and then I spilled all the condensed moonlight I had gathered into the stream. It flowed uphill against the current of the water—back toward its source, which hung over Paradise Peak immense and globose. And, for me, unreachable. I would answer the call.

We said goodbye to Gene on a rocky outcropping about a mile from our last camp. At some point last night he had stopped off the panning of the stream and had gone to Eva's tent. They emerged together from it in the morning. Eva was now carrying away a little of Gene inside her, both physically and emotionally and seemed less distraught to be leaving him behind.

We all shook hands.

"Well," I said. I took out my map. "For the moment, it's mostly a matter of climbing down."

"I have something for you," Gene said. "For all of you."

He pulled a bandana from his pocket and unwrapped it. Inside the fabric were three fly fishing lures. He gave one to each of us. I lay my lure in the palm of my hand.

"One day you may come back to the commons," Gene said. "And you may want to find me."

"Of course we will find you," Haller said.

Eva was clutching her lure and was crying.

"They'll disappear when we leave," she said.

"Don't worry about that," Gene said, and gave her a freshly washed bandana to wipe her tears. "Nothing will be lost."

I looked down at my lure. It was an exquisite thing of feather and bone. And in the center was a moonstone. Well, a moon-pebble, actually, hardly bigger than a grain of sand. So that was what he'd been panning for. They were extremely rare, and only found in these high lands.

"All day yesterday I was thinking about what each of you would look like to me," Gene said, "from the other side. The way a fish sees a mayfly above the water."

"So this is me," I said, folding my palm over the lure.

"Yes, Tan."

"And this is me," said Eva.

"And me," Hellar said.

"No matter what I become while you're gone," Gene said. "These will always draw me back to you."

We trekked down from the mountains into snow that later became a steady rain. Our hot breath formed a foggy haze about us so that we seemed to be continually walking out of a cloud. The stream veered away and then rejoined us at various times and at the bottom of the last alluvial hill, it emptied out into the river. Our canoes were where we'd left them, hidden in some willows. We secured the gear and took the boats out into the current.

We were a fortnight on the Time river. We had been nearly a month and a half paddling up it. After the river turned against the January Hills, we grounded the canoes. The January Hills had not been here when everyone first arrived. They had risen over time as people had walked through them. Most of the trails cut straight through the hills in straight lines along gorges that were nearly a mile deep in places.

We came out of the January Hills into the vineyards on the outskirts of the Interport City. The last of those who were answering the call emerged with us, and we walked together, eating grapes and drinking from the caches of young red wine that the grape growers had left for those who would come behind them. After we had passed, the wilderness would reclaim these lands and the commons would flow back into civilization once again.

We arrived at the port fifty days after we'd left Gene in the mountains. The sea was the mottled green of a spread of lichen. There were wheelbarrows and hospital gurneys, which people had used to cart the infirm down to the waters, all along the boardwalk margin. I lashed my map to a rusted anchor I'd dragged from a ruined wharf nearby to keep the map from floating up and away, back to the moon. I buried it beneath a stand of six palm trees several hundred feet from the beach and marked the spot with a stack of gurneys with a wheelbarrow on top. This was mild Resolution Gulf, and no storms would disturb my monument.

At sunset of the fifty-first day—it was a day of a traveling east-west sun—Hellar, Eva and I went down to the beach.

"I have something to tell you both," Eva said. "Before we go in."

"What is it?" Hellar asked, but I had already guessed. I was Eva's confidante, the one to whom she brought her doubts and frustrations, and she always told me she had her period. She hadn't told me.

"Is it Gene's?" I said. I stared out at the sparkling surf and smiled.

"What?" said Hellar. He bit his lips, thought for a moment. "Oh. I see."

"It's Gene's," Eva said. "I used a potion that last night. I'd been preparing it for days." She looked at me and winked. "You aren't the only alchemist among us; I have learned a craft of my own, you know."

"And that," Hellar said, "may be a neat solution to the problem of the bad dogs. If the baby somehow comes along with us."

"Yes," Eva said. "I suppose you could think of it that way. But what will it mean—after we answer the call?"

"Surely only good will come of this," I said. "But let's go and find out."

We held hands, Eva between Hellar and me, and walked naked across the sand, returning the way we had come forth: naked, except that each of us had in our hands the fishing lure that Gene had given us. I could feel Eva's lure pressed against my skin where she held my palm.

The water was warm, as it should be with the sun sinking into it like a hot stone and heating it up. We stood in the lap of the waves and watched the top of the sun disappear, steaming and red, beneath the ocean in the west.

"Do you think it will be the same dream we left before," Eva said, "or another one?"

"*This* is the dream," Hellar said. "I thought we were straight on that."

"I wouldn't be so sure," I told him, "of anything."

We walked into the sea, and it covered us over, and we breathed in the water and drowned.

I rose from the holding casket and stretched. After a moment, my eyes cleared. After another moment, I had feeling in my fingers and toes. The others were standing near me, also stretching and yawning. Grooming robots hovered near us and the whisk of their vacuuming wands sucked away the dandruff of dry skin cells that sloughed from us in tiny avalanches.

"Aaah," I said, priming my vocal cords as I'd been taught. So were the others.

"Aaaah," we all said. "Aaah, aaah."

I turned to the nearest robot. "What time is it?" I asked.

"Two thirty p.m.," it said, "November 19, 23,596 AD. Thursday."

"Thank you," I said. "Did you say twenty-three?"

"Yes."

"How far are we from Earth?"

"Just under two hundred lightyears. West, along the short arm of the Milky Way, of course."

"Of course. That was the way we were headed when I went to sleep. Eleven thousand years ago."

"We have found a very nice planet," said the robot. "I have been instructed, sir, to ask you if you feel that mental reintegration is complete."

"Come again?"

"During the lengthy virtual dreaming stage of our journey, your mentality was separated out to prevent systemic deterioration and the random creep of neurosis that a journey of such a time scale might induce. A side effect was the possibility that some portions of you might fail to reintegrate. Might settle, so to speak." The robot shot a puff of air over me as a final touch in the cleaning. "How are you? Are you quite re-mixed and stable, sir?"

I rubbed my eyes, blinked several times. "I . . . don't know about that," I said.

"In that case, sir, I have been instructed by the ship's mind to ask you to look at your hand."

"Look at my hand?"

"Yes, sir. The ship's consensus virtuality bids you to have a look at your left hand. While you were asleep, some mild genetic restructuring was performed by the sleeping casket mechanism."

I glanced down. There, in my left palm, were the three lures. They seemed to be embedded just beneath the surface, but I touched them with my right index finger and they actually *were* the surface. If you looked closely, you could see that each lure was made from my own skin. There were tiny capillaries of blood flowing through them. Three signs of contentment—lost or gained? I could not say.

I could feel them, Hellar and Eva, within me, in a way I never could before the voyage, before we journeyed into the commons. I was conscious of being a *voice*, their voice, as I'd never been conscious of it before. And the voice of the other, the new one, growing with the part of me that was Eva. Little Gene. Who knew what strange aspect he would add to the totality of our personality when he came into his own. What was I going to become? Something that had not been before. When the time came, would I have the words to say what it was like being me?

But, for now, there were other things that needed doing, and the one thing Tan—me—*was* good at was taking care of the business of the moment. I am the ego, after all. Those within me need me to speak and to act for them. That's why I came out from the commons. Otherwise, I might have stayed. I was very happy there.

And I almost touched the moon.

I went forward to see where we were. A robot stood at the helm, where it had stood for thousands of years, ready to adjust the course if the helm veered from true. It had not veered. The tiny singularity which supplied our gravity had neither disappeared nor engulfed us. All the machinery had done its job; we had found the place for which we were looking. I walked past the robot and gazed out the viewport.

The planet *was* a beautiful place, at least from up here. And though a part of me was going down there soon, a part of me would always stay above it all—the old man in the moon, hanging tranquilly in the sky, no matter what might befall those below. It was a funny way for people to end up after all these years.

"The ship's mind bids you good morning, sir," said the robot at the helm. "It says to wish you . . . good fishing."

"Good morning," I said, still considering the planet below us. "Good morning, Gene. From the rest of you."

HOME FRONT

by Sarah A. Hoyt & Jeff Greason

Pioneers on Earth frequently had to worry about local inhabitants who were unfriendly (often with good reason), but the Moon has no such dangerous neighbors; unless they're imported . . . or self-imported.

★🪐★

WE WERE BEING INVADED and it was impossible.

I know it happens all the time on Earth. We studied history and I've read and watched movies about invasions and wars and countries fighting each other. Dad was in the military, before he got his degree and came to the Moon. He said there was hardly ever a time when some place on Earth wasn't at war with some other place.

But we were on the Moon. There were only twenty adults and five kids, at least in our part of it. The adults were all scientists, and none of them military. Mom said it was a chance at a new beginning, a clean break with the old Earth rivalries. That with infinite space there would be less war.

I was the first baby born on the Moon. Mom had wanted to name me Eos Prometheus, but dad laughed and said no. Our last name is MacDonald, so he knew just what to name me.

My name is Robert Anson MacDonald. I don't think Mom ever got the joke. I only did because I have the same reading tastes as dad.

My first hint that something was wrong came when I was exercising in the centrifuge room. Okay, it wasn't a room exactly. The entire place we live in is a vast cavern, a tube really, created by lava flow.

But the tube has two branches. In the upper one we have laboratories and living quarters. The skylight entrance from the outside of the Moon leads to the lab, and then there's living quarters, and then the lower branch. Where the upper branch was a later flow that blocked the entrance to the lower branch. Later, as the lava that blocked that join cooled, it cracked and you got a rockfall, which still looks like it blocks the way, until you look closely. The centrifuges were past that rock fall, and then, past the centrifuges was the long cavern. It was part of our pressure and all, but not living space or labs. Eventually, the adults said it would be labs. For now it was recreational space, most of the recreation being clearing the floor of rockfall and scree. But we also shot and ran there.

So, we were in the centrifuge space, and there were lights, and beyond it was the long cavern, not very obvious because it was dark.

We had the type of centrifuges where you lay on your back and are centrifuged around your head. Dad calls them short-arm centrifuges. He says they used to have another type, but people used to get sick.

We didn't get sick. It wasn't bad. It was just really, really boring. There were four of us kids—there were more kids, but some people sent them to Earth. Mom's parents had never forgiven her not sending me to them when I was born—and we used the centrifuges while the adults were working, during the "day". We also used them way more than the adults, because no one knew what growing up with 1/6th gravity would do to us. Considering how much we were prodded, measured and examined, I think we were as much guinea pigs as the guinea pigs in the lab.

And I didn't mind, not really, except as I said, the centrifuges were boring. Most of the other kids used headscreens or watched movies. Except Mary, who was six months old and just slept.

Me? I used to go into my head and design space ships. In six months I was going to go to Earth to study aerospace engineering. I'd gone through most of what I could learn long-distance. So, I was lying there and designing a space ship.

Which I think is why I was the only one to hear the shots.

The first one sounded odd, and I thought it was just some lab equipment malfunctioning. Then there was another one, and this time I was sure it was a shot. My dad and Mrs. Li, my friend Laura's mother, used to be sharp shooters, and they both practice shoot—and taught us kids how—in the long cavern. It's not real shooting. It's a computer system with a mechanical device on the pistol, but it simulates the whole thing, the recoil and the sound, and it records it all so you can better your performance. Dad said it was the only way to give us kids something competitive to do. I wasn't that great at it, but I enjoyed it. And I knew the sound really well.

So when there was another shot, I was sure. Then Mom screamed. I'd know Mom's voice anywhere. Before she became a scientist, she was an opera singer. Dad said you could hear her voice all over the habitat when she was enthusiastic. Now she sounded half-angry and half scared.

It didn't make any sense. Yes, sure, I read dad's books and the science fiction of the twentieth century, where people in colonies went mad and all shot each other. In this particular colony the worst people did was shout at each other when they disagreed on scientific hypothesis, and not even much of that, since every person had a different specialty or slant on a specialty.

There is a way to stop the centrifuge before the programmed time. I reached for it and turned it off, then waited for the centrifuge to slow to a full stop.

Even with it stopped, most of what I could hear was the sound of the other three centrifuges that were working.

I held my breath. It seemed to me there were unusual noises coming from the lab on the higher arm of the habitat. Like stuff being pushed, and thrown over. But my heart was beating so hard it was difficult to be sure.

I got out of the centrifuge, trying to make as little noise as possible, not that anyone would hear me above the centrifuges, and crept to the rock pile that blocked view of the entrance.

The centrifuge room was lit, but on sort of dim light, so as not to interfere with people reading or watching movies on their devices.

The corridor outside was far more brightly lit. It was the "back end" of living quarters. No one has separate rooms, really, but living quarters for the various families are separated with plant shelves and "walls" made of packing materials. Each "front door" to a family's space opened onto a "hallway" which was really around four feet of the original space left open. That hallway was always lit, so people could come and go to the centrifuge room, or the lab, on the other side of the living quarters, or even the long cavern.

So, I was behind a rock pile and in the semi-dark looking out at a brightly lit space. Which meant I was practically invisible. Which was good because there was an invader in the hallway.

The colony—Luna City as the adults call it—was established and is financed by private companies, even if we're all American. That means that we get people who are employed by the child companies of our company from all over the world visiting, sometimes for a week or two, to look at what we were doing. We were always kept out of the way for that, but of course we spied.

My head had been so full of going back to Earth to study and all, that it was entirely possible I'd have missed the announcement of a visitor. Except that this was not a scientist, or even one of the investors. None of them had ever worn a uniform or carried a machine gun.

As I stood there, watching the man look around at the rock pile, then trot out of sight into this relatively small space that was like a side-flow where the two lava flows had met, and which led to a long tapering area, used mostly for storage.

He came back, looked again at the rock pile, then towards living quarters, and, obviously thinking it was the end of the habitat, turned around and went back the way he'd come. I watched. The back of my brain told me that this was a People's Republic of China soldier.

I knew it from the star on the helmet.

Look, I hadn't paid a ton of attention to tensions on Earth, or Earth politics. I suspected I'd do more of that once I was actually on Earth, but it had always seemed remote and unimportant from here on the Moon. But I'd seen the news programs the adults watched, I remembered Dad saying that China was like a beautiful lacquered vase with the smooth surface hiding the cracks, and that the fact that they were in trouble made them more dangerous. I also remembered the uniform and the star on the hat. Oh, the man was Chinese, too, but that didn't mean anything. So were Laura Li's family, but they were Americans.

I didn't think this man was. Another thing I noticed as he walked away was that he wasn't used to 1/6th gravity. Sure, he was somewhat used, and he must have trained for it. But he walked funny as people did when they were new here. Like . . . they were doing a slow walk that looked almost comical. The visiting people did that and worse, the first few times they came up. They got better if they came up fairly regularly.

And again, none of the visitors ever had machine guns.

As he walked back up the hallway in front of the quarters, I slid back into the room. I was sweating.

Suppose that the People's Liberation Army had come in. I couldn't understand how, since the Earth's skies were watched by multiple security satellites, and people kept an eye on launches. But suppose they'd made a Moon shot and got here, somehow, unwatched, and came in . . . I suppose through the skylight and airlock outside the labs.

I listened. There were still sounds of thumps, and shouts that sounded like orders, but I couldn't even tell the language. They'd have rounded up all the adults. They'd have them under guard. One of the invaders, probably followed closely by others, had come to the end of the living quarters, and looked and, from that angle, had thought it was a rockfall and the end of the tunnel. He or they had gone back. Did they even know there were kids here? If they found out what would they do?

When we had visitors, they were all from our company, and we were kept out of the way, because otherwise, Dad said, we'd become the Child Protective Services cause celebre, since no one was quite sure what physiological changes we'd have from growing up on the moon. I mean, the company knew we were here and appreciated the data, but casual visitors didn't need to know.

As for what the invaders would do, that question couldn't be answered because I had no idea why China would invade a private facility. I knew a lot of the research was secret, but there would be other ways to intercept the information. So why were they here?

I couldn't answer that, so I had no idea what they'd do to us. Or to the adults, for that matter. It could be anything from killing to holding us hostage. In either case, it wouldn't be good. I tried really hard not to think they might be killing Mom and dad right now.

I wasn't a child. I was one of the "kids" just because I wasn't one of the scientist-colonists, but I wasn't a baby who needed his parents. Still, odd couple though they were, and even if I wasn't utterly dependent on them, I didn't like to think of Mom and dad getting killed, much less by an unexpected invasion for which they hadn't been prepared.

I got my screen from my pocket, and brought up Laura's number, and texted "Stop your centrifuge. Don't say anything."

For a long while, it seemed like she didn't respond. I now wonder if it was in fact only a minute or two, but it seemed longer. Her centrifuge slowed down and stopped, and she got out of it, and looked around. When she saw me, her eyebrows went way up.

She comes about to my armpit, but she's fifteen, and in general she's very sensible.

I shook my head at her, then got close and whispered what I had seen. Her eyebrows went up more, and it looked like she was going to argue, but she didn't. Instead, she went to the entrance to the centrifuge area, staying behind the rock pile, and listened for a while. Then she came back. She took my screen and silenced it, then she silenced her own, then she texted me, "I hear strangers' voices."

I nodded.

She stopped there, looking at me, as though she expected me to have some kind of answer. I texted back, "I don't know what to do, but I think they're holding our parents captive."

She nodded. Then she texted, and Colton's centrifuge slowed down, even as I was reading the three way text, with her telling Colton everything we had figured out. Colton is fourteen and resents that we're older and that we're planning to go to Earth soon. It's like we're doing it on purpose to leave him behind with only Mary who can't even talk, and all the scientists obsessed with their own projects. Sometimes I think he suspects us of being older just to upset him.

So I wasn't surprised when he came up to us scowling. Before he could open his mouth, both Laura and I had fingers on our lips, indicating silence, which made him scowl harder.

He headed to the rock pile, then out of it. I texted "What are you doing?"

"Going to figure out what's going on. What are you two going to do? Just sit around and wait till someone finds you?"

I looked at Laura. She shrugged. I also had nothing to say to that. I mean, he was right that we needed to know exactly what we were up against. Making any kind of plan before knowing that was stupid. On the other hand, I suppose making a plan at all was stupid. After all we were just three kids, and if these were really members of the Chinese Army, they were trained soldiers and were armed, and would have no trouble at all taking us down. They'd had no trouble taking our parents down.

I had a brief wild hope that maybe dad had escaped somewhere and was hiding ready to rescue us all, but it was just a fantasy. This time of day my dad would have been in the lab taking the vital signs of lab rats or something. The only gun he had didn't shoot. It was really a computer device, that "recorded" simulated shots.

Even if we had a gun it wouldn't make any difference. I had no experience of machine guns but what I'd seen on videos and heard from dad's stories from his military service.

Yeah, if you're facing a guy with a machine gun it's better to have a pistol than nothing. If you're a really good shot—I was so so—you can take the guy out before he kills you.

But if you're facing more than one guy with a machine gun, you're going to get killed in the next few seconds. At most you can take a couple out, before the third shoots you.

I very much doubted the Chinese had sent a force of only one man. Or only three for that matter.

Must have thought so long that Colton came walking back. He was walking funny. Not like he was hurt, but kind of like he wanted to run but was preventing himself from doing it.

The floor of the habitat and the labs is basalt, cut in thin slabs and fused in place, everywhere but in the long cavern.

So Colton wouldn't make that much noise even if he pelted down the hallway, but he was walking like he wanted to go on tiptoe, and he kept looking over his shoulder.

Before coming into the centrifuge space, he stood there a long time, looking down the hallway. Then he slipped past the rock fall, and stood there. He was very pale.

"Are you all right?" I risked a whisper.

He nodded. Then shook his head. "There are a lot of them. Twelve?" He spoke in the same sort of whisper. "They're all over the lab and the communication room." He paused. "They have your father in the com room. They're trying to get him to read a message to Earth."

I felt like my throat was closing. "Dad?" I said, more lip movement than sound.

I had a wild, Momentary suspicion that Colton was just saying that, because I hadn't gone with him to scout out our situation. But I knew, even as I thought it, that it wasn't true. Sure. Colton could be jealous of my going to Earth, and he could be a pain and sulk. But he wouldn't say something like that just to wind me up.

Besides, he looked really pale.

"So?" I said.

"Dr. McGown. Mr. McGown, I mean," he said, having apparently remembered that there were after all two doctors McGown. "They must have shot him in his living quarters. He's dead on the floor, and there's blood all over." Pause. "I've never seen anyone dead."

I put my hand on his shoulder, just a touch, trying to communicate comfort, not knowing what else I could do. The doctors McGown had sent their three children down to Earth to be raised by relatives, but he was always very nice to us, like, you know, he regretted not having his kids with him.

"Oh, no," Laura said, and folded Colton into her arms. Which is a funny thing to say, since she was shorter than him too. But she folded him in her arms like he was a little kid and she was the adult.

I was thinking of my dad in the com room with all

those soldiers. If there's one thing my dad is, it's stubborn. If they'd shot Mr. McGown they might shoot dad too. Part of me wanted to go right out to the com room and start punching or shooting people. But it really made no sense, did it? I mean, again, what was I going to do? Even if I could get one of their machine guns, I'd never shot one of them. And from the comments dad made when we watched movies, there was more to machine guns than what he called "spray and pray."

"We have to do something," Laura said. And she and Colton both looked at me.

Look, I guess it was fair. I was the oldest. I had absolutely no experience with resisting invasions, but then neither did they.

"Yeah," I said.

All I could think of was the stuff they kept telling us about how we had to be careful of the air mixture.

The entire habitat, labs and living quarters, and even the long cavern was all the same pressure. Well, no. Not quite. There were portions of the lab that were these big plastic tents, which were kept at a different oxygen concentration. And other parts where people could only enter after thorough decontamination and wearing dust proof suits. We kids never went into those parts of the habitat, of course. Nor did most of the adults. Only the ones responsible for the stuff there.

Those tents had separate alarms. But the main habitat had one place and one regulator of air and pressure, and if we tampered with that and found some sort of fuel, we could . . .

I must have been talking aloud, because Laura looked

at me like I'd lost my mind. "And what?" she whispered furiously. "Blow the whole habitat up? Or set it on fire? How will that help?"

I shook my head. "No," I said. And I was thinking. We could seal the lab. I knew where they kept the plastic that they made the "tents" with for isolated experiments. I could seal it, and increase the oxygen and blow it up. But then . . .

But then, the com room being part of the lab, that would mean blowing dad up as well, and I really didn't want to do that.

"Where are the other people?" I asked Colton. "The other adults?"

He shook his head. "From the sound, somewhere in the lab."

I was chewing my lip again. "If we could get our people out of the lab, we could blow the lab up."

Laura opened her mouth as though she were going to protest. She had got paid money this last summer for cleaning the rabbit cages, and she had named the rabbits and really liked them. But she just shook her head. "How can we get them out?" she said.

"I don't know, I'm just . . . thinking aloud."

"Right," she said.

"Or if we could get the bad guys out," I said. "Or most of them. Somewhere we could seal and pump full of oxygen, then blow up."

"Seems . . . a long shot?" she was frowning, as if trying to think.

"Yeah," I said. "But we're not exactly well armed here. If there's a dozen of the invaders . . ."

"There could be more," Colton said. "I didn't count. It was like twelve, maybe, but only the ones I could see looking around the door of the com room. There might be others guarding the rest of the people."

"We don't have much time," I said. Even right now my father could be getting killed for talking back or refusing to transmit the message they wanted, or—I strained for sounds, but couldn't hear anything.

Laura looked towards the centrifuge, where little Mary was still being spun and looked sound asleep within a centrifuge-adapting child seat. "Yeah, at some point she'll awake, and you remember the racket she makes if she's dirty or hungry."

Hungry. I hadn't even thought of that. There was a refectory in the living quarters, since there was neither space nor any point to each family having a kitchen of their own. When you needed a pressure cooker to cook anything, it was easier to have it centralized. It was at the other end of the living quarters, near the labs. My guess was that our going near it would risk detection. But if we waited much longer we were going to need water. In fact, of course, the minute I thought of it, I wanted water. I said, through a dry throat, "that would be awful."

"I don't know," Colton said. "We could put her somewhere where she's crying, then pump that full of oxygen and blow it up, once all the invaders are in there."

"No," Laura said almost too loudly. "You're not going to blow Mary up."

"It might be the smallest sacrifice we can make!" Colton said.

"It's not your sacrifice to make," she said. "Her life is not yours to dispose of."

"But—"

But my mind had gone off on a track of its own. "A recording. Colton is right."

Two shocked faces turned towards me.

"You can't mean you want to sacrifice Mary, because—"

I put my finger to my lips, signaling Laura to quiet down. I tiptoed to the entrance and looked out, but the area outside was clear and all the noise still came from far away. If dad—No. I couldn't think of that, not right now. "No, listen," I said, coming back to them and whispering, as I tried to assemble my thoughts. "if we take that storage area, where the two lava tunnels flow together, the one that dead-ends, where we have all the shelves with oxygen bottles and stuff on them, and get one of the tents from the lab, the ones they get to isolate experiments, and assemble it at the end of that tunnel. It self-seals, though you can unseal the door to go in. Then we fill it with a lot of oxygen from the tanks used for surface walking or emergency. Then we rig a recording to bring them running, and once they're inside, we blow it up."

Laura looked confused. "I don't think a recording of Laura crying will bring them running!" she said.

"No," I said. "But a recording of gunfire will." And as she stared blankly at me, "Our shooting practice," I said. "It records the shoot, so you can analyze your performance on your screen. I can rig it to fast repeat, so that it looks like a person firing again and again. I can loop it. And they'll come running if they hear gunfire. They'll have to. They'll think there's someone armed here, in the habitat."

There was silence for a few seconds and then both of them nodded.

Laura whispered, "I'm going to add to Mary's centrifuge time. She rarely wakes when she's being centrifuged. That should give us a little time."

Then she and I and Colton divided tasks.

The oxygen wasn't a big deal. A lot of the tanks for surface walks, or in case of depressurization came from that same storage space, all we had to do was open them. And there were already a lot of shelves in the place we were going to use up. They were filled with odds and end the adults hadn't got around to putting anywhere else: discarded equipment from old experiments, the oxygen tanks for surface walks, all sorts of things, some of which I didn't know what they were. There were ten rows of shelves, ten feet tall, and each shelf was crowded with assorted junk. This was good because if we set the tent over the shelves we could put my screen at the back, and the invaders wouldn't be able to see all of the inside of the tent right away. I thought the tent would just about be large enough and tall enough.

The hard part was getting one of the tents.

They were kept in the laboratory, see, because they were only used there, when someone's experiment needed a different mix of oxygen, or a different temperature, or even just to keep biological or chemical contaminants away.

I knew where they were because I had helped Mom put one up the last one she'd needed for her experiments. There was a supply area right by the entrance to the labs.

"I can go get it," Colton offered, but you could tell from his extremely pale face he didn't want to do. On his last reconnaissance, not only had he gotten scared, but he'd come face to face with death for the first time.

"No," I said. "I'm the oldest, and I should go. Besides," I added, as he looked like he would protest, "I need to go make sure dad is still alive."

This last wasn't precisely true, mostly because I was afraid that dad wasn't, and that I'd find he was dead. And I didn't want to know. Certainly not any time soon.

But we needed the tent. And if I knew about dad, then I'd at least know what I was dealing with.

I made my way out of the centrifuge room. It seemed weird being outside and fully exposed, under the light. I wanted to unplug the light, as if being in the dark would protect me, instead of the lights going off probably alerting the invaders.

I walked close to the plant-walls of the living quarters, ready to duck into a curtain-entry way at the slightest sound or movement ahead.

But there were none. The sounds continued to come from where they'd been coming: from the lab. It was the sound of many voices, and the cadences were not English, even if the speakers were speaking English, which I couldn't tell from this far off.

The closer I got to the lab, the more carefully I moved, the more carefully I listened.

Which is why I heard sounds ahead, and ducked into one of the living quarters, staying very still, almost not breathing, crouched in a corner, where the people who lived there had hung clothes.

The curtain twitched. A face in a star-helmet peeked in. I swear I almost stopped breathing. But his gaze ran right over me, where I stood, half-enveloped in a lab coat. I heard him walk back towards the lab and held my breath and waited.

The only explanation I could think of for his having come here is that he'd heard something. This both showed me it was possible to alarm them with sounds and perhaps that I'd been making way too much noise.

I don't know how long I waited to stop hearing the footsteps. It felt like forever. Even when I made it out, I was convinced the soldier would be waiting at the entrance to the lab to jump me, so my progress was excruciatingly slow, or felt that way.

Eventually, though, I saw the entrance to the lab. The door was open. I shifted from one side to the other to look inside. I studied the shadows upon the doorway. I couldn't find any reason to be suspicious. And I had to go in and get the tent, or all this was in vain.

Thing is, this up close, I could hear dad's voice, and he sounded so tired, and also like he was reading from something. I felt both relieved he was obviously alive, and scared. What had they done to make dad sound defeated?

"The glorious People's Republic of China—" dad was reciting. I couldn't imagine his saying those words of his free will or even parroting them without major persuasion.

The lab looked mostly undisturbed, when I went in, except for some tables pushed out of the way, a table overturned and a track that I was fairly sure was blood on the floor.

"In demonstration of the failures of capitalism—"

dad's voice droned. The com room is normally soundproof. Mom and dad joked that it had become sound proof after the entire community heard the big argument Mom had with her Mom over not wanting to send me Earthside to be raised.

But for it to be soundproof, you had to close the door. The door was open. Just as I noticed this, a face peered out, as though to look over the lab. But this time it couldn't be because he had heard a sound. Not that I didn't make sounds, but because the glance was perfunctory, like he was just reassuring himself everything was fine out here.

I noted there were also half a dozen soldiers in a corner of the lab, blocking the opening between two tall sets of shelves, and assumed that's where the rest of the people were. It wasn't likely that they'd killed everyone else, and left only dad alive. And anyway, I could hear sobs and whispers form that corner.

Also, I couldn't be sure and wasn't going to go much further in to make sure, but I thought the blood trail, meandering between shelves and tables, led to that corner.

I waited to make sure that no one was looking out of the com room. Dad's voice droned on saying the most unlikely things. I assumed they had a gun pointed at his head, and I wasn't going to try to see him.

Instead, ten steps inside the lab entrance, I slid left, staying close to shelves and things, and ducked to a set of shelves against the wall where the sealed packages of tents were.

There were many sizes of these, I knew, but the

smallest was the size of a family's living quarters. That
should be both small enough to fill with oxygen quickly,
and large enough to contain a dozen or so soldiers. Then
I thought again, and reached for the next biggest. We'd
need to put it over a lot of the shelves, so we could hide
the source of noise behind it. If they could see it, they
wouldn't go in. We'd want them to go in, and try to push
shelves aside, to get at the people firing guns. It had to be
plausible that there were people with guns behind there.

On the way out, I grabbed one of the laboratory
lighters, a kind I'd used before while helping Mom, and
which I knew how to wedge on. We'd have to use leaf
litter for fuel. There was a receptacle for them—before
putting them in the compost pile—in the lab, but there
was another in the hallway outside the living quarters.
One of the jobs we kids did since we were little was
remove fallen leaves from the plant shelves. We kept the
oxygen at about 24% because any more than that and
things became flammable. We were about to make things
flammable.

When I got back to the storage area, Colton and Laura
had got the leaves and set them in a big pile in the center
of the shelf upfront. They were trying to move things
around to create a series of obstacles.

We decided from the measurements of the tent that
we could put it over six of the shelf systems. So we
decided to make it the center ones. That way the two first
shelves, up front, would obscure the tent some more, and
the invaders would have to run down the space in
between the shelves to enter the tent.

Putting the tent over those things was easier said than

done. The tents were clear plastic, with a sort of superfine "structure" also in plastic. The front plastic has two overlapping flaps that are "gummy" so that they seal together, but open under pressure of a hand pushing them, or even someone running at them. Once freed from the packaging and unfolded, the plastic supports snapped free, and the plastic "walls" fell into place.

Normally you opened the tent in a clear space, and then filled it with whatever you needed.

"We're going to have to move all those shelves," Laura said. "Move them away, set the tent up and then move all the shelves back."

I looked at the shelves dubiously. Sure. I know, the adults were always saying "things don't weigh that much on the moon" which was usually a ploy to make one of us go fetch something. It was second only to "your knees aren't as old as mine." But even if we could move the shelves, they were like six feet long each and ten feet tall, and they were modular. Parts of them could detach and fall. Not to mention the stuff on them could detach and fall.

"We don't have time," I said. "And it risks attracting attention before we're ready."

But we were putting the tent over three sets of shelves. Six shelves, side by side, with about three feet space between them. And we had five sets of those shelves. Ten shelves in all. "I know," I said. I managed to stop Colton before he opened the tent and possibly ripped the side walls against one of the shelves. Fortunately we had space above, about ninety feet or so.

"I climb on the front right shelf, all the way to the top,

and Colton on the front left shelf. Laura, you take one of the back shelves. I wish we had four people."

Laura looked dubious. "What if I kick something down from the shelves?"

"Try not to," I said. I was scared too, but it was the only thing I could think to do. I took the tent. It was going to be a trick and a half to open it atop the rickety shelves, and get a corner to each of the others, but that's what we had to do.

We climbed the shelves. I opened the tent and it sprang free, like jelly fish in water, floating around in the tank in the lab. Colton leaned so far forward, I thought he was going to fall off the shelf, but he didn't, and he got hold of it, and Laura got hold of the back corner.

Since the entire structure was super fine and light, it wasn't heavy. It was merely unwieldy, like trying to walk in a pressure suit the very first time.

We lowered the tent slowly over the six central shelves. I swear I was holding my breath for fear it wouldn't be quite wide enough or would snag on one of the corners of the shelf, or something on it, as we shifted our hold on it and lowered it, slowly, slowly.

It was hard enough, and we came so close to tearing the walls that I almost offered to go get another tent, and then we'd move everything out of the way and open it, then fill it.

Two things stopped me: I had a gut feeling we didn't have that kind of time, and I didn't know if I could make myself go into the lab again, with all those soldiers around and my father's voice droning on in a dispirited way.

So, we shoved and angled and maneuvered the tent into position, each of us perched unsteadily on a set of storage shelves, while the fourth corner of the tent wasn't held up by anyone and threatened to drag the whole thing out of position. It would have too, if the tent were even slightly heavy.

Even when we got it down over the shelves, I had to face climbing down from the shelves. I'm not afraid of heights, and normally I'd simply have jumped down. But now, I was afraid suddenly that the shelves would tumble under me and bring vengeance on us before we had our trap set up.

I guess the others went through the same hesitation, because by the time we all got down, we were all looking pale and shaken, and Laura, who normally jumped and moved with uncaring grace, took almost as long to get to the ground as I did.

We walked around the tent in silence, sealing it to the floor. It had a strip on the bottom of the walls that you could seal to the floor by walking on it.

Then it was a matter of walking in and setting up the pile of leaves on one of the front shelves in front of where the flaps opened when pressed. I put recording on my screen, with twenty minutes delay and we opened the valves on the oxygen tanks.

I was sure there was an apparatus, probably more than one, in the lab that would allow me to start a fire on a timer. There were two problems with that: I didn't know what it was or what it looked like and I didn't know what time it would take, from the moment the sounds started to having the maximum number of invaders in the tent.

I mean, it could all backfire. We might only get two or three of them.

But at least we had to try. And the best way to get the most effect was that balance between the most invaders in the tent and the repeated openings of the front flaps— which were designed to seal between passages, by overlapping and having some kind of quality that made them stick together but give way at push or force—letting too much oxygen out so that the mixture inside wouldn't explode.

Unfortunately as in such things, someone needed to do it, and the someone was me. I'd have to shove the self-sealing tent flap open and throw the lighter at the leaves.

I led Colton and Laura into the centrifuge room, and then pointed them at the long cavern. "Go there," I said. "As far deep as you can. I have no idea how far the explosion will go. There could be a fire ball. Use your screens for light."

Laura grabbed my arm. "Don't you sacrifice—"

"I'm not going to sacrifice myself," I said. "Just going to try to blow it up and get away as fast as possible."

The gunfire sounds had started. We'd put the screen on a shelf, in an empty area, and hoped it would echo. It did. It sounded like there were several people firing weapons inside the tent.

I guess if they'd thought about it, they wouldn't fall for it. But the invaders thought they'd secured the area, that there were no hidden people on the loose. They were in the middle of making their victory broadcast and then suddenly gunfire.

I heard them running down the hallway outside, and

risked a peek in time to see a handful of them go into the tent, followed by more of them.

I was very afraid that as I thrust my arm in there to set fire to the leaves, one of them would grab me. Or that I'd be caught in the fire. But it had to be done.

There were sounds of gunfire, again, from the lab, but I had no time to worry or think about who might be getting hurt or which side. There were screams too, but I couldn't tell whose voices they might be.

The last straggler of the invaders to come down the hallway hesitated and looked puzzled. I thought he was the guy who had come down there before, and he was probably trying to figure out where the tent had come from. He'd looked at those storage shelves and there wasn't a tent over them.

He opened the flap of the tent, put his head in and started shouting something, urgently. I couldn't risk it. Also, his head and upper body were thrust into the flap, unsealing the space above him, and leaving a triangular space over his head.

I was taller than him. I wasn't the world's best at throwing things, but we kids played ball in the long cavern, and I wasn't the world's worst, either.

One good throw. I needed one good throw.

I took the lighter from my pocket, wedged it open, and ran, hell for leather out of the centrifuge room, and past the tent, flinging the lighter hard. It went sailing into the triangular opening above the soldier's head and, I thought, straight into the pile of leaf litter on the shelf on the right.

I wanted to know if it worked, but it if worked, I

couldn't stick around. I ran on, down the living quarters corridor as fast as I could, not knowing if my plot had worked, or if there were now several invaders on my heels. I thought I saw a flash behind me, illuminating everything, suddenly, and I swear I smelled burning, but then, I was so scared I couldn't be sure.

The only thing I knew for sure was that there was an art to running on the Moon and that those of us who had been born and raised on it were much better at it than even our parents who had lived here for decades, and always better than any visitors.

I half slid, half dove into the laboratory, and—

And met with the people of the colony. Bedraggled, a few of them crying, and Mom with blood trickling down her arm.

Only after that did I take in that there were four, no, five dead invaders on the floor, one of them half in half out of the com room. There was one who might be dead or unconscious by the animal cages.

And dad, with a blood smear on his forehead, was holding one of the invaders' machine guns. He looked at me, and you could see tension leaking out of him. "Robert," he said. "Oh, thank God."

Mrs. Jones pushed from between the group, "Where is Mary? The explosion . . . Is she all right?"

As though on cue, Mary's cry came from the direction of the hallway, and moments later Colton walked in with Laura. Laura was carrying Mary in full screaming fit.

"It worked?" I asked, turning around, remembering having heard an explosion while I was running, even though I hadn't really noticed it in my mad dash. Okay it wasn't really an explosion, more of a fwoosh, but same thing.

Laura nodded. "It worked. They're either dead or too burned to do much."

The Jones, the Lis and the Cordovas came from the crowd to embrace their kids. Mom just held me and started crying, even though her shirt was the one soaked in blood.

Dad and a few other men went out the door, carrying machine guns.

Turns out they'd thought we were dead, since the invaders never made any references to us. They thought they'd found us and killed us.

I really thought Mom would be upset we'd done something that led to the death of people. But she wasn't. Even though she always tried to get us kids to solve our problems by non violent means, and flinched a little when dad told war stories.

She said that there was nothing to be ashamed of in defending yourself, then cried over me again, until Doctor Marston, who is our medic and also animal experimenter, dragged her away to take care of her wound. It turned out it was only a graze, and she didn't have any problems recovering from it.

It also turned out that the Chinese had decided to take this laboratory as a publicity coup aimed, mostly, at quelling internal dissension in China, by showing that not only could China make a Moon shot, but it could take over a private, capitalist base and win. They'd made their shot disguised as the testing of an anti-satellite weapon, which in turn was announced as a satellite launch. The people who'd observed an explosion in orbit thought the Chinese were being sneaky by testing anti-satellite weapons, not by firing a capsule full of soldiers at the Moon.

They had forced open our skylight and pressure lock, and invaded through the laboratory, where they'd caught the adults unawares. Except poor Mr. McGowan who had gone to the living quarters for something, and come out of his lodging to meet a soldier who'd shot him, probably out of reflex.

As it turned out the attempt on the colony was the last of a long list of blunders, and the one that caused a revolution in China. I asked dad if that meant they'd now get a better government. He said one could only hope, but history indicated it was unlikely.

And then he said, "I feel better about you going to Earth now, Robert. I've been afraid you'd been raised too protected, because of how small the colony is, and how you've known everyone since birth. But now I know you can and will do what it takes to survive, and to protect those who depend on you." He put his hand on my shoulder and said, "You've nothing to be afraid of, son. You're a survivor."

INCIDENT ON CALYPSO

by Murray Leinster

The rocket pilot hadn't planned on being an explorer or pioneer until mechanical failure stranded his ship on a moon of Jupiter. And then he discovered a group of explorers who weren't human but who were in the same predicament and had been for long, long time.

Interestingly, there is no moon of Jupiter named Calypso, though a very tiny moon or moonlet of Saturn now has that name. Since Mr. Leinster was well up on scientific knowledge, I can only conjecture (since he isn't around to be asked) that perhaps he liked the name and decided to put one there, back in the days when the best equipment we had to find moons were telescopes operating under a murky atmosphere, and such a moon might be there awaiting discovery.

STEVE BARING didn't expect to find human—well, call them humanoid—footprints on Calypso. He didn't expect to find anything. He'd expected to land there and die when his air gave out. The automatic pilot of his space-cruiser had jammed on four-gravities acceleration when a short-circuit developed somewhere in its innards, and when the main fuel tanks were empty and Steve could stir from the flat of his back, he had only his emergency fuel left.

He was then well past the main asteroid belts—he'd been heading for Mars, originally—and speeding for outer space like a bat out of hell. He simply didn't have enough fuel to stop and come back. So he edged over to use Jupiter's mass as a brake, spent lavishly what fuel he did have left, and came in for a landing on Calypso with just twelve hours' drive at one-gravity acceleration left to him. Which was just about enough to enable him to take off again and be sure of falling into Jupiter itself. As a matter of purely illogical preference, he decided to stay and die on Calypso.

He had no hope of any sort. Calypso had been surveyed back in 1982 and offered no inducements for further exploration. It is four hundred million miles out from Earth, it is in Jupiter's gravitational field, and it is airless. Which last means that its surface is all pock-marked with ring-mountains made at the same time as those on Luna and Io by that unthinkable mass of stuff that barged through the solar system a hundred-odd-million years ago. Nobody else would be turning up on Calypso to rescue him. He was through when his air gave out. Finished. Period.

But then he saw the footprints.

His cruiser was lying slightly askew not far from the riven cliffs of a ring-mountain's outer perimeter. Steve had settled down, eaten a fairly hearty meal—he had more food than air—and tried to savor the fact that he was just as dead as if he'd hit a planet head-on at one hundred miles a second and was already reduced to his constituent atoms.

He found himself stonily calm. He even smoked. But time passes slowly when you're newly quick and dead at the same time. He went restlessly to the ports of the cruiser to stare out.

He saw the monstrous disk of Jupiter, coming up past Calypso's irregular horizon. Opposite was the high wall of the nearby ring-mountain. Other ring-mountains in other directions. Pits, where smaller things had struck. Craters within craters, and desolation as complete as that of Luna itself.

The sun was a small, fiercely flaring spot of light. Stars were clearly visible. The ground was simply shattered talus, loosely filled in with the dust which had settled slowly in airlessness after that insensate, incredible bombardment from the farther rim of space.

But then, in the dust at the very base of the ring-mountain cliffs, he saw a single line of regularly spaced depressions. They were regular footprints, as of somebody walking. But humans do not walk on low-gravity terrain! The odd, skating gait which men use on Luna and the other lesser satellites does not leave tracks like that.

Steve stared blankly, smoking. Once he made an irresolute movement as if to turn a scanning telescope upon them. But it is hard to think of any action as worthwhile when everything is futile, when you're simply waiting until your air gives out and you die.

When his cigarette was finished, he shook himself and got into a spacesuit. He went out the airlock, stared about him for a moment, and loneliness hit him like a blow. He was actually the only human being in two hundred million miles. But he swallowed and went toward the cliff-wall. He moved with the finicky skating motion appropriate to Calypso's low gravity, it is not a series of bounding hops, but something much more practical. He made the necessary gradual halt and the tippy-toe approach to the line of depressions.

They were footprints. They were narrow, and they were arched, and they had not been made by any spaceboots that humans ever wore. There were no toes, but there was a heel, and they looked as if they had been made by something very like a human shoe, only of course they hadn't. They were absolutely distinct. They looked perfectly fresh. Steve felt a moment's wild flare of emotion before common sense told him that in airlessness a footprint will remain fresh forever.

Then he shrugged. He could tell the direction of motion by the sidewalls. He followed it. He had nothing to lose but his sanity. His life was already gone. He set off in the direction the footprints led.

They went on sturdily for miles. Once Steve looked up and realized that he was out of sight of the cruiser. There was no familiar formation in view. He felt a little flicker of apprehension. Then he grinned wryly. His own tracks and the ones he followed would be a guide back. And if he didn't get back it wasn't important.

The footprints rounded a place where a column of rock—thrown out in the formation of a crater—had fallen upright without breaking. It made a sixty-foot, irregular monolith. The footprints skirted it. Other footprints of precisely the same sort came from a new direction and joined the first set. They took a new line and headed for the monstrous wall of a mountain. A third set came in a mathematically straight line and joined them. The three went on. An opening loomed in the cliff. Yet more footprints came along the cliff-face and entered. There was darkness within.

Steve hesitated. He looked at the sky. Jupiter was still only a quarter-way across the horizon, though the sun was low down against a jagged mountain-scarp. He turned on his helmet-light and went doggedly inside.

Before he was actually within the cliff he saw everything that he ever discovered in this spot. There were six things in the shallow cave. They were metal, and they were the things which had made the footprints, and they were utterly motionless. There was no dust here, of course. There had been no air to swirl it in. The six things sat—there is no other word for it—in something like a circle. And that was absolutely all there was in the cave.

The things themselves were plainly robots with curiously android bodies, two legs which ended in gracefully formed feet, and two arms. There was a head with a small, gracefully curved rod bent above it, like a receiving or transmitting antenna for very short radio waves. There were eye-spaces which were definitely not fitted with scanners. And the robots in their entirety had the peculiar, satisfying cleanness of line of an object which is perfect engineering. Like a suspension bridge or a race horse, or a perfectly streamlined atmospheric plane.

They sat in a circle, seeming to regard each other. They might have been sitting there for one hour or for a million years. On Calypso, without atmosphere, metal does not rust or apparatus deteriorate.

Steve stared at them for a long time. They were quite impossible. Then he suddenly moved forward purposefully. From one standpoint, nothing that he could do was worthwhile because nothing could change his fate. If he took one of these robots back to the ship, though, and examined its workings, he would at least have an occupation. He might keep himself sane.

He looked at all of them and heaved one to his shoulder. Examination might tell where it came from. At least it would be a sort of technical solitaire he could play until his air ran out. He had no faintest idea that the robots could affect his personal future, except by providing a sort of game of patience he might play like any other condemned man.

He went back to the space-cruiser, pleased with the robot as a thing to investigate, but nagged by the fact that he was here on Calypso to die, and nothing else really mattered. He left the robot in the airlock for a while. A puddle of furiously boiling liquid air formed about its feet as air filled the lock. The robot had been at the normal temperature of Calypso—say eight degrees absolute—and it took time to warm up. But presently Steve carted it into the main cabin and set to work to find out what made it tick.

In ten minutes he knew he was looking at the absolute

perfection of engineering design. Half of it was unintelligible, of course, but the thing had muscles, which were of flexible plastic with a magnetizing coil about them. They shortened in exact proportion to the magnetizing current. It had eyes which were not scanners, but lenses focused directly on a flat close spiral of infinitely fine wire, it had what must have been tactile nerves which were almost microscopically small variable-resistance units.

The whole interior of the robot was contrived to slide out as units, once the torso was opened, whether for examination or for replacement. The power was undoubtedly electric and it was generated by a thermo-unit Steve could not begin to understand.

He spent half a Calypsian day in mere examination, being careful to remove nothing. It was absorbing. It was fascinating. He discovered an enormous number of things he could see the use of, but whose workings he could not fathom. In the skull case, for example, a thick sheath of fine wires from all over the robot led to a mass of black substance with a faintly visible external pattern of crystal-outlines on it. It was apparently the coordinating factor for the operation of the robot. There was a minute bit of apparatus with a recognizable variable condenser adjusted by a tiny "muscle." That must be a short-wave radio unit for communication.

In spite of these mechanical details, however, the robot had an extraordinarily manlike look when it was closed up again. The head was not round, but a laterally flattened ovoid, set on a turnable neck, with the highest part at the rear. But for its slender gracefulness, the robot might have been taken for a suit of golden armor, designed by a genius for an impossibly wiry human being. And it was small. Its total height was under five feet.

"Whoever designed you," said Steve warmly, "did a job of work! I understand about ten percent of your works! If I had you back on Earth, we'd make some real machines!"

The thing was motionless. But it looked amazingly human. Erect, it would have a gallant briskness in its air.

"I'm going to see if I can't start you going," said Steve suddenly. "You can't do any harm, anyhow!"

Power was derived from a thermo-generator, far ahead of anything similar that Steve knew of. It was the logical power-unit for a robot, though. No battery will store as much power as its own weight of fuel will yield. Steve had seen where fuel from a tiny double tank had been fed through a hairlike capillary tube to what must have been a catalyzing-chamber.

He set to work with a tiny brazing-torch and a wisp of platinized asbestos. An hour later he carefully funneled almost a full pint of rocket fuel into the robot's tank. With a platinum catalyst, the temperature attained would be relatively low and the efficiency ridiculously small, but it should work. He made as careful an adjustment as he could and closed the torso.

The golden figure stirred. Its arms and legs shifted from slackness to something like tenseness. The head came around. The robot, in effect, sat up. It looked at him, and all about the cruiser's cabin, and then sharply back at him.

"Hello!" said Steve, grinning, though his heart pounded oddly. "I'm Steve Baring. Who are you?"

The golden figure made no sound. It suddenly occurred to Steve that he had seen no signs of either hearing-apparatus or of sound-producing means in the robot's works. For a machine designed to operate in airlessness, of course, sound would not exist.

"Oh-oh!" said Steve. "You don't talk. Want to look around?"

He stood up. He beckoned. The golden figure stood, with a complete effortlessness that was grace itself. Steve led the way to a port and pointed. The golden figure tilted its head and stared out. It looked back at Steve. It was extraordinarily like a living thing. There was no jerkiness in any movement. There was no clumsiness.

"If you are remote-controlled," said Steve, "the lad who's running you knows his stuff! But somehow, I don't think you are. Let's look around."

He led the way to the control room. The robot followed, sure-footed and light upon its feet. Steve halted suddenly. The robot moved to one side to give him space to move. It looked from him to the instruments and to the star map. It regarded the star map steadily for several seconds. It was nearer the door back into the cabin, and when Steve moved toward the door it stepped aside to let him lead the way. It was incredibly like the courtesy of a reasoning being. Steve jumped a little.

He did not know whether he felt idiotic or frightened, but either sensation was preferable to continued contemplation of his predicament as a castaway on Calypso. He led the way to the tiny engine room. The robot followed with light, sure steps.

It was glittering golden metal. It was all graceful smooth lines and strictly functional curves. It was a thing of beauty, with the crestlike metal spur which must be a radio antenna giving it a trace of cockiness that was irresistibly appealing.

It scrutinized the drive, its twin vision devices moving back and forth among the fuel pumps, the catalyzers, and the field-generator which turned the catalyzed but still relatively inert organic compound into the continually detonating stuff which drove the ship—when one had enough of it to count.

The robot looked, but always it paid close attention to Steve. It was so lifelike that it actually had a manner. It was absorbed, it was brisk and it was—well—human.

"I'd give a half-hour of my oxygen to know how they made that black stuff in your brain case," Steve mused.

He crossed the cabin and took out a volume of the Celestial Pilot with its orbit-constants for all the larger bodies of the solar system, landing-ports and regulations for the different planets, and photographs of all moons and most of the asteroids from every possible angle of approach.

"Your eyes ought to take this stuff," said Steve. "Let's see if I can get a reaction out of you."

He flipped the pages to the photographs of Calypso and pointed outside. The robot regarded the pictures attentively. Steve pointed out the photographs of Jupiter, recognizable from its huge disk overhead. Then he turned to a map of the Jovian system of satellites.

The robot looked up at him. With a curiously tentative pressure it took the book into its own hands and fumbled with the pages. It caught the trick of turning them and went through the entire pilot from beginning to end, disregarding the text, but eagerly regarding the photographs and maps.

Steve sat down. He lighted a cigarette and smoked

reflectively, putting the lighter on the table beside his chair. He watched the robot with a curious mingling of pleasure and wistfulness.

"Fella," said Steve wryly, "you intrigue me. You can't do me any harm because my killing's already attended to. You can't harm other humans, because you can't get off Calypso with what fuel's left in this ship. And anyhow, the stuff in your fuel tank will run out presently. So you and I can be chummy. I need a friend to chat with, right now. You're elected."

The robot looked at him, having seen his movement. It put down the book and waited. Steve grinned wryly again.

"Maybe you know some games?" he asked humorously.

The robot looked at the bookshelves, reached out, took a book, and offered it to Steve with a quaint air of asking permission.

"Go ahead!" said Steve. "Maybe you're only a glorified set of clockworks, but I like your manners. Wait a minute, though! That's a novel, with no pictures. I'll find something."

He hunted. He found a suitable book. He opened it and fumbled in his pocket for a cigarette. The robot crossed the cabin and came back with the lighter he'd put down beside his chair. Steve's jaw dropped.

"Now, what the devil! You're human!"

He showed the robot pictures. Once or twice he sketched diagrams—talking busily the while—to make some illustration clear. Presently the robot seemed able to go on by itself. Steve sat back and watched with a sort of quasi-parental pride as the robot looked at pictures.

He fell asleep in his chair, while pondering the problem of how to establish two-way communication with his mental protégé. So far, it was only one-way. He could tell the robot things, in a limited way, but the robot could not communicate in return.

When he awoke, the robot was gone. And on the table beside him was a tiny bit of copper tubing with a wisp of platinized asbestos inside it. It was the improvised catalyzer he'd spent an hour on the day before, to fit the robot's thermo-generator to use rocket fuel.

"Jupiter!" said Steve sourly. "That dummy figured I must've opened him up and fueled him, so he opened himself up to see. And he didn't like my work and took it out and went home."

Then he heard the airlock. It was being worked with precision and exact knowledge. There were footsteps on the metal plating. The outer door closed. There was the soughing sound of air admitted.

The robot came lightly into the cabin, clothed in mist. It carried a round, flat object in its hands. It regarded the frosting which formed upon it because of its temperature, and looked at Steve, and made what could only be described as a deprecatory gesture. It put the flat object down and waited patiently.

"You've been out a long time!" said Steve, growling in spite of an illogical elation at the robot's return. "You had to, to get that cold! You should've used a suit."

But he was extraordinarily cheered. He was in the almost unthinkable situation of a man with no purpose and no plans. He could have none. He was waiting to die when his air ran out. So the robot was companionship or it was nothing. He stood up and looked at the flat thing the robot had brought.

"An apple for teacher, eh?" he growled again. "Let's see what it is."

He turned a heater on robot and flat object together. In minutes the frost vanished from both. But it did have a tendency to return as the unwarmed inner mechanisms took heat from the outer surface.

The robot pointed to the flat thing. Pictures formed under a transparent dial. It was a vision-plate; a television receiver. And it showed Steve's face, speaking. He wasn't speaking. It showed the pages of the Celestial Pilot being turned, one by one. They weren't being turned. Then it showed Steve, without a spacesuit, walking on the airless outer surface of Calypso. He wasn't. He hadn't.

"Good Lord!" said Steve explosively. "I get it! I think in words, and short waves will carry 'em. You think in pictures, and short waves will carry them too! I get it! We talk two-way now!"

He settled down zestfully to talk with the only companion he could possibly have before his air ran out. Talking was an involved process, involving sketches and hastily-looked-up photographs on Steve's part, and pictures coming into view on the flat dial, on the part of the robot. It probably should have resulted in a marvelously educational technical session for Steve, but instead it brought the unfolding of a story.

It began with the picture of a planet, which was frost and ice from pole to pole. The pale, bluish light of a distant sun played upon it faintly. But that picture melted into another, of a snow-clad city of such infinitely graceful lines and such perfect grouping of masses that it was breathtaking. And that, in turn, melted into other pictures within the city, which was peopled by brisk, gallantly erect and lightly stepping metal figures such as the one who now stood beside Steve Baring.

There were flying things which descended swiftly to the city, and others which took off and went away, and then a swift panorama of planets upon planets, and suns upon suns, and brisk bright metal figures everywhere, but always the visiscreen image returned to the frozen planet and the city which had been shown first of all.

Then there was a picture of a small object alone in space. It was a spaceship, and it moved, because the pattern of stars behind it changed slowly. But presently it wavered upon the screen. It ceased to point steadily in one direction. It careered crazily about among the stars. It made monstrous swoops and cavortings. And then— superimposed upon the image of the crazily darting ship—there came a picture of a giant double star, its components seemingly motionless. The twin stars moved visibly, faster and faster about each other until their movement in their orbit was a mere blur, while still the spaceship hung itself crazily about.

The motion of the phantom double star ceased, and the spaceship was seen to be tumbling slowly and purposelessly through space.

"That first was your home planet," said Steve, nodding. "And you're telling me that the controls of your spaceship went haywire, just like mine, and the ship was acting up so crazily you couldn't control it for as long as it took that double star to spin about itself all those times—"

He felt that he had failed to notice something. But the pictures began again. He saw inside the spaceship, now. Six space-suited figures regarded utterly cryptic machinery and worked precisely upon it, repairing it, evidently. Then one of them opened its torso and removed the half of its own fuel tank. It applied that tiny tank to a larger tank beside the contrivance just repaired.

A picture showed the spaceship moving steadily. Another figure seeming to disembowel itself to provide fuel for the ship, and still others. Then the spaceship came down in a clumsy landing on Calypso. It was a bad landing, a crash landing. The spaceship buckled and spouted odd parts.

Six golden figures spread out from the wreckage, desperately searching. After a long time they met again. They had found nothing. They entered a shallow cave beside a monstrous irregular monolith. Then the screen ceased to move, with six golden figures seated in the cave.

"You got control again," said Steve, "when the fuel in your main tanks ran out. Like me. But you had to use the stuff your bodies run on to power it to a landing, and Calypso was the best you could do. You must've figured it mighty close, to crash-land like you did. Then you couldn't take off. Again like me. So you sat down and—well—died, like I'm going to do. Only I came along and brought you back to life."

The robot looked at him. Steve said sourly, "And now you're asking me to wake up the rest of your friends, huh? I'll think about it."

He felt a curious, somber jealousy. He had no plans. He could have none. He could only act upon impulse, because reason had no sense to it now, and he wanted company for his lonely last hours. Now, with one robot active, he had company of a sort. If he fueled all the rest, they would be company for each other, but he would be an interloper. He would be left out. He would be more lonely than before, because he would see these brisk metal figures in a companionship he could not share. So he was jealous.

He rather anxiously brought out a vision-record and put it on the projector to entertain the robot who was his guest. The golden figure watched intently. When the first record was finished, it watched hopefully for another. It watched the insertion of the record and the starting of the projector. When that was ended, it briskly changed to a third record without fumbling.

"Jupiter!" said Steve, "You've got brains! A robot wouldn't've thought of bringing a visiplate to talk with! But you are a robot!"

He fumbled for a cigarette. The robot handed him his case. There was no hint of servility in the act. It went back to the watching of the vision records.

Steve felt an angry resentment within him. He had wakened the robot to life, and in a sense it was at his mercy and would share his fate. He would live while he had air, and it would live while he supplied it with fuel. When he died, it would die. It was reasonable enough that it should devote itself to him. But it must feel an added loneliness because it could have the companionship of its fellows, which Steve denied it.

Steve said, "Jupiter!" in a disgusted voice. He got up and climbed into his spacesuit. He came back to the cabin to say, "Stay here!" and reinforced the command with gestures. He went out the airlock and over to the line of footsteps he had first followed. He followed them for the second time.

"Sentimental fool!" he muttered. "He's a machine. A machine can't be lonely! I'm giving him a personality like people do with dogs and babies!"

But he went on because reason was no longer reasonable. In his situation, only impulses had meaning, because only impulses made a difference. He knew where he was headed for, and the way to the irregular monolith and the shallow cave did not seem long.

When he saw the asymmetrical opening of the cave he felt an absurd but pleasurable warming of his heart. He was being absurd, getting a machine to be company for another machine. But he was going to die and he felt uncomfortable at the thought of being unkind even to a machine.

He reached the shallow cave. He turned on his helmet-light. And the cave was empty.

For a moment he was shocked numb. Then came a fierce anger. He saw the whole thing at once. The robot in the space-cruiser had gone out the airlock only partly to get the vision-plate it had brought back. Essentially, it had gone out to share its fuel with these others! And it hadn't been alone or lonely. All the time it was with him, it had been in communication with its fellows by shortwave radio!

He swung about and came out of the cave, seething. He had only to look at the ground to see where the other robots had gone. He knew, in any case. Where had the vision-plate come from if not from the wrecked spaceship? Where had the robots gone, if not to the same place?

Steve made for that spaceship. He knew how to find it. He followed the six fresh sets of footprints in the dust of Calypso's surface. He used the skating gait in which a space-suited human being seems to glide just above the surface with a sort of magic ease. He moved swiftly.

He saw the spaceship while still a mile or more away. It was exactly as it had been shown him in the vision-plate, but it was no longer smashed. Five brisk, graceful figures moved busily about it. They put shattered plates together, and something glowed fiercely along the jagged line of the break for the barest fraction of an instant and the plates were whole again. The ship had been wrecked. Markings in the dust told of fragments flung here and there. Those fragments now were gone. They had been fitted back into place.

Steve came up to the scene of activity. The five golden figures turned to face him. They were impassive, of course, but one moved as if to allow him a clearer view of the spaceship on which they worked. He had the feeling of an elaborate courtesy extended to him. His rage deepened. He felt that he was being patronized—and by robots!

"Very nice!" he snarled within his helmet. "Make fun of me, let that partner of yours kid me along to get the trick of finding more fuel and fix up your own ship! But what good will it do you? There's not enough to do you any good! You don't know that!"

He found a door leading into the ship. He stalked in. His helmet-lights showed the interior as the very perfection of functional design. Everything within him that was engineer or artist responded. But he raged.

The robots followed him in, politely. They made way for him without servility. One of them pointed as if proudly to the focus of all the design within the ship. It was a machine whose principle was inscrutable. Its function, though, was plain. It was the space-drive.

The few visible parts had that beautiful precision of workmanship that a machine which is both simple and efficient must have, and an insane jealousy came to Steve. This ship and that machine and these gallant golden figures were the products of a civilization Earth could not match. He could not believe that his own helplessness for lack of rocket fuel had not been understood and discounted by the metal men. They had a purpose now. He had wakened one, and that one had wakened the rest, and now they prepared to return to their home planet, while he would remain behind to die.

He was jealous because he counted as nothing, either to the slender figures here about him, or their fellow in his own spaceship. He was jealous because they moved in brisk and comradely companionship, with apparent certain hope, and he was lonely to the brink of madness as he waited to die.

Since he had given them life and hope, he could take it away. There was a massive bar of metal lying beside the space-drive. He seized it. He raised it in a savage, hate-filled swing to destroy the space-drive utterly.

And he was helpless. Mechanical muscles move more swiftly and more strongly than human ones. Two of the metal men held him fast. Without effort. Without even any appearance of resentment. Just as they would have restrained a child.

He struggled, while a choking maniacal fury swept him, beside which despair was calmness. He felt the metal bar wrested from his space-gloves in a gentle withdrawal.

Then there was stillness. The five slim metal figures looked at him. They looked at each other, and Steve hated them because they could communicate with each other and he knew nothing of what they said.

One moved away. He returned with a flat plate which was the duplicate of the one that had been brought to the space-cruiser. He held it before Steve. A picture formed on it.

It was a picture of Steve in the space-cruiser, putting rocket-fuel into the tiny double tank of the first robot's torso. It was the happening which had meant the revival of all six.

That picture faded, and another formed. This was of Steve striking savage blows at the mechanism now before him with the metal bar. That faded in turn and a completely arbitrary symbol took its place.

Suddenly, he was released. One of the five metal men handed the metal bar to him. All of them stood back and looked at him. It was so astounding a thing that if shocked him back to calm.

"You mean," he growled furiously, "I woke you up, so I'm entitled to smash your drive. It's an equation, eh? That's what that symbol meant. All right—"

He raised the bar. None of the metal men stirred. They waited to see their space-drive smashed. Steve glared at them and flung the bar to one side.

"You know where you can go!" he said bitterly. "All of you!"

He stalked out of the spaceship. None of the metal men followed. He turned and stared back at it, then headed for the cruiser.

On the way, his bitterness increased. He began to see many things. His companion in the space-cruiser had discarded the tiny catalyzer he'd built, because it was inefficient. With sudden startled insight, Steve awoke to the sort of efficiency that would enable the metal men to fuel their ship for operation with the contents of such minute reservoirs of fuel. What would enable one metal man to share a pint of fuel with five companions, and have power to weld and repair metal—?

The detonation of a single molecule of rocket-compound will raise the temperature of that molecule close to the hundred-thousand-degree mark. And it was not difficult to envision—though Steve could not design—a forcefield which would raise a molecule already at that temperature to disintegration temperature.

Ordinary matter would never reach such a temperature, which is usually found only in stars. Only rocket fuel or something similar, fed molecule by molecule into a tiny disintegration chamber, would, by its detonation, acquire a starting temperature the field could carry to the breakdown point.

The metal men, then, had atomic power, using an organic-base fuel and working on individual molecules so that they could make power-units for individual robots— or for spaceships or giant machines which could shift planets.

"Fine thing!" raged Steve. He'd given the first robot a pint of rocket fuel. Used in atomic-power generators, that would fuel all six for thousands of years. No wonder they could afford to let him smash their space-drive if he wished! With ten thousand years in which to repair it— he'd be dead in less than two months. They could take the space-cruiser apart, inch by inch, and find the rocket-fuel he had left. They would have all the time there was—

"I can set it off!" snarled Steve. "Then let 'em try to laugh at me!" He moved onward, vengefully. He reached the space-cruiser.

His companion, the one he had thought of as a friend to comfort him until his air was gone, that companion rose and looked at him.

Steve got out of his spacesuit, scowling. The slender golden figure reached for the flat vision-plate. He held it out to Steve. Pictures formed on it. Steve would not look at them.

"Take it away!" he said bitterly. "You've been laughing at me! I don't want to see what you've got to say! Get out! I'm going to get rid of you!"

There were loose papers where the robot had been sitting. Looking at everything, it had found paper and notes in Steve's handwriting, and pens and pencils to write with. It had experimented, and it had been writing. Steve saw diagrams, each with a minute and beautifully executed sketch beside it to make it lucid.

"Going to amuse me, eh?" he snarled. "You're going to get out!"

He was jealous. He was lonely. He was bitter. And he was humiliated that the metal men had been prepared to let him smash their space-drive because he had brought them back to life. He went savagely into the engine room. He wrenched at fastenings. He came back with two tubes of rocket-fuel, the amount that should be left over after the servicing of the ship past his death. He thrust the tubes angrily upon the slender metal man.

"Get out!" he raged. "You're not my friend! I won't be patronized by a pack of clockworks! I won't let 'em feel superior! Take this to your friends and don't come back!"

He shoved the quietly yielding robot to the airlock. He thrust him in. He worked the controls which opened the outer door swiftly, wasting a lockful of air.

Minutes later he saw the robot marching sturdily across the desolate, airless surface of Calypso, carrying the tubes of fuel.

Steve drove himself to eat. He smoked, prodigally wasting his air. He coddled his rage, because there was no sense in being reasonable. He saw moving things on the flat vision-plate, but for a long time he would not look. Presently he yielded. He saw the robots' spaceship lift from its resting place. He saw the ring-mountains of Calypso from that spaceship in flight. Then he looked down upon his own space-cruiser as it would be seen from above. It enlarged swiftly, as if the ship which saw it was descending.

There was an indescribable crunching vibration underfoot, and he knew. He scowled out the port. The other spaceship had landed close beside his own. Metal figures got out of it. One carried a burden, lightly. They advanced to the cruiser's airlock.

Steve stood still, frozen. He heard metal footprints on

metal plates. The soughing of air. The metal man he had thrust out a few hours since came back—and another.

The second man carried a contrivance which looked remarkably like an ordinary metal bar, but it had been finished since Steve had planned to use it as a maul. Now it was a space-drive like the one on the robots' own ship, though smaller. It had been made while the repair work on the space-ship was under way.

The golden figure which carried it moved assuredly toward the engine room. The other made a somehow appealing gesture to Steve and offered the vision-plate urgently. With an attempt at cold dignity, Steve uncompromisingly looked. Presently he swore softly.

"The devil! You looked at all my vision records, eh? You know what people are like. So you are people too! But we build houses to live in, and you build robots. And then we make cities for our houses to be in, and you make cities for your robots to occupy. Of course," he said generously, "you've an advantage in that you're not material, and you use that black stuff in your skull cases as a way of affecting matter—"

Then he paused. A moment later he said awkwardly, "But, after all, we're not material either. We use the gray stuff in our skull cases to affect matter, too. Only our robots, our bodies, aren't as tough as yours. But we're pretty much alike—"

The second golden figure came out of the engine room, with a strand of compacted wires trailing behind it. It paid them out carefully and went into the control room.

"You aren't a dummy, though. If you were," said Steve

uncomfortably, "I couldn't accept a favor from you. I wouldn't be beholden to a machine! But since you're people, why, I can. So, thanks. Maybe when our two races get together we'll be friends. I hope so—"

The other robot came out of the control room. Steve knew exactly what had been done. A new space-drive had been attached to the old one, which served now purely as a mounting. A bare two ounces of rocket fuel, included in the space-drive device, would drive his ship half a dozen times across the solar system.

From a man with a ship which was useless because it had only twelve hours' one-gravity drive left, he had become a man who'd given the robots means to cross the galaxy, and still had a ship more prodigally fueled than any other spaceship ever made by men.

He had, moreover, the design of the drive and the conversion-unit which made rocket fuel into atomic power. And his essential instruments had been connected to the new drive so that he could operate his ship exactly as before. He could drive the cruiser at three gravities all the way to the halfway point, and decelerate as recklessly, so that his air would be more than ample.

"I guess," said Steve, "you'll be going on. If you had any queer notions about conquest by your race, you wouldn't turn me loose. So I won't worry about that! When you've taken off, I'll start home."

The erect and gallant small figure before him could not smile, of course. It had probably understood little or nothing of what Steve actually said, but it had looked at a lot of vision-records. It knew a lot about human beings now. It held out a metal, articulated hand.

ALL THE TRAPS OF EARTH

by Clifford D. Simak

Many a pioneer in the past became one in order to get beyond the reach of the law, to avoid jail or even a necktie party. This accidental pioneer was facing something perhaps worse, and the hero's not being human doesn't keep this from being a typically warm and, yes, human story by Mr. Simak.

★🌑★

THE INVENTORY LIST was long. On its many pages, in his small and precise script, he had listed furniture, paintings, china, silverware and all the rest of it—all the personal belongings that had been accumulated by the Barringtons through a long family history.

And now that he had reached the end of it, be noted down himself, the last item of them all:

One domestic robot, Richard Daniel, antiquated but in good repair.

He laid the pen aside and shuffled all the inventory sheets together and stacked them in good order, putting a paper weight upon them—the little exquisitely carved ivory paper weight that Aunt Hortense had picked up that last visit she had made to Peking.

And having done that, his job came to an end.

He shoved back the chair and rose from the desk and slowly walked across the living room, with all its clutter of possessions from the family's past. There, above the mantel, hung the sword that ancient Jonathon had worn in the War Between the States, and below it, on the mantelpiece itself, the cup the Commodore had won with his valiant yacht, and the jar of moon-dust that Tony had brought back from Man's fifth landing on the Moon, and the old chronometer that had come from the long-scrapped family spacecraft that had plied the asteroids.

And all around the room, almost cheek by jowl, hung the family portraits, with the old dead faces staring out into the world that they had helped to fashion.

And not a one of them from the last six hundred years, thought Richard Daniel, staring at them one by one, that he had not known.

There, to the right of the fireplace, old Rufus Andrew Barrington, who had been a judge some two hundred years ago. And to the right of Rufus, Johnson Joseph Barrington, who had headed up that old lost dream of mankind, the Bureau of Paranormal Research. There, beyond the door that led out to the porch, was the scowling pirate face of Danley Barrington, who had first built the family fortune.

And many others—administrator, adventurer, corporation chief. All good men and true.

But this was at an end. The family had run out.

Slowly, Richard Daniel began his last tour of the house—the family room with its cluttered living space, the den with its old mementos, the library and its rows of ancient books, the dining hall in which the crystal and the china shone and sparkled, the kitchen gleaming with the copper and aluminum and the stainless steel, and the bedrooms on the second floor, each of them with its landmarks of former occupants. And finally, the bedroom where old Aunt Hortense had finally died, at long last closing out the line of Barringtons.

The empty dwelling held a not-quite-haunted quality, the aura of a house that waited for the old gay life to take up once again. But it was a false aura. All the portraits, all the china and the silverware, everything within the house would be sold at public auction to satisfy the debts. The rooms would be stripped and the possessions would be scattered and, as a last indignity, the house itself be sold.

Even he, himself, Richard Daniel thought, for he was chattel, too. He was there with all the rest of it, the final item on the inventory.

Except that what they planned to do with him was worse than simple sale. For he would be changed before he was offered up for sale. No one would be interested in putting up good money for him as he stood. And, besides, there was the law—the law that said no robot could legally have continuation of a single life greater than a hundred years. And he had lived in a single life six times a hundred years.

He had gone to see a lawyer and the lawyer had been sympathetic, but had held forth no hope.

"Technically," he had told Richard Daniel in his short, clipped lawyer voice, "you are at this moment much in violation of the statute. I completely fail to see how your family got away with it."

"They liked old things," said Richard Daniel. "And, besides, I was very seldom seen. I stayed mostly in the house. I seldom ventured out."

"Even so," the lawyer said, "there are such things as records. There must be a file on you . . ."

"The family," explained Richard Daniel, "in the past had many influential friends. You must understand, sir, that the Barringtons, before they fell upon hard times, were quite prominent in politics and in many other matters."

The lawyer grunted knowingly.

"What I can't quite understand," he said, "is why you should object so bitterly. You'll not be changed entirely. You'll still be Richard Daniel."

"I would lose my memories, would I not?"

"Yes, of course you would. But memories are not too important. And you'd collect another set."

"My memories are dear to me," Richard Daniel told him. "They are all I have. After some six hundred years, they are my sole worthwhile possession. Can you imagine, counselor, what it means to spend six centuries with one family?"

"Yes, I think I can," agreed the lawyer. "But now, with the family gone, isn't it just possible the memories may prove painful?"

"They're a comfort. A sustaining comfort. They make me feel important. They give me perspective and a niche."

"But don't you understand? You'll need no comfort, no importance once you're reoriented. You'll be brand new. All that you'll retain is a certain sense of basic identity—*that* they cannot take away from you even if they wished. There'll be nothing to regret. There'll be no leftover guilts, no frustrated aspirations, no old loyalties to hound you."

"I must be myself," Richard Daniel insisted stubbornly. "I've found a depth of living, a background against which my living has some meaning. I could not face being anybody else."

"You'd be far better off," the lawyer said wearily. "You'd have a better body. You'd have better mental tools. You'd be more intelligent."

Richard Daniel got up from the chair. He saw it was no use.

"You'll not inform on me?" he asked.

"Certainly not," the lawyer said. "So far as I'm concerned, you aren't even here."

"Thank you," said Richard Daniel. "How much do I owe you?"

"Not a thing," the lawyer told him. "I never make a charge to anyone who is older than five hundred."

He had meant it as a joke, but Richard Daniel did not smile. He had not felt like smiling.

At the door he turned around. "Why?" he was going to ask. "Why this silly law." But he did not have to ask—it was not hard to see.

Human vanity, he knew. No human being lived much

longer than a hundred years, so neither could a robot. But a robot, on the other hand, was too valuable simply to be junked at the end of a hundred years of service, so there was this law providing for the periodic breakup of the continuity of each robot's life. And thus no human need undergo the psychological indignity of knowing that his faithful serving man might manage to outlive him by several thousand years.

It was illogical, but humans were illogical.

Illogical, but kind. Kind in many different ways.

Kind, sometimes, as the Barringtons had been kind, thought Richard Daniel. Six hundred years of kindness. It was a prideful thing to think about. They had even given him a double name. There weren't many robots nowadays who had double names. It was a special mark of affection and respect.

The lawyer having failed him, Richard Daniel had sought another source of help. Now, thinking back on it, standing in the room where Hortense Barrington had died, he was sorry that he'd done it. For he had embarrassed the religico almost unendurably. It had been easy for the lawyer to tell him what he had. Lawyers had the statutes to determine their behavior, and thus suffered little from agonies of personal decision.

But a man of the cloth is kind if he is worth his salt. And this one had been kind instinctively as well as professionally, and that had made it worse.

"Under certain circumstances," he had said somewhat awkwardly, "I could counsel patience and humility and prayer. Those are three great aids to anyone who is willing to put them to his use. But with you I am not certain."

"You mean," said Richard Daniel, "because I am a robot?"

"Well, now . . ." said the minister, considerably befuddled at this direct approach.

"Because I have no soul?"

"Really," said the minister miserably, "you place me at a disadvantage. You are asking me a question that for centuries has puzzled and bedeviled the best minds in the church."

"But one," said Richard Daniel, "that each man in his secret heart must answer for himself."

"I wish I could," cried the distraught minister. "I truly wish I could."

"If it is any help," said Richard Daniel, "I can tell you that sometimes I suspect I have a soul."

And that, he could see, had been most upsetting for this kindly human. It had been, Richard Daniel told himself, unkind of him to say it. For it must have been confusing, since coming from himself it was not opinion only, but expert evidence.

So he had gone away from the minister's study and come back to the empty house to get on with his inventory work.

Now that the inventory was all finished and the papers stacked where Dancourt, the estate administrator, could find them when he showed up in the morning, Richard Daniel had done his final service for the Barringtons and now must begin doing for himself.

He left the bedroom and closed the door behind him and went quietly down the stairs and along the hallway to the little cubby, back of the kitchen, that was his very own.

And that, he reminded himself with a rush of pride, was of a piece with his double name and his six hundred years. There were not too many robots who had a room, however small, that they might call their own.

He went into the cubby and turned on the light and closed the door behind him.

And now, for the first time, he faced the grim reality of what he meant to do.

The cloak and hat and trousers hung upon a hook and the galoshes were placed precisely underneath them. His attachment kit lay in one corner of the cubby and the money was cached underneath the floor board he had loosened many years ago to provide a hiding place.

There was, he told himself, no point in waiting. Every minute counted. He had a long way to go and he must be at his destination before morning light.

He knelt on the floor and pried up the loosened board, shoved in a hand and brought out the stacks of bills, money hidden through the years against a day of need.

There were three stacks of bills, neatly held together by elastic bands—money given him throughout the years as tips and Christmas gifts, as birthday presents and rewards for little jobs well done.

He opened the storage compartment located in his chest and stowed away all the bills except for half a dozen which he stuffed into a pocket in one hip.

He took the trousers off the hook and it was an awkward business, for he'd never worn clothes before except when he'd tried on these very trousers several days before. It was a lucky thing, he thought, that long-dead

Uncle Michael had been a portly man, for otherwise the trousers never would have fit.

He got them on and zippered and belted into place, then forced his feet into the overshoes. He was a little worried about the overshoes. No human went out in the summer wearing overshoes. But it was the best that he could do. None of the regular shoes he'd found in the house had been nearly large enough.

He hoped no one would notice, but there was no way out of it. Somehow or other, he had to cover up his feet, for if anyone should see them, they'd be a giveaway.

He put on the cloak and it was a little short. He put on the hat and it was slightly small, but he tugged it down until it gripped his metal skull and that was all to the good, he told himself; no wind could blow it off.

He picked up his attachments—a whole bag full of them that he'd almost never used. Maybe it was foolish to take them along, he thought, but they were a part of him and by rights they should go with him. There was so little that he really owned—just the money he had saved, a dollar at a time, and this kit of his.

With the bag of attachments clutched underneath his arm, he closed the cubby door and went down the hall.

At the big front door he hesitated and turned back toward the house, but it was, at the moment, a simple darkened cave, empty of all that it once had held. There was nothing here to stay for—nothing but the memories, and the memories he took with him.

He opened the door and stepped out on the stoop and closed the door behind him.

And now, he thought, with the door once shut behind

him, he was on his own. He was running off. He was wearing clothes. He was out at night, without the permission of a master. And all of these were against the law.

Any officer could stop him, or any citizen. He had no rights at all. And he had no one who would speak for him, now that the Barringtons were gone.

He moved quietly down the walk and opened the gate and went slowly down the street, and it seemed to him the house was calling for him to come back. He wanted to go back, his mind said that he should go back, but his feet kept going on, steadily down the street.

He was alone, he thought, and the aloneness now was real, no longer the mere intellectual abstract he'd held in his mind for days. Here he was, a vacant hulk, that for the moment had no purpose and no beginning and no end, but was just an entity that stood naked in an endless reach of space and time and held no meaning in itself.

But he walked on and with each block that he covered he slowly fumbled back to the thing he was, the old robot in old clothes, the robot running from a home that was a home no longer.

He wrapped the cloak about him tightly and moved on down the street and now he hurried, for he had to hurry.

He met several people and they paid no attention to him. A few cars passed, but no one bothered him.

He came to a shopping center that was brightly lighted and he stopped and looked in terror at the wide expanse of open, brilliant space that lay ahead of him. He could detour around it, but it would use up time and he stood there, undecided, trying to screw up his courage to walk into the light. Finally, he made up his mind and strode briskly out, with his cloak wrapped tight about him and his hat pulled low.

Some of the shoppers turned and looked at him and he felt agitated spiders running up and down his back. The galoshes suddenly seemed three times as big as they really were and they made a plopping, squashy sound that was most embarrassing.

He hurried on, with the end of the shopping area not more than a block away.

A police whistle shrilled and Richard Daniel jumped in sudden fright and ran. He ran in slobbering, mindless fright, with his cloak streaming out behind him and his feet slapping on the pavement.

He plunged out of the lighted strip into the welcome darkness of a residential section and he kept on running.

Far off, he heard the siren and he leaped a hedge and tore across the yard. He thundered down the driveway and across a garden in the back and a dog came roaring out and engaged in noisy chase.

Richard Daniel crashed into a picket fence and went through it to the accompaniment of snapping noises as the pickets and the rails gave way. The dog kept on behind him and other dogs joined in.

He crossed another yard and gained the street and pounded down it. He dodged into a driveway, crossed another yard, upset a birdbath and ran into a clothesline, snapping it in his headlong rush.

Behind him lights were snapping on in the windows of the houses and screen doors were banging as people hurried out to see what the ruckus was.

He ran on a few more blocks, crossed another yard and ducked into a lilac thicket, stood still and listened. Some dogs were still baying in the distance and there was some human shouting, but there was no siren.

He felt a thankfulness well up in him that there was no siren, and a sheepishness, as well. For he had been panicked by himself, he knew; he had run from shadows, he had fled from guilt.

But he'd thoroughly roused the neighborhood and even now, he knew, calls must be going out and in a little while the place would be swarming with police.

He'd raised a hornet's nest and he needed distance, so he crept out of the lilac thicket and went swiftly down the street, heading for the edge of town,

He finally left the city and found the highway. He loped along its deserted stretches. When a car or truck appeared, he pulled off on the shoulder and walked along sedately. Then when the car or truck had passed, he broke into his lope again.

He saw the spaceport lights miles before he got there. When he reached the port, he circled off the road and came up outside a fence and stood there in the darkness, looking.

A gang of robots was loading one great starship and there were other ships standing darkly in their pits.

He studied the gang that was loading the ship, lugging the cargo from a warehouse and across the area lighted by the floods. This was just the setup he had planned on, although he had not hoped to find it immediately—he had been afraid that he might have to hide out for a day or two before he found a situation that he could put to use. And it was a good thing that he had stumbled on this opportunity, for an intensive hunt would be on by now for a fleeing robot, dressed in human clothes.

He stripped off the cloak and pulled off the trousers and the overshoes; he threw away the hat. From his attachments bag he took out the cutters, screwed off a hand and threaded the cutters into place. He cut the fence and wiggled through it, then replaced the hand and put the cutters back into the kit.

Moving cautiously in the darkness, he walked up to the warehouse, keeping in its shadow.

It would be simple, he told himself. All he had to do was step out and grab a piece of cargo, clamber up the ramp and down into the hold. Once inside, it should not be difficult to find a hiding place and stay there until the ship had reached first planet-fall.

He moved to the corner of the warehouse and peered around it and there were the toiling robots in what amounted to an endless chain, going up the ramp with the packages of cargo, coming down again to get another load.

But there were too many of them and the line was too tight. And the area too well-lighted. He'd never be able to break into that line.

And it would not help if he could, he realized despairingly—because he was different from those smooth and shining creatures. Compared to them, he was like a man in another century's dress; he and his six-hundred-year-old body would stand out like a circus freak.

He stepped back into the shadow of the warehouse and he knew that he had lost. All his best-laid plans, thought out in sober, daring detail, as he had labored at the inventory, had suddenly come to naught.

It all came, he told himself, from never going out, from having no real contact with the world, from not keeping up with robot-body fashions, from not knowing what the score was. He'd imagined how it would be and he'd got it all worked out and when it came down to it, it was nothing like he thought.

Now he'd have to go back to the hole he'd cut in the fence and retrieve the clothing he had thrown away and hunt up a hiding place until he could think of something else.

Beyond the corner of the warehouse he heard the harsh, dull grate of metal, and he took another look.

The robots had broken up their line and were streaming back toward the warehouse and a dozen or so of them were wheeling the ramp away from the cargo port. Three humans, all dressed in uniform, were walking toward the ship, heading for the ladder, and one of them carried a batch of papers in his hand.

The loading was all done and the ship about to lift and here he was, not more than a thousand feet away, and all that he could do was stand and see it go.

There had to be a way, he told himself, to get in that ship. If he could only do it his troubles would be over— or at least the first of his troubles would be over.

Suddenly it struck him like a hand across the face. There was a way to do it! He'd stood here, blubbering, when all the time there had been a way to do it!

In the ship, he'd thought. And that was not necessary. He didn't have to be *in* the ship.

He started running, out into the darkness, far out so he could circle round and come upon the ship from the other side, so that the ship would be between him and the flood lights on the warehouse. He hoped that there was time.

He thudded out across the port, running in an arc, and came up to the ship and there was no sign as yet that it was about to leave.

Frantically, he dug into his attachments bag and found the things he needed—the last things in that bag he'd ever thought he'd need. He found the suction discs and put them on, one for each knee, one for each elbow, one for each sole and wrist.

He strapped the kit about his waist and clambered up one of the mighty fins, using the discs to pull himself awkwardly along. It was not easy. He had never used the discs and there was a trick to using them, the trick of getting one clamped down and then working loose another so that he could climb.

But he had to do it. He had no choice but to do it.

He climbed the fin and there was the vast steel body of the craft rising far above him, like a metal wall climbing to the sky, broken by the narrow line of a row of anchor posts that ran lengthwise of the hull—and all that huge extent of metal painted by the faint, illusive shine of starlight that glittered in his eyes.

Foot by foot he worked his way up the metal wall. Like a humping caterpillar, he squirmed his way and with each foot he gained he was a bit more thankful.

Then he heard the faint beginning of a rumble and with the rumble came terror. His suction cups, he knew, might not long survive the booming vibration of the wakening rockets, certainly would not hold for a moment when the ship began to climb.

Six feet above him lay his only hope—the final anchor post in the long row of anchor posts.

Savagely, he drove himself up the barrel of the shuddering craft, hugging the steely surface like a desperate fly.

The rumble of the tubes built up to blot out all the world and he climbed in a haze of almost prayerful, brittle hope. He reached that anchor post or he was as good as dead. Should he slip and drop into that pit of flaming gases beneath the rocket mouths and he was done for.

Once a cup came loose and he almost fell, but the others held and he caught himself.

With a desperate, almost careless lunge, he hurled himself up the wall of metal and caught the rung in his fingertips and held on with a concentration of effort that wiped out all else.

The rumble was a screaming fury now that lanced through brain and body. Then the screaming ended and became a throaty roar of power and the vibration left the ship entirely. From one corner of his eye he saw the lights of the spaceport swinging over gently on their side.

Carefully, slowly, he pulled himself along the steel until he had a better grip upon the rung, but even with the better grip he had the feeling that some great hand had him in its fist and was swinging him in anger in a hundred-mile-long arc.

Then the tubes left off their howling and there was a terrible silence and the stars were there, up above him and to either side of him, and they were steely stars with no twinkle in them. Down below, he knew, a lonely Earth was swinging, but he could not see it.

He pulled himself up against the rung and thrust a leg beneath it and sat up on the hull.

There were more stars than he'd ever seen before, more than he'd dreamed there could be. They were still and cold, like hard points of light against a velvet curtain; there was no glitter and no twinkle in them and it was as if a million eyes were staring down at him. The Sun was underneath the ship and over to one side; just at the edge of the left-hand curvature was the glare of it against the silent metal, a sliver of reflected light outlining one edge of the ship. The Earth was far astern, a ghostly blue-green ball hanging in the void, ringed by the fleecy halo of its atmosphere.

It was as if he were detached—a lonely, floating brain that looked out upon a thing it could not understand nor could ever try to understand; as if he might even be afraid of understanding it—a thing of mystery and delight so long as he retained an ignorance of it, but something fearsome and altogether overpowering once the ignorance had gone.

Richard Daniel sat there, flat upon his bottom, on the metal hull of the speeding ship and he felt the mystery and delight and the loneliness and the cold and the great uncaring and his mind retreated into a small and huddled, compact defensive ball.

He looked. That was all there was to do. It was all right now, he thought. But how long would he have to look at it? How long would he have to camp out here in the open—the most deadly kind of open?

He realized for the first time that he had no idea where

the ship was going or how long it might take to get there. He knew it was a starship, which meant that it was bound beyond the solar system, and that meant that at some point in its flight it would enter hyperspace. He wondered, at first academically, and then with a twinge of fear, what hyperspace might do to one sitting naked to it. But there was little need, he thought philosophically, to fret about it now, for in due time he'd know, and there was not a thing that he could do about it—not a single thing.

He took the suction cups off his body and stowed them in his kit and then with one hand he tied the kit to one of the metal rungs and dug around in it until he found a short length of steel cable with a ring on one end and a snap on the other. He passed the ring end underneath a rung and threaded the snap end through it and snapped the snap onto a metal loop underneath his armpit. Now he was secured; he need not fear carelessly letting go and floating off the ship.

So here he was, he thought, neat as anything, going places fast, even if he had no idea where he might be headed, and now the only thing he needed was patience. He thought back, without much point, to what the religico had said in the study back on Earth. Patience and humility and prayer, he'd said, apparently not realizing at the moment that a robot has a world of patience.

It would take a lot of time, Richard Daniel knew, to get where he was going. But he had a lot of time, a lot more than any human, and he could afford to waste it. There were no urgencies, he thought—no need of food or air or water, no need of sleep or rest. There was nothing that could touch him.

Although, come to think of it, there might be.

There was the cold, for one. The space-hull was still fairly warm, with one side of it picking up the heat of the Sun and radiating it around the metal skin, where it was lost on the other side, but there would be a time when the Sun would dwindle until it had no heat and then he'd be subjected to the utter cold of space.

And what would the cold do to him. Might it make his body brittle? Might it interfere with the functioning of his brain? Might it do other things he could not even guess?

He felt the fears creep in again and tried to shrug them off and they drew off, but they still were there, lurking at the fringes of his mind.

The cold, and the loneliness, he thought—but he was one who could cope with loneliness. And if he couldn't, if he got too lonely, if he could no longer stand it, he could always beat a devil's tattoo on the hull and after a time of that someone would come out to investigate and they would haul him in.

But that was the last move of desperation, he told himself. For if they came out and found him, then he would be caught. Should he be forced to that extremity, he'd have lost everything—there would then have been no point in leaving Earth at all.

So he settled down, living out his time, keeping the creeping fears at bay just beyond the outposts of his mind, and looking at the universe all spread out before him.

The motors started up again with a pale blue flickering in the rockets at the stern and although there was no sense of acceleration he knew that the ship, now well off the

Earth, had settled down to the long, hard drive to reach the speed of light.

Once they reached that speed they would enter hyperspace. He tried not to think of it, tried to tell himself there was not a thing to fear—but it hung there just ahead of him, the great unknowable.

The Sun shrank until it was only one of many stars and there came a time when he could no longer pick it out. And the cold clamped down but it didn't seem to bother him, although he could sense the coldness.

Maybe, he said in answer to his fear, that would be the way it would be with hyperspace as well. But he said it unconvincingly. The ship drove on and on with the weird blueness in the tubes.

Then there was the instant when his mind went splattering across the universe.

He was aware of the ship, but only aware of it in relation to an awareness of much else, and it was no anchor point, no rallying position. He was spread and scattered; he was opened out and rolled out until he was very thin. He was a dozen places, perhaps a hundred places, all at once, and it was confusing, and his immediate reaction was to fight back somehow against whatever might have happened to him—to fight back and pull himself together. The fighting did no good at all, but made it even worse, for in certain instances it seemed to drive parts of him farther from other parts of him and the confusion was made greater.

So he quit his fighting and his struggling and just lay there, scattered, and let the panic ebb away and told himself he didn't care, and wondered if he did.

Slow reason returned a dribble at a time and he could think again and he wondered rather bleakly if this could be hyperspace and was pretty sure it was. And if it were, he knew, he'd have a long time to live like this, a long time in which to become accustomed to it and to orient himself, a long time to find himself and pull himself together, a long time to understand this situation if it were, in fact, understandable.

So he lay, not caring greatly, with no fear or wonder, just resting and letting a fact seep into him here and there from many different points.

He knew that, somehow, his body—that part of him which housed the rest of him—was still chained securely to the ship, and that knowledge, in itself, he knew, was the first small step towards reorienting himself. He had to reorient, he knew. He had to come to some sort of terms, if not to understanding, with this situation.

He had opened up and he had scattered out—that essential part of him, the feeling and the knowing and the thinking part of him, and he lay thin across a universe that loomed immense in unreality.

Was this, he wondered, the way the universe should be, or was it the unchained universe, the wild universe beyond the limiting disciplines of measured space and time.

He started slowly reaching out, cautious as he had been in his crawling on the surface of the ship, reaching out toward the distant parts of him, a little at a time. He did not know how he did it, he was conscious of no particular technique, but whatever he was doing, it seemed to work, for he pulled himself together, bit by knowing bit, until he had gathered up all the scattered fragments of him into several different piles.

Then he quit and lay there, wherever there might be, and tried to sneak up on those piles of understanding that he took to be himself.

It took a while to get the hang of it, but once he did, some of the incomprehensibility went away, although the strangeness stayed. He tried to put it into thought and it was hard to do. The closest he could come was that he had been unchained as well as the universe—that whatever bondage had been imposed upon him by that chained and normal world had now become dissolved and he no longer was fenced in by either time or space.

He could see—and know and sense—across vast distances, if distance were the proper term, and he could understand certain facts that he had not even thought about before, could understand instinctively, but without the language or the skill to coalesce the facts into independent data.

Once again the universe was spread far out before him and it was a different and in some ways a better universe, a more diagrammatic universe, and in time, he knew, if there were such a thing as time, he'd gain some completer understanding and acceptance of it.

He probed and sensed and learned and there was no such thing as time, but a great foreverness.

He thought with pity of those others locked inside the ship, safe behind its insulating walls, never knowing all the glories of the innards of a star or the vast panoramic sweep of vision and of knowing far above the flat galactic plane.

Yet he really did not know what he saw or probed; he

merely sensed and felt it and became a part of it, and it became a part of him—he seemed unable to reduce it to a formal outline of fact or of dimension or of content. It still remained a knowledge and a power so overwhelming that it was nebulous. There was no fear and no wonder, for in this place, it seemed, there was neither fear nor wonder. And he finally knew that it was a place apart, a world in which the normal space-time knowledge and emotion had no place at all and a normal space-time being could have no tools or measuring stick by which he might reduce it to a frame of reference.

There was no time, no space, no fear, no wonder—and no actual knowledge, either.

Then time came once again and suddenly his mind was stuffed back into its cage within his metal skull and he was again one with his body, trapped and chained and small and cold and naked.

He saw that the stars were different and that he was far from home and just a little way ahead was a star that blazed like a molten furnace hanging in the black.

He sat bereft, a small thing once again, and the universe reduced to package size.

Practically, he checked the cable that held him to the ship and it was intact. His attachments kit was still tied to its rung. Everything was exactly as it had been before.

He tried to recall the glories he had seen, tried to grasp again the fringe of knowledge which he had been so close to, but both the glory and the knowledge, if there had ever been a knowledge, had faded into nothingness.

He felt like weeping, but he could not weep, and he

was too old to lie down upon the ship and kick his heels in tantrum.

So he sat there, looking at the sun that they were approaching and finally there was a planet that he knew must be their destination, and he found room to wonder what planet it might be and how far from Earth it was.

He heated up a little as the ship skipped through atmosphere as an aid to braking speed and he had some rather awful moments as it spiraled into thick and soupy gases that certainly were a far cry from the atmosphere of Earth. He hung most desperately to the rungs as the craft came mushing down onto a landing field, with the hot gases of the rockets curling up about him. But he made it safely and swiftly clambered down and darted off into the smog-like atmosphere before anyone could see him.

Safely off, he turned and looked back at the ship and despite its outlines being hidden by the drifting clouds of swirling gases, he could see it clearly, not as an actual structure, but as a diagram. He looked at it wonderingly and there was something wrong with the diagram, something vaguely wrong, some part of it that was out of whack and not the way it should be.

He heard the clanking of cargo haulers coming out upon the field and he wasted no more time, diagram or not.

He drifted back, deeper in the mists, and began to circle, keeping a good distance from the ship. Finally he came to the spaceport's edge and the beginning of the town.

He found a street and walked down it leisurely and there was a wrongness in the town.

He met a few hurrying robots who were in too much of a rush to pass the time of day. But he met no humans.

And that, he knew quite suddenly, was the wrongness of the place. It was not a human town.

There were no distinctly human buildings—no stores or residences, no churches and no restaurants. There were gaunt shelter barracks and sheds for the storing of equipment and machines, great sprawling warehouses and vast industrial plants. But that was all there was. It was a bare and dismal place compared to the streets that he had known on Earth.

It was a robot town, he knew. And a robot planet. A world that was barred to humans, a place where humans could not live, but so rich in some natural resource that it cried for exploitation. And the answer to that exploitation was to let the robots do it.

Luck, he told himself. His good luck still was holding. He had literally been dumped into a place where he could live without human interference. Here, on this planet, he would be with his own.

If that was what he wanted. And he wondered if it was. He wondered just exactly what it was he wanted, for he'd had no time to think of what he wanted. He had been too intent on fleeing Earth to think too much about it. He had known all along what he was running from, but had not considered what he might be running to.

He walked a little further and the town came to an end. The street became a path and went wandering on into the wind-blown fogginess. So he turned around and went back up the street. There had been one barracks, he remembered, that had a TRANSIENTS sign hung out, and he made his way to it.

Inside, an ancient robot sat behind the desk. His body

was old-fashioned and somehow familiar. And it was familiar, Richard Daniel knew, because it was as old and battered and as out-of-date as his.

He looked at the body, just a bit aghast, and saw that while it resembled his, there were little differences. The same ancient model, certainly, but a different series. Possibly a little newer, by twenty years or so, than his.

"Good evening, stranger," said the ancient robot. "You came in on the ship?"

Richard Daniel nodded.

"You'll be staying till the next one?"

"I may be settling down," said Richard Daniel. "I may want to stay here."

The ancient robot took a key from off a hook and laid it on the desk.

"You representing someone?"

"No," said Richard Daniel.

"I thought maybe that you were. We get a lot of representatives. Humans can't come here, or don't want to come, so they send robots out here to represent them."

"You have a lot of visitors?"

"Some. Mostly the representatives I was telling you about. But there are some that are on the lam. I'd take it, mister, you are on the lam."

Richard Daniel didn't answer.

"It's all right," the ancient one assured him. "We don't mind at all, just so you behave yourself. Some of our most prominent citizens, they came here on the lam."

"That is fine," said Richard Daniel. "And how about yourself? You must be on the lam as well."

"You mean this body. Well, that's a little different. This here is punishment."

"Punishment?"

"Well, you see, I was the foreman of the cargo warehouse and I got to goofing off. So they hauled me up and had a trial and they found me guilty. Then they stuck me into this old body and I have to stay in it, at this lousy job, until they get another criminal that needs punishment. They can't punish no more than one criminal at a time because this is the only old body that they have. Funny thing about this body. One of the boys went back to Earth on a business trip and found this old heap of metal in a junkyard and brought it home with him—for a joke, I guess. Like a human might buy a skeleton for a joke, you know."

He took a long, sly look at Richard Daniel. "It looks to me, stranger, as if your body . . ."

But Richard Daniel didn't let him finish.

"I take it," Richard Daniel said, "you haven't many criminals."

"No," said the ancient robot sadly, "we're generally a pretty solid lot."

Richard Daniel reached out to pick up the key, but the ancient robot put out his hand and covered it.

"Since you are on the lam," he said, "it'll be payment in advance."

"I'll pay you for a week," said Richard Daniel, handing him some money.

The robot gave him back his change.

"One thing I forgot to tell you. You'll have to get plasticated."

"Plasticated?"

"That's right. Get plastic squirted over you. To protect you from the atmosphere. It plays hell with metal. There's a place next door will do it."

"Thanks. I'll get it done immediately."

"It wears off," warned the ancient one. "You have to get a new job every week or so."

Richard Daniel took the key and went down the corridor until he found his numbered cubicle. He unlocked the door and stepped inside. The room was small, but clean. It had a desk and chair and that was all it had.

He stowed his attachments bag in one corner and sat down in the chair and tried to feel at home. But he couldn't feel at home, and that was a funny thing—he'd just rented himself a home.

He sat there, thinking back, and tried to whip up some sense of triumph at having done so well in covering his tracks. He couldn't.

Maybe this wasn't the place for him, he thought. Maybe he'd be happier on some other planet. Perhaps he should go back to the ship and get on it once again and have a look at the next planet coming up.

If he hurried, he might make it. But he'd have to hurry, for the ship wouldn't stay longer than it took to unload the consignment for this place and take on new cargo.

He got up from the chair, still only half-decided.

And suddenly he remembered how, standing in the swirling mistiness, he had seen the ship as a diagram rather than a ship, and as he thought about it, something clicked inside his brain and he leaped toward the door.

For now he knew what had been wrong with the

spaceship's diagram—an injector valve was somehow out of kilter; he had to get back there before the ship took off again.

He went through the door and down the corridor. He caught sight of the ancient robot's startled face as he ran across the lobby and out into the street. Pounding steadily toward the spaceport, he tried to get the diagram into his mind again, but it would not come complete—it came in bits and pieces, but not all of it.

And even as he fought for the entire diagram, he heard the beginning take-off rumble.

"Wait!" he yelled. "Wait for me! You can't . . ."

There was a flash that turned the world pure white and a mighty invisible wave came swishing out of nowhere and sent him reeling down the street, falling as he reeled. He was skidding on the cobblestones and sparks were flying as his metal scraped along the stone. The whiteness reached a brilliance that almost blinded him and then it faded swiftly and the world was dark.

He brought up against a wall of some sort, clanging as he hit, and he lay there, blind from the brilliance of the flash, while his mind went scurrying down the trail of the diagram.

The diagram, he thought—why should he have seen a diagram of the ship he'd ridden through space, a diagram that had shown an injector out of whack? And how could he, of all robots, recognize an injector, let alone know there was something wrong with it. It had been a joke back home, among the Barringtons, that he, a mechanical thing himself, should have no aptitude at all for mechanical contraptions. And he could have saved those people and the ship—he could have saved them all if he'd immediately recognized the significance of the diagram. But he'd been too slow and stupid and now they all were dead.

The darkness had receded from his eyes and he could see again and he got slowly to his feet, feeling himself all over to see how badly he was hurt. Except for a dent or two, he seemed to be all right.

There were robots running in the street, heading for the spaceport, where a dozen fires were burning and where sheds and other structures had been flattened by the blast.

Someone tugged at his elbow and he turned around. It was the ancient robot.

"You're the lucky one," the ancient robot said. "You got off it just in time."

Richard Daniel nodded dumbly and had a terrible thought: What if they should think he did it? He had gotten off the ship; he had admitted that he was on the lam; he had rushed out suddenly, just a few seconds before the ship exploded. It would be easy to put it all together—that he had sabotaged the ship, then at the last instant had rushed out, remorseful, to undo what he had done. On the face of it, it was damning evidence.

But it was all right as yet, Richard Daniel told himself. For the ancient robot was the only one that knew—he was the only one he'd talked to, the only one who even knew that he was in town.

There was a way, Richard Daniel thought—there was an easy way. He pushed the thought away, but it came back. You are on your own, it said. You are already beyond the law. In rejecting human law, you made yourself an outlaw. You have become fair prey. There is just one law for you—self-preservation.

But there are robot laws, Richard Daniel argued. There are laws and courts in this community. There is a place for justice.

Community law, said the leech clinging in his brain, provincial law, little more than tribal law—and the stranger's always wrong.

Richard Daniel felt the coldness of the fear closing down upon him and he knew, without half-thinking, that the leech was right.

He turned around and started down the street, heading for the transients barracks. Something unseen in the street caught his foot and he stumbled and went down. He scrambled to his knees, hunting in the darkness on the cobblestones for the thing that tripped him. It was a heavy bar of steel, some part of the wreckage that had been hurled this far. He gripped it by one end and arose.

"Sorry," said the ancient robot. "You have to watch your step."

And there was a faint implication in his words, a hint of something more than the words had said, a hint of secret gloating in a secret knowledge.

You have broken other laws, said the leech in Richard Daniel's brain. What of breaking just one more? Why, if necessary, not break a hundred more. It is all or nothing. Having come this far, you can't afford to fail. You can allow no one to stand in your way now.

The ancient robot half-turned away and Richard

Daniel lifted up the bar of steel, and suddenly the ancient robot no longer was a robot, but a diagram. There, with all the details of a blueprint, were all the working parts, all the mechanism of the robot that walked in the street before him. And if one detached that single bit of wire, if one burned out that coil, if—

Even as he thought it, the diagram went away and there was the robot, a stumbling, falling robot that clanged on the cobblestones.

Richard Daniel swung around in terror, looking up the street, but there was no one near.

He turned back to the fallen robot and quietly knelt beside him. He gently put the bar of steel down into the street. And he felt a thankfulness—for, almost miraculously, he had not killed.

The robot on the cobblestones was motionless. When Richard Daniel lifted him, he dangled. And yet he was all right. All anyone had to do to bring him back to life was to repair whatever damage had been done his body. And that served the purpose, Richard Daniel told himself, as well as killing would have done.

He stood with the robot in his arms, looking for a place to hide him. He spied an alley between two buildings and darted into it. One of the buildings, he saw, was set upon stone blocks sunk into the ground, leaving a clearance of a foot or so. He knelt and shoved the robot underneath the building. Then he stood up and brushed the dirt and dust from his body.

Back at the barracks and in his cubicle, he found a rag and cleaned up the dirt that he had missed. And, he thought hard.

He'd seen the ship as a diagram and, not knowing what it meant, hadn't done a thing. Just now he'd seen the ancient robot as a diagram and had most decisively and neatly used that diagram to save himself from murder— from the murder that he was fully ready to commit.

But how had he done it? And the answer seemed to be that he really had done nothing. He'd simply thought that one should detach a single wire, burn out a single coil—he'd thought it and it was done.

Perhaps he'd seen no diagram at all. Perhaps the diagram was no more than some sort of psychic rationalization to mask whatever he had seen or sensed. Seeing the ship and robot with the surfaces stripped away from them and their purpose and their function revealed fully to his view, he had sought some explanation of his strange ability, and his subconscious mind had devised an explanation, an analogy that, for the moment, had served to satisfy him.

Like when he'd been in hyperspace, he thought. He'd seen a lot of things out there he had not understood. And that was it, of course, he thought excitedly. Something had happened to him out in hyperspace. Perhaps there'd been something that had stretched his mind. Perhaps he'd picked up some sort of new dimension-seeing, some new twist to his mind.

He remembered how, back on the ship again, with his mind wiped clean of all the glory and the knowledge, he had felt like weeping. But now he knew that it had been much too soon for weeping. For although the glory and the knowledge (if there'd been a knowledge) had been lost to him, he had not lost everything. He'd gained a new perceptive device and the ability to use it somewhat fumblingly—and it didn't really matter that he still was at a loss as to what he did to use it. The basic fact that he possessed it and could use it was enough to start with.

Somewhere out in front there was someone calling—someone, he now realized, who had been calling for some little time . . .

"Hubert, where are you? Hubert, are you around? Hubert . . ."

Hubert?

Could Hubert be the ancient robot? Could they have missed him already?

Richard Daniel jumped to his feet for an undecided moment, listening to the calling voice. And then sat down again. Let them call, he told himself. Let them go out and hunt. He was safe in this cubicle. He had rented it and for the moment it was home and there was no one who would dare break in upon him.

But it wasn't home. No matter how hard he tried to tell himself it was, it wasn't. There wasn't any home.

Earth was home, he thought. And not all of Earth, but just a certain street and that one part of it was barred to him forever. It had been barred to him by the dying of a sweet old lady who had outlived her time; it had been barred to him by his running from it.

He did not belong on this planet, he admitted to himself, nor on any other planet. He belonged on Earth, with the Barringtons, and it was impossible for him to be there.

Perhaps, he thought, he should have stayed and let them reorient him. He remembered what the lawyer had said about memories that could become a burden and a torment. After all, it might have been wiser to have started over once again.

For what kind of future did he have, with his old outdated body, his old outdated brain? The kind of body that they put a robot into on this planet by way of punishment. And the kind of brain—but the brain was different, for he had something now that made up for any lack of more modern mental tools.

He sat and listened, and he heard the house—calling all across the light years of space for him to come back to it again. And he saw the faded living room with all its vanished glory that made a record of the years. He remembered, with a twinge of hurt, the little room back of the kitchen that had been his very own.

He arose and paced up and down the cubicle—three steps and turn, and then three more steps and turn for another three.

The sights and sounds and smells of home grew close and wrapped themselves about him and he wondered wildly if he might not have the power, a power accorded him by the universe of hyperspace, to will himself to that familiar street again.

He shuddered at the thought of it, afraid of another power, afraid that it might happen. Afraid of himself, perhaps, of the snarled and tangled being he was—no longer the faithful, shining servant, but a sort of mad thing that rode outside a spaceship, that was ready to kill another being, that could face up to the appalling sweep of hyperspace, yet cowered before the impact of a memory.

What he needed was a walk, he thought. Look over

the town and maybe go out into the country. Besides, he remembered, trying to become practical, he'd need to get that plastication job he had been warned to get.

He went out into the corridor and strode briskly down it and was crossing the lobby when someone spoke to him.

"Hubert," said the voice, "just where have you been? I've been waiting hours for you."

Richard Daniel spun around and a robot sat behind the desk. There was another robot leaning in a corner and there was a naked robot brain lying on the desk.

"You are Hubert, aren't you?" asked the one behind the desk.

Richard Daniel opened up his mouth to speak, but the words refused to come.

"I thought so," said the robot. "You may not recognize me, but my name is Andy. The regular man was busy, so the judge sent me. He thought it was only fair we make the switch as quickly as possible. He said you'd served a longer term than you really should. Figures you'd be glad to know they'd convicted someone else."

Richard Daniel stared in horror at the naked brain lying on the desk.

The robot gestured at the metal body propped into the corner.

"Better than when we took you out of it," he said with a throaty chuckle. "Fixed it up and polished it and got out all the dents. Even modernized it some. Brought it strictly up to date. You'll have a better body than you had when they stuck you into that monstrosity."

"I don't know what to say," said Richard Daniel, stammering. "You see, I'm not . . ."

"Oh, that's all right," said the other happily. "No need for gratitude. Your sentence worked out longer than the judge expected. This just makes up for it."

"I thank you, then," said Richard Daniel. "I thank you very much."

And was astounded at himself, astonished at the ease with which he said it, confounded at his sly duplicity. But if they forced it on him, why should he refuse? There was nothing that he needed more than a modern body!

It was still working out, he told himself. He was still riding luck. For this was the last thing that he needed to cover up his tracks.

"All newly plasticated and everything," said Andy. "Hans did an extra special job."

"Well, then," said Richard Daniel, "let's get on with it."

The other robot grinned. "I don't blame you for being anxious to get out of there. It must be pretty terrible to live in a pile of junk like that."

He came around from behind the desk and advanced on Richard Daniel.

"Over in the corner," he said, "and kind of prop yourself. I don't want you tipping over when I disconnect you. One good fall and that body'd come apart."

"All right," said Richard Daniel. He went into the corner and leaned back against it and planted his feet solid so that he was propped.

He had a rather awful moment when Andy disconnected the optic nerve and he lost his eyes and there was considerable queasiness in having his skull lifted off his shoulders and he was in sheer funk as the final disconnections were being swiftly made.

Then he was a blob of greyness without a body or a head or eyes or anything at all. He was no more than a bundle of thoughts all wrapped around themselves like a pail of worms and this pail of worms was suspended in pure nothingness.

Fear came to him, a taunting, terrible fear. What if this were just a sort of ghastly gag? What if they'd found out who he really was and what he'd done to Hubert? What if they took his brain and tucked it away somewhere for a year or two—or for a hundred years? It might be, he told himself, nothing more than their simple way of justice.

He hung onto himself and tried to fight the fear away, but the fear ebbed back and forth like a restless tide.

Time stretched out and out—far too long a time, far more time than one would need to switch a brain from one body to another. Although, he told himself, that might not be true at all. For in his present state he had no way in which to measure time. He had no external reference points by which to determine time.

Then suddenly he had eyes.

And he knew everything was all right. One by one his senses were restored to him and he was back inside a body and he felt awkward in the body, for he was unaccustomed to it.

The first thing that he saw was his old and battered body propped into its corner and he felt a sharp regret at the sight of it and it seemed to him that he had played a dirty trick upon it. It deserved, he told himself, a better fate than this—a better fate than being left behind to serve as a shabby jailhouse on this outlandish planet. It had served him well for six hundred years and he should not be deserting it. But he was deserting it. He was, he told himself in contempt, becoming very expert at deserting his old friends. First the house back home and now his faithful body.

Then he remembered something else—all that money in the body!

"What's the matter, Hubert?" Andy asked.

He couldn't leave it there, Richard Daniel told himself, for he needed it. And besides, if he left it there, someone would surely find it later and it would be a giveaway. He couldn't leave it there and it might not be safe to forthrightly claim it. If he did, this other robot, this Andy, would think he'd been stealing on the job or running some side racket. He might try to bribe the other, but one could never tell how a move like that might go. Andy might be full of righteousness and then there'd be hell to pay. And, besides, he didn't want to part with any of the money.'

All at once he had it—he knew just what to do. And even as he thought it, he made Andy into a diagram.

That connection there, thought Richard Daniel, reaching out his arm to catch the falling diagram that turned into a robot. He eased it to the floor and sprang across the room to the side of his old body. In seconds, he had the chest safe open and the money safely out of it and locked inside his present body.

Then he made the robot on the floor become a diagram again and got the connection back the way that it should be.

Andy rose shakily off the floor. He looked at Richard Daniel in some consternation.

"What happened to me?" he asked in a frightened voice.

Richard Daniel sadly shook his head. "I don't know. You just keeled over. I started for the door to yell for help, then I heard you stirring and you were all right."

Andy was plainly puzzled. "Nothing like this ever happened to me before," he said.

"If I were you," counseled Richard Daniel, "I'd have myself checked over. You must have a faulty relay or a loose connection."

"I guess I will," the other one agreed. "It's downright dangerous."

He walked slowly to the desk and picked up the other brain, started with it toward the battered body leaning in the corner.

Then he stopped and said: "Look, I forgot. I was supposed to tell you. You better get up to the warehouse. Another ship is on its way. It will be coming in any minute now."

"Another one so soon?"

"You know how it goes," Andy said, disgusted. "They don't even try to keep a schedule here. We won't see one for months and then there'll be two or three at once."

"Well, thanks," said Richard Daniel, going out the door.

He went swinging down the street with a newborn confidence. And he had a feeling that there was nothing that could lick him, nothing that could stop him.

For he was a lucky robot!

Could all that luck, he wondered, have been gotten out in hyperspace, as his diagram ability, or whatever one might call it, had come from hyperspace? Somehow hyperspace had taken him and twisted him and changed him, had molded him anew, had made him into a different robot than he had been before.

Although, so far as luck was concerned, he had been lucky all his entire life. He'd had good luck with his human family and had gained a lot of favors and a high position and had been allowed to live for six hundred years. And that was a thing that never should have happened. No matter how powerful or influential the Barringtons had been, that six hundred years must be due in part to nothing but sheer luck.

In any case, the luck and the diagram ability gave him a solid edge over all the other robots he might meet. Could it, he asked himself, give him an edge on Man as well? *No*—that was a thought he should not think, for it was blasphemous. There never was a robot that would be the equal of a man.

But the thought kept on intruding and he felt not nearly so contrite over this leaning toward bad taste, or poor judgment, whichever it might be, as it seemed to him he should feel.

As he neared the spaceport, he began meeting other robots and some of them saluted him and called him by the name of Hubert and others stopped and shook him by the hand and told him they were glad that he was out of pokey.

This friendliness shook his confidence. He began to wonder if his luck would hold, for some of the robots, he was certain, thought it rather odd that he did not speak to them by name, and there had been a couple of remarks that he had some trouble fielding. He had a feeling that when he reached the warehouse he might be sunk without a trace, for he would know none of the robots there and he had not the least idea what his duties might include. And, come to think of it, he didn't even know where the warehouse was.

He felt the panic building in him and took a quick involuntary look around, seeking some method of escape. For it became quite apparent to him that he must never reach the warehouse.

He was trapped, he knew, and he couldn't keep on floating, trusting to his luck. In the next few minutes, he'd have to figure something.

He started to swing over into a side street, not knowing what he meant to do, but knowing he must do something, when he heard the mutter far above him and glanced up quickly to see the crimson glow of belching rocket tubes shimmering through the clouds.

He swung around again and sprinted desperately for the spaceport and reached it as the ship came chugging down to a steady landing. It was, he saw, an old ship. It had no burnish to it and it was blunt and squat and wore a hangdog look.

A tramp, he told himself, that knocked about from port to port, picking up whatever cargo it could, with perhaps now and then a paying passenger headed for some backwater planet where there was no scheduled service.

He waited as the cargo port came open and the ramp came down and then marched purposefully out onto the field, ahead of the straggling cargo crew, trudging toward the ship. He had to act, he knew, as if he had a perfect right to walk into the ship as if he knew exactly what he might be doing. If there were a challenge he would pretend he didn't hear it and simply keep on going.

He walked swiftly up the ramp, holding back from running, and plunged through the accordion curtain that served as an atmosphere control. His feet rang across the metal plating of the cargo hold until he reached the catwalk and plunged down it to another cargo level.

At the bottom of the catwalk he stopped and stood tense, listening. Above him he heard the clang of a metal door and the sound of footsteps coming down the walk to the level just above him. That would be the purser or the first mate, he told himself, or perhaps the captain, coming down to arrange for the discharge of the cargo.

Quietly, he moved away and found a corner where he could crouch and hide.

Above his head he heard the cargo gang at work, talking back and forth, then the screech of crating and the thump of bales and boxes being hauled out to the ramp.

Hours passed, or they seemed like hours, as he huddled there. He heard the cargo gang bringing something down from one of the upper levels and he made a sort of prayer that they'd not come down to this lower level—and he hoped no one would remember seeing him come in ahead of them, or if they did remember, that they would assume that he'd gone out again.

Finally it was over, with the footsteps gone. Then came the pounding of the ramp as it shipped itself and the banging of the port.

He waited for long minutes, waiting for the roar that, when it came, set his head to ringing, waiting for the monstrous vibration that shook and lifted up the ship and flung it off the planet.

Then quiet came and he knew the ship was out of atmosphere and once more on its way.

And knew he had it made.

For now he was no more than a simple stowaway. He was no longer Richard Daniel, runaway from Earth. He'd dodged all the traps of Man, he'd covered all his tracks, and he was on his way.

But far down underneath he had a jumpy feeling, for it all had gone too smoothly, more smoothly than it should.

He tried to analyze himself, tried to pull himself in focus, tried to assess himself for what he had become.

He had abilities that Man had never won or developed or achieved, whichever it might be. He was a certain step ahead of not only other robots, but of Man as well. He had a thing, or the beginning of a thing, that Man had sought and studied and had tried to grasp for centuries and had failed.

A solemn and a deadly thought: was it possible that it was the robots, after all, for whom this great heritage had been meant? Would it be the robots who would achieve the paranormal powers that Man had sought so long, while Man, perforce, must remain content with the materialistic and the merely scientific? Was he, Richard Daniel, perhaps, only the first of many? Or was it all explained by no more than the fact that he alone had been exposed to hyperspace? Could this ability of his belong to anyone who would subject himself to the full, uninsulated mysteries of that mad universe unconstrained by time?

Could Man have this, and more, if he too should expose himself to the utter randomness of unreality?

He huddled in his corner, with the thought and speculation stirring in his mind and he sought the answers, but there was no solid answer.

His mind went reaching out, almost on its own, and there was a diagram inside his brain, a portion of a blueprint, and bit by bit was added to it until it all was there, until the entire ship on which he rode was there, laid out for him to see.

He took his time and went over the diagram resting in his brain and he found little things—a fitting that was working loose and he tightened it, a printed circuit that was breaking down and getting mushy and he strengthened it and sharpened it and made it almost new, a pump that was leaking just a bit and he stopped its leaking.

Some hundreds of hours later one of the crewmen found him and took him to the captain.

The captain glowered at him. "Who are you?" he asked.

"A stowaway," Richard Daniel told him.

"Your name," said the captain, drawing a sheet of paper before him and picking up a pencil, "your planet of residence and owner."

"I refuse to answer you," said Richard Daniel sharply and knew that the answer wasn't right, for it was not right and proper that a robot should refuse a human a direct command.

But the captain did not seem to mind. He laid down the pencil and stroked his black beard slyly.

"In that case," he said, "I can't exactly see how I can

force the information from you. Although there might be some who'd try, you are very lucky that you stowed away on a ship whose captain is a most kind-hearted man."

He didn't look kind-hearted. He did look foxy.

Richard Daniel stood there, saying nothing.

"Of course," the captain said, "there's a serial number somewhere on your body and another on your brain. But I suppose that you'd resist if we tried to look for them."

"I am afraid I would."

"In that case," said the captain, "I don't think for the moment we'll concern ourselves with them."

Richard Daniel still said nothing, for he realized that there was no need to. This crafty captain had it all worked out and he'd let it go at that.

"For a long time," said the captain, "my crew and I have been considering the acquiring of a robot, but it seems we never got around to it. For one thing, robots are expensive and our profits are not large."

He sighed and got up from his chair and looked Richard Daniel up and down.

"A splendid specimen," he said. "We welcome you aboard. You'll find us congenial."

"I am sure I will," said Richard Daniel. "I thank you for your courtesy."

"And now," the captain said, "you'll go up on the bridge and report to Mr. Duncan. I'll let him know you're coming. He'll find some light and pleasant duty for you."

Richard Daniel did not move as swiftly as he might, as sharply as the occasion might have called for, for all at once the captain had become a complex diagram. Not like the diagrams of ships or robots, but a diagram of strange symbols, some of which Richard Daniel knew were frankly chemical, but others which were not.

"You heard me!" snapped the captain. "Move!"

"Yes, sir," said Richard Daniel, willing the diagram away, making the captain come back again into his solid flesh.

Richard Daniel found the first mate on the bridge, a horse-faced, somber man with a streak of cruelty ill-hidden, and slumped in a chair to one side of the console was another of the crew, a sodden, terrible creature.

The sodden creature cackled. "Well, well, Duncan, the first non-human member of the *Rambler's* crew."

Duncan paid him no attention. He said to Richard Daniel: "I presume you are industrious and ambitious and would like to get along."

"Oh, yes," said Richard Daniel, and was surprised to find a new sensation—laughter—rising in himself.

"Well, then," said Duncan, "report to the engine room. They have work for you. When you have finished there, I'll find something else."

"Yes, sir," said Richard Daniel, turning on his heel.

"A minute," said the mate. "I must introduce you to our ship's physician, Dr. Abram Wells. You can be truly thankful you'll never stand in need of his services."

"Good day, Doctor," said Richard Daniel, most respectfully.

"I welcome you," said the doctor, pulling a bottle from his pocket "I don't suppose you'll have a drink with me. Well, then, I'll drink to you."

Richard Daniel turned around and left. He went down to the engine room and was put to work at polishing and scrubbing and generally cleaning up. The place was in need of it. It had been years, apparently, since it had been cleaned or polished and it was about as dirty as an engine room can get—which is terribly dirty. After the engine room was done there were other places to be cleaned and furbished up and he spent endless hours at cleaning and in painting and shining up the ship. The work was of the dullest kind, but he didn't mind. It gave him time to think and wonder, time to get himself sorted out and to become acquainted with himself, to try to plan ahead.

He was surprised at some of the things he found in himself. Contempt, for one—contempt for the humans on this ship. It took a long time for him to become satisfied that it was contempt, for he'd never held a human in contempt before.

But these were different humans, not the kind he'd known. These were no Barringtons. Although it might be, he realized, that he felt contempt for them because he knew them thoroughly. Never before had he known a human as he knew these humans. For he saw them not so much as living animals as intricate patternings of symbols. He knew what they were made of and the inner urgings that served as motivations, for the patterning was not of their bodies only, but of their minds as well. He had a little trouble with the symbology of their minds, for it was so twisted and so interlocked and so utterly confusing that it was hard at first to read. But he finally got it figured out and there were times he wished he hadn't.

The ship stopped at many ports and Richard Daniel took charge of the loading and unloading, and he saw the planets, but was unimpressed. One was a nightmare of fiendish cold, with the very atmosphere turned to drifting snow. Another was a dripping, noisome jungle world, and still another was a bare expanse of broken, tumbled rock without a trace of life beyond the crew of humans and their robots who manned the huddled station in this howling wilderness.

It was after this planet that Jenks, the cook, went screaming to his bunk, twisted up with pain—the victim of a suddenly inflamed vermiform appendix.

Dr. Wells came tottering in to look at him, with a half-filled bottle sagging the pocket of his jacket. And later stood before the captain, holding out two hands that trembled, and with terror in his eyes.

"But I cannot operate," he blubbered. "I cannot take the chance. I would kill the man!"

He did not need to operate. Jenks suddenly improved. The pain went away and he got up from his bunk and went back to the galley and Dr. Wells sat huddled in his chair, bottle gripped between his hands, crying like a baby.

Down in the cargo hold, Richard Daniel sat likewise huddled and aghast that he had dared to do it—not that he had been able to, but that he had dared, that he, a robot, should have taken on himself an act of interference, however merciful, with the body of a human.

Actually, the performance had not been too difficult. It was, in a certain way, no more difficult than the repairing of an engine or the untangling of a faulty circuit. No more difficult—just a little different. And he wondered what he'd done and how he'd gone about it, for he did not know. He held the technique in his mind, of that there was ample demonstration, but he could in no wise isolate or pinpoint the pure mechanics of it. It was like an instinct, he thought—unexplainable, but entirely workable.

But a robot had no instinct. In that much he was different from the human and the other animals. Might not, he asked himself, this strange ability of his be a sort of compensating factor given to the robot for his very lack of instinct? Might that be why the human race had failed in its search for paranormal powers? Might the instincts of the body be at certain odds with the instincts of the mind?

For he had the feeling that this ability of his was just a mere beginning, that it was the first emergence of a vast body of abilities which some day would be rounded out by robots. And what would that spell, he wondered, in that distant day when the robots held and used the full body of that knowledge? An adjunct to the glory of the human race, or equals of the human race, or superior to the human race—or, perhaps, a race apart?

And what was his role, he wondered. Was it meant that he should go out as a missionary, a messiah, to carry to robots throughout the universe the message that he held? There must be some reason for his having learned this truth. It could not be meant that he would hold it as a personal belonging, as an asset all his own.

He got up from where he sat and moved slowly back to the ship's forward area, which now gleamed spotlessly from the work he'd done on it, and he felt a certain pride.

He wondered why he had felt that it might be wrong, blasphemous, somehow, to announce his abilities to the world? Why had he not told those here in the ship that it had been he who had healed the cook, or mentioned the many other little things he'd done to maintain the ship in perfect running order?

Was it because he did not need respect, as a human did so urgently? Did glory have no basic meaning for a robot? Or was it because he held the humans in this ship in such utter contempt that their respect had no value to him?

And this contempt—was it because these men were meaner than other humans he had known, or was it he now was greater than any human being? Would he ever again be able to look on any human as he had looked upon the Barringtons?

He had a feeling that if this were true, he would be the poorer for it. Too suddenly, the whole universe was home and he was alone in it and as yet he'd struck no bargain with it or himself.

The bargain would come later. He need only bide his time and work out his plans and his would be a name that would be spoken when his brain was scaling flakes of rust. For he was the emancipator, the messiah of the robots; he was the one who had been called to lead them from the wilderness.

"You!" a voice cried.

Richard Daniel wheeled around and saw it was the captain.

"What do you mean, walking past me as if you didn't see me?" asked the captain fiercely.

"I am sorry," Richard Daniel told him.

"You snubbed me!" raged the captain.

"I was thinking," Richard Daniel said.

"I'll give you something to think about," the captain yelled. "I'll work you till your tail drags. I'll teach the likes of you to get uppity with me!"

"As you wish," said Richard Daniel.

For it didn't matter. It made no difference to him at all what the captain did or thought. And he wondered why the respect even of a robot should mean so much to a human like the captain, why he should guard his small position with so much zealousness.

"In another twenty hours," the captain said, "we hit another port."

"I know," said Richard Daniel. "Sleepy Hollow on Arcadia."

"All right, then," said the captain, "since you know so much, get down into the hold and get the cargo ready to unload. We been spending too much time in all these lousy ports loading and unloading. You been dogging it."

"Yes, sir," said Richard Daniel, turning back and beading for the hold.

He wondered faintly if he were still robot—or was he something else? Could a machine evolve, he wondered, as Man himself evolved? And if a machine evolved, whatever would it be? Not Man, of course, for it never could be that, but could it be machine?

He hauled out the cargo consigned to Sleepy Hollow and there was not too much of it. So little of it, perhaps, that none of the regular carriers would even consider its delivery, but dumped it off at the nearest terminal, leaving it for a roving tramp, like the *Rambler,* to carry eventually to its destination.

When they reached Arcadia, he waited until the

thunder died and the ship was still. Then he shoved the lever that opened up the port and slid out the ramp.

The port came open ponderously and he saw blue skies and the green of trees and the far-off swirl of chimney smoke mounting in the sky.

He walked slowly forward until he stood upon the ramp and there lay Sleepy Hollow, a tiny, huddled village planted at the river's edge, with the forest as a background. The forest ran on every side to a horizon of climbing folded hills. Fields lay near the village, yellow with maturing crops, and he could see a dog sleeping in the sun outside a cabin door.

A man was climbing up the ramp toward him and there were others running from the village.

"You have cargo for us?" asked the man.

"A small consignment," Richard Daniel told him. "You have something to put on?"

The man had a weather-beaten look and he'd missed several haircuts and he had not shaved for days. His clothes were rough and sweat-stained and his hands were strong and awkward with hard work.

"A small shipment," said the man. "You'll have to wait until we bring it up. We had no warning you were coming. Our radio is broken."

"You go and get it," said Richard Daniel. "I'll start unloading."

He had the cargo half-unloaded when the captain came storming down into the hold. What was going on, he yelled. How long would they have to wait? "God knows we're losing money as it is even stopping at this place."

"That may be true," Richard Daniel agreed, "but you

knew that when you took the cargo on. There'll be other cargoes and goodwill is something—"

"Goodwill be damned!" the captain roared. "How do I know I'll ever see this place again?"

Richard Daniel continued unloading cargo.

"You," the captain shouted, "go down to that village and tell them I'll wait no longer than an hour . . ."

"But this cargo, sir?"

"I'll get the crew at it. Now, jump!"

So Richard Daniel left the cargo and went down into the village.

He went across the meadow that lay between the spaceport and the village, following the rutted wagon tracks, and it was a pleasant walk. He realized with surprise that this was the first time he'd been on solid ground since he'd left the robot planet. He wondered briefly what the name of that planet might have been, for he had never known. Nor what its importance was, why the robots might be there or what they might be doing. And he wondered, too, with a twinge of guilt, if they'd found Hubert yet.

And where might Earth be now? he asked himself. In what direction did it lie and how far away? Although it didn't really matter, for he was done with Earth.

He had fled from Earth and gained something in his fleeing. He had escaped all the traps of Earth and all the snares of Man. What he held was his, to do with as he pleased, for he was no man's robot, despite what the captain thought.

He walked across the meadow and saw that this planet was very much like Earth. It had the same soft feel about it, the same simplicity. It had far distances and there was a sense of freedom.

He came into the village and heard the muted gurgle of the river running and the distant shouts of children at their play and in one of the cabins a sick child was crying with lost helplessness.

He passed the cabin where the dog was sleeping and it came awake and stalked growling to the gate. When he passed it followed him, still growling, at a distance that was safe and sensible.

An autumnal calm lay upon the village, a sense of gold and lavender, and tranquility hung in the silences between the crying of the baby and the shouting of the children.

There were women at the windows looking out at him and others at the doors and the dog still followed, but his growls had stilled and now he trotted with prick-eared curiosity.

Richard Daniel stopped in the street and looked around him and the dog sat down and watched him and it was almost as if time itself had stilled and the little village lay divorced from all the universe, an arrested microsecond, an encapsulated acreage that stood sharp in all its truth and purpose.

Standing there, he sensed the village and the people in it, almost as if he had summoned up a diagram of it, although if there were a diagram, he was not aware of it.

It seemed almost as if the village were the Earth, a transplanted Earth with the old primeval problems and hopes of Earth—a family of peoples that faced existence with a readiness and confidence and inner strength.

From down the street he heard the creak of wagons

and saw them coming around the bend, three wagons piled high and heading for the ship.

He stood and waited for them and as he waited the dog edged a little closer and sat regarding him with a not-quite-friendliness.

The wagons came up to him and stopped.

"Pharmaceutical materials, mostly," said the man who sat atop the first load, "It is the only thing we have that is worth the shipping."

"You seem to have a lot of it," Richard Daniel told him.

The man shook his head. "It's not so much. It's almost three years since a ship's been here. We'll have to wait another three, or more perhaps, before we see another."

He spat down on the ground.

"Sometimes it seems," he said, "that we're at the tail-end of nowhere. There are times we wonder if there is a soul that remembers we are here."

From the direction of the ship, Richard Daniel heard the faint, strained violence of the captain's roaring.

"You'd better get on up there and unload," he told the man. "The captain is just sore enough he might not wait for you."

The man chuckled thinly. "I guess that's up to him," he said.

He flapped the reins and clucked good-naturedly at the horses.

"Hop up here with me," he said to Richard Daniel. "Or would you rather walk?"

"I'm not going with you," Richard Daniel said. "I am staying here. You can tell the captain."

For there was a baby sick and crying. There was a radio to fix. There was a culture to be planned and guided. There was a lot of work to do. This place, of all the places he had seen, had actual need of him.

The man chuckled once again. "The captain will not like it."

"Then tell him," said Richard Daniel, "to come down and talk to me. I am my own robot. I owe the captain nothing. I have more than paid any debt I owe him."

The wagon wheels began to turn and the man flapped the reins again.

"Make yourself at home," he said. "We're glad to have you stay."

"Thank you, sir," said Richard Daniel. "I'm pleased you want me."

He stood aside and watched the wagons lumber past, their wheels lifting and dropping thin films of powdered earth that floated in the air as an acrid dust.

Make yourself at home, the man had said before he'd driven off. And the words had a full round ring to them and a feel of warmth. It had been a long time, Richard Daniel thought, since he'd had a home.

A chance for resting and for knowing—that was what he needed. And a chance to serve, for now he knew that was the purpose in him. That was, perhaps, the real reason he was staying—because these people needed him . . . and he needed, queer as it might seem, this very need of theirs. Here on this Earth-like planet, through the generations, a new Earth would arise. And perhaps, given only time, he could transfer to the people of the planet all the powers and understanding he would find inside himself.

And stood astounded at the thought, for he'd not believed that he had it in him, this willing, almost eager, sacrifice. No messiah now, no robotic liberator, but a simple teacher of the human race.

Perhaps that had been the reason for it all from the first beginning. Perhaps all that had happened had been no more than the working out of human destiny. If the human race could not attain directly the paranormal power he held, this instinct of the mind, then they would gain it indirectly through the agency of one of their creations. Perhaps this, after all, unknown to Man himself, had been the prime purpose of the robots.

He turned and walked slowly down the length of village street, his back turned to the ship and the roaring of the captain, walked contentedly into this new world he'd found, into this world that he would make—not for himself, nor for robotic glory, but for a better Mankind and a happier. Less than an hour before he'd congratulated himself on escaping all the traps of Earth, all the snares of Man. Not knowing that the greatest trap of all, the final and the fatal trap, lay on this present planet.

But that was wrong, he told himself. The trap had not been on this world at all, nor any other world. It had been inside himself.

He walked serenely down the wagon-rutted track in the soft, golden afternoon of a matchless autumn day, with the dog trotting at his heels.

Somewhere, just down the street, the sick baby lay crying in its crib.

THE CAVE OF NIGHT

by James E. Gunn

As I've said in the introduction, this anthology is not intended as a history of space travel, and this story could only have happened in a universe parallel to the one which you, gentle reader, are sitting in. And yet, if Russia hadn't launched that beeping metal basketball on October 4, 1957 and panicked the US, something like this might have been necessary. Along with three associated stories, "The Cave of Night" was knit together into a paste-up novel, Station in Space *(currently not in print, damfino why), and that novel would fit the theme of* Space Pioneers *to a T (or maybe a P, for "pioneer") but there wouldn't have been room for it. So here's the opening shot, one heard (pardon the cliché) around the world.*

THE PHRASE was first used by a poet disguised in the cynical hide of a newspaper reporter. It appeared on the first day and was widely reprinted. He wrote:

At eight o'clock, after the Sun has set and
*   the sky is darkening, look up!*
There's a man up there where no man has ever been.
He is lost in the cave of night . . .

The headlines demanded something short, vigorous and descriptive. That was it. It was inaccurate, but it stuck.

If anybody was in a cave, it was the rest of humanity. Painfully, triumphantly, one man had climbed out. Now he couldn't find his way back into the cave with the rest of us.

What goes up doesn't always come back down.

That was the first day. After it came twenty-nine days of agonized suspense.

The cave of night. I wish the phrase had been mine.

That was it, the tag, the symbol. It was the first thing a man saw when he glanced at the newspaper. It was the way people talked about it: "What's the latest about the cave?" It summed it all up, the drama, the anxiety, the hope.

Maybe it was the Floyd Collins influence. The papers dug up their files on that old tragedy, reminiscing, comparing; and they remembered the little girl—Kathy Fiscus, wasn't it?—who was trapped in that abandoned California drain pipe; and a number of others.

Periodically, it happens, a sequence of events so accidentally dramatic that men lose their hatreds, their terrors, their shynesses, their inadequacies, and the human race momentarily recognizes its kinship.

The essential ingredients are these: a person must be

in unusual and desperate peril. The peril must have duration. There must be proof that the person is still alive. Rescue attempts must be made. Publicity must be widespread.

One could probably be constructed artificially, but if the world ever discovered the fraud, it would never forgive.

Like many others, I have tried to analyze what makes a niggling, squabbling, callous race of beings suddenly share that most human emotion of sympathy, and, like them, I have not succeeded. Suddenly a distant stranger will mean more than their own comfort. Every waking moment, they pray: Live, Floyd! Live, Kathy! Live, Rev!

We pass on the street, we who would not have nodded, and ask, "Will they get there in time?"

Optimists and pessimists alike, we hope so. We all hope so.

In a sense, this one was different. This was purposeful. Knowing the risk, accepting it because there was no other way to do what had to be done. Rev had gone into the cave of night. The accident was that he could not return.

The news came out of nowhere—literally—to an unsuspecting world. The earliest mention the historians have been able to locate was an item about a ham radio operator in Davenport, Iowa. He picked up a distress signal on a sticky-hot June evening.

The message, he said later, seemed to fade in, reach a peak, and fade out:

". . . and fuel tanks empty receiver broke . . . transmitting in clear so someone can pick this up, and . . . no way to get back . . . stuck . . ."

A small enough beginning.

The next message was received by a military base radio watch near Fairbanks, Alaska. That was early in the morning. Half an hour later, a night-shift worker in Boston heard something on his short-wave set that sent him rushing to the telephone.

That morning, the whole world learned the story. It broke over them, a wave of excitement and concern. Orbiting 1,075 miles above their heads was a man, an officer of the United States Air Force, in a fuelless spaceship.

All by itself, the spaceship part would have captured the world's attention. It was achievement as monumental as anything Man has ever done and far more spectacular. It was liberation from the tyranny of Earth, this jealous mother who had bound her children tight with the apron strings of gravity.

Man was free. It was a symbol that nothing is completely and finally impossible if Man wants it hard enough and long enough.

There are regions that humanity finds peculiarly congenial. Like all Earth's creatures, Man is a product and a victim of environment. His triumph is that the slave became the master. Unlike more specialized animals, he distributed himself across the entire surface of the Earth, from the frozen Antarctic continent to the Arctic icecap.

Man became an equatorial animal, a temperate zone animal, an arctic animal. He became a plain dweller, a valley dweller, a mountain dweller. The swamp and the desert became equally his home.

Man made his own environment.

With his inventive mind and his dexterous hands, he fashioned it, conquered cold and heat, dampness, aridness, land, sea, air. Now, with his science, he had conquered everything. He had become independent of the world that bore him.

It was a birthday cake for all mankind, celebrating its coming of age.

Brutally, the disaster was icing on the cake.

But it was more, too. When everything is considered, perhaps it was the aspect that, for a few, brief days, united humanity and made possible what we did.

It was a sign: Man is never completely independent of Earth; he carries with him his environment; he is always and forever a part of humanity. It was a conquest mellowed by a confession of mortality and error.

It was a statement: Man has within him the qualities of greatness that will never accept the restraints of circumstance, and yet he carries, too, the seeds of fallibility that we all recognize in ourselves.

Rev was one of us. His triumph was our triumph; his peril—more fully and finely—was our peril.

Reverdy L. McMillen, III, first lieutenant, U.S.A.F. Pilot. Rocket jockey. Man. Rev. He was only a thousand miles away, calling for help, but those miles were straight up. We got to know him as well as any member of our own family.

The news came as a great personal shock to me. I knew Rev. We had become good friends in college, and fortune had thrown us together in the Air Force, a writer and a pilot. I had got out as soon as possible, but Rev had stayed in. I knew, vaguely, that he had been testing rocket-powered aeroplanes with Chuck Yeager. But I had no idea that the rocket programme was that close to space.

Nobody did. It was a better-kept secret that the Manhattan Project.

I remember staring at Rev's picture in the evening newspaper: the straight black hair; the thin, rakish moustache; the Clark Gable ears; the reckless, rueful grin and I felt again, like a physical thing, his great joy in living. It expressed itself in a hundred ways. He loved widely, but with discrimination. He ate well, drank heartily, reveled in expert jazz and artistic inventiveness, and talked incessantly.

Now he was alone and soon all that might be extinguished. I told myself that I would help.

That was a time of wild enthusiasm. Men mobbed the Air Force Proving Grounds at Cocoa, Florida, wildly volunteering their services. But I was no engineer. I wasn't even a welder or a riveter. At best, I was only a poor word mechanic.

But words, at least, I could contribute.

I made a hasty verbal agreement with a local paper and caught the first plane to Washington, D.C. For a long time, I liked to think that what I wrote during the next few days had something to do with subsequent events, for many of my articles were picked up for reprint by other newspapers.

The Washington fiasco was the responsibility of the Senate Investigating Committee. It subpoenaed everybody in sight—which effectively removed them from the vital work they were doing. But within a day, the

Committee realized that it had bitten off a bite it could neither swallow nor spit out.

General Beauregard Finch, head of the research and development programme, was the tough morsel the Committee gagged on. Coldly, accurately, he described the development of the project, the scientific and technical research, the tests, the building of the ship, the training of the prospective crewmen, and the winnowing of the volunteers down to one man.

In words more eloquent because of their clipped precision, he described the take-off of the giant three-stage ship, shoved upward on a lengthening arm of combining hydrazine and nitric acid. Within fifty-six minutes, the remaining third stage had reached its orbital height of 1,075 miles.

It had coasted there. In order to maintain that orbit, the motors had to flicker on for fifteen seconds.

At that moment, disaster laughed at Man's careful calculations.

Before Rev could override the automatics, the motors had flamed for almost half a minute. The fuel he had depended upon to slow the ship so that it would drop, re-enter the atmosphere and be reclaimed by Earth was almost gone. His efforts to counteract the excess resulted only in an approximation of the original orbit.

The fact was this: Rev was up there. He would stay there until someone came and got him. And there was no way to get there. The Committee took that as an admission of guilt and incompetence; they tried to lever themselves free with it, but General Finch was not to be intimidated. A manned ship had been sent up because no mechanical or electronic computer could contain the vast possibilities for decision and action built into a human being.

The original computer was still the best all-purpose computer. There had been only one ship built, true. But there was good reason for that, a completely practical reason—money.

Leaders are, by definition, ahead of the people. But this wasn't a field in which they could show the way and wait for the people to follow. This was no expedition in ancient ships, no light exploring party, no pilot-plant operation. Like a parachute jump, it had to be successful first time.

This was an enterprise into new, expensive fields. It demanded money (billions of dollars), brains (the best available), and the hard, dedicated labour of men (thousands of them).

General Finch became a national hero that afternoon. He said, in bold words, "With the limited funds you gave us, we have done what we set out to do. We have demonstrated that space flight is possible, that a space platform is feasible.

"If there is an inefficiency, if there is any blame for what has happened, it lies at the door of those who lacked confidence in the courage and ability of their countrymen to fight free of Earth to the greatest glory. Senator, how did you vote on that?"

But I am not writing a history. The shelves are full of them. I will touch on the international repercussions only enough to show that the event was no more a respecter of national boundaries than was Rev's orbiting ship.

★ ★ ★

The orbit was almost perpendicular to the equator. The ship travelled as far north as Nome, as far south as Little America on the Antarctic continent. It completed one giant circle every two hours. Meanwhile, the Earth rotated beneath. If the ship had been equipped with adequate optical instruments, Rev could have observed every spot on Earth within twenty-four hours. He could have seen fleets and their dispositions, aircraft carriers and the planes taking off their decks, troop maneuvers.

In the General Assembly of the United Nations, the Russian ambassador protested this unwarranted and illegal violation of its national boundaries. He hinted darkly that it would not be allowed to continue. The U.S.S.R. had not been caught unprepared, he said. If the violation went on—*"every few hours!"*—drastic steps would be taken.

World opinion reared up in indignation. The U.S.S.R. immediately retreated and pretended, as only it could, that its belligerence had been an unwarranted inference and that it had never said anything of the sort, anyway. This was not a military observer above our heads. It was a man who would soon be dead unless help reached him.

A world offered what it had. Even the U.S.S.R. announced that it was outfitting a rescue ship, since its space programme was already on the verge of success. And the American public responded with more than a billion dollars within a week. Congress appropriated another billion. Thousands of men and women volunteered.

The race began.

Would the rescue party reach the ship in time? The world prayed.

And it listened daily to the voice of a man it hoped to buy back from death.

The problem shaped up like this: the trip had been planned to last for only a few days. By careful rationing, the food and water might be stretched out for more than a month, but the oxygen, by cutting down activity to conserve it, couldn't possibly last more than thirty days. That was the absolute outside limit.

I remember reading the carefully detailed calculations in the paper and studying them for some hopeful error. There was none.

Within a few hours, the discarded first stage of the ship had been located floating in the Atlantic Ocean. It was towed back to Cocoa, Florida. Almost a week was needed to find and return to the Proving Grounds the second stage, which had landed nine hundred and six miles away.

Both sections were practically undamaged; their fall had been cushioned by ribbon parachute. They could be cleaned, repaired and used again. The trouble was the vital third stage—the nose section. A new one had to be designed and built within a month.

Space-madness became a new form of hysteria. We read statistics, we memorized insignificant details, we studied diagrams, we learned the risks and the dangers and how they would be met and conquered. It all became part of us. We watched the slow progress of the second ship and silently, tautly, urged it upward.

The schedule overhead became part of everyone's daily

life. Work stopped while people rushed to windows or outside or to their television sets, hoping for a glimpse, a glint from the high, swift ship, so near, so untouchably far.

And we listened to the voice from the cave of night: "I've been staring out of the portholes. I never tire of that. Through the one on the right, I see what looks like a black velvet curtain with a strong light behind it. There are pinpoint holes in the curtain and the light shines through, not winking the way stars do, but steady. There's no air up here. That's the reason. The mind can understand and still misinterpret.

"My air is holding out better than I expected. By my figures, it should last twenty-seven days more. I shouldn't use so much of it talking all the time, but it's hard to stop. Talking, I feel as if I'm still in touch with Earth, still one of you, even if I am way up here.

"Through the left-hand window is San Francisco Bay, looking like a dark, wandering arm extended by the ocean octopus. The city itself looks like a heap of diamonds with trails scattered from it. It glitters up cheerfully, an old friend. It misses me, it says. Hurry home, it says. It's gone now, out of sight. Good-bye, Frisco!

"Do you hear me down there? Sometimes I wonder. You can't see me now. I'm in the Earth's shadow. You'll have to wait for the dawn. I'll have mine in a few minutes.

"You're all busy down there. I know that. If I know you, you're all worrying about me, working to get me down, forgetting everything else. You don't know what a feeling that is. I hope to Heaven you never have to, wonderful though it is.

"Too bad the receiver was broken, but if it had to be

one or the other, I'm glad it was the transmitter that came through. There's only one of me. There are billions of you to talk to.

"I wish there were some way I could be sure you were hearing me. Just that one thing might keep me from going crazy."

Rev, you were one in millions. We read all about your selection, your training. You were our representative, picked with our greatest skill.

Out of a thousand who passed the initial rigid requirements for education, physical and emotional condition and age, only five could qualify for space. They couldn't be too tall, too stout, too young, too old. Medical and psychiatric tests weeded them out.

One of the training machines—Lord, how we studied this—reproduces the acceleration strains of a blasting rocket. Another trains men for maneuvering in the weightlessness of space. A third duplicates the cramped, sealed conditions of a spaceship cabin. Out of the final five, you were the only one who qualified.

No, Rev, if any of us could stay sane, it was you.

There were thousands of suggestions, almost all of them useless. Psychologists suggested self-hypnotism; cultists suggested yoga. One man sent a detailed sketch of a giant electromagnet with which Rev's ship could be drawn back to Earth.

General Finch had the only practical idea. He outlined a plan for letting Rev know that we were listening. He picked out Kansas City and set the time. "Midnight," he said. "On the dot. Not a minute earlier or later. At that moment, he'll be right overhead."

And at midnight, every light in the city went out and came back on and went out and came back on again.

For a few awful moments, we wondered if the man up there in the cave of night had seen. Then came the voice we knew now so well that it seemed it had always been with us, a part of us, our dreams and our waking.

The voice was husky with emotion: "Thanks . . . Thanks for listening. Thanks, Kansas City. I saw you winking at me. I'm not alone. I know that now. I'll never forget. Thanks."

And silence then as the ship fell below the horizon. We pictured it to ourselves sometimes, continually circling the Earth, its trajectory exactly matching the curvature of the globe beneath it. We wondered if it would ever stop.

Like the Moon, would it be a satellite of the Earth forever?

We went through our daily chores like automatons while we watched the third stage of the rocket take shape. We raced against a dwindling air supply, and death raced to catch a ship moving at fifteen thousand eight hundred miles per hour.

We watched the ship grow. On our television screens, we saw the construction of the cellular fuel tanks, the rocket motors, and the fantastic multitude of pumps, valves, gauges, switches, circuits, transistors, and tubes.

The personnel space was built to carry five men instead of one man. We watched it develop, a Spartan simplicity in the middle of the great complex, and it was as if we ourselves would live there, would watch those dials and instruments, would grip those chair-arm controls for the infinitesimal sign that the automatic pilot had faltered, would feel the soft flesh and the softer internal organs being wrenched away from the unyielding bone, and would hurtle upward into the cave of night.

We watched the plating wrap itself protectively around the vitals of the nose section. The wings were attached; they would make the ship a huge, metal glider in its unpowered descent to Earth after the job was done.

We met the men who would man the ship. We grew to know them as we watched them train, saw them fighting artificial gravities, testing spacesuits in simulated vacuums, practicing maneuvers in the weightless condition of free fall.

That was what we lived for.

And we listened to the voice that came to us out of the night: "Twenty-one days. Three weeks. Seems like more. Feel a little sluggish, but there's no room for exercise in a coffin. The concentrated foods I've been eating are fine, but not for a steady diet. Oh, what I'd give for a piece of home-baked apple pie!

"The weightlessness got me at first. Felt I was sitting on a ball that was spinning in all directions at once. Lost my breakfast a couple of times before I learned to stare at one thing. As long as you don't let your eyes roam, you're okay.

"There's Lake Michigan! My God, but it's blue today! Dazzles the eyes! There's Milwaukee, and how are the Braves doing? It must be a hot day in Chicago. It's a little muggy up here, too. The water absorbers must be overloaded.

"The air smells funny, but I'm not surprised. I must

smell funny, too, after twenty-one days without a bath. Wish I could have one. There are an awful lot of things I used to take for granted and suddenly want more than—

"Forget that, will you? Don't worry about me, I'm fine. I know you're working to get me down. If you don't succeed, that's okay with me. My life wouldn't just be wasted. I've done what I've always wanted to do. I'd do it again.

"Too bad, though, that we only had the money for one ship."

And again: "An hour ago, I saw the Sun rise over Russia. It looks like any other land from here, green where it should be green, farther north a sort of mud color, and then white where the snow is still deep.

"Up here, you wonder why we're so different when the land is the same. You think, we're all children of the same mother planet. Who says we're different?

"Think I'm crazy. Maybe you're right. It doesn't matter much what I say as long as I say something. This is one time I won't be interrupted. Did any man ever have such an audience?"

No, Rev. Never.

The voice from above, historical now, preserved: "I guess the gadgets are all right. You slide-rule mechanics! You test-tube artists! You finding what you want? Getting the dope on cosmic rays, meteoric dust, those islands you could never map, the cloud formations, wind movements, all the weather data? Hope the telemetering gauges are working. They're more important than my voice."

I don't think so, Rev. But we got the data. We built some of it into the new ships. *Ships,* not *ship,* for we didn't stop with one. Before we were finished, we had two complete three-stages and a dozen nose sections.

The voice: "Air's bad tonight. Can't seem to get a full breath. Sticks in the lungs. Doesn't matter, though. I wish you could all see what I have seen, the vast-spreading universe around Earth, like a bride in a soft veil. You'd know, then, that we belong out here."

We know, Rev. You led us out. You showed us the way.

We listened and we watched. It seems to me now that we held our breath for thirty days.

At last we watched the fuel pumping into the ship nitric acid and hydrazine. A month ago, we did not know their names; now we recognize them as the very substance of life itself. It flowed through the long special hoses, dangerous, cautiously grounded, over half a million dollars' worth of rocket fuel.

Statisticians estimate that more than a hundred million Americans were watching their television sets that day. Watching and praying.

Suddenly, the view switched to the ship fleeing south above us. The technicians were expert now. The telescopes picked it up instantly, the focus perfect the first time, and tracked it across the sky until it dropped beyond the horizon. It looked no different now than when we had seen it first.

But the voice that came from our speakers was different. It was weak. It coughed frequently and paused for breath.

"Air very bad. Better hurry. Can't last much longer . . . Silly I . . . Of course, you'll hurry.

"Don't want anyone feeling sorry for me . . . I've been living fast . . . Thirty days? I've seen three hundred sixty sunrises, three hundred sixty sunsets . . . I've seen what no man has ever seen before . . . I was the first. That's something . . . worth dying for . . .

"I've seen the stars, clear and undiminished. They look cold, but there's warmth to them and life. They have families of planets like our own Sun, some of them . . . They must. God wouldn't put them there for no purpose . . . They can be homes for our future generations. Or, if they have inhabitants, we can trade with them: goods, ideas, the love of creation . . .

"But—more than this—I have seen the Earth. I have seen it—as no man has ever seen it—turning below me like a fantastic ball, the seas like blue glass in the Sun . . . or lashed into grey storm-peaks . . . and the land green with life . . . the cities of the world in the night, sparkling . . . and the people . . .

"I have seen the Earth—there where I have lived and loved . . . I have known it better than any man and loved it better and known its children better . . . It has been good . . .

"Good-bye . . . I have a better tomb than the greatest conqueror Earth ever bore . . . Do not disturb—"

We wept. How could we help it?

Rescue was so close and we could not hurry it. We watched impotently. The crew were hoisted far up into the nose section of the three-stage rocket. It stood as tall as a twenty-four-story building. *Hurry*! we urged. But they could not hurry. The interception of a swiftly moving target is precision business. The takeoff was all calculated and impressed on the metal and glass and free electrons of an electronic computer.

The ship was tightened down methodically. The spectators scurried back from the base of the ship. We waited. The ship waited. Tall and slim as it was, it seemed to crouch. Someone counted off the seconds to a breathless world: ten—nine—eight . . . five, four, three . . . one—*fire*!

There was no flame, and then we saw it spurting into the air from the exhaust tunnel several hundred feet away. The ship balanced, unmoving, on a squat column of incandescence; the column stretched itself, grew tall; the huge ship picked up speed and dwindled into a point of brightness.

The telescopic lenses found it, lost it, found it again. It arched over on its side and thrust itself seaward. At the end of eighty-four seconds, the rear jets faltered, and our hearts faltered with them. Then we saw that the first stage had been dropped. The rest of the ship moved off on a new fiery trail. A ring-shaped ribbon parachute blossomed out of the third stage and slowed it rapidly.

The second stage dropped away one hundred twenty-four seconds later. The nose section, with its human cargo, its rescue equipment, went on alone. At sixty-three miles altitude, the flaring exhaust cut out. The third stage would coast up the gravitational hill more than a thousand miles.

Our stomachs were knotted with dread as the rescue ship disappeared beyond the horizon of the farthest television camera. By this time, it was on the other side of the world, speeding towards a carefully planned rendezvous with its sister.

Hang on, Rev! Don't give up!

Fifty-six minutes. That was how long we had to wait. Fifty-six minutes from the take-off until the ship was in its orbit. After that, the party would need time to match speeds, to send a space-suited crewman drifting across the emptiness between, over the vast, eerily turning sphere of the Earth beneath.

In imagination, we followed them.

Minutes would be lost while the rescuer clung to the ship, opened the airlock cautiously so that none of the precious remnants of air would be lost, and passed into the ship where one man had known utter loneliness.

We waited. We hoped.

Fifty-six minutes. They passed. An hour. Thirty minutes more. We reminded ourselves—and were reminded—that the first concern was Rev. It might be hours before we would get any real news.

The tension mounted unbearably. We waited—a nation, a world—for relief.

At eighteen minutes less than two hours—*too soon,* we told ourselves, lest we hope too much—we heard the voice of Captain Frank Pickrell, who was later to become the first commander of the *Doughnut.*

"I have just entered the ship," he said slowly. "The airlock was open." He paused. The implication stunned our emotions; we listened mutely. "Lieutenant McMillen is dead. He died heroically, waiting until all hope was gone, until every oxygen gauge stood at zero. And then— well, the airlock was open when we arrived.

"In accordance with his own wishes, his body will be left here in its eternal orbit. This ship will be his tomb for all men to see when they look up towards the stars. As long as there are men on Earth, it will circle above them, an everlasting reminder of what men have done and what men can do.

"That was Lieutenant McMillen's hope. This he did not only as an American, but as a man, dying for all humanity, and all humanity can glory for it.

"From this moment, let this be his shrine, sacred to all the generations of spacemen, inviolate. And let it be a symbol that Man's dreams can be realized, but sometimes the price is steep.

"I am going to leave here now. My feet will be the last to touch this deck. The oxygen I released is almost used up. Lieutenant McMillen is in his control chair, staring out towards the stars. I will leave the airlock doors open behind me. Let the airless, frigid arms of space protect and preserve for all eternity the man they would not let go."

Good-bye, Rev! Farewell! Good night!

Rev was not long alone. He was the first, but not the last to receive a space burial and a hero's farewell.

This, as I said, is no history of the conquest of space. Every child knows the story as well as I and can identify the make of a spaceship more swiftly.

The story of the combined efforts that built the orbital platform irreverently called the *Doughnut* has been told by others. We have learned at length the political triumph that placed it under United Nations control.

Its contribution to our daily lives has received the

accolade of the commonplace. It is an observatory, a laboratory, and a guardian. Startling discoveries have come out of that weightless, airless, heartless place. It has learned how weather is made and predicted it with incredible accuracy. It has observed the stars clear of the veil of the atmosphere. And it has insured our peace . . .

It has paid its way. No one can question that. It and its smaller relay stations made possible today's worldwide television and radio network. There is no place on Earth where a free voice cannot be heard or the face of freedom be seen. Sometimes we find ourselves wondering how it could have been any other way.

And we have had adventure. We have travelled to the dead gypsum seas of the Moon with the first exploration party. This year, we will solve the mysteries of Mars. From our armchairs, we will thrill to the discoveries of our pioneers—our stand-ins, so to speak. It has given us a common heritage, a common goal, and for the first time we are united.

This I mention only for background; no one will argue that the conquest of space was not of incalculable benefit to all mankind.

The whole thing came back to me recently, an overpowering flood of memory. I was skirting Times Square, where every face is a stranger's, and suddenly I stopped, incredulous.

"Rev!" I shouted.

The man kept on walking. He passed me without a glance. I turned around and stared after him. I started to run. I grabbed him by the arm. "Rev!" I said huskily, swinging him around. "Is it really you?"

The man smiled politely. "You must have mistaken me for someone else." He undamped my fingers easily and moved away. I realized then that there were two men with him, one on each side. I felt their eyes on my face, memorizing it.

Probably it didn't mean anything. We all have our doubles. I could have been mistaken.

But it started me remembering and thinking.

The first thing the rocket experts had to consider was expense. They didn't have the money. The second thing was weight. Even a medium-sized man is heavy when rocket payloads are reckoned, and the stores and equipment essential to his survival are many times heavier.

If Rev had escaped alive, why had they announced that he was dead? But I knew the question was all wrong.

If my speculations were right, Rev had never been up there at all. The essential payload was only a thirty-day recording and a transmitter. Even if the major feat of sending up a manned rocket was beyond their means and their techniques, they could send up that much.

Then they got the money; they got the volunteers and the techniques.

I suppose the telemetered reports from the rocket helped. But what they accomplished in thirty days was an unparalleled miracle.

The timing of the recording must have taken months of work; but the vital part of the scheme was secrecy. General Finch had to know and Captain—now Colonel—Pickrell. A few others—workmen, administrators—and Rev . . .

What could they do with him? Disguise him? Yes. And then hide him in the biggest city in the world. They would have done it that way.

It gave me a funny, sick kind of feeling, thinking about it. Like everybody else, I don't like to be taken in by a phony plea. And this was a fraud perpetrated on all humanity.

Yet it had led us to the planets. Perhaps it would lead us beyond, even to the stars. I asked myself: could they have done it any other way?

I would like to think I was mistaken. This myth has become part of us. We lived through it ourselves, helped make it. Someday, I tell myself, a spaceman whose reverence is greater than his obedience will make a pilgrimage to that swift shrine and find only an empty shell.

I shudder then.

This pulled us together. In a sense, it keeps us together. Nothing is more important than that.

I try to convince myself that I was mistaken. The straight black hair was gray at the temples now and cut much shorter. The moustache was gone. The Clark Gable ears were flat to the head; that's a simple operation, I understand.

But grins are hard to change. And anyone who lived through those thirty days will never forget that voice.

I think about Rev and the life he must have now, the things he loved and can never enjoy again, and I realize perhaps he made the greater sacrifice.

I think sometimes he must wish he were really in the cave of night, seated in that icy control chair, 1,075 miles above, staring out at the stars.

★ ★ ★

This story was first published in February 1955, two and a half years before the first satellite was orbited, and six and a half years before the first man was put into orbit.

It is interesting to see in what ways James Gunn (who now works in an administrative position at the University of Kansas) foresaw events correctly, and in what ways he did not.

Gunn felt, as science fiction writers had always felt, that it was logical for a man to be inside the first object orbited. Actually, this proved not to be the case. All sorts of objects (including animals) were placed in orbit before the men in charge of the space programmes in either the U.S.A. or the U.S.S.R. would trust men to ride a spaceship safely.

Gunn's final twist has a recording orbited before a man after all (and that is much more nearly correct) and he uses that recording as a device to force mankind of all nations to be willing to invest in a space programme. This was, actually, a remarkable piece of prophecy. The first orbiting vehicle, even though it was very simple, transmitted only a bleep, and did not represent a human life in danger, did arouse enough interest to bring about the spending of billions.

The space effort that resulted, however, was not a united drive aimed at an errand of mercy, but was a nationalistic push on the part of two competing nations, each determined to pull prestige-coups over the other. (This no science fiction writer foresaw.)

Gunn assumed (as all American science fiction writers did) that the American effort would be the first to succeed. He does say the U.S.S.R. announced "its space programme was already on the verge of success" but Gunn may have intended this ironically as the sort of thing the vainglorious Russians would be bound to say for propaganda reasons. He must have been surprised (as I was) when, in 1957, it was the Russians, after all, who managed to put up a satellite first.

Gunn had the centre of the effort at Cocoa, Florida, which is only fifteen miles west of Cape Canaveral (later Cape Kennedy) where the launchings eventually did take place. On the other hand, his picture of Earth as seen from space seems to envisage a planet with all its land and ocean clearly in view. As it turned out, the most prominent feature visible from space is Earth's cloud cover and very little of its land features can be made out easily at any given moment.

HE FELL INTO A DARK HOLE

by Jerry E. Pournelle

A little reading of history will show that pioneers on Earth are not necessarily nice people. In this case, the governments backing the pioneers may be downright despicable, particularly when the rulers have convinced themselves that they are the only thing holding back a planet-killing nuclear holocaust so that anything they do is justified. This is one of the late Dr. Pournelle's future history series in which the USA and the USSR formed the CoDominium to control the Earth and colony planets beyond, taking on the worst aspects of both systems in the process.

CDSN Captain Bartholomew Ramsey watched his men check out, each man leaving the oval entry port under the satanic gaze of the master-at-arms. After nearly two years in space the men deserved something more exciting than twenty hours dirtside at Ceres Base, but they were eager for even that much. CDSS *Daniel Webster* got all the long patrols and dirty out-system jobs in the Navy because her captain didn't protest. Now, when these men got to Luna Base and Navy Town, Lord help the local girls . . .

Well, they'd be all right here, Ramsey thought. The really expensive pleasures were reserved for Belt prospectors and the crews of Westinghouse mining ships. Bart glanced at the screens displaying ships docked at Ceres. None of the big ore-processing ships were in Thorstown. Things should be pretty quiet. Nothing Base Marines couldn't handle, even if *Daniel Webster*'s crew hadn't been on a good drunker for twenty months. Ramsey turned away from the entry port to go back to his cabin.

It was difficult to walk in the low gravity of Ceres. Very inconvenient place, he thought. But of course low gravity was a main reason for putting a Navy yard there. That and the asteroid mines . . .

He walked carefully through gray steel bulkheads to the central corridor. Just outside the bridge entrance he met Dave Trevor, the first lieutenant.

"Not going ashore?" Ramsey asked.

"No, sir." Trevor's boyish grin was infectious. Ramsey had once described it as the best crew morale booster in the Navy. And at age twenty-four, Dave Trevor had been in space eleven years, as ship's boy, midshipman, and officer. He would know every pub in the Solar System and a lot outside it . . . "Never cared much for the girls on Ceres," he said. "Too businesslike."

Captain Ramsey nodded sagely. With Trevor's looks he wouldn't have to shell out money for an evening's fun anywhere near civilization. Ceres was another matter. "I'd appreciate it if you'd make a call on the provost's office, Mr. Trevor. We might need a friend there by morning."

The lieutenant grinned again. "Aye, aye, Captain."

Bart nodded and climbed down the ladder to his cabin. Trevor's merry whistling followed him until he closed the door. Once Ramsey was inside he punched a four-digit code on the intercom console.

"Surgeon's office, Surgeon's Mate Hartley, sir."

"Captain here. Make sure we have access to a good dental repair unit in the morning, Hartley. Even if we have to use Base facilities."

"Aye, aye, sir."

Ramsey switched the unit off and permitted himself a thin smile. The regeneration stimulators aboard *Daniel Webster* worked but there was something wrong with the coding information in the dental unit. It produced buck teeth, not enormous but quite noticeable, and when his men were out drinking and some dirtpounder made a few funny remarks . . .

The smile faded as Ramsey sat carefully in the regulation chair. He glanced around the sterile cabin. There were none of the comforts other captains provided themselves. Screens, charts, built-in cabinets and tables, his desk, everything needed to run his ship, but no photographs and solidos, no paintings and rugs. Just Ramsey and his ship, his wife with the masculine name. He took a glass of whiskey from the arm of the chair. It was Scotch and the taste of burnt malt was very strong.

Bart tossed it off and replaced it to be refilled. The intercom buzzed. "Captain here."

"Bridge, sir. Call from Base Commandant Torrin."

"Put him on."

"Aye, aye, sir." The watch midshipman's face vanished and Rap Torrin's broad features filled the screen. The rear admiral looked at the bare cabin, grimaced, then smiled at Ramsey.

"I'm going to pull rank on you, Bart," Torrin said. "Expect that courtesy call in an hour. You can plan on having dinner with me, too."

Ramsey forced a smile. "Very good, sir. My pleasure. In an hour, then."

"Right." The screen went blank and Ramsey cursed. He drank the second whiskey and cursed again, this time at himself.

What's wrong with you? he thought. *Rap Torrin is as good a friend as you have in the Navy. Shipmate way back in Ajax under Sergei Lermontov. Now Rap has a star, well, that was expected. And Lermontov is Vice Admiral Commanding, the number two man in the whole CoDominium Space Navy.*

And so what? I could have had stars. As many as I wanted. I'm that good, or I was. And with Martin Grant's influence in the Grand Senate and Martin's brother John in charge of United States security, Senator Martin Grant's son-in-law could have had any post no matter how good . . .

Ramsey took another whiskey from the chair and looked at it for a long time. He'd once had his star, polished and waiting, nothing but formalities to go, while

Rap and Sergei grinned at his good luck. Sergei Lermontov had just made junior vice admiral then. Five years ago.

Five years. Five years ago, Barbara Jean Ramsey and their son Harold were due back from Meiji. Superstitiously, Bart had waited for them before accepting his promotion. When he took it, he'd have to leave *Daniel Webster* for something dirtside and wait until a spacing admiral was needed. That wouldn't have been long. The Danube situation was heating up back then. Ramsey could have commanded the first punitive expedition, but it had gone out under an admiral who botched the job. Barbara Jean had never come home from Meiji.

Her ship had taken a new direct route along an Alderson path just discovered. It never came out into normal space. A scoutcraft was sent to search for the liner, and Senator Grant had enough influence to send a frigate after that. Both vanished, and there weren't any more ships to send. Bartholomew Ramsey stayed a captain. He couldn't leave his ship because he couldn't face the empty house in Luna Base compound.

He sighed, then laughed cynically at himself. Time to get dressed. Rap wanted to show off his star, and it would be cruel to keep him waiting.

The reunion was neither more nor less than he'd expected, but Admiral Torrin cut short the time in his office. "Got to get you home, Bart. Surprise for you there. Come along, man, come along."

Bart followed woodenly. *Something really wrong with me,* he thought. *Man doesn't go on like this for five years.*

I'm all right aboard Old Danny Boy. It's only when I leave my ship, now why should that be? But a man can marry a ship, even a slim steel whiskey bottle four hundred meters long and sixty across; he wouldn't be the first captain married to a cruiser.

Most of Ceres Base was underground, and Bart was lost in the endless rock corridors. Finally they reached a guarded area. They returned the Marines' salutes and went through to broader hallways lined with carpets. There were battle paintings on the walls. Some reached back to wet navy days and every CD base, insystem or out, had them. There were scenes from all the great navies of the world. Russian, Soviet, U.S., British, Japanese . . . there weren't any of Togo at Tshushima, though. Or Pearl Harbor. Or Bengal Bay.

Rap kept up his hearty chatter until they got inside his apartment. The admiral's quarters were what Bart had visualized before he entered: richly furnished, filled with the gifts and mementos that a successful independent command captain could collect on a dozen worlds after more than twenty years in service. Shells and stuffed exotic fauna, a cabinet made of the delicately veined snakewood of Tanith, a table of priceless Spartan roseteak. There was a house on Luna Base that had been furnished like this . . .

Bart caught sight of the man who entered the room and snapped to attention in surprise. Automatically, he saluted.

Vice Admiral Lermontov returned the salute. The admiral was a tall, slim man who wore rimless spectacles which made his gray eyes look large and round as they bored through his subordinates. Men who served under Lermontov either loved him or hated him. Now his thin features distorted in genuine pleasure. "Bartholomew, I am sorry to surprise you like this."

Lermontov inspected Ramsey critically. The smile faded slightly. "You have not taken proper care of yourself, my friend. Not enough exercise."

"I can still beat you. Arm wrestling, anything you name—uh, sir."

Lermontov's smile broadened again. "That is better. But you need not call me 'sir'. You would say 'sir' only to Vice Admiral Lermontov, and it is quite obvious that the Vice Admiral Commanding cannot possibly be on Ceres. So, since you have not seen me . . ."

"I see," Ramsey said.

Lermontov nodded. "It is rather important. You will know why in a few moments. Rap, can you bring us something to drink?"

Torrin nodded and fussed with drinks from the snakewood cabinet. The ringing tone of a crystal glass was very loud in the quiet apartment. Ramsey was vaguely amused as he took a seat at the roseteak table in the center of the lush room. A rear admiral waiting on a captain, and no enlisted spacers to serve the Vice Admiral Commanding, who, after all, wasn't really there in the first place . . . the whiskey was from Inverarry and was very good.

"You have been in space nearly two years," Lermontov said. "You have not seen your father-in-law in that time?"

"More like three since Martin and I really talked about

anything," Ramsey said. "We—we remind each other too much of Barbara Jean and Harold."

The pain in Ramsey's face was reflected as a pale shadow in Lermontov's eyes. "But you knew he had become chairman of the appropriations committee."

"Yes."

"The Navy's friend, Grand Senator Grant. Without him these last years would have been disaster for us all. For the Navy, and for Earth as well if those politicians could only see it." Lermontov cut himself off with an angry snap. The big eyes matching his steel gray hair focused on Bart. "The new appropriations are worse," the admiral growled. "While you have been away, everything has become worse. Millington, Harmon, Bertram, they all squeeze President Lipscomb's Unity Party in your country, and Kaslov gains influence every day in mine. I think it will not be long before one or the other of the CoDominium sponsors withdraws from the treaties, Bart. And after that, war."

"War." Ramsey said it slowly, not believing. After a hundred and fifty years of uneasy peace between the United States and the Soviets, war again, and with the weapons they had . . .

"Any spark might set it off," Lermontov was saying. "We must be ready to step in. The fleet must be strong, strong enough to cope with the national forces and do whatever we must do."

Ramsey felt as if the admiral had struck him. War? Fleet intervention? "What about the Commanding Admiral? The Grand Senate?"

Lermontov shrugged. "You know who are the good

men, who are not. But so long as the fleet is strong, something perhaps can be done to save Earth from the idiocy of the politicians. Not that the masses are better, screaming for a war they can never understand." Lermontov drank quietly, obviously searching for words, before he turned back to Ramsey. "I have to tell you something painful, my friend. Your father-in-law is missing."

"Missing—where? I told Martin to be careful, that Millington's Liberation Army people . . ."

"No. Not on Earth. Outsystem. Senator Grant went to Meiji to visit relatives there . . ."

"Yes." Ramsey felt the memory like a knife in his vitals. "His nephew, Barbara Jean's cousin, an officer in the Diplomatic Corps on Meiji. Grew up in the senator's home. Barbara Jean was visiting him when . . ."

"Yes." Lermontov leaned closer to Ramsey so that he could touch his shoulder for a moment. Then he took his hand away. "I do not remind you of these things because I am cruel, my friend. I must know—would the senator have tried to find his daughter? After all these years?"

Bart nodded. "She was his only child. As Harold was mine. If I thought there was any chance, I'd look myself. You think he tried it?"

"We do." Lermontov signaled Torrin to bring him another drink. "Senator Grant went to Meiji with the visit to his relatives as cover. With the Japanese representation question to come up soon, and the budget after that. Meiji is important. The Navy provided a frigate for transportation. It took the usual route through Colby and around, and was supposed to return the same way. But we have confirmed reports that Senator Grant's ship went instead to the jump-off point for the direct route."

"What captain in his right mind would let him get away with that?"

"His name was Commander John Grant, Jr. The senator's nephew."

"Oh." Bart nodded again, exaggerating the gesture as he realized the full situation. "Yeah. Johnny would do it if the old man asked. So you came all the way out here for my opinion, Sergei? I can give it quick. Senator Grant was looking for Barbara Jean. So you can write him off and whatever other plans you've got for the goddam Navy, you can write off, too. Learn to live without him, Sergei. The goddam jinx has another good ship and another good man. Now if you'll excuse me, I want to get back to my ship and get drunk."

Captain Ramsey strode angrily toward the door. Before he reached it, the vice admiral's voice crackled through the room. "Captain, you are not excused."

"Sir." Ramsey whirled automatically. "Very well, sir. Your orders?"

"My orders are for you to sit down and finish your drink, Captain." There was a long silence as they faced each other. Finally, Ramsey sat at the expensive table.

"Do you think so badly of me, Bart, that you believe I would come all the way out here, meet you secretly, for as little as this?"

Bart looked up in surprise. Emotions welled up inside him, emotions he hadn't felt in years, and he fought desperately to force them back. *No, God, don't let me hope again. Not that agony. Not hope . . .* But Lermontov was still speaking.

"I will let Professor Stirner explain it to you, since I am not sure any of us understand him. But he has a theory, Bart. He believes that the senator may be alive, and that there may be a chance to bring him home before the Senate knows he is missing. For years, the Navy has preserved the peace, now a strong fleet is needed more than ever. We have no choice, Bart. If there is any chance at all, we must take it."

Professor Hermann Stirner was a short Viennese with thinning red hair, improbable red freckles, and a neat round belly. Ramsey thought him about fifty, but the man's age was indeterminate. It was unlikely that he was younger, but with regeneration therapy he could be half that again. Rap Torrin brought the professor in through a back entrance.

"Dr. Stirner is an intelligence adviser to the fleet," Lermontov said. "He is not a physicist."

"No, no physicist," Stirner agreed quickly. "Who would want to live under the restrictions of a licensed physicist? CoDominium intelligence officers watching every move, suppressing most of your discoveries . . ." He spoke intently giving the impression of great emotion no matter what he said. "And most physicists I have met are not seeing beyond the end of their long noses. Me, I worry mostly about politics, Captain. But when the Navy loses ships, I want to know what happened to them. I have a theory about those ships, for years."

Ramsey gripped the arms of his chair until his

knuckles were white, but his voice was deadly calm. "Why didn't you bring up your theory before now?"

Stirner eyed him critically. Then he shrugged. "As I said, I am no physicist. Who would listen to me? But now, with the senator gone . . ."

"We need your father-in-law badly," Lermontov interrupted. "I do not really believe Professor Stirner's theories, but the fleet needs Senator Grant so desperately we will try anything. Let Dr. Stirner explain."

"Ja. You are a bright young CoDominium Navy captain, I am going to tell you things you know already, maybe. But I do not myself understand everything I should know, so you let me explain my own way, ja?" Stirner paced briskly for a moment, then sat restlessly at the table. He gave no chance to answer his question. but spoke rapidly, so that he gave the impression of interrupting himself.

"You got five forces in this universe we know about, ja? Only one of them maybe really isn't in this universe, we do not quibble about that, let the cosmologists worry. Now we look at two of those forces, we can forget the atomics and electromagnetics. Gravity and the Alderson force, these we look at. Now you think about the universe as flat like this table, eh?" He swept a pudgy hand across the roseteak surface. "And wherever you got a star, you got a hill that rises slowly, gets all the time steeper until you get near the star when it's so steep you got a cliff." And you think of your ships like roller coasters. You get up on the hill, aim where you want to go, and pop on the hyperspace drivers. Bang, you are in a universe where the Alderson effect acts like gravity. You are rolling downhill, across the table, and up the side of the next hill, not using up much potential energy, so you are ready to go again somewhere else if you can get lined up right. O.K.?"

Ramsey frowned. "It's not quite what we learned as middies—you've got ships repelled from a star rather than—"

"Ja, ja, plenty of quibble we can make if we want to. Now, Captain, how is it you get out of hyperspace when you want to?"

"We don't," Ramsey said. "When we get close enough to a gravity source, the ship comes out into normal space whether we want it to or not."

Stirner nodded. "Ja. And you use your photon drivers to run around in normal space where the stars is like wells, not hills, at least thinkin' about gravities. Now, suppose you try to shoot past one star to another, all in one jump?"

"It doesn't work," Ramsey said. "You'd get caught in the gravity field of the in-between star. Besides, the Alderson paths don't cross each other. They're generated by stellar nuclear activities, and you can only travel along lines of equal flux. In practice that means almost line of sight, with range limits, but they aren't really straight lines . . ."

"Ja. O.K. That's what I think is happening to them. I think there is a star between A-7820 and 82 Eridani. which is the improbable name Meiji's sun is stuck with."

"Now wait a minute," Admiral Torrin protested. "There can't be a star there, Professor. There's no question of missing it, not with our observations. Man, do you think the Navy didn't look for it? A liner and an explorer class frigate vanished on that route. We looked, first thing we thought of."

"Suppose there is a star there but you are not seeing it?"

"How could that be?" Torrin asked.

"A Black Hole, Admiral. Ja," Stirner continued triumphantly, "I think Senator Grant fell into a Black Hole."

Ramsey looked puzzled. "I seem to remember hearing something about Black Holes, but I don't remember what."

"Theoretical concept," Stirner said. "Hundred, hundred and fifty years ago, before the CoDominium Treaty puts a stop to scientific research. Nobody ever finds any Black Holes, so no appropriations for licensed physicists to work on them. But way back then, a man named Schwarzschild, Viennese perhaps, thinks of them." Stirner puffed with evident pride. "A Black Hole is like a neutron star that goes all the way. Collapsed down so far, down to maybe two, three kilometers, that nothing gets out of the gravity well. Infinite red shift of light. Some ways a Black Hole isn't even theoretically inside the universe."

The others looked incredulous and Stirner laughed. "You think that is strange? There was even talk once about whole galaxies collapsed to less than a tenth AU in size. They wouldn't be in the universe for real either."

"Then how would Black Holes interact with—oh," Rap Torrin said, "gravity. It still has that."

Stirner's round face bobbed in agreement. "Ja, ja, which is how we know is no black galaxy out there. Would be too much gravity, but there is plenty room for a star. Now one thing I do not understand though, why the survey ship gets through, others do not. Maybe gravity changes for one of those things, ja?"

"No, look, the Alderson path really isn't a line of sight, it can shift slightly—maybe just enough!" Torrin spoke rapidly. "If the geometry were just right, then sometimes the Hole wouldn't be in the way . . ."

"O.K.," Stirner said. "I leave that up to you Navy boys. But you see what happens, the ship is taking sights or whatever you do when you are making a jump, the captain pushes the button, and maybe you come out in normal space near this Black Hole. Nothing to see anywhere around you. *And no way to get back home.*"

"Of course." Ramsey stood, twisted his fingers excitedly. "The Alderson effect is generated by nuclear reactions. And the dark holes—"

"Either got none of those, or the Alderson force stuffs is caught inside the Black Hole like light and everything else. So you are coming home in normal space or you don't come home at all."

"Which is light-years. You'd never make it." Ramsey found himself near the bar. Absently, he poured a drink. "But in that case—the ships can sustain themselves a long time on their fuel!"

"Yes." Lermontov said it carefully. "It is at least possible that Senator Grant is alive. If his frigate dropped into normal space at a sufficient distance from the Black Hole so that it did not vanish down it."

"Not only Martin," Bart Ramsey said wonderingly. His heart pounded. "Barbara Jean. And Harold. They were on a Norden Lines luxury cruiser, only half the passenger berths taken. There should have been enough supplies and hydrogen to keep them going five years, Sergei. More than enough!"

Vice Admiral Lermontov nodded slowly. "That is why we thought you should go. But you realize that . . ."

"I haven't dared hope. I've wanted to die for five years, Sergei. Found that out about myself, had to be careful. Not fair to my crew to be so reckless. I'll go after Martin and—I'll go. But what does that do for us? If I do find them, I'll be as trapped as they are."

"Maybe. Maybe not." Stirner snorted. "Why you think we came out here, just to shake up a captain and maybe lose the Navy a cruiser? What made me think about this Black Hole business, I am questioning a transportee. Sentence to the labor market on Tanith, the charge is unauthorized scientific research. I look into all those crazies, might be something the Navy can use, ja? This one was fooling around with gravity waves, theories about Black Holes. Hard to see how the Navy could use it. I was for letting them take this one to Tanith when I start to think, we are losing those ships coming from Meiji, and click! So I pulled the prisoner off the colony ship."

"And he says he can get us home from a dark hole in blank space?" Ramsey asked. He tried to suppress the wave of excitement that began in his bowels and crept upward until he could hardly speak. Not hope! Hope was an agony, something to be dreaded. It was much easier to live with resignation . . .

"Ja. Only is not a him. Is a her. Not very attractive her. She *says* she can do this." Stirner paused significantly.

"Miss   Ward   hates   the   CoDominium,   Bart,"

Lermontov said carefully. "With what she thinks is good reason. She won't tell us how she plans to get the ship home."

"By God, she'll tell me!" *Why can't anything be simple? To know Barbara Jean is dead, or to know what mountain to climb to save her* . . . "If I can't think of something we can borrow a State Security man from the—"

"No." Lermontov's voice was a flat refusal. "Leave aside the ethics of the situation, we need this girl's creative energies. You can't get that with brainscrubs."

"Maybe." *And maybe I'll try it anyway if nothing else works. Barbara Jean, Barbara Jean* . . . "Where is this uncooperative scientist?"

"On Ceres." Vice Admiral Lermontov stretched a long arm toward the bar and poured for everyone. Stirner swished his brandy appreciatively in a crystal snifter. "Understand something, Bart," the Admiral said. "Miss Ward may not know a thing. She may hate us enough to destroy a CD ship even at the cost of her life. You're gambling on a theory we don't know exists and could be wrong even if she has one."

"So I'm gambling. My God, Sergei, do you know what I've been through these last years? It isn't normal for a man to brood like I do. You think I don't know that? That I don't know you whisper about it when I'm not around? Now you say there's a chance but it might cost my life. *You're* gambling a cruiser you can't spare, my ship is worth more to the Navy than I am."

Lermontov ignored Ramsey's evaluation, and Bart wished it had been challenged. But it was probably true, although the old Bart Ramsey was something else again, a man headed for the job Sergei held now . . .

"I am gambling a ship because if we do not get Martin Grant back in time for the appropriations hearings, I will lose more than a ship. We might lose half the fleet."

"Ja, ja," Stirner sighed. He shook his round head sadly, slowly, a big gesture. "It is not usual that one man may be so important. I do not believe in the indispensable-man theory myself. Yet, without Senator Grant I do not see how we are getting the ships in time or even keeping what we have, and without those ships . . . but maybe it is too late anyway, maybe even with the senator we cannot get the ships, or with the ships we can still do nothing when a planet full of people are determined to kill themselves."

"That's as it may be," Lermontov said. "But for now we need Senator Grant. I'll have the prisoner aboard *Daniel Webster* in four hours, Bart. You'll want to fill the tanks. Trim the crew down to minimum also. We must try this, but I do not really give very good odds on your coming home."

"STAND BY FOR JUMPOFF. Jump stations, man your jump stations." The unemotional voice of the officer of the watch monotoned through steel corridors, showing no more excitement than he would have used to announce an off-watch solido show. It took years to train that voice into Navy officers, but it made them easier to understand in battle. "Man your jump stations."

Bart Ramsey looked up from his screens as First Lieutenant Trevor ushered Marie Ward onto the bridge. She was a round, dumpy woman, her skin a faint red color.

Shoulder-length hair fell almost straight down to frame her face, but dark brown wisps poked out at improbable angles despite combings and hair ribbons. Her hands were big, as powerful as a man's, and the nails, chewed to the quick, were colorless. When he met her, Ramsey had estimated her age in the mid-thirties and was surprised to learn she was only twenty-six.

"You may take the assistant helmsman's acceleration chair," Ramsey told her. He forced a smile. "We're about to make the jump to Meiji." In his lonely ship. She'd been stripped down, empty stations all through her.

"Thank you, Captain." Marie sat and allowed Trevor to strap her in. The routine for jumpoff went on. As he listened to the reports, Ramsey realized Marie Ward was humming. "What is that?" he asked. "Catchy tune . . ."

"Sorry. It's an old nursery thing. 'The bear went over the mountain, the bear went over the mountain, the bear went over the mountain, to see what he could see.' "

"Oh. Well, we haven't seen anything yet."

" 'The other side of the mountain, was all that he could see.' But it's the third verse that's interesting. 'He fell into a dark hole, and covered himself over with charcoal—' "

"Warning, warning, take your posts for jumpoff."

Ramsey examined his screens. His chair was surrounded by them. "All right, Trevor, make your search."

"Aye, aye, sir."

Lieutenant Trevor would be busy for a while. He had been assigned the job of looking after Marie Ward, but for the moment Ramsey would have to be polite to her. "You haven't told us much about what we're going to see on the other side of that mountain. Why?"

"Captain, if you knew everything I did, you wouldn't need to take me along," she said. "I wish they'd hurry up. I *don't like* starjumps."

"It won't be long now—" Just what do you say to a convict genius? The whole trip out she'd been in everybody's hair, seldom talking about anything but physics. She'd asked the ship's officers about the drive, astrogation, instruments, the guns, nearly everything. Sometimes she was humorous, but more often scathingly sarcastic. And she wouldn't say a word about Black Holes, except to smile knowingly. More and more Ramsey wished he'd borrowed a KGB man from the Soviets . . .

"WARNING, WARNING. Jumpoff in one minute," the watch officer announced. Alarm bells sounded through the ship.

"Lined up, Captain," Trevor said. "For all I can tell, we're going straight through to 81 Eridani. If there's anything out there, I can't see it."

"Humph," Marie Ward snorted. "Why should you?"

"Yes, but if the Alderson path's intact, the Hole won't have any effect on us," Trevor protested. "And to the best we can measure, that path is there."

"No, no," Marie insisted. "You don't measure the Alderson path at all! You only measure the force, Lieutenant. Then your computer deduces the existence of the path from the stellar geometry. I'd have thought they'd teach you that much anyway. And that you could remember it."

"FINAL WARNING. Ten seconds to jump." A series of chimes, descending in pitch. Marie grimaced. Her mannish hands clutched the chair arms as she braced herself. At the tenth tone, everything blurred for an instant that stretched to a million years.

There is no way to record the time a jump takes. The best chronological instruments record nothing whatever. Ships vanish into the state of nonbeing conveniently called "hyperspace" and reappear somewhere else. Yet it always *seems* to take forever, and while it happens everything in the universe is wrong, *wrong*, WRONG . . .

Ramsey shook his head. The screens around his command seat remained blurred. "Jump completed. Check ship," he ordered.

Crewmen moved fuzzily to obey despite the protests of tortured nerves. Electronic equipment, computers, nearly everything complex suffers from jump induced transients although there is no known permanent effect.

"Captain, we're nowhere near Meiji!" the astrogator exclaimed. "I don't know *where* we are . . ."

"Stand by to make orbit," Ramsey ordered.

"Around *what?*" Lieutenant Trevor asked. "There's no star out there, Captain. There's nothing!"

"Then we'll orbit nothing." Ramsey turned to Marie Ward. "Well, we've found the damn thing. You got any suggestions about locating it? I'd as soon not fall into it."

"Why not?" she asked. Ramsey was about to smile politely when he realized she was speaking seriously. "According to some theories, a Black Hole is a time/space gate. You could go into it and come out—somewhere else. In another century. Or another universe."

"Is that why the hell you brought us out here? To kill

yourself testing some theory about Black Holes and space/time?"

"I am here because the CoDominium Marines put me aboard," she said. Her voice was carefully controlled. "And I have no desire to test any theory. Yet." She turned to Lieutenant Trevor. "Dave, is it really true? There's no star out there at all?"

"It's true enough."

She smiled. A broad, face-cracking smile that, with the thousand-meter stare in her eyes, made her look strangely happy. Insanely happy, in fact. "My God, it worked! There really is a Black Hole . . ."

"Which we haven't found yet," Trevor reminded her.

"Oh. Yes. Let's see—it should have started as about five stellar masses in size. That's my favorite theory, anyway. When it began to collapse it would have radiated over eighty percent of its mass away. X-rays, mostly. Lots of them. And if it had planets, they might still be here . . . Anyway, it should be about as massive as Sol. There won't be any radiation coming out. X-rays, light, nothing can climb out of that gravity well . . . just think of it, infinite red shift! It really happens!"

"Infinite red shift," Ramsey repeated carefully. "Yes, ma'am. Now, just how do we find this source of tired light?"

"It isn't tired light! That's a very obsolete theory. Next I suppose you'll tell me you think photons slow down when they lose energy."

"No, I—"

"Because they don't. They wouldn't *be* photons if they *could* slow down. They just lose energy until they vanish."

"Fine, but *how do we find it?*"

"It can't reach out and grab you, Captain," she said. The grin wasn't as wide as before, but still she smiled softly to herself. It made her look much better, although the mocking tone didn't help Ramsey's appreciation. "It's just a star, Captain. A very small star, very dense, as heavy as most other stars, but it doesn't have any more gravity than Sol. You could get quite close and still pull away—"

"If we knew which direction was away."

"Yes. Hm-m-m. It will bend light rays, but you'd have to be pretty close to see any effect at all from that . . ."

"Astrogation!" Ramsey ordered crisply. "How do we find a star we can't see?"

"We're about dead in space relative to whatever stopped us," the astrogator told him. "We can wait until we accelerate toward it and get a vector from observation of other stars. That will take a while. Or we can see if it's left any planets, but with nothing to illuminate them they'll be hard to find—"

"Yeah. Do the best you can, Mister." Marie Ward was still looking happily at the screens. They showed absolutely nothing. Ramsey punched another button in the arm of his command chair. "Comm room, sir."

"Eyes, there are ships out there somewhere." *God, I hope there are. Or one ship.* "Find them and get me communications."

"Aye, aye, sir. I'll use the distress frequencies. They might be monitoring those."

"Right. And Eyes, see if your bright electronics and physics boys can think of a way to detect gravity. So far as

I can make out that's the only effect that Black Hole has on the real universe."

"On *our* real universe, Captain," Marie Ward said.

"Huh?"

"On *our* real universe. Imagine a universe in which there are particles with non-zero rest masses able to move faster than light. Where you get rid of energy to go faster. Sentient beings in that universe would think of it as real. It might even be where our ships go when they make an Alderson jump. And the Black Holes could be gates to get you there."

"Yes, Miss Ward," Ramsey said carefully. Two enlisted spacers on the other side of the bridge grinned knowingly at each other and waited for the explosion. They'd been waiting ever since Marie Ward came aboard, and it ought to be pretty interesting. But Ramsey's voice became even softer and more controlled. "Meanwhile, have you any useful suggestions on what we should do now?"

"Find the Hole, of course. Your astrogator seems quite competent. His approach is very reasonable. Yes, quite competent. For a Navy man."

Carefully, his hands moving very slowly, Captain Bartholomew Ramsey unstrapped himself from his command chair and launched himself across the bridge to the exit port. "Take the con, Mr. Trevor," he said. And left.

For fifty hours, *Daniel Webster* searched for the other ships. Then, with no warning at all, Ramsey was caught in the grip of a giant vise.

For long seconds, he felt as if titanic hands were

squeezing him. They relaxed, ending the agony for a brief moment. And tried to pull him apart. The screens blurred, and he heard the sound of rending metal as the hands alternately crushed, then pulled.

Somehow, the watch officer sounded General Quarters. Klaxons blared through the ship as she struggled with her invisible enemy. Ramsey screamed, as much in rage and frustration as pain, hardly knowing he had made a sound. He had to take control of his ship before she died, but there were no orders to give. This was no attack by an enemy, but what, what?

The battle damage screen flared red. Ramsey was barely able to see as it showed a whole section of the ship's outer corridors evacuated to space. How many men were in there? Most wouldn't be in armor. *My God!* Daniel Webster *too? My wife and now my ship?*

Slowly it faded away. Ramsey pulled himself erect. Around him on the bridge the watch crew slumped at their stations. The klaxons continued, adding their confusion, until Ramsey shut them off.

"What—what was it?" Lieutenant Trevor gasped. His usually handsome features were contorted with remembered pain, and he looked afraid.

"All stations report damage," Ramsey ordered. "I don't know what it was, Lieutenant."

"I do!" Marie Ward gasped excitedly. Her eyes darted about in wonder. "I know! Gravity waves from the Black Hole! A tensor field! And these were tensor, not scalar—"

"Gravity waves?" Ramsey asked stupidly. "But gravity waves are weak things, only barely detectable."

Marie Ward snorted. "In your experience, Captain.

And in mine. But according to one Twentieth-Century theory—they had lots of theories then, when intellectuals were free, Captain—according to one theory, if a Black Hole is rotating and a mass enters the Schwarzschild Limit, part of the mass will be converted to gravity waves. *They* can escape from the Hole and affect objects outside it. So can Alderson forces, I think. But they didn't know about the Alderson force then . . ."

"But—is that going to happen again?" Ramsey demanded. Battle damage reports appeared on his screens. "We can't live through much of that."

"I really don't know how often it will happen," Marie answered. She chewed nervously on her right thumbnail. "I do know one thing. We have a chance to get home again."

"Home?" Ramsey took a deep breath. That depended on what had been done to Danny Boy. A runner brought him another report. Much of the ship's internal communications were out, but the chief engineer was working with a damage-control party. Another screen came on, and Ramsey heard the bridge speaker squawk.

"Repairable damage to normal space drive in main engine room," the toneless voice said. "Alderson drive appears unaffected."

"Gunnery reports damage to laser lenses in number one battery. No estimate of time to repair."

Big rigid objects had broken. Ramsey later calculated the actual displacement at less than a millimeter/meter; not very much, but enough to damage the ship and kill half a dozen crewmen unable to get into battle armor. Explosive decompression wasn't a pretty death, but it was quick.

With all her damage, *Daniel Webster* was only hurt. She could sail, his ship wasn't dead. Not yet. Ramsey gave orders to the damage control parties. When he was sure they were doing everything they could, he turned back to the dumpy girl in the assistant helmsman's seat. "How do we get home?"

She had been scribbling on a pad of paper, but her pencil got away from her when she tried to set it down without using the clips set into the arm of the seat. Now she stared absently at her notes, a thin smile on her lips. "I'm sorry, Captain. What did you say?"

"I asked, how do we get home?"

"Oh." She tried to look serious but only succeeded in appearing sly. "I was hasty in saying that. I don't know."

"Sure. Don't you want to get home?"

"Of course, Captain. I'd just love to get back on a colony ship. I understand Tanith has such a wonderful climate."

"Come off it. The Navy doesn't forget people who've helped us. You aren't going to Tanith." He took a deep breath. "We have a rescue mission, Miss Ward. Some of those people have been out here for five years." Five years of that? Nobody could live through five years of that. *O God, where is she? Crushed, torn apart, again and again, her body drifting out there in black space without even a star? Rest eternal grant them, O Lord, and let light perpetual shine upon them . . .*

"How do we get home?"

"I told you, I don't know."

But you do. And come to think of it, so do I. "Miss Ward, you implied that if we knew when a mass would enter the Black Hole, we could use the resulting Alderson forces to get us out of here."

"I'll be damned." She looked at Ramsey as if seeing him for the first time. "The man can actually—yes, of course." She smiled faintly. "I *thought* so before we left Ceres. Theory said that would work . . ."

"But we'd have to know the timing rather precisely, wouldn't we?"

"Yes. Depending on the size of the mass. The larger it is, the longer the effect would last. I think. Maybe not, though."

Ramsey nodded to himself. There was only one possible mass whose entry into the Hole they could predict. "Trevor."

"Sir?"

"One way you might amuse yourself is in thinking of ways to make a ship impact a solar mass not much more than two kilometers in diameter: a star you can't see and whose location you can't know precisely."

"Aye, aye, skipper." Dave Trevor frowned. He didn't often do that and it distorted his features. "Impact, Captain? But unless you were making corrections all the way in, you'd probably miss—as it is, the ship would pick up so much velocity that it's more likely to whip right around—"

"Exactly, Lieutenant. But it's the only way home."

One hundred and eight hours after breakout, Chief Yeoman Karabian located the other ships. *Daniel Webster*'s call was answered by the first frigate sent out to find the Norton liner:

DANIEL WEBSTER THIS IS HENRY HUDSON BREAK BREAK WE ARE IN ORBIT ELEVEN ASTRONOMICAL UNITS FROM WHATEVER THAT THING DOWN THERE IS STOP WE WILL SEND A CW SIGNAL TO GIVE YOU A BEARING STOP

THE NORTON LINER LORELEI AND CDSN CONSTELLATION ARE WITH US STOP YOUR SIGNAL INDICATES THAT YOU ARE LESS THAN ONE AU FROM THE DARK STAR STOP YOU ARE IN EXTREME DANGER REPEAT EXTREME DANGER STOP ADVISE YOU MOVE AWAY FROM DARK STAR IMMEDIATELY STOP THERE ARE STRONG GRAVITY FLUXES NEAR THE DARK STAR STOP THEY CAN TEAR YOU APART STOP ONE SCOUTSHIP ALREADY DESTROYED BY GRAVITY WAVES STOP REPEAT ADVISE YOU MOVE AWAY FROM DARK STAR IMMEDIATELY AND HOME ON OUR CW SIGNAL STOP

REQUEST FOLLOWING INFORMATION COLON WHO IS MASTER ABOARD DANIEL WEBSTER INTERROGATIVE BREAK BREAK MESSAGE ENDS

Ramsey read the message on his central display screen, then punched the intercom buttons. "Chief, get this out:

"HENRY HUDSON THIS IS DANIEL WEBSTER

BREAK BREAK CAPTAIN BARTHOLOMEW RAMSEY COMMANDING STOP WE WILL HOME ON YOUR BEACON STOP HAVE EXPERIENCED GRAVITY STORM ALREADY STOP SHIP DAMAGED BUT SPACEWORTHY STOP

"IS SENATOR MARTIN GRANT ABOARD CONSTELLATION INTERROGATIVE IS MRS RAMSEY THERE INTERROGATIVE BREAK MESSAGE ENDS."

The hundred-and-sixty-minute round trip for message and reply would be a lifetime.

"Trevor, get us moving when you've got that beacon," Ramsey ordered. "Pity he couldn't tell us about the gravity waves before we found out the hard way."

"Yes, sir." The acceleration alarm rang through the ship as Trevor prepared the new course. "We can only make about a half-G, Captain. We're lucky to get that. We took more damage from that gravity storm than Danny Boy's ever got from an enemy."

"Yeah." *Pity indeed. But communications did all they could. Space is just too big for omni signals, and we had maser damage to boot. Had to send in narrow cones, lucky we made contact this soon even sweeping messages. And no ecliptic here either. Or none we know of.*

"Communications here," Ramsey's speaker announced.

"Yes, Eyes."

"We're getting that homing signal. Shouldn't be any problem."

"Good." Ramsey studied the figures that flowed across his screen. "Take the con, Mr. Trevor. And call me when there's an answer from *Henry Hudson*. I'll wait in my patrol cabin." *And a damn long wait that's going to be. Barbara Jean, Barbara Jean, are you out there?*

The hundred and sixty minutes went past. Then another hour, and another. It was nearly six hours before there was a message from the derelicts; and it was in code the Navy used for the eyes of commanding officers only.

Captain Ramsey sat in his bare room and stared at the message flimsy. In spite of the block letters from the coding printer, his eyes wouldn't focus on the words.

DANIEL WEBSTER THIS IS HENRY HUDSON BREAK THE FOLLOWING IS PERSONAL MESSAGE FOR CAPTAIN BARTHOLOMEW RAMSEY FROM GRAND SENATOR MARTIN GRANT BREAK BREAK PERSONAL MESSAGE BEGINS

"BART WE ARE ALL HERE AND ALIVE STOP THE SCOUTSHIP WAS LOST TO GRAVITY WAVES STOP THE LINER LORELEI THE FRIGATE HENRY HUDSON AND THE FRIGATE CONSTELLATION ARE DAMAGED STOP LORELEI IN SPACEWORTHY CONDITION WITH MOST OF CREW SURVIVING DUE TO HEROIC EFFORTS OF MASTER OF HENRY HUDSON STOP

"BOTH BARBARA JEAN AND HAROLD ARE WELL STOP REGRET TO INFORM YOU THAT

BARBARA JEAN MARRIED COMMANDER JAMES
HARRIMAN OF HENRY HUDSON THREE YEARS
AGO STOP BREAK END PERSONAL MESSAGE
BREAK BREAK MESSAGE ENDS."

Ramsey automatically reached for a drink, then angrily
tossed the glass against a bare steel wall. It wouldn't be
fair to the crew. Or to his ship. And *Daniel Webster* was
still the only wife he had.

The intercom buzzed. "Bridge Captain."

"Go ahead, Trevor."

"Two hundred eighty plus hours to rendezvous,
Captain. We're on course."

"Thank you." *Damn long hours those are going to be.
How could she—but that's simple. For all Barbara Jean
could know, she and the boy were trapped out here
forever. I can bet there were plenty of suicides on those
ships. And the boy would be growing up without a father.*

*Not that I was so much of one. Half the time, I was out
on patrol anyway. But I was home when he caught
pneumonia from going with us to Ogden Base. Harold just
had to play in that snow . . .*

He smiled in remembrance. They'd built a snowman
together. But Harold wasn't used to Earth gravity, and
that more than the cold weakened him. The boy never did
put in enough time in the centrifuge on Luna Base. Navy
kids grew up on the Moon because the Navy was safe only
among its own . . .

Ramsey made a wry face. Hundreds of Navy kids
crowding into the big centrifuge . . . they were hard to
control, and Barbara Jean like most mothers hated to take

her turn minding them. She needed a hairdo. Or had to go shopping. Or something . . .

She should have remarried. Of course she should. He pictured Barbara Jean with another man. *What did she say to him when they made love? Did she use the same words? Like our first time, when we—oh, damn.*

He fought against the black mood. *Harriman. James Harriman. Fleet spatball champ seven years ago. A good man. Tough. Younger than Barbara Jean. Harriman used to be a real comer before he vanished. Never married and the girls at Luna Base forever trying to get—never married until now.*

Stop it! Would you rather she was dead? The thought crept through unwanted. *If you would, you'll godammit not admit it, you swine. Not now and not ever.*

She's alive! Bart Ramsey, you remember that and forget the rest of it. Barbara Jean is alive!

Savagely he punched the intercom buttons.

"Bridge. Aye, aye, Captain."

"We on course, Mister?"

"Yes, sir."

"Damage control parties working?"

"Yes, sir." Trevor's voice was puzzled. He was a good first lieutenant, and it wasn't like Ramsey to ride him . . .

"Excellent." Ramsey slapped the off button, waited a moment, and reached for another whiskey. This time he drank it. And waited.

There was little communication as *Daniel Webster* accelerated, turned over, and slowed again to approach the derelicts. Messages took energy, and they'd need it all. To get out, or to survive if Marie Ward proved wrong with her theories. Someday there'd be a better theory. Lermontov might come up with something, and even now old Stirner would be examining ancient records at Stanford and Harvard. If Ward was wrong, they still had to survive . . .

"Getting them on visual now," the comm officer reported. The unemotional voice broke. "Good God, Captain!"

Ramsey stared at the screens. The derelicts were worse than he could have imagined. *Lorelei* was battered, although she seemed intact, but the other ships seemed *bent*. The frigate *Constellation* was a wreck, with gaping holes in her hull structure. *Henry Hudson* was crumpled, almost unrecognizable. The survivors must all be on the Norton liner.

Ramsey watched in horror as the images grew on the screens. *Five years, with all hope going, gone. Harriman must be one hell of a man to keep anyone alive through that.*

When they were alongside, Navy routine carried Ramsey through hours that were lifetimes. Like one long continuous Jump. Everything *wrong*.

Spacers took *Daniel Webster*'s cutter across to *Lorelei* and docked. After another eternity she lifted away with passengers. CDSN officers, one of the merchant service survivors from *Lorelei*—and the others. Senator Grant. Johnny Grant. Commander Harriman. Barbara Jean, Harold—and Jeanette Harriman, age three.

"I'll be in my cabin, Trevor."

"Yes, sir."

"And get some spin on the ship as soon as that boat's fast aboard."

"Aye, aye, sir."

Ramsey waited. Who would come? It was his ship, he could send for anyone he liked. Instead he waited. Let Barbara Jean make up her own mind. Would she come? And would Harriman be with her?

Five years. Too long, he's had her for five years. But we had ten years together before that. Damned if I don't feel like a Middie on his first prom.

He was almost able to laugh at that.

The door opened and she came in. There was no one with her, but he heard voices in the corridor outside. She stood nervously at the bulkhead, staring around the bare cabin, at the empty desk and blank steel walls.

Her hair's gone. The lovely black hair that she never cut, whacked off short and tangled—God, you're beautiful. Why can't I say that? Why can't I say anything?

She wore shapeless coveralls, once white, but now grimy, and her hands showed ground-in dirt and grease. They'd had to conserve water, and there was little soap. Five years is a long time to maintain a closed ecology—

"No pictures, Bart? Not even one of me?"

"I—I thought you were dead." He stood, and in the small cabin they were very close. "There wasn't anybody else to keep a picture of."

Her tightly kept smile faded. "I—I would have waited, Bart. But we were dead. I don't even know why we tried to stay alive. Jim drove everybody, he kept us going, and then—he needed help."

Ramsey nodded. It was going to be all right. Wasn't it? He moved closer and put his hands on her shoulders, pulling her to him. She responded woodenly, then broke away.

"Give me—give me a little time to get used to it, Bart."

He backed away from her. "Yeah. The rest of you can come in now," he called.

"Bart, I didn't mean—"

"It's all right, Barbara Jean. We'll work it out." Somehow.

The boy came in first. He was very hesitant. Harold didn't look so very different. He still had a round face, a bit too plump. But he was *big*. And he was leading a little girl, a girl with dark hair and big round eyes, her mother's eyes.

Harold stood for a long moment. "Sir—ah," he began formally, but then he let go of the girl and rushed to his father. "Daddy! I knew you'd come get us, I told them you'd come!" He was tall enough that his head reached Bart's shoulder, and his arms went all the way around him.

Finally, he broke away. "Dad, this is my little sister." He said it defiantly, searchingly, watching his father's face. Finally, he smiled. "She's a nuisance sometimes, but she grows on you."

"I'm sure she does," Ramsey said. It was very still in the bare cabin. Ramsey wanted to say something else, but he had trouble with his voice.

Daniel Webster's wardroom was crowded. There was barely room at the long steel table for all the surviving astrogation officers to sit with Ramsey, Senator Grant, and Marie Ward. They waited tensely.

The senator was thinner than Ramsey had ever seen him despite the short time he'd been marooned. *Constellation* had been hit hard by a gravity storm—it was easier to think of them that way, although the term was a little silly. Now the senator's hands rested lightly on the wardroom table, the tips of the fingers just interlocked, motionless. Like everyone else, Senator Grant watched Commander Harriman.

Harriman paced nervously. He had grown a neatly trimmed beard, brown, with both silver and red hairs woven through it. His uniform had been patched a dozen times, but it was still the uniform of the Service, and Harriman wore it proudly. There was no doubt of who had been in command.

"The only ship spaceworthy is *Lorelei*," Harriman reported. "*Henry Hudson* was gutted to keep *Lorelei* livable, and Johnny Grant's *Constellation* took it hard in the gravity storms before we could get him out far enough from that thing."

Senator Grant sighed loudly. "I hope never to have to live through anything like that again. Even out this far you can feel the gravity waves, although it's not dangerous. But in close, before we knew where to go . . . ."

"But *Lorelei* can space?" Ramsey asked. Harriman nodded. "Then *Lorelei* it'll have to be. Miss Ward, explain what it takes to get home again."

"Well, I'm not *sure*, Captain. I think we should wait."

"We can't wait. I realize you want to stay out here and look at the Black Hole until doomsday, but these people want to go home. Not to mention my orders from Lermontov."

Reluctantly, she explained her theory, protesting all the while that they really ought to make a better study. "And the timing will have to be perfect," she finished. "The ship must be at the jumpoff point and turn on the drive at just the right time."

"Throw a big mass down the hole," Harriman said. "Well, there's only the one mass to throw. *Lorelei.*" He stopped pacing for a moment and looked thoughtful. "And that means somebody has to ride her in."

"Gentlemen?" Ramsey looked around the table. One by one, the astrogation officers nodded mutely. Trevor, seeing his captain's face, paused for a long second before he also nodded agreement.

"There's no way to be sure of a hit if we send her in on automatic," Trevor said. "We can't locate the thing close enough from out here. We can't send *Lorelei* on remote, either. The time lag's too long."

"Couldn't you build some kind of homing device?" Senator Grant asked. His voice was carefully controlled, and it compelled attention. In the Grand Senate, Martin Grant's speeches were worth listening to, although senators usually voted from politics anyway.

"What would you home on?" Marie asked caustically. "There's nothing to detect. In close enough you should see bending light rays, but I'm not sure. I'm just not sure of anything, but I know we couldn't build a homing device."

"Could we wait for a gravity storm and fly out on that?" Trevor asked. "If we were ready for it, we could make the jump . . ."

"Nonsense," Harriman snapped. "Give me credit for

a little sense, Lieutenant. We tried that. I didn't know what we were up against, but I figured those were gravity waves after they'd nearly wrecked my ships. Where there's gravity there may be Alderson forces. But you can't predict the damn gravity storms. We get one every thousand hours, sometimes close together, sometimes a long time apart, but about a thousand-hour average. How can you be in position for a jump when you don't know it's coming? And the damn gravity waves do things to the drives."

"Every thousand hours!" Marie demanded excitedly. "But that's impossible! What could cause that—so much matter! Commander Harriman, have you observed asteroids in this system?"

"Yeah. There's a whole beehive of them, all in close to the dark star. Thousands and thousands of them, it looks like. But they're *really* close, it's a swarm in a thick plane, a ring about ten kilometers thick. It's hard to observe anything, though. They move so fast, and if you get in close the gravity storms kill you. From out here we don't see much."

"A ring—are they large bodies?" Marie asked. Her eyes shone.

Harriman shrugged. "We've bounced radar off them and we deduce they're anywhere from a few millimeters to maybe a full kilometer in diameter, but it's hard to tell. There's nothing stable about the system, either."

Marie chewed both thumbnails. "There wouldn't be," she said. She began so softly that it was difficult to hear her. "There wouldn't be if chunks keep falling into the Hole. Ha! We won't be able to use the asteroids to give a position on the Black Hole. Even if you had better observations, the Hole is rotating. There must be enormous gravitational anomalies."

Harriman shrugged again, this time helplessly. "You understand, all we ever really observed was some bending light and a fuzzy occultation of stars. We deduced there was a dark star, but there was nothing in our data banks about them. Even if we'd known what a Black Hole was, I don't know how much good it would have done. I burned out the last of the Alderson drives three years ago trying to ride out. We were never in the right position . . . I was going to patch up *Constellation* and have another stab at it."

Just like that, Ramsey thought. *Just go out and patch up that wreck of a ship.* How many people would even try, much less be sure they could . . . so three years ago they'd lost their last hope of getting out of there. And after that, Barbara Jean had . . .

"Did you ever try throwing something down the Hole yourself?" Trevor asked.

"No. Until today we had no idea what we were up against. I still don't, but I'll take your word for it." Harriman drew in a deep breath and stopped pacing. "I'll take *Lorelei* down."

Bart looked past Harriman to a painting on the wardroom bulkhead. Trevor had liked it and hung it there long ago. John Paul Jones strode across the blazing decks of his flagship. Tattered banners blew through sagging rigging, blood ran in the scuppers, but Jones held his old cutlass aloft.

Well, why not? Somebody's got to do it, why not Harriman? But—but what will Barbara Jean think?

"I want to go, too." Marie Ward spoke softly, but

everyone turned to look at her. "I'll come with you, Commander Harriman."

"Don't be ridiculous," Harriman snapped.

"Ridiculous? What's ridiculous about it? This is an irreplaceable opportunity. We can't leave the only chance we'll ever have to study Black Holes for an amateur. There is certainly nothing ridiculous about a trained observer going." Her voice softened. "Besides, you'll be too busy with the ship to take decent observations."

"Miss Ward." Harriman compelled attention although it was difficult to say exactly why. Even though Ramsey was senior officer present, Harriman seemed to dominate the meeting. "Miss Ward, we practically rebuilt *Lorelei* over the past five years. I doubt if anyone else could handle her, so I've *got* to go. But just why do you want to?"

"Oh—" the arrogant tone left her voice. "Because this is my one chance to do something important. Just what am I? I'm not pretty." She paused, as if she hoped someone would disagree, but there was only silence.

"And no one ever took me seriously as an intellectual. I've no accomplishments at all. No publications. Nothing. But as the only person ever to study a Black Hole, I'll be recognized!"

"You've missed a point." Ramsey spoke quickly before anyone else could jump in. His voice was sympathetic and concerned. "We take you seriously. Admiral Lermontov took you so seriously he sent this cruiser out here. And you're our only expert on Black Holes. If Commander Harriman's attempt fails or for any other reason we don't get out of this system on this try, you'll have to think of something else for us."

"But—"

Harriman clucked his tongue impatiently. "Will *Lorelei* be mass enough, Miss Ward?"

"I don't know." She'd answered softly, but when they all stared at her she pouted defensively. "Well, I don't! How could I! There should be more than enough energy but I don't *know!*" Her voice rose higher. "If you people hadn't suppressed everything we'd have more information. But I've had to work all by myself, and I—"

Dave Trevor put his hand gently on her arm. "It'll be all right. You haven't been wrong yet."

"Haven't I?"

Senator Grant cleared his throat. "This isn't getting us anywhere at all. We have only one ship capable of sailing down to that Hole and only one theory of how to get away from here. We'll just have to try it."

There was a long silence before Bart spoke. "You sure you want to do this, Commander?" Ramsey cursed himself for the relief he felt, knowing what Harriman's answer would be.

"I'll do it, Captain. Who else could? Let's get started."

Ramsey nodded. *If 'twere done, 'twere best done quickly . . . what was that from? Shakespeare?* "Mr. Trevor, take an engineering crew over to *Lorelei* and start making her ready. Get all the ships' logs too."

"Logs!" Marie smiled excitedly. "Dave, I want to see those as soon as possible."

As Trevor nodded agreement, Ramsey waved dismissal to the officers. "Commander Harriman, if you'd stay just a moment . . ."

The wardroom emptied. There was a burst of chatter as the others left. Their talk was too spirited, betraying their relief. *They* didn't have to take *Lorelei* into a Black Hole. Ramsey and Harriman sat for what seemed like a long time.

"Is there something I can say?" Ramsey asked.

"No. I'd fight you for her if there wasn't a way home. But if there's any chance at all—you'll take care of Jeanette, of course." Harriman looked at the battered mug on the table, then reached for the coffee pot. After years in space, he didn't notice the strange angle the liquid made as it flowed into the cup under spin gravity. "That's fine coffee, Captain. We ran out, must be three, four years ago. You get to miss coffee after a while."

"Yeah." *What the Hell can I say to him? Do I thank him for not making me order him to take that ship in? He really is the only one who could do it, and we both knew that.* Unwanted, the image of Barbara Jean in this man's arms came to him. Ramsey grimaced savagely. "Look, Harriman, there's got to be some way we can—"

"There isn't and we both know it. Sir. Even if there were, what good would it do? We can't both go back with her."

And I'm glad it's me who's going home, Ramsey thought. *Hah. The first time in five years I've cared about staying alive. But will she ever* really *be mine again?*

Was that all that was wrong with me?

"Your inertial navigation gear working all right?" Harriman asked. "Got an intact telescope?"

"Eh? Yeah, sure."

"You shouldn't have too much trouble finding the jumpoff point, then."

"I don't expect any." Marie Ward's ridiculous song came back to him. "He fell into a dark hole, and covered himself over with charcoal, he went back over the mountain—" But Harriman wouldn't be going back over the mountain. Or would he? What was a Black Hole, anyway? Could it really be a time tunnel?

Harriman poured more coffee. "I better get over to *Lorelei* myself. Can you spare a pound of coffee?"

"Sure."

Harriman stood. He drained the mug. "Don't see much point in coming back to *Daniel Webster* in that case. Your people can plot me a course and send it aboard *Lorelei*." He flexed his fingers as if seeing them for the first time, then brushed imaginary lint from his patched uniform. "Yeah. I'll go with the cutter. Now."

"Now? But don't you want to—"

"No, I think not. What would I say?" Harriman very carefully put the coffee mug into the table rack. "Tell her I loved her, will you? And be sure to send that coffee over. Funny the things you can get to miss in five years."

DANIEL WEBSTER THIS IS LORELEI BREAK BREAK TELL TREVOR HIS COURSE WAS FINE STOP I APPEAR TO BE ONE-HALF-MILLION KILOMETERS FROM THE BLACK HOLE WITH NO OBSERVABLE ORBITAL VELOCITY STOP WILL PROCEED AT POINT 1-G FROM HERE STOP STILL CANNOT SEE THAT BEEHIVE AT ALL WELL STOP NOTHING TO OBSERVE IN BEST CALCULATED POSITION OF BLACK HOLE STOP

TELL MARIE WARD SHE IS NOT MISSING A
THING STOP BREAK MESSAGE ENDS

Barbara Jean and her father sat in Captain Ramsey's
cabin. Despite the luxury of a shower, she didn't feel
clean. She read the message flimsy her father handed her.

"I ought to say something to him, hadn't I? Shouldn't
I? Dad, I can't just let him die like this."

"Leave him alone, kitten," Senator Grant told her.
"He's got enough to do, working that half-dead ship by
himself. And he has to work fast. One of those gravity
storms while he's this close and—" Grant shuddered
involuntarily.

"But—God, I've made a mess of things, haven't I?"

"How? Would you rather it was Bart taking that ship
in there?"

"No. No, no, no! But I still—wasn't there any other
way, Daddy? Did somebody *really* have to do it?"

"As far as I can tell, Barbara Jean. I was there when
Jim volunteered. Bart tried to talk him out of it. you
know."

She didn't say anything.

"You're right, of course," Grant sighed. "He didn't try
very hard. There wasn't any point in it anyway.
Commander Harriman was the obvious man to do it. You
didn't enter the decision at all."

"I wish I could believe that."

"Yes. So does your husband. But it's still true. Are you
coming down to the bridge? I don't think it's a good idea,
but you can."

"No. You go on, though. I have to take care of

Jeanette. Bill Hartley has her in the sick bay. Daddy, what am I going to do?"

"You're going to go home with your husband and be an admiral's lady. For a while, anyway. And when there aren't any admirals because there isn't any fleet, God knows what you'll do. Make the best of it like all the rest of us, I guess."

The bridge was a blur of activity as they waited for *Lorelei* to approach the Black Hole. As the minutes ticked off, tension grew. A gravity storm just now would wipe out their only chance.

Finally, Ramsey spoke. "You can get the spin off the ship, Mr. Trevor. Put the crew to jump stations."

"Aye, aye, sir."

"Can we talk to Harriman still?" Senator Grant asked.

Ramsey's eyes flicked to the screens, past the predicted time of impact to the others, taking in every detail. "No." He continued to look at the data pouring across the screens. Their position had to be right. Everything had to be right, they'd get only the one chance at best . . . "Not to get an answer. You could get a message to *Lorelei*, but before we'd hear a reply it'll be all over."

Grant looked relieved. "I guess not, then."

"Damnedest thing." Harriman's voice was loud over the bridge speaker. "Star was occulted by the Hole. Made a bright ring in space. Real bright. Just hanging there, never saw anything like it."

"Nobody else ever will," Marie Ward said quietly. "Or will they? Can the Navy send more ships out here to study it? Oh, I wish I could *see!*"

They waited forever until Harriman spoke again. "Got a good position fix," they heard. "Looks good, Ramsey, damn good."

"Stand by for jumpoff," Bart ordered. Alarm bells rang through *Daniel Webster*.

"Another bright ring. Must be getting close."

"What's happening to his voice?" Senator Grant demanded.

"Time differential," Marie Ward answered. "His ship is accelerating to a significant fraction of light velocity. Time is slowing down for him relative to us."

"Looks good for jump here, skipper," Trevor announced.

"Right." Bart inspected his screens again. The predicted time to impact ticked off inexorably, but it was only a prediction. Without a more exact location of the Hole it couldn't be perfect. As Ramsey watched, the ship's computers updated the prediction from Harriman's signals.

Ramsey fingered the keys on his console. The Alderson drive generators could be kept on for less than a minute in normal space, but if they weren't on when *Lorelei* hit . . . he pressed the key. *Daniel Webster* shuddered as the ship's fusion engines went to full power, consuming hydrogen and thorium catalyst at a prodigal rate, pouring out energy into the drive where it—vanished.

Into hyperspace, if that was a real place. Or on the other side of the Lepton Barrier. Maybe to where you went when you fell through a Black Hole if there was anything to that theory. Marie Ward had been fascinated by it and had seen nothing to make her give it up.

Wherever the energy went, it left the measurable universe. But not all of it. The efficiency wasn't that good. The drive generators screamed . . .

"There's another bright ring. Quite a sight. Best damn view in the universe." The time distortion was quite noticeable now. Time to impact loomed big on Ramsey's screens, seconds to go.

Marie Ward hummed her nursery rhyme. Unwanted, the words rang through Ramsey's head. "He fell into a dark hole—" The time to impact clicked off to zero. Nothing happened.

"Ramsey, you lucky bastard," the speaker said. "Did you know she kept your damned picture the whole time? The whole bloody time, Ramsey. Tell her—"

The bridge blurred. There was a twisted, intolerable, eternal instant of agony. And confusion. Ramsey shook his head. The screens remained blurred.

"We—we're in the 81 Eridani system, skipper!" Trevor shouted. "We—hot damn, we made it!"

Ramsey cut him off. "Jump completed. Check ship."

"It worked," Marie Ward said. Her voice was low, quiet, almost dazed. "It really worked." She grinned at Dave Trevor, who grinned back. "Dave, it worked! There *are* Black Holes, and they *do* bend light, and they *can* generate Alderson forces, and I'm the first person to ever study one! Oh!" Her face fell.

"What's wrong?" Trevor asked quickly.

"I can't publish." She pouted. That was what had got her in trouble in the first place. The CoDominium couldn't keep people from thinking. *Die Gedanken, Sie sind frei.* But CDI could ruthlessly suppress books and letters and arrest everyone who tried to tell others about their unlicensed speculations.

"I can arrange something," Senator Grant told her. "After all, you're *the* expert on Black Holes. We'll see that you get a chance to study them for the fleet." He sighed and tapped the arm of his acceleration chair, then whacked it hard with his open palm. "I don't know. Maybe the CoDominium Treaty wasn't such a good idea. We got peace, but—you know, all we ever wanted to do was keep national forces from getting new weapons. Just suppress *military* technology. But that turned out to be nearly everything. And did we really get peace?"

"We'll need a course, Mr. Trevor," Ramsey growled. "This is still a Navy ship. I want the fastest route home."

Home. Sol System, and the house in Luna Base compound. It's still there. And I'll leave you, Daniel Webster, but I'll miss you, old girl, old boy, whatever you are. I'll miss you, but I can leave you.

Or can I? Barbara Jean, are you mine now? Some of you will always belong to Jim Harriman. Five goddam years that man kept his crew and passengers alive, five years when there wasn't a shred of hope they'd get home again. She'll never forget him.

And that's unworthy, Bart Ramsey. Neither one of us ought to forget him.

"But I still wonder," Marie Ward said. Her voice was very low and quiet, plaintive in tone. "I don't suppose I'll ever know."

"Know what?" Ramsey asked. It wasn't hard to be polite to her now.

"It's the song." She hummed her nursery rhyme. "What did he really see on the other side of the mountain?"

WHAT'S IT LIKE OUT THERE?

by Edmond Hamilton

Although Edmond Hamilton was one of the biggest and most popular names in the fields of both science fiction and horror in the 1940s, he was unable to sell this story when he wrote it. Later on, taking note of a more realistic trend in sf, he rewrote it in a leaner style, and it was published in 1952 with a blurb announcing a "new Edmond Hamilton." Not really, of course—even with more pulpish prose, this story that dared to picture space exploration as something that would be hard, brutal, and deadly was ahead of its time, and the field had needed time to catch up with the "new" Hamilton.

I HADN'T WANTED TO WEAR my uniform when I left the hospital, but I didn't have any other clothes there

and I was too glad to get out to argue about it. But as soon
as I got on the local plane I was taking to Los Angeles, I
was sorry I had it on.

People gawked at me and began to whisper. The
stewardess gave me a special big smile. She must have
spoken to the pilot, for he came back and shook hands,
and said, "Well, I guess a trip like this is sort of a
comedown for *you*."

A little man came in, looked around for a seat, and
took the one beside me. He was a fussy, spectacled guy of
fifty or sixty, and he took a few minutes to get settled.
Then he looked at me, and stared at my uniform and at
the little brass button on it that said "TWO."

"Why," he said, "you're one of those Expedition Two
men!" And then, as though he'd only just figured it out,
"Why, you've been to Mars!"

"Yeah," I said. "I was there."

He beamed at me in a kind of wonder. I didn't like it,
but his curiosity was so friendly that I couldn't quite resent
it.

"Tell me," he said, "what's it like out there?"

The plane was lifting, and I looked out at the Arizona
desert sliding by close underneath.

"Different," I said. "It's different."

The answer seemed to satisfy him completely. "I'll just
bet it is," he said. "Are you going home, Mr. . . . ."

"Haddon. Sergeant Frank Haddon."

"You going home, Sergeant?"

"My home's back in Ohio," I told him. "I'm going in
to L.A. to look up some people before I go home."

"Well, that's fine. I hope you have a good time,

Sergeant. You deserve it. You boys did a great job out there. Why, I read in the newspapers that after the U.N. sends out a couple more expeditions, we'll have cities out there, and regular passenger lines, and all that."

"Look," I said, "that stuff is for the birds. You might as well build cities down there in Mojave, and have them a lot closer. There's only one reason for going to Mars now, and that's uranium."

I could see he didn't quite believe me. "Oh, sure," he said, "I know that's important too, the uranium we're all using now for our power stations—but that isn't all, is it?"

"It'll be all, for a long, long time," I said.

"But look, Sergeant, this newspaper article said . . ."

I didn't say anything more. By the time he'd finished telling me about the newspaper article, we were coming down into L.A. He pumped my hand when we got out of the plane.

"Have yourself a time, Sergeant! You sure rate it. I hear a lot of chaps on Two didn't come back."

"Yeah," I said. "I heard that."

I was feeling shaky by the time I got to downtown L.A. I went in a bar and had a double bourbon and it made me feel a little better. Then I went out and found a cabby and asked him to drive me out to San Gabriel. He was a fat man with a broad red face.

"Hop right in, buddy," he said. "Say, you're one of those Mars guys, aren't you?"

I said, "That's right."

"Well, well," he said. "Tell me, how was it out there?"

"It was a pretty dull grind, in a way," I told him.

"I'll bet it was!" he said, as we started through traffic.

"Me, I was in the Army in World War Two, twenty years ago. That's just what it was, a dull grind nine-tenths of the time. I guess it hasn't changed any."

"This wasn't any Army expedition," I explained. "It was a United Nations one, not an Army one—but we had officers and rules of discipline like the Army."

"Sure, it's the same thing," said the cabby. "You don't need to tell me what it's like, buddy. Why, back there in 'forty-two, or was it 'forty-three?—anyway, back there I remember that . . ."

I leaned back and watched Huntington Boulevard slide past. The sun poured in on me and seemed very hot, and the air seemed very thick and soupy. It hadn't been so bad up on the Arizona plateau, but it was a little hard to breathe down here.

The cabby wanted to know what address in San Gabriel. I got the little packet of letters out of my pocket and found the one that had "Martin Valinez" and a street address on the back. I told the cabby and put the letters back into my pocket.

I wished now that I'd never answered them.

But how could I keep from answering when Joe Valinez' parents wrote to me at the hospital? And it was the same with Jim's girl, and Walter's family. I'd had to write back, and the first thing I knew I'd promised to come and see them, and now if I went back to Ohio without doing it I'd feel like a heel. Right now, I wished I'd decided to be a heel.

The address was on the south side of San Gabriel, in a section that still had a faintly Mexican tinge to it. There was a little frame grocery store with a small house beside it, and a picket fence around the yard of the house; very neat, but a queer, homely place after all the slick California stucco.

I went into the little grocery and a tall, dark man with quiet eyes took a look at me and called a woman's name in a low voice and then came around the counter and took my hand.

"You're Sergeant Haddon," he said. "Yes. Of course. We've been hoping you'd come."

His wife came in a hurry from the back. She looked a little too old to be Joe's mother, for Joe had been just a kid; but then she didn't look so old either, but just sort of worn.

She said to Valinez, "Please, a chair. Can't you see he's tired? And just from the hospital."

I sat down and looked between them at a case of canned peppers, and they asked me how I felt, and wouldn't I be glad to get home, and they hoped all my family were well.

They were gentlefolk. They hadn't said a word about Joe, just waited for me to say something. And I felt in a spot, for I hadn't known Joe well, not really. He'd been moved into our squad only a couple of weeks before take-off, and since he'd been our first casualty, I'd never got to know him much.

I finally had to get it over with, and all I could think to say was, "They wrote you in detail about Joe, didn't they?"

Valinez nodded gravely. "Yes—that he died from shock within twenty-four hours after take-off. The letter was very nice."

His wife nodded too. "Very nice," she murmured. She

looked at me, and I guess she saw that I didn't know quite what to say, for she said, "You can tell us more about it. Yet you must not if it pains you."

I could tell them more. Oh, yes, I could tell them a lot more, if I wanted to. It was all clear in my mind, like a movie film you run over and over till you know it by heart.

I could tell them all about the take-off that had killed their son. The long lines of us, uniformed backs going up into Rocket Four and all the other nineteen rockets—the lights flaring up there on the plateau, the grind of machinery and blast of whistles and the inside of the big rocket as we climbed up the ladders of its center well.

The movie was running again in my mind, clear as crystal, and I was back in Cell Fourteen of Rocket Four, with the minutes ticking away and the walls quivering every time one of the other rockets blasted off, and us ten men in our hammocks, prisoned inside that odd-shaped windowless metal room, waiting. Waiting, till that big, giant hand came and smacked us down deep into our recoil springs, crushing the breath out of us, so that you fought to breathe, and the blood roared into your head, and your stomach heaved in spite of all the pills they'd given you, and you heard the giant laughing, *b-r-room! b-r-r-room! b-r-r-oom!*

Smash, smash, again and again, hitting us in the guts and cutting our breath, and someone being sick, and someone else sobbing, and the *b-r-r-oom! b-r-r-oom!* laughing as it killed us; and then the giant quit laughing, and quit slapping us down, and you could feel your sore and shaky body and wonder if it was still all there.

Walter Millis cursing a blue streak in the hammock

underneath me, and Breck Jergen, our sergeant then, clambering painfully out of his straps to look us over, and then through the voices a thin, ragged voice saying uncertainly, "Breck, I think I'm hurt . . ."

Sure, that was their boy Joe, and there was blood on his lips, and he'd had it—we knew when we first looked at him that he'd had it. A handsome kid, turned waxy now as he held his hand on his middle and looked up at us. Expedition One had proved that take-off would hit a certain percentage with internal injuries every time, and in our squad, in our little windowless cell, it was Joe that had been hit.

If only he'd died right off. But he couldn't die right off, he had to lie in the hammock all those hours and hours. The medics came and put a strait-jacket around his body and doped him up, and that was that, and the hours went by. And we were so shaken and deathly sick ourselves that we didn't have the sympathy for him we should have had—not till he started moaning and begging us to take the jacket off.

Finally Walter Millis wanted to do it, and Breck wouldn't allow it, and they were arguing and we were listening when the moaning stopped, and there was no need to do anything about Joe Valinez anymore. Nothing but call the medics, who came into our little iron prison and took him away.

Sure, I could tell the Valinezes all about how their Joe died, couldn't I?

"Please," whispered Mrs. Valinez, and her husband looked at me and nodded silently.

So I told them. I said, "You know Joe died in space.

He'd been knocked out by the shock of take-off, and he was unconscious, not feeling a thing. And then he woke up, before he died. He didn't seem to be feeling any pain, not a bit. He lay there, looking out the window at the stars. They're beautiful, the stars out there in space, like angels. He looked, and then he whispered something and lay back and was gone."

Mrs. Valinez began to cry softly. "To die out there, looking at stars like angels . . ."

I got up to go, and she didn't look up. I went out the door of the little grocery store, and Valinez came with me.

He shook my hand. "Thank you, Sergeant Haddon. Thank you very much."

"Sure," I said.

I got into the cab. I took out my letters and tore that one into bits. I wished to God I'd never got it. I wished I didn't have any of the other letters I still had.

★ 2 ★

I TOOK THE EARLY PLANE for Omaha. Before we got there I fell asleep in my seat, and then I began to dream, and that wasn't good.

A voice said, "We're coming down." And we were coming down, Rocket Four was coming down, and there we were in our squad cell, all of us strapped into our hammocks, waiting and scared, wishing there was a window so we could see out, hoping our rocket wouldn't be the one to crack up, hoping none of the rockets cracked up, but if one does, don't let it be *ours* . . .

"We're coming down . . ."

Coming down, with the blasts starting to boom again underneath us, hitting us hard, not steady like at take-off, but *blast-blast-blast,* and then again, *blast-blast.*

Breck's voice, calling to us from across the cell, but I couldn't hear for the roaring that was in my ears between blasts. No, it was *not* in my ears; that roaring came from the wall beside me: we had hit atmosphere, we were coming in.

The blasts in lightning succession without stopping, *crash-crash-crash-crash-crash!* Mountains fell on me, and this was it, and don't let it be ours, please, God, don't let it be ours . . .

Then the bump and the blackness, and finally somebody yelling hoarsely in my ears, and Breck Jergen, his face deathly white, leaning over me.

"Unstrap and get out, Frank! All men out of hammocks—all men out!"

We'd landed, and we hadn't cracked up, but we were half-dead and they wanted us to turn out, right this minute, and we couldn't.

Breck yelling to us, "Breathing masks on! Masks on! We've got to go out!"

"My God, we've just landed, we're torn to bits, we can't!"

"We've got to! Some of the other rockets cracked up in landing and we've got to save whoever's still living in them! Masks on! Hurry!"

We couldn't, but we did. They hadn't given us all those months of discipline for nothing. Jim Clymer was already on his feet, Walter was trying to unstrap underneath me, whistles were blowing like mad somewhere and voices shouted hoarsely.

My knees wobbled under me as I hit the floor. Young Lassen, beside me, tried to say something and then crumpled up. Jim bent over him, but Breck was at the door yelling, "Let him go! Come on!"

The whistles screeching at us all the way down the ladders of the well, and the mask clip hurting my nose, and down at the bottom a disheveled officer yelling at us to get out and join Squad Five, and the gangway reeling under us.

Cold. Freezing cold, and a wan sunshine from the shrunken little sun up there in the brassy sky, and a rolling plain of ocherous red sand stretching around us, sand that slid away under our feet as our squads followed Captain Wall toward the distant metal bulk that lay oddly canted and broken in a little shallow valley.

"Come on, men—hurry! Hurry!"

Sure, all of it a dream, the dreamlike way we walked with our lead-soled shoes dragging our feet back after each step, and the voices coming through the mask resonators muffled and distant.

Only not a dream, but a nightmare, when we got up to the canted metal bulk and saw what had happened to Rocket Seven—the metal hull ripped like paper, and a few men crawling out of the wreck with blood on them, and a gurgling sound where shattered tanks were emptying, and voices whimpering, "First aid! First aid!"

Only it hadn't happened, it hadn't happened yet at all, for we were still back in Rocket Four coming in, we hadn't landed yet at all but we were going to any minute.

"We're coming down . . ."

I couldn't go through it all again. I yelled and fought my hammock straps and woke up, and I was in my plane seat and a scared hostess was a foot away from me, saying, "This is Omaha, Sergeant. We're coming down."

They were all looking at me, all the other passengers, and I guessed I'd been talking in the dream—I still had the sweat down my back like all those nights in the hospital when I'd keep waking up.

I sat up, and they all looked away from me quick and pretended they hadn't been staring.

We came down to the airport. It was midday, and the hot Nebraska sun felt good on my back when I got out. I was lucky, for when I asked at the bus depot about going to Cuffington, there was a bus all ready to roll.

A farmer sat down beside me, a big young fellow who offered me cigarettes and told me it was only a few hours' ride to Cuffington.

"Your home there?" he asked.

"No, my home's back in Ohio," I said. "A friend of mine came from there. Name of Clymer."

He didn't know him, but he remembered that one of the town boys had gone on that second expedition to Mars.

"Yeah," I said. "That was Jim."

He couldn't keep it in any longer. "What's it like out there, anyway?"

I said, "Dry. Terrible dry."

"I'll bet it is," he said. "To tell the truth, it's too dry here, this year, for good wheat weather. Last year it was fine. Last year . . ."

Cuffington, Nebraska, was a wide street of stores, and other streets with trees and old houses, and yellow wheat fields all around as far as you could see. It was pretty hot, and I was glad to sit down in the bus depot while I went through the thin little phone book.

There were three Graham families in the book, but the first one I called was the right one—Miss Ila Graham. She talked fast and excited, and said she'd come right over, and I said I'd wait in front of the bus depot.

I stood underneath the awning, looking down the quiet street and thinking that it sort of explained why Jim Clymer had always been such a quiet, slow-moving sort of guy. The place was sort of relaxed, like he'd been.

A coupe pulled up, and Miss Graham opened the door. She was a brown-haired girl, not especially good-looking, but the kind you think of as a nice girl, a very nice girl.

She said, "You look so tired that I feel guilty now about asking you to stop."

"I'm all right," I said. "And it's no trouble stopping over a couple of places on my way back to Ohio."

As we drove across the little town, I asked her if Jim hadn't had any family of his own here.

"His parents were killed in a car crash years ago," Miss Graham said. "He lived with an uncle on a farm outside Grandview, but they didn't get along, and Jim came into town and got a job at the power station." She added, as we turned a corner, "My mother rented him a room. That's how we got to know each other. That's how we— how we got engaged."

"Yeah, sure," I said.

It was a big square house with a deep front porch, and some trees around it. I sat down in a wicker chair, and Miss Graham brought her mother out. Her mother talked a little about Jim, how they missed him, and how she declared he'd been just like a son.

When her mother went back in, Miss Graham showed me a little bunch of blue envelopes. "These were the letters I got from Jim. There weren't very many of them, and they weren't very long."

"We were only allowed to send one thirty-word message every two weeks," I told her. "There were a couple of thousand of us out there, and they couldn't let us jam up the message transmitter all the time."

"It was wonderful how much Jim could put into just a few words," she said, and handed me some of them.

I read a couple. One said, "I have to pinch myself to realize that I'm one of the first Earthmen to stand on an alien world. At night, in the cold, I look up at the green star that's Earth and can't quite realize I've helped an age-old dream come true."

Another one said, "This world's grim and lonely, and mysterious. We don't know much about it yet. So far, nobody's seen anything living but the lichens that Expedition One reported, but there might be anything here."

Miss Graham asked me, "Was that all there was, just lichens?"

"That, and two or three kinds of queer cactus things," I said. "And rock and sand. That's all."

As I read more of those little blue letters, I found that now that Jim was gone I knew him better than I ever had.

There was something about him I'd never suspected: he was romantic inside. We hadn't suspected it, he was always so quiet and slow, but now I saw that all the time he was more romantic about the thing we were doing than any of us.

He hadn't let on. We'd have kidded him, if he had. Our name for Mars, after we got sick of it, was the Hole. We always talked about it as the Hole. I could see now that Jim had been too shy of our kidding to ever let us know that he glamorized the thing in his mind.

"This was the last one I got from him before his sickness," Miss Graham said.

That one said, "I'm starting north tomorrow with one of the mapping expeditions. We'll travel over country no human has ever seen before."

I nodded. "I was on that party myself. Jim and I were on the same half-track."

"He was thrilled by it, wasn't he, Sergeant?"

I wondered. I remembered that trip, and it was hell. Our job was simply to run a preliminary topographical survey, checking with Geigers for possible uranium deposits. It wouldn't have been so bad, if the sand hadn't started to blow. It wasn't sand like Earth sand. It was ground to dust by billions of years of blowing around that dry world. It got inside your breathing mask, and your goggles, and the engines of the half-tracks, in your food and water and clothes. There was nothing for three days but cold, and wind, and sand.

Thrilled? I'd have laughed at that before, but now I didn't know. Maybe Jim had been, at that. He had lots of patience, a lot more than I ever had. Maybe he glamorized that hellish trip into wonderful adventure on a foreign world.

"Sure, he was thrilled," I said. "We all were. Anybody would be."

Miss Graham took the letters back, and then said, "You had Martian sickness too, didn't you?"

I said, yes, I had, just a touch, and that was why I'd had to spend a stretch in reconditioning hospital when I got back.

She waited for me to go on, and I knew I had to. "They don't know yet if it's some sort of virus or just the effect of Martian conditions on Earthmen's bodies. It hit forty percent of us. It wasn't really so bad—fever and dopiness, mostly."

"When Jim got it, was he well cared for?" she asked. Her lips were quivering a little.

"Sure, he was well cared for. He got the best care there was," I lied.

The best care there was? That was a laugh. The first cases got decent care, maybe. But they'd never figured on so many coming down. There wasn't any room in our little hospital—they just had to stay in their bunks in the aluminum Quonsets when it hit them. All our doctors but one were down, and two of them died.

We'd been on Mars six months when it hit us, and the loneliness had already got us down. All but four of our rockets had gone back to Earth, and we were alone on a dead world, our little town of Quonsets huddled together under that hateful, brassy sky, and beyond it the sand and rocks that went on forever.

You go up to the North Pole and camp there, and find

out how lonely that is. It was worse out there, a lot worse. The first excitement was gone long ago, and we were tired, and homesick in a way nobody was ever homesick before—we wanted to see green grass, and real sunshine, and women's faces, and hear running water; and we wouldn't until Expedition Three came to relieve us. No wonder guys blew their tops out there. And then came Martian sickness, on top of it.

"We did everything for him that we could," I said.

Sure we had. I could still remember Walter and me tramping through the cold night to the hospital to try to get a medic, while Breck stayed with him, and how we couldn't get one. I remember how Walter had looked up at the blazing sky as we tramped back, and shaken his fist at the big green star of Earth.

"People up there are going to dances tonight, watching shows, sitting around in warm rooms laughing! Why should good men have to die out here to get them uranium for cheap power?"

"Can it," I told him tiredly. "Jim's not going to die. A lot of guys got over it."

The best care there was? That was real funny. All we could do was wash his face, and give him the pills the medic left, and watch him get weaker every day till he died.

"Nobody could have done more for him than was done," I told Miss Graham.

"I'm glad," she said. "I guess—it's just one of those things."

When I got up to go she asked me if I didn't want to see Jim's room. They'd kept it for him just the same, she said.

I didn't want to, but how are you going to say so? I went up with her and looked and said it was nice. She opened a big cupboard. It was full of neat rows of old magazines.

"They're all the old science fiction magazines he read when he was a boy," she said. "He always saved them."

I took one out. It had a bright cover, with a spaceship on it, not like our rockets but a streamlined thing, and the rings of Saturn in the background.

When I laid it down, Miss Graham took it up and put it back carefully into its place in the row, as though somebody was coming back who wouldn't like to find things out of order.

She insisted on driving me back to Omaha, and out to the airport. She seemed sorry to let me go, and I suppose it was because I was the last real tie to Jim, and when I was gone it was all over then for good.

I wondered if she'd get over it in time, and I guessed she would. People do get over things. I supposed she'd marry some other nice guy, and I wondered what they'd do with Jim's things—with all those old magazines nobody was ever coming back to read.

★ 3 ★

I WOULD NEVER have stopped at Chicago at all if I could have got out of it, for the last person I wanted to talk to anybody about was Walter Millis. It would be too easy for me to make a slip and let out stuff nobody was supposed to know.

But Walter's father had called me at the hospital a couple of times. The last time he called, he said he was having Breck's parents come down from Wisconsin so they could see me, too, so what could I do then but say, yes, I'd stop. But I didn't like it at all, and I knew I'd have to be careful.

Mr. Millis was waiting at the airport and shook hands with me and said what a big favor I was doing them all, and how he appreciated my stopping when I must be anxious to get back to my own home and parents.

"That's all right," I said. "My dad and mother came out to the hospital to see me when I first got back."

He was a big, fine-looking important sort of man, with a little bit of the stuffed shirt about him, I thought. He seemed friendly enough, but I got the feeling he was looking at me and wondering why I'd come back and his son, Walter, hadn't. Well, I couldn't blame him for that.

His car was waiting, a big car with a driver, and we started north through the city. Mr. Millis pointed out a few things to me to make conversation, especially a big atomic-power station we passed.

"It's only one of thousands, strung all over the world," he said. "They're going to transform our whole economy. This Martian uranium will be a big thing, Sergeant."

I said, yes, I guessed it would.

I was sweating blood, waiting for him to start asking about Walter, and I didn't know yet just what I could tell him. I could get myself in Dutch plenty if I opened my big mouth too wide, for that one thing that had happened to Expedition Two was supposed to be strictly secret, and we'd all been briefed on why we had to keep our mouths shut.

But he let it go for the time being, and just talked other stuff. I gathered that his wife wasn't too well, and that Walter had been their only child. I also gathered that he was a very big shot in business, and dough-heavy. I didn't like him. Walter I'd liked plenty, but his old man seemed a pretty pompous person, with his heavy business talk.

He wanted to know how soon I thought Martian uranium would come through in quantity, and I said I didn't think it'd be very soon.

"Expedition One only located the deposits," I said, "and Two just did mapping and setting up a preliminary base. Of course, the thing keeps expanding, and I hear Four will have a hundred rockets. But Mars is a tough setup."

Mr. Millis said decisively that I was wrong, that the world was power-hungry, that it would be pushed a lot faster than I expected.

He suddenly quit talking business and looked at me and asked, "Who was Walter's best friend out there?"

He asked it sort of apologetically. He was a stuffed shirt, but all my dislike of him went away then.

"Breck Jergen," I told him. "Breck was our sergeant. He sort of held our squad together, and he and Walter cottoned to each other from the first."

Mr. Millis nodded, but didn't say anything more about it. He pointed out the window at the distant lake and said we were almost to his home.

It wasn't a home, it was a big mansion. We went in and he introduced me to Mrs. Millis. She was a limp, pale-looking woman, who said she was glad to meet one of Walter's friends. Somehow I got the feeling that even though he was a stuffed shirt, he felt it about Walter a lot more than she did.

He took me up to a bedroom and said that Breck's parents would arrive before dinner, and that I could get a little rest before then.

I sat looking around the room. It was the plushiest one I'd ever been in, and, seeing this house and the way these people lived, I began to understand why Walter had blown his top more than the rest of us.

He'd been a good guy, Walter, but high-tempered and I could see now he'd been a little spoiled. The discipline at training base had been tougher on him than on most of us, and this was why.

I sat and dreaded this dinner that was coming up, and looked out the window at a swimming pool and tennis court, and wondered if anybody ever used them now that Walter was gone. It seemed a queer thing for a fellow with a setup like this to go out to Mars and get himself killed.

I took the satin cover off the bed so my shoes wouldn't dirty it, and lay down and closed my eyes, and wondered what I was going to tell them. The trouble was, I didn't know what story the officials had given them.

"The Commanding Officer regrets to inform you that your son was shot down like a dog . . ."

They'd never got any telegram like that. But just what line *had* been handed them? I wished I'd had a chance to check on that.

Damn it, why didn't all these people let me alone? They started it all going through my mind again, and the psychos had told me I ought to forget it for a while, but how could I? It might be better just to tell them the truth. After all, Walter wasn't the only one who'd blown his top out there. In that grim last couple of months, plenty of guys had gone around sounding off.

Expedition Three isn't coming!

We're stuck, and they don't care enough about us to send help!

That was the line of talk. You heard it plenty, in those days. You couldn't blame the guys for it, either. A fourth of us down with Martian sickness, the little grave markers clotting up the valley beyond the ridge, rations getting thin, medicine running low, everything running low, all of us watching the sky for rockets that never came.

There'd been a little hitch back on Earth, Colonel Nichols explained. (He was our C.O. now that General Rayen had died.) There was a little delay, but the rockets would be on their way soon, we'd get relief, we just had to hold on.

Holding on—that's what we were doing. Nights we'd sit in the Quonset and listen to Lassen coughing in his bunk, and it seemed like wind-giants, cold-giants, were bawling and laughing around our little huddle of shelters.

"Damn it, if they're not coming, why don't we go home?" Walter said. "We've still got the four rockets—they could take us all back."

Breck's serious face got graver. "Look, Walter, there's too much of that stuff being talked around. Lay off."

"Can you blame the men for talking it? We're not storybook heroes. If they've forgotten about us back on Earth, why do we just sit and take it?"

"We have to," Breck said. "Three will come." I've always thought that it wouldn't have happened, what did happen, if we hadn't had that false alarm. The one that set the whole camp wild that night, with guys shouting, "Three's here! The rockets landed over west of Rock Ridge!" Only when they charged out there, they found they hadn't seen rockets landing at all, but a little shower of tiny meteors burning themselves up as they fell.

It was the disappointment that did it, I think. I can't say for sure, because that same day was the day I conked out with Martian sickness, and the floor came up and hit me and I woke up in the bunk, with somebody giving me a hypo, and my head big as a balloon. I wasn't clear out, it was only a touch of it, but it was enough to make everything foggy, and I didn't know about the mutiny that was boiling up until I woke up once with Breck leaning over me and saw be wore a gun and an M.P. brassard now.

When I asked him how come, he said there'd been so much wild talk about grabbing the four rockets and going home that the M.P. force had been doubled and Nichols had issued stern warnings.

"Walter?" I said, and Breck nodded. "He's a leader and he'll get hit with a court-martial when this is over. The blasted idiot!"

"I don't get it—he's got plenty of guts, you know that," I said.

"Yes, but he can't take discipline, he never did take it very well, and now that the squeeze is on he's blowing up. Well, see you later, Frank."

I saw him later, but not the way I expected. For that was the day we heard the faint echo of shots, and then the alarm siren screaming, and men running, and half-tracks starting up in a hurry. And when I managed to get out of my bunk and out of the hut, they were all going toward the big rockets, and a corporal yelled to me from a jeep, "That's blown it! The damn fools swiped guns and tried to take over the rockets and make the crews fly 'em home!"

I could still remember the sickening slidings and bouncings of the jeep as it took us out there, the milling little crowd under the looming rockets, milling around and hiding something on the ground, and Major Weiler yelling himself hoarse giving orders.

When I got to see what was on the ground, it was seven or eight men and most of them dead. Walter had been shot right through the heart. They told me later it was because he'd been the leader, out in front, that he got it first of the mutineers.

One M.P. was dead, and one was sitting with red all over the middle of his uniform, and that one was Breck, and they were bringing a stretcher for him now.

The corporal said, "Hey, that's Jergen, your squad leader!" And I said, "Yes, that's him." Funny how you can't talk when something hits you—how you just say words, like, "Yes, that's him."

Breck died that night without ever regaining consciousness, and there I was, still half-sick myself, and with Lassen dying in his bunk, and five of us were all that was left of Squad Fourteen, and that was that.

How could H.Q. let a thing like that get known? A fine advertisement it would be for recruiting more Mars expeditions, if they told how guys on Two cracked up and did a crazy thing like that. I didn't blame them for telling us to keep it top secret. Anyway, it wasn't something we'd want to talk about.

But it sure left me in a fine spot now, a sweet spot. I was going down to talk to Breck's parents and Walter's parents, and they'd want to know how their sons died, and I could tell them, "Your sons probably killed each other, out there." Sure, I could tell them that, couldn't I? But what *was* I going to tell them? I knew H.Q. had reported those casualties as "accidental deaths," but what kind of accident?

Well, it got late, and I had to go down, and when I did, Breck's parents were there. Mr. Jergen was a carpenter, a tall, bony man with level blue eyes like Breck's. He didn't say much, but his wife was a little woman who talked enough for both of them.

She told me I looked just like I did in the pictures of us Breck had sent home from training base. She said she had three daughters too—two of them married, and one of the married ones living in Milwaukee and one out on the Coast. She said that she'd named Breck after a character in a book by Robert Louis Stevenson, and I said I'd read the book in high school.

"It's a nice name," I said.

She looked at me with bright eyes and said, "Yes. It was a nice name."

That was a fine dinner. They'd got everything they thought I might like, and all the best, and a maid served it, and I couldn't taste a thing I ate.

Then afterward, in the big living room, they all just sort of sat and waited, and I knew it was up to me.

I asked them if they'd had any details about the

accident, and Mr. Millis said, No, just "accidental death" was all they'd been told.

Well, that made it easier. I sat there, with all four of them watching my face, and dreamed it up.

I said, "It was one of those one-in-a-million things. You see, more little meteorites hit the ground on Mars than here, because the air's so much thinner it doesn't burn them up so fast. And one hit the edge of the fuel dump and a bunch of little tanks started to blow. I was down with the sickness, so I didn't see it, but I heard all about it."

You could hear everybody breathing, it was so quiet as I went on with my yarn.

"A couple of guys were knocked out by the concussion and would have been burned up if a few fellows hadn't got in there fast with foamite extinguishers. They kept it away from the big tanks, but another little tank let go, and Breck and Walter were two of the fellows who'd gone in, and they were killed instantly."

When I'd got it told, it sounded corny to me and I was afraid they'd never believe it. But nobody said anything, until Mr. Millis let out a sigh and said, "So that was it. Well . . . well, if it had to be, it was mercifully quick, wasn't it?"

I said, yes, it was quick.

"Only, I can't see why they couldn't have let us know. It doesn't seem fair."

I had an answer for that. "It's hush-hush because they don't want people to know about the meteor danger. That's why."

Mrs. Millis got up and said she wasn't feeling so well, and would I excuse her and she'd see me in the morning. The rest of us didn't seem to have much to say to each other, and nobody objected when I went up to my bedroom a little later.

I was getting ready to turn in when there was a knock on the door. It was Breck's father, and he came in and looked at me steadily.

"It was just a story, wasn't it?" he said.

I said, "Yes, it was just a story."

His eyes bored into me and he said, "I guess you've got your reasons. Just tell me one thing. Whatever it was, did Breck behave right?"

"He behaved like a man, all the way," I said. "He was the best man of us, first to last."

He looked at me, and I guess something made him believe me. He shook hands and said, "All right, son. We'll let it go."

I'd had enough. I wasn't going to face them again in the morning. I wrote a note, thanking them all and making excuses, and then went down and slipped quietly out of the house.

It was late, but a truck coming along picked me up, and the driver said he was going near the airport. He asked me what it was like on Mars and I told him it was lonesome. I slept in a chair at the airport, and I felt better, for next day I'd be home, and it would be over.

That's what I thought.

★ **4** ★

IT WAS GETTING toward evening when we reached the village, for my father and mother hadn't known I was coming on an earlier plane, and I'd had to wait for them up at Cleveland Airport. When we drove into Market Street, I saw there was a big painted banner stretching across: "HARMONVILLE WELCOMES HOME ITS SPACEMAN!"

Spaceman—that was me. The newspapers had started calling us that, I guess, because it was a short word good for headlines. Everybody called us that now. We'd sat cooped up in a prison cell that flew, that was all—but now we were "spacemen."

There were bright uniforms clustered under the banner, and I saw that it was the high-school band. I didn't say anything, but my father saw my face.

"Now, Frank, I know you're tired, but these people are your friends and they want to show you a real welcome."

That was fine. Only it was all gone again, the relaxed feeling I'd been beginning to get as we drove down from Cleveland.

This was my home country, this old Ohio country with its neat little white villages and fat, rolling farms. It looked good, in June. It looked very good, and I'd been feeling better all the time. And now I didn't feel so good, for I saw that I was going to have to talk some more about Mars.

Dad stopped the car under the banner, and the high-school band started to play, and Mr. Robinson, who was the Chevrolet dealer and also the mayor of Harmonville, got into the car with us.

He shook hands with me and said, "Welcome home, Frank! What was it like out on Mars?"

I said, "It was cold, Mr. Robinson. Awful cold."

"You should have been here last February!" he said. "Eighteen below—nearly a record."

He leaned out and gave a signal, and Dad started driving again, with the band marching along in front of us and playing. We didn't have far to go, just down Market Street under the big old maples, past the churches and the old white houses to the square white Grange Hall.

There was a little crowd in front of it, and they made a sound like a cheer—not a real loud one, you know how people can be self-conscious about really cheering—when we drove up. I got out and shook hands with people I didn't really see, and then Mr. Robinson took my elbow and took me on inside.

The seats were all filled and people standing up, and over the little stage at the far end they'd fixed up a big floral decoration—there was a globe all of red roses with a sign above it that said "Mars" and beside it a globe all of white roses that said "Earth" and a little rocket ship made out of flowers was hung between them.

"The Garden Club fixed it up," said Mr. Robinson. "Nearly everybody in Harmonville contributed flowers."

"It sure is pretty," I said.

Mr. Robinson took me by the arm, up onto the little stage, and everyone clapped. They were all people I knew—people from the farms near ours, my high-school teachers, and all that.

I sat down in a chair and Mr. Robinson made a little speech about how Harmonville boys had always gone out when anything big was doing, how they'd gone to the War of 1812 and the Civil War and the two World Wars, and how now one of them had gone to Mars.

He said, "Folks have always wondered what it's like out there on Mars, and now here's one of our own Harmonville boys come back to tell us all about it."

And he motioned me to get up, and I did, and they clapped some more, and I stood wondering what I could tell them.

And all of a sudden, as I stood there wondering, I got the answer to something that had always puzzled us out there. We'd never been able to understand why the fellows who had come back from Expedition One hadn't tipped us off how tough it was going to be. And now I knew why. They hadn't because it would have sounded as if they were whining about all they'd been through. And now I couldn't, for the same reason.

I looked down at the bright, interested faces, the faces I'd known almost all my life, and I knew that what I could tell them was no good anyway. For they'd all read those newspaper stories, about "the exotic red planet" and "heroic spacemen," and if anyone tried to give them a different picture now, it would just upset them.

I said, "It was a long way out there. But flying space is a wonderful thing—flying right off the Earth, into the stars—there's nothing quite like it."

Flying space, I called it. It sounded good, and thrilling. How could they know that flying space meant lying strapped in that blind stokehold listening to Joe Valinez dying, and praying and praying that it wouldn't be our rocket that cracked up?

"And it's a wonderful thrill to come out of a rocket and step on a brand-new world, to look up at a different-looking sun, to look around at a whole new horizon . . ."

Yes, it was wonderful. Especially for the guys in Rockets Seven and Nine who got squashed like flies and lay around there on the sand, moaning, "First aid!" Sure, it was a big thrill, for them and for us who had to try to help them. "There were hardships out there, but we all knew that a big job had to be done . . ."

That's a nice word, too, "hardships." It's not coarse and ugly like fellows coughing their hearts out from too much dust; it's not like having your best friend die of Martian sickness right in the room you sleep in. It's a nice, cheerful word, "hardships."

". . . and the only way we could get the job done, away out there so far from Earth, was by teamwork."

Well, that was true enough in its way, and what was the use of spoiling it by telling them how Walter and Breck had died?

"The job's going on, and Expedition Three is building a bigger base out there right now, and Four will start soon. And it'll mean plenty of uranium, plenty of cheap atomic power, for all Earth."

That's what I said, and I stopped there. But I wanted to go on and add, "And it wasn't worth it! It wasn't worth all those guys, all the hell we went through, just to get cheap atomic power so you people can run more electric washers and television sets and toasters!"

But how are you going to stand up and say things like that to people you know, people who like you? And who was I to decide? Maybe I was wrong, anyway. Maybe lots of things I'd had and never thought about had been squeezed out of other good guys, back in the past. I wouldn't know.

Anyway, that was all I could tell them, and I sat down, and there was a big lot of applause, and I realized then that I'd done right, I'd told them just what they wanted to hear, and everyone was all happy about it.

Then things broke up, and people came up to me, and I shook a lot more hands. And finally, when I got outside, it was dark—soft, summery dark, the way I hadn't seen it for a long time. And my father said we ought to be getting on home, so I could rest.

I told him, "You folks drive on ahead, and I'll walk. I'll take the short cut. I'd sort of like to walk through town."

Our farm was only a couple of miles out of the village, and the short cut across Heller's farm I'd always taken when I was a kid was only a mile. Dad didn't think maybe I ought to walk so far, but I guess he saw I wanted to, so they went on ahead.

I walked on down Market Street, and around the little square, and the maples and elms were dark over my head, and the flowers on the lawns smelled the way they used to, but it wasn't the same either—I'd thought it would be, but it wasn't.

When I cut off past the Odd Fellows' Hall, beyond it I met Hobe Evans, the garage hand at the Ford place, who was humming along half-tight, the same as always on a Saturday night.

"Hello, Frank, heard you were back," he said. I waited for him to ask the question they all asked, but he didn't. He said, "Boy, you don't look so good! Want a drink?"

He brought out a bottle, and I had one out of it, and he had one, and he said he'd see me around, and went humming on his way. He was feeling too good to care much where I'd been.

I went on, in the dark, across Heller's pasture and then along the creek under the big old willows. I stopped there like I'd always stopped when I was a kid, to hear the frog noises, and there they were, and all the June noises, the night noises, and the night smells.

I did something I hadn't done for a long time. I looked up at the starry sky, and there it was, the same little red dot I'd peered at when I was a kid and read those old stories, the same red dot that Breck and Jim and Walter and I had stared away at on nights at training base, wondering if we'd ever really get there.

Well, they'd got there, and weren't ever going to leave it now, and there'd be others to stay with them, more and more of them as time went by.

But it was the ones I knew that made the difference, as I looked up at the red dot.

I wished I could explain to them somehow why I hadn't told the truth, not the whole truth. I tried, sort of, to explain. "I didn't want to lie," I said. "But I had to—at least, it seemed like I had to—"

I quit it. It was crazy, talking to guys who were dead and forty million miles away. They were dead, and it was over, and that was that. I quit looking up at the red dot in the sky and started on home again.

But I felt as though something was over for me too. It was being young. I didn't feel old. But I didn't feel young either, and I didn't think I ever would, not ever again.

THE MAN WHO LOST THE SEA

by Theodore Sturgeon

This one, frankly, is not safe to describe, without damaging its impact. At first, you may wonder what it has to do with space pioneers, but all will be revealed. Maybe I should mention that one of your editors (HD) considers this to be not only Sturgeon's finest short story, but, if challenged at gunpoint to name the finest sf story ever written, would say, this one. Trust me . . .

★🌀★

SAY YOU'RE A KID, and one dark night you're running along the cold sand with this helicopter in your hand, saying very fast witchy-witchy-witchy. You pass the sick man and he wants you to shove off with that thing. Maybe he thinks you're too old to play with toys. So you squat next to him in the sand and tell him it isn't a toy, it's a

339

model. You tell him look here, here's something most people don't know about helicopters. You take a blade of the rotor in your fingers and show him how it can move in the hub, up and down a little, back and forth a little, and twist a little, to change pitch. You start to tell him how this flexibility does away with the gyroscopic effect, but he won't listen. He doesn't want to think about flying, about helicopters, or about you, and he most especially does not want explanations about anything by anybody. Not now. Now, he wants to think about the sea. So you go away.

The sick man is buried in the cold sand with only his head and his left arm showing. He is dressed in a pressure suit and looks like a man from Mars. Built into his left sleeve is a combination time-piece and pressure gauge, the gauge with a luminous blue indicator which makes no sense, the clock hands luminous red. He can hear the pounding of surf and the soft swift pulse of his pumps. One time long ago when he was swimming he went too deep and stayed down too long and came up too fast, and when he came to it was like this: they said, "Don't move, boy. You've got the bends. Don't even try to move." He had tried anyway. It hurt. So now, this time, he lies in the sand without moving, without trying.

His head isn't working right. But he knows clearly that it isn't working right, which is a strange thing that happens to people in shock sometimes. Say you were that kid, you could say how it was, because once you woke up lying in the gym office in high school and asked what had happened. They explained how you tried something on the parallel bars and fell on your head. You understood exactly, though you couldn't remember falling. Then a minute later you asked again what had happened and they told you. You understood it. And a minute later . . . forty-one times they told you, and you understood. It was just that no matter how many times they pushed it into your head, it wouldn't stick there; but all the while you *knew* that your head would start working again in time. And in time it did. . . . Of course, if you were that kid, always explaining things to people and to yourself, you wouldn't want to bother the sick man with it now.

Look what you've done already, making him send you away with that angry shrug of the mind (which, with the eyes, are the only things which will move just now). The motionless effort costs him a wave of nausea. He has felt seasick before but he has never *been* seasick, and the formula for that is to keep your eyes on the horizon and stay busy. Now! Then he'd better get busy—now; for there's one place especially not to be seasick in, and that's locked up in a pressure suit. Now!

So he busies himself as best he can, with the seascape, landscape, sky. He lies on high ground, his head propped on a vertical wall of black rock. There is another such outcrop before him, whip-topped with white sand and with smooth flat sand. Beyond and down is valley, salt-flat, estuary; he cannot yet be sure. He is sure of the line of footprints, which begin behind him, pass to his left, disappear in the outcrop shadows, and reappear beyond to vanish at last into the shadows of the valley.

Stretched across the sky is old mourning-cloth, with starlight burning holes in it, and between the holes the black is absolute—wintertime, mountaintop sky-black.

(Far off on the horizon within himself, he sees the swell and crest of approaching nausea; he counters with an undertow of weakness, which meets and rounds and settles the wave before it can break. Get busier. Now.)

Burst in on him, then, with the X-15 model. That'll get him. Hey, how about this for a gimmick? Get too high for the thin air to give you any control, you have these little jets in the wingtips, see? and on the sides of the empennage: bank, roll, yaw, whatever, with squirts of compressed air.

But the sick man curls his sick lip: oh, git, kid, git, will you?—that has nothing to do with the sea. So you git.

Out and out the sick man forces his view, etching all he sees with a meticulous intensity, as if it might be his charge, one day, to duplicate all this. To his left is only starlit sea, windless. In front of him across the valley, rounded hills with dim white epaulettes of light. To his right, the jutting corner of the black wall against which his helmet rests. (He thinks the distant moundings of nausea becalmed, but he will not look yet.) So he scans the sky, black and bright, calling Sirius, calling Pleiades, Polaris, Ursa Minor, calling that . . . that . . . Why, it *moves*. Watch it: yes, it moves! It is a fleck of light, seeming to be wrinkled, fissured, rather like a chip of boiled cauliflower in the sky. (Of course, he knows better than to trust his own eyes just now.) But that movement . . .

As a child he had stood on cold sand in a frosty Cape Cod evening, watching Sputnik's steady spark rise out of the haze (madly, dawning a little north of west); and after that he had sleeplessly wound special coils for his receiver, risked his life restringing high antennas, all for the brief capture of an unreadable *tweetle-eep-tweetle* in his earphones from Vanguard, Explorer, Lunik, Discoverer, Mercury. He knew them all (well, some people collect match-covers, stamps) and he knew especially that unmistakable steady sliding in the sky.

This moving fleck was a satellite, and in a moment, motionless, uninstrumented but for his chronometer and his part-brain, he will know which one. (He is grateful beyond expression—without that sliding chip of light, there were only those footprints, those wandering footprints, to tell a man he was not alone in the world.)

Say you were a kid, eager and challengeable and more than a little bright, you might in a day or so work out a way to measure the period of a satellite with nothing but a timepiece and a brain; you might eventually see that the shadow in the rocks ahead had been there from the first only because of the light from the rising satellite. Now if you check the time exactly at the moment when the shadow on the sand is equal to the height of the outcrop, and time it again when the light is at the zenith and the shadow gone, you will multiply this number of minutes by 8—think why, now: horizon to zenith is one-fourth of the orbit, give or take a little, and halfway up the sky is half that quarter—and you will then know this satellite's period. You know all the periods—ninety minutes, two, two-and-a-half hours; with that and the appearance of this bird, you'll find out which one it is.

But if you were that kid, eager or resourceful or whatever, you wouldn't jabber about it to the sick man, for not only does he not want to be bothered with you, he's thought of all that long since and is even now watching the shadows for that triangular split second of measurement. Now! His eyes drop to the face of his chronometer: 0400, near as makes no never mind.

He has minutes to wait now—ten? . . . thirty? . . . twenty-three?—while this baby moon eats up its slice of shadowpie; and that's too bad, the waiting, for though the inner sea is calm there are currents below, shadows that shift and swim. Be busy. Be busy. He must not swim near that great invisible amoeba, whatever happens: its first cold pseudopod is even now reaching for the vitals.

Being a knowledgeable young fellow, not quite a kid any more, wanting to help the sick man too, you want to tell him everything you know about that cold-in-the-gut, that reaching invisible surrounding implacable amoeba. You know all about it—listen, you want to yell at him, don't let that touch of cold bother you. Just know what it is, that's all. Know what it is that is touching your gut. You want to tell him, listen:

Listen, this is how you met the monster and dissected it. Listen, you were skin-diving in the Grenadines, a hundred tropical shoal-water islands; you had a new blue snorkel mask, the kind with face-plate and breathing-tube all in one, and new blue flippers on your feet, and a new blue spear-gun—all this new because you'd only begun, you see; you were a beginner, aghast with pleasure at your easy intrusion into this underwater otherworld. You'd been out in a boat, you were coming back, you'd just reached the mouth of the little bay, you'd taken the notion to swim the rest of the way. You'd said as much to the boys and slipped into the warm silky water. You brought your gun.

Not far to go at all, but then beginners find wet distances deceiving. For the first five minutes or so it was only delightful, the sun hot on your back and the water so warm it seemed not to have any temperature at all and you were flying. With your face under the water, your mask was not so much attached as part of you, your wide blue flippers trod away yards, your gun rode all but weightless in your hand, the taut rubber sling making an occasional hum as your passage plucked it in the sunlit green. In your ears crooned the breathy monotone of the snorkel tube, and through the invisible disk of plate glass you saw wonders. The bay was shallow—ten, twelve feet or so—and sandy, with great growths of brain-, bone-, and fire-coral, intricate waving sea-fans, and fish—such fish! Scarlet and green and aching azure, gold and rose and slate-color studded with sparks of enamel-blue, pink and peach and silver. And that *thing* got into you, that . . . monster.

There were enemies in this otherworld: the sand-colored spotted sea-snake with his big ugly head and turned-down mouth, who would not retreat but lay watching the intruder pass; and the mottled moray with jaws like bolt-cutters; and somewhere around, certainly, the barracuda with his undershot face and teeth turned inward so that he must take away whatever he might strike. There were urchins—the plump white sea-egg with its thick fur of sharp quills and the black ones with the long slender spines that would break off in unwary flesh and fester there for weeks; and file-fish and stone-fish with their poisoned barbs and lethal meat; and the stingaree who could drive his spike through a leg bone. Yet these were not *monsters*, and could not matter to you, the invader churning along above them all. For you were above them in so many ways—armed, rational, comforted by the close shore (ahead the beach, the rocks on each side) and by the presence of the boat not too far behind. Yet you were . . . attacked.

At first it was uneasiness, not pressing, but pervasive, a contact quite as intimate as that of the sea; you were sheathed in it. And also there was the touch—the cold inward contact. Aware of it at last, you laughed: for Pete's sake, what's there to be scared of?

The monster, the amoeba.

You raised your head and looked back in air. The boat had edged in to the cliff at the right; someone was giving a last poke around for lobster. You waved at the boat; it was your gun you waved, and emerging from the water it gained its latent ounces so that you sank a bit, and as if you had no snorkel on, you tipped your head back to get a breath. But tipping your head back plunged the end of the tube under water; the valve closed; you drew in a hard lungful of nothing at all. You dropped your face under; up came the tube; you got your air, and along with it a bullet of seawater which struck you somewhere inside the throat. You coughed it out and floundered, sobbing as you sucked in air, inflating your chest until it hurt, and the air you got seemed no good, no good at all, a worthless devitalized inert gas.

You clenched your teeth and headed for the beach, kicking strongly and knowing it was the right thing to do; and then below and to the right you saw a great bulk mounding up out of the sand floor of the sea. You knew it was only the reef, rocks and coral and weed, but the sight of it made you scream; you didn't care what you knew. You turned hard left to avoid it, fought by as if it would reach for you, and you couldn't get air, couldn't get air, for all the unobstructed hooting of your snorkel tube. You couldn't bear the mask, suddenly, not for another second, so you shoved it upward clear of your mouth and rolled over, floating on your back and opening your mouth to the sky and breathing with a quacking noise.

It was then and there that the monster well and truly engulfed you, mantling you round and about within itself—formless, borderless, the illimitable amoeba. The beach, mere yards away, and the rocky arms of the bay, and the not-too-distant boat—these you could identify but no longer distinguish, for they were all one and the same thing . . . the thing called unreachable.

You fought that way for a time, on your back, dangling the gun under and behind you and straining to get enough warm sun-stained air into your chest. And in time some particles of sanity began to swirl in the roil of your mind, and to dissolve and tint it. The air pumping in and out of your square-grinned frightened mouth began to be meaningful at last, and the monster relaxed away from you.

You took stock, saw surf, beach, a leaning tree. You felt the new scend of your body as the rollers humped to become breakers. Only a dozen firm kicks brought you to where you could roll over and double up; your shin struck coral with a lovely agony and you stood in foam and waded ashore. You gained the wet sand, hard sand, and ultimately, with two more paces powered by bravado, you crossed high-water mark and lay in the dry sand, unable to move.

You lay in the sand, and before you were able to move or to think, you were able to feel a triumph—a triumph because you were alive and knew that much without thinking at all.

When you were able to think, your first thought was of the gun, and the first move you were able to make was to let go at last of the thing. You had nearly died because you had not let it go before; without it you would not have been burdened and you would not have panicked. You had (you began to understand) kept it because someone else would have had to retrieve it—easily enough—and you could not have stood the laughter. You had almost died because They might laugh at you.

This was the beginning of the dissection, analysis, study of the monster. It began then; it had never finished. Some of what you had learned from it was merely important; some of the rest—vital.

You had learned, for example, never to swim farther with a snorkel than you could swim back without one. You learned never to burden yourself with the unnecessary in an emergency: even a hand or a foot might be as expendable as a gun; pride was expendable, dignity was. You learned never to dive alone, even if They laugh at you, even if you have to shoot a fish yourself and say afterward "we" shot it. Most of all, you learned that fear has many fingers, and one of them—a simple one, made of too great a concentration of carbon dioxide in your blood, as from too-rapid breathing in and out of the same tube—is not really fear at all but feels like fear, and can turn into panic and kill you.

Listen, you want to say, listen, there isn't anything

wrong with such an experience or with all the study it leads to, because a man who can learn enough from it could become fit enough, cautious enough, foresighted, unafraid, modest, teachable enough to be chosen, to be qualified for. . . .

You lose the thought, or turn it away, because the sick man feels that cold touch deep inside, feels it right now, feels it beyond ignoring, above and beyond anything that you, with all your experience and certainty, could explain to him even if he would listen, which he won't. Make him, then; tell him the cold touch is some simple explainable thing like anoxia, like gladness even: some triumph that he will be able to appreciate when his head is working right again.

Triumph? Here he's alive after . . . whatever it is, and that doesn't seem to be triumph enough, though it was in the Grenadines, and that other time, when he got the bends, saved his own life, saved two other lives. Now, somehow, it's not the same: there seems to be a reason why just being alive afterward isn't a triumph.

Why not triumph? Because not twelve, not twenty, not even thirty minutes is it taking the satellite to complete its eighth-of-an-orbit: fifty minutes are gone, and still there's a slice of shadow yonder. It is this, this which is placing the cold finger upon his heart, and he doesn't know why, he doesn't know why, he will not know why; he is afraid he shall when his head is working again. . . .

Oh, where's the kid? Where is any way to busy the mind, apply it to something, anything else but the watchhand which outruns the moon? Here, kid: come over here—what you got there?

If you were the kid, then you'd forgive everything and hunker down with your new model, not a toy, not a helicopter or a rocket-plane, but the big one, the one that looks like an overgrown cartridge. It's so big, even as a model, that even an angry sick man wouldn't call it a toy. A giant cartridge, but watch: the lower four-fifths is Alpha—all muscle—over a million pounds thrust. (Snap it off, throw it away.) Half the rest is Beta—all brains—it puts you on your way. (Snap it off, throw it away.) And now look at the polished fraction which is left. Touch a control somewhere and see—see? it has wings—wide triangular wings. This is Gamma, the one with wings, and on its back is a small sausage; it is a moth with a sausage on its back. The sausage (click! it comes free) is Delta. Delta is the last, the smallest: Delta is the way home.

What will they think of next? Quite a toy. Quite a toy. Beat it, kid. The satellite is almost overhead, the sliver of shadow going—going—almost gone and . . . gone.

Check: 0459. Fifty-nine minutes? give or take a few. Times eight . . . 472 . . . is, uh, 7 hours 52 minutes.

Seven hours fifty-two minutes? Why, there isn't a satellite round earth with a period like that. In all the solar system there's only . . .

The cold finger turns fierce, implacable.

The east is paling and the sick man turns to it, wanting the light, the sun, an end to questions whose answers couldn't be looked upon. The sea stretches endlessly out to the growing light, and endlessly, somewhere out of sight, the surf roars. The paling east bleaches the sandy hilltops and throws the line of footprints into aching relief. That would be the buddy, the sick man knows, gone for help. He cannot at the moment recall who the buddy is, but in time he will, and meanwhile the footprints make him less alone.

The sun's upper rim thrusts itself above the horizon with a flash of green, instantly gone. There is no dawn, just the green flash and then a clear white blast of unequivocal sunup. The sea could not be whiter, more still, if it were frozen and snow-blanketed. In the west, stars still blaze, and overhead the crinkled satellite is scarcely abashed by the growing light. A formless jumble in the valley below begins to resolve itself into a sort of tent-city, or installation of some kind, with tubelike and sail-like buildings. This would have meaning for the sick man if his head were working right. Soon, it would. Will. (Oh . . .)

The sea, out on the horizon just under the rising sun, is behaving strangely, for in that place where properly belongs a pool of unbearable brightness, there is instead a notch of brown. It is as if the white fire of the sun is drinking dry the sea—for look, look! the notch becomes a bow and the bow a crescent, racing ahead of the sunlight, white sea ahead of it and behind it a cocoa-dry stain spreading across and down toward where he watches.

Beside the finger of fear which lies on him, another finger places itself, and another, making ready for that clutch, that grip, that ultimate insane squeeze of panic. Yet beyond that again, past that squeeze when it comes, to be savored if the squeeze is only fear and not panic, lies triumph—triumph, and a glory. It is perhaps this which constitutes his whole battle: to fit himself, prepare himself to bear the utmost that fear could do, for if he can do that, there is a triumph on the other side. But . . . not yet. Please, not yet awhile.

Something flies (or flew, or will fly—he is a little confused on this point) toward him, from the far right where the stars still shine. It is not a bird and it is unlike any aircraft on earth, for the aerodynamics are wrong. Wings so wide and so fragile would be useless, would melt and tear away in any of earth's atmosphere but the outer fringes. He sees then (because he prefers to see it so) that it is the kid's model, or part of it, and for a toy it does very well indeed.

It is the part called Gamma, and it glides in, balancing, parallels the sand and holds away, holds away slowing, then, settles, all in slow motion, throwing up graceful sheet-fountains of fine sand from its skids. And it runs along the ground for an impossible distance, letting down its weight by the ounce and stingily the ounce, until *look out* until a skid *look out* fits itself into a bridged crevasse *look out, look out!* and still moving on, it settles down to the struts. Gamma then, tired, digs her wide left wingtip carefully into the racing sand, digs it in hard; and as the wing breaks off, Gamma slews, sidles, slides slowly, pointing her other triangular tentlike wing at the sky, and broadside crushes into the rocks at the valley's end.

As she rolls smashing over, there breaks from her broad back the sausage, the little Delta, which somersaults away to break its back upon the rocks, and through the broken hull spill smashed shards of graphite from the moderator of her power-pile. *Look out! Look out!* and at the same instant from the finally checked mass of Gamma there explodes a doll, which slides and tumbles into the sand, into the rocks and smashed hot graphite from the wreck of Delta.

The sick man numbly watches this toy destroy itself: what will they think of next?—and with a gelid horror prays at the doll lying in the raging rubble of the atomic pile: *don't stay there, man—get away! get away! that's hot, you know?* But it seems like a night and a day and half another night before the doll staggers to its feet and, clumsy in its pressure-suit, runs away up the valleyside, climbs a sand-topped outcrop, slips, falls, lies under a slow cascade of cold ancient sand until, but for an arm and the helmet, it is buried.

The sun is high now, high enough to show the sea is not a sea, but brown plain with the frost burned off it, as now it burns away from the hills, diffusing in air and blurring the edges of the sun's disk, so that in a very few minutes there is no sun at all, but only a glare in the east. Then the valley below loses its shadows, and, like an arrangement in a diorama, reveals the form and nature of the wreckage below: no tent city this, no installation, but the true real ruin of Gamma and the eviscerated hulk of Delta. (Alpha was the muscle, Beta the brain; Gamma was a bird, but Delta, Delta was the way home.)

And from it stretches the line of footprints, to and by the sick man, above to the bluff, and gone with the sandslide which had buried him there. Whose footprints?

He knows whose, whether or not he knows that he knows, or wants to or not. He knows what satellite has (give or take a bit) a period like that (want it exactly?—it's 7.66 hours). He knows what world has such a night, and such a frosty glare by day. He knows these things as he knows how spilled radioactives will pour the crash and mutter of surf into a man's earphones.

Say you were that kid: say, instead, at last, that you are the sick man, for they are the same; surely then you can understand why of all things, even while shattered, shocked, sick with radiation calculated (leaving) radiation computed (arriving) and radiation past all bearing (lying in the wreckage of Delta) you would want to think of the sea. For no farmer who fingers the soil with love and knowledge, no poet who sings of it, artist, contractor, engineer, even child bursting into tears at the inexpressible beauty of a field of daffodils—none of these is as intimate with Earth as those who live on, live with, breathe and drift in its seas. So of these things you must think; with these you must dwell until you are less sick and more ready to face the truth.

The truth, then, is that the satellite fading here is Phobos, that those footprints are your own, that there is no sea here, that you have crashed and are killed and will in a moment be dead. The cold hand ready to squeeze and still your heart is not anoxia or even fear, it is death. Now, if there is something more important than this, now is the time for it to show itself.

The sick man looks at the line of his own footprints, which testify that he is alone, and at the wreckage below, which states that there is no way back, and at the white east and the mottled west and the paling flecklike satellite above. Surf sounds in his ears. He hears his pumps. He hears what is left of his breathing. The cold clamps down and folds him round past measuring, past all limit.

Then he speaks, cries out: then with joy he takes his triumph at the other side of death, as one takes a great fish, as one completes a skilled and mighty task, rebalances at the end of some great daring leap; and as he used to say "we shot a fish" he uses no "I":

"God," he cries, dying on Mars, "God, we made it!"

THE PARLIAMENT OF OWLS

by Christopher Ruocchio

Pioneering is big business, and big business means big crime. Young Christopher's story is the second all-original story in this anthology of reprints, after Sarah A. Hoyt and Jeff Greason's "Home Front." In fact, it's also only the second short story he's ever published. (Did I say short? It's one of the longer tales in the book!) Sometimes the frontier isn't all it's cracked up to be. Sometimes a man just wants to go fishing—too bad he's a repo man for a terraforming company, and too bad their latest order was just stolen. . . .

THE SKY ABOVE Abhanri City was gray as the city itself. Concrete and steel and mirrored glass vanished into low cloud only to emerge again, higher and higher until—like shadows vanishing into the arriving night—they were lost in the heavens above.

Kalas missed trees. He missed the wheat fields and the rolling meadows of his home. Missed the grape vines ripening on the old trellis, and the way the trees would bend when fliers streaked low above their boughs, making for the village where he'd been born. Anything would have been a welcome relief to all that grayness and the neon flash of advertisements tall as houses that shone from the sides of buildings.

He missed home, though he had not seen Maglona in twenty-four years, and it had not seen him for going on eighty. He had shipped out on the Emperor's coin, taken commission with the 212th Centaurine Legion. He'd wanted an excuse to see the galaxy, wanted an excuse to leave his dusty old village and a life as farmer and make a name for himself. He hadn't thought to ever be looking back.

He hadn't ever thought to be trapped in a place like Abhanri either, on Kanthi, beyond the borders of his Empire. Hadn't expected to be working for the Consortium either, doing enforcement. He'd always pictured himself fishing. He wasn't sure why. Maybe because there weren't any oceans back home on Maglona—but there were no oceans on Kanthi either. Just *gray*.

"I've got eyes on our guy here, Kal," Gant said, voice coming in through Kalas's ear piece. "Coming out of the lift."

"Good," Kalas replied, subvocalizing. He checked his phase disruptor was set to stun and moved to station himself in the shadow of the curtains that hung to one side of glass wall that overlooked the city. He shut one eye, kept the other fixed on the door. For a moment, all was perfectly still. The apartment's climate control had stopped running when Kalas had disabled the suite's security, and even the white noise hum of electronics was dead. Once upon a time, this would have been the moment where the rush of blood pounding in his ears deafened him. But Kalas had been a hunter a long time, and moments like these had ceased to frighten him.

Gant's voice came low in his ear, as if his Kanthite partner stood at his ear. "At the door. Look sharp now." Kalas didn't reply. He waited, pointed his disruptor at the door, his reflection a faint greenish blur on the brushed metal wall.

The airlock cycled red to blue, and the inner seal came unglued, admitting the doctor back into his home. Anwen Sen was a small man, on the young side of middle age, with thick black hair and the copper complexion that marked him as a descendant of Kanthi's first wave of colonists. He hadn't seen Kalas, was busy undoing his nose-tubes and unzipping the puffy dun jacket he wore against the planet's interminable chill.

The hunter watched him go, hardly bothering to control his breathing as the small doctor crossed to the little kitchen unit, fussing with the contents of his pockets.

"You know the trouble with thieving?" Kalas asked, leveling the stunner at the doctor. The man froze, hands on the blond stone of the counter. "There's always something *missing*. People notice."

Dr. Sen did not turn. He did not move. That was good. That meant Kalas didn't have to shoot him and tie him to a chair. Yet. In a high, nasal voice, the geneticist said, "You're from the Consortium? One of their dogs?"

Kalas took one careful step closer, footfall light on the thick carpets. He did not lower his arm. "Same as you."

"I'm not a dog," the man said. "I do research."

"You're a rat," Kalas cut him off. "What did you do with them, Sen? Are they here?"

He could see sweat beginning to well up on the back of the man's neck. For all that, Kalas had to admit the man was surprisingly calm. Most of the bonecutters Kalas had known would have fainted already from the stress. "You've turned the place inside out, haven't you?"

"He doesn't have them, Kal, I'm telling you," Gant said over the comm. Kalas ignored him, but he knew Gant was right.

The hunter took another measured step closer, adjusted his aim. "Who did you sell them to?"

Sen whirled.

Bang!

Where he'd gotten the handgun Kalas wasn't sure. Had it been in his coat? His sleeve? The bullet went wide, shattered against the metal wall behind him and he lunged to the right, firing back. The stunner bolt struck the cabinetry just above Sen's shoulder, leaving a smoking mark on the glass there. Sen fired again, but he was no marksman.

His hand was shaking. Kalas could see it. The man was afraid of his own gun, as such men so often were. He regained his footing. His balance. His aim. The stunner bolt took Dr. Sen in the shoulder, and he dropped his gun, eyes wide with mingled terror and frustration. The nerve damage had cascaded down his side, and his right leg buckled, tipping him back into the range. Kalas cleared the space between him and the doctor in three bounds, scooping up the old-style autorevolver. Without breaking stride, he threw an elbow across the doctor's face, and while the man was reeling slid his stunner back into his pocket before he seized the man by his shirtfront.

In a voice of forced and practiced calm, Kalas said, "You know why I'm here."

"I sold them!" Sen said, then yelped as Kalas shook him.

"To who?"

"To whom!" Gant corrected, forcing a snarl from between Kalas's teeth.

Kalas placed the mouth of Sen's own revolver against the man's shoulder, the weapon awkward in his left hand. "Who'd you sell to?"

The man's eyes widened, "I don't remember! Some fence in the Narrows!"

The hunter tightened his grip on the doctor's shirt, "Which is it?" The doctor made a confused noise, and Kalas said, evenly, "Do you not remember? Or was it a fence in the Narrows?"

The doctor shook his head furiously, tried to dislodge Kalas's hand with his still functional one. Moving deliberately, Kalas moved the autorevolver down to the man's thigh and fired. Dr. Sen made a choking sound, then bit back his cry, blood beginning to soak down his leg. He swore, breath coming in hissing gasps, "You shot me!"

"And I will again if you don't answer my questions, doctor," Kalas said. Not hurried. He'd seen worse on the battlefield from his time in the Legions. He'd done worse. He'd had to. "Who did you sell to?" Sen wheezed, stun-lame arm flapping as he tried to put pressure on his gunshot wound. Kalas brushed the weak arm away with the autorevolver. "None of that now. Who did you sell to?"

The geneticist shook his head more fiercely, "Said she had a client looking for seed stock. Some offworlder looking to jump-start their own colony in the Veil. I didn't ask questions."

"I do." Kalas shot the man in his other thigh.

"You hunters . . ." the doctor hissed, teeth clenched.

"Answer my questions and you can call the health service," Kalas said. It was a lie, and perhaps the doctor knew it. He was a hunter for the Wong-Hopper Consortium, and the Consortium was not so forgiving of those who stole its product to sell on the black market.

Kalas hoped the apartment walls were a thick. There was little law enforcement on Kanthi worth the name, but the last thing he wanted was a shootout with prefects of the colonial authority or—more likely—whichever enforcement syndicate Sen's apartment tower had on the payroll.

Kalas pressed his knee into one of the doctor's wounds. Sen whimpered. He didn't cry out—for which Kalas was grateful—he only clenched his jaw to stop from screaming. Words shaking, Sen said, "Vela! Vela—her name's Vela. She works out of one of those old stockhouses in the Narrows, down by the reservoir and the fisheries, you know?"

"I know!" Gant's voice chimed over the ear piece. Kalas had almost forgotten the younger man was there.

The hunter eased the pressure on Sen's knee, glad the hydrophobic wicking in his long coat and pants had kept the blood off. "Good, good. And the buyer?"

"I don't know! For Earth's sake! I don't know!"

Kalas let the little man go, and taking a step back he shook his head, "Doctor, I *will* shoot you again. I swear by Earth and Emperor, I will."

Anwen Sen allowed himself to slip down to the floor to sit amidst the smeared blood—the red of it stark against the pale tiling. Thus freed, he pressed his good hand to one thigh, wincing. "Black planet . . . I . . . I don't know much, all right? She said something about someone called Giacomo."

"Giacomo?" Kalas repeated, keeping the gun pointed at Sen from his hip. "What is he? Jaddian?"

"Hell if I know," Sen said, gritting his teeth. "I told you I don't *know*, you bastard."

"Two names is more than nothing, friend," Kalas replied, crouching down so that he looked Sen directly in the eye. "Now tell me everything, and this will go easier for you."

Gant's voice came low in one ear, "Still nothing on the comm channels, Kal. But it's almost too quiet. I don't like it."

Kalas didn't move, kept his elbow propped on his knee, the gun leveled at Sen's head. He didn't need to ask any questions, the man knew what he wanted.

Sen tried to speak, but the pain caught in his throat, and he choked. "The . . . the Parliament of Owls," he managed after a moment's strain. "Giacomo and the Parliament of Owls, that was what she said. Vela, I mean."

"The what now?" Gant's confusion over the comm was thick enough to scrape over bread.

Kalas understood how he felt, "The what now?"

"That was what she said," said Anwen Sen once more. "The Parliament of Owls. That's really all I know."

"What is it? A company?"

"Sounds more like a cult to me," Gant put in, unhelpfully.

The little man was shaking his head. "I don't know, I really don't know. Maybe a company, maybe a ship, maybe it's the name of some colony state—I don't know, man. I sequence genomes. That's all I know!" His fingers squeezed the wound, blood welling up between his fingers. Tears brimmed in the doctor's eyes, "You're going to kill me."

Kalas nodded once, "Yes."

Sen swallowed, "I just wanted . . . just wanted to get offworld. Needed the money." He sniffed, sucking back the panic that was starting to run down his face.

"You and me both, pal," Kalas said. And fired.

Dr. Sen's head hit the door of the oven behind him, blood and brain spattering as the black glass cracked. At once it was very quiet again, the only sound the distant rush and murmur of the city: the faint beep and squeal of groundcars, the whine of fliers. Kalas stood, slid the autorevolver into the pocket of his coat and returned his phase disruptor to his shoulder holster. He turned, found a gray cat watching him from atop one neatly arranged bookcase. The useless thing hadn't so much as raised a paw to aid its master. Kalas looked back at Dr. Sen's body, not sure if it was the man or the little beast he felt sorry for.

Kanthi was a gray purgatory Kalas had come to at the end of a long campaign. Sen had been born here, near as Kalas could guess. He couldn't blame the man for wanting to get out. When he'd been a boy, the Legion recruitment posters on Maglona had told of strange places and foreign peoples, enticing the grubby peasant boy he'd been to strike out among the stars, following in the footsteps of those first pilgrim-pioneers that had left Old Earth so many thousand years ago.

It hadn't been worth it.

Home—Maglona—had been as near to Earth as terraforming and hard work could make it. Blue skies. Green hills. No seas, of course, but lakes and little rivers. So many of the worlds Kalas had seen were not. They had been places where the sun was strange, weak and red, reflected by the glare of orbital mirrors. Places where the gravity pulled too heavily on the bones, or not heavily enough—as was the case here on Kanthi. Places where the people seemed hardly people at all, so changed were they by their environs.

Places where the air was poison.

Places like Kanthi.

Kalas fished his nose-tubes out of the collar of his coat. He passed the line up over his ear and plugged the things into place. Turning on his osmosis pack, he felt the chilly flow of clean oxygen start, and turned towards the airlock and the bitter world beyond.

★ ★ ★

"You're awfully quiet," Gant said from the driver's seat. As he spoke, he tipped the controls, steering the flier in low over a block of drab tenement buildings. "That doctor get to you?"

Kalas glanced at the younger man. Gant had the manners of a cat. He dressed like one of the lordlings Kalas had seen swanning about so many an Imperial palace in his day: in a long suit of gray and black, the lapels of crushed velvet, twirling vines embroidered about silver buttons. He wore a wide-brimmed hat that matched, a white feather in its band—and in place of boots he wore buckled shoes and a pair of tight gaiters patterned white-on-white that accentuated the flare of his jodhpurs. He didn't look like a thug at all. He looked like a procurer, one of the *leno* who used to come round selling women and boys to the legionnaires when they put in at port. He was the sort of man as like to smile as shoot, the sort of man who fussed about getting blood on his hands but not about the trigger. Kalas did *not* like him, but he was efficient, and he knew Abhanri City.

"No, no, just thinking's all," Kalas said, and massaged one hand with another. "Sounds like someone paid this Vela to find the seed and Sen was the first nut she could crack, paid him to smuggle it out of the of Consortium park." He could see the park buildings towering away in the distance: three massive white cubes more than half a mile high standing on the tundra between downtown Abhanri and the starport. From their height he could see the horizon curling away on all sides, see the CO_2 plants in the air farm belching greenhouse gas into an atmosphere that needed it so desperately. Maybe one day people could breathe on Kanthi without air tubes and osmosis packs. Maybe not. He'd heard there was talk of plantings being done in the equatorial regions: beans and peas and the like trying to enrich the quality of the thin and rocky soil.

It was a start, but it would be centuries—maybe millennia—before Kanthi flowered the way Maglona did. How had he been so stupid not to see it? Why had he ever left?

"You think there are others?"

"No, that's what I'm saying," Kalas replied. "Not that it wouldn't hurt to warn the folks in HR, tell them to scan company and personal communiques—but I reckon this was a one-off. This Giacomo person . . . Sen said he was an offworlder. I bet my boots he came here knowing we had a Consortium center but very little planetary government—no Empire, say. Figured that'd make the heist easy, just pay off a disgruntled employee to smuggle the stock out of cold storage. If he'd wanted more I think we'd have more stolen property on our hands. So I figure either there was more as got stolen that we haven't heard about, or they tried to steal more and only Sen carried it off proper. Or what Sen took was all this Giacomo guy asked for."

Gant sucked on his teeth, angled the flier into a sweeping arc that brought it down towards the car park at one end of a high street in the Narrows. "Still seems like a lot of effort to go through for seed, be better off just paying." Smoke stacks rose like the turrets of some ugly castle from the gray mist, rust red or black. Even from the comfort of the flier Kalas could feel the damp already, the damp bricks and sweating metal walls of the low town.

"Shit's expensive. Paying someone like Vela for the heist's gotta be cheaper. Paying off a disgruntled employee like Sen definitely is."

The younger man grunted. "You're probably right."

"I'm definitely right," said Kalas, checking the seal on his nose-tubes again. "You ready?"

"Man, you know I'm always ready." Gant flashed his artificially bright smile. He'd had his real teeth shattered two years back when he'd been caught by a lowtown gang, and rather than pay to have a bonecutter regrow them, Gant had opted for ceramic implants.

The flier's door seals hissed—although Gant had never bothered to scrub the internal compartment—and the two hunters slung out from under the big gull wing doors and hit the street. It had snowed again not two days past, and the black slush stood piled against the curb and the sides of the buildings, soot-stained and filthy. The heat of the buildings would melt it eventually, or the street sweepers would clear it away—but it would never really melt. Kanthi had not experienced anything any reasonable human being would have called summer in perhaps millions of years. Kalas popped his over-sized collar and clicked the magnetic clasps to baffle the thing over his lower face like a scarf, and added warm air and sunshine to the list of things he missed.

Adri's was still there, crouched beneath the shadow of a warehouse, the bright neon in its windows contrasting against the dead-eyed frosted glass of the buildings around, inviting in that threatening way all such dives were inviting.

They brushed past a trio of big men in striped nylon racing suits crouching at the stoop and through the airlock with a gesture. Kalas knew the men on sight. Mother Earth knew he drank at Adri's often enough. Despite the fact that it was only mid-afternoon, there was a fair crowd inside already. Doubtless some were poorer spacers on different clocks than the planetside natives, but Kalas recognized a few old stalwarts, and tapped his fist to his chest in quiet salute to the old man watching from the bar. He'd been a veteran of the 225th, a centurion—which meant he was owed Kalas's respect.

"Kalas, you old goat! Is that you?"

"Yes, ma'am!" Kalas replied, unclipping his collar from his face and pulling out his nose tubes with relief and a big sigh.

The woman behind the bar set down the mug she was cleaning and came round the table to give the older hunter a hug. "Been a couple weeks, we were starting to worry you'd been done for." She kissed him on the cheek, one hand lingering on his arm as she pulled away, looking up at him. Adri had owned the little pub for more than a decade—going on two, maybe—at any rate far longer than Kalas had been on Kanthi. She'd started it young, and might have been only a year or two his junior. She smiled crookedly up at him, the heavy makeup around her eyes making her look more tired than beautiful—not that Kalas didn't think she was beautiful. She was the sort of woman they said had aged gracefully, who'd come to the good side of middle aged looking only a little older than she had as a girl. A little wiser, perhaps. A little more sad, with a knowing light in those blue eyes. She was an offworlder like him, yellow hair shot now with gray she hadn't bothered to hide.

Kalas smiled back at her, "I've been working. You know how it is."

Glancing at Gant, she said, "The peacock's looking a bit drab today. Where's all the purple, Gant?"

"He's in mourning," Kalas said wryly, stepping aside as Adri thrust out her hand.

"Mourning?" she echoed, "What for?"

"His fashion sense, mostly," Kalas said.

Adri thrust out her hand for Gant to kiss it, which he did, saying, "You're looking lovely as ever, Miss Adri. Did you change your hair?" She hadn't.

"Do you like it?" Adri asked, tossing her head.

"I'm sure you'd put a palatine duchess to shame." Gant grinned, looking like nothing so much a satyr with his sculpted goatee.

Adri swatted at him and returned to stand behind the bar, leaning over the half-cleaned mug in such a way that Kalas could see down her loose blouse. He looked—as he was meant to—then tracked to her face as she said, "So what can I get you?"

"Zvanya for me," Kalas replied, leaning over the bar, "the peacock will doubtless take something questionable—"

"But delicious," Gant interjected, "Sunrise Sultana, please."

Adri groaned.

"Someone's going to kick the shit out of you for ordering that drink there, Gant," Kalas said, settling against one of the stools bolted to the floor.

The other man shrugged. "Let them try. You're the one drinking that Jaddian piss that smells like someone set a cinnamon tree on fire."

"You don't make it sound so bad when you put it that way." The proprietor busied herself cleaning the glass she'd abandoned and set it back in the chiller before she poured Kalas his drink and set about mixing Gant's. "What are you boys in for? Because I know this ain't a social call."

Kalas threw the Jaddian liquor back in one shot, grimacing, but Gant beat him to the response, "Vela."

The barkeep stopped midway through shaking Gant's drink, "I don't know what you're talking about."

"Now see, if that were true, Adri," Gant said smoothly, propping his elbows on the surface of the bar, "you'd have just said, 'Who?'" The younger man leaned in over the bar as he spoke, the shadow of his wide-brimmed hat drawing a line across Adri's painted face.

Kalas put a hand on the younger man's arm to stay his advance. "You know what we do, Adri. That's no secret. Word is she fenced or is fencing a supply of Consortium seed stock boosted from Park Towers three days back."

Still clutching the silver mixer in her hands, "You know I don't want any trouble . . ."

"And we're not looking to bring it," Kalas said, glancing round the dingy room. Another group of men sat in the far corner, huddled around a hookah that stank of jubala, while not far off a mixed group of men and women watched a recorded Colosso match projected in miniature on a holograph table. No one was really listening, not even the old centurion in his cups. Still, Kalas was too much the former Sollan legionnaire to lose the sense that they might be being listened to. Speaking more softly then, he said, "We're just trying to find the tech's all."

Blue eyes narrowed and Adri shook her head, "You're missing my point. It's not you I'm scared of. It's *her*."

"Vela?"

The barkeep flashed Gant a look that probably soured the liquor in her mixer, which she still clutched to her breast like a talisman. To Kalas she said, "Now you being new from offworld I can understand you not knowing, even in your line of work, but *you?*" She glared at Gant, not breaking eye contact as she poured the man's violently orange drink into a broad cocktail glass. The drink immediately began to separate in the grimy yellow light, the lowest portions turning a bright, sunny blue. "How in Earth's name do you not know about her?"

Gant sipped the Sultana, a puzzled look indicating that a thought had penetrated his perfectly coiffed haircut and the skull beneath it. "She's not the one who did for old Arturo and his lot, is she?"

Adri nodded. Gant swore.

"Does the name 'Parliament of Owls' mean anything to you?" Kalas asked, shaking his glass to signal for a second shot, which Adri obliged.

Putting the glass stopper back in the bottle, she said, "No. What is it?"

"The buyer, I think," Kalas replied, downing the cinnamon liquor, "that was all our . . . informant said. Said this Vela of yours was selling our contraband to someone called Giacomo and the Parliament of Owls."

"Sounds like a sex club to me," Gant put in, speaking around the rim of his cocktail glass, "a *weird* sex club."

"You'd know," Kalas said, turning his glass over.

"Would not."

"What's Vela's deal?" Kalas asked Adri, jerking his chin up, "Why's she got you so tight-lipped?"

Adri's deep blue eyes swept over her attendees, taking in the sights. "She's a big fish is all. Eyes everywhere, fingers in everything. Been knocking off a bunch of the small timers for years now. Making noise. Surprised you lot haven't heard of her, or did you pop your eardrums living so high up in those Consortium towers?"

Both men snorted at the same time, prompting Kalas to glare at his partner. "Big fish . . ." he repeated, thinking it a strange expression to bring this world where fish were so few. "Heard she works out of a stockhouse down here. Any idea which one?"

"You know the old Narayan Shipping offices? Right on the reservoir?"

"Sure."

The barkeep looked down and away, as if unsure she'd said the right thing.

"What is it about this Vela woman's got you so scared?" Kalas asked, and thinking of his time in the Legions added, "I've met worse."

Adri looked him in the face, eyes narrowing, searching for her answer in Kalas's face. "Word is she's the one you go to if you want to trade with the Extras."

Gant choked on his drink, "The Extras? You sure?"

The Extrasolarians. The word had a special sharpness for Kalas. As a boy—in the Empire—the Extrasolarians were the stuff of nightmares. Monsters his gran had threatened him with, pirates who dwelt between the stars, who kidnapped children and turned them into their mindless machine servants.

Adri looked from Gant to Kalas, gave them a slow nod.

But Kalas had lived long enough and fought long enough to take this in stride. It was a rumor—and even if it was true, it didn't change the fact that he had a job to do. He stood, drew out his credit chit. Seeing her cue, the barkeep keyed a number into the scanner—the price of three drinks and a bit of information—and Kalas paid. No matter. It was Wong-Hopper money anyway. Gant hadn't stirred for any of this, and Kalas had to haul him off his stool even as he struggled to drain the last of his garish drink. "Thank you for the drink, Adri," Kalas said.

"That's it?" Adri asked, stunned. "Just like that?"

"Unless you know more." Kalas shrugged, "What am I supposed to do? Gant and me—we don't get paid unless we recover the Consortium's property."

The woman only shook her head, muttered, "I guess a hunter is a hunter . . ."

They turned to go.

"And Kalas!" the barkeep's words caught them before they'd gone five paces. He turned. Waited. "We still on for next week?"

The old hunter bobbed his head ever so slightly and gave her a neat half-salute, tapping his chest with his fist. "Yes ma'am."

In a small voice—so small that Kalas wasn't quite sure or not if he was meant to hear it—she said, "You be careful."

The Narayan building was easy enough to find. Like

most of the oldest buildings in Abhanri City, it wasn't gray, but white: assembled from prefabricated units brought in from offworld on some super-carrier and assembled on the ground. It wasn't tall—Kalas only counted twelve stories—but it dwarfed the massive concrete drums of the water reservoir and the fisheries around it. Even with his nose-tubes in place, Kalas could smell the mercury stink of fish and of the algaes living and dead that helped feed the fish and clean Kanthi's poisonous airs. It would take a lot more of such algae to make the planet's poisonous air breathable, and for that it would take a lot more water. The experts said that water was trapped in permafrost and the ice caps far to the north and south, but Kalas wasn't sure.

He'd believe it when he saw it, and he'd be dead by then.

"You sure this'll work there, Kal?" Gant's voice came clear through the earpiece.

The old hunter grimaced and did not respond, but clambered up onto the top of one of the great fishery vats, looking down on turgid green waters tossed here and there by rippling movement. Great plumes of white steam rose from stacks on the low buildings around, and his osmosis pack buzzed to indicate that it was safe to remove his nose-tubes.

He didn't, turned instead to the height of the tower near at hand.

Subvocalizing again, he said, "There it is, see?"

"Ooh . . ." He could hear Gant's grin over the line. "I knew I liked you."

The old Narayan building was separated from the top

of the fishery by a space only perhaps a dozen feet wide, near enough that a man might leap to it if he started high. "These prefab units are almost all Wong-Hopper standard kit, the sort they sell to new colonies," Kalas said. "Used to see a lot of them back in the Legions. Colonists buy them cheap and in bulk." He squinted, judging his chances. He didn't like them.

The building units were all built to a similar plan, and Kalas had been in and out of hundreds on them on a dozen worlds in his day. Towers like the Narayan building were built simply by stacking the same ugly white block of a unit atop its duplicate over and over and over—in this case, twelve times. The windows were in the same place on every level, as were the exterior lights. Perhaps the units' inner walls varied floor to floor, perhaps not—it wasn't important.

What was important was the door, or *doors,* rather. The Narayan Shipping company had built the tower when Abhanri City was just a few thousand people brought in to mine the massive vein of tungsten that had attracted the first wave colonists. They'd built cheap and fast. The prefab units came in sets of three, which meant every third floor on the tower had the same doors as the first floor. Someone had come after and built balconies outside the main doors, but the *side* doors? The emergency exits? No. There was only a narrow shelf, perhaps eighteen inches deep, set beside a fire-escape ladder that stood hiked up to the third story.

"But are you sure this'll work?" Gant asked again.

"Consortium hasn't changed factory codes in seven thousand years, Gant," Kalas replied, lips barely moving.

"You know that just as well as me." Theoretically, it should be possible to use the manufacturer's override codes to open that back door without triggering any internal alarms. And they *were* the manufacturers—or their hired guns. The Wong-Hopper Consortium had its fingers in everything: interstellar trade, starship manufacture, raw materials prospecting . . . even politics. But it was the colonial trade that had catapulted them to power and prominence. Terraforming equipment, construction gear, orbital mirrors, hightower anchor stations and counterweights, prefabricated housing, industrial, and commercial buildings. And genetic seed stock: everything from super-oxygenating designer algaes and plastic-eating fungi to dogs and oaks and moray eels.

Everything.

"You, uh . . . you gonna make the jump there?"

"In a minute," Kalas said, squaring his shoulder and turning away from the edge. "You want to do this instead? I'll wait until you can get down here." He glanced up towards the factory smokestack where Gant crouched, nestled in the scaffolding.

Gant liked to run *support* when it came to this part of the job. *I'm just not a blunt instrument,* he often said, pressing one hand to his chest. How the fellow had survived in this line of work for so long Kalas could never quite understand. At least not until Gant started shooting, that was.

"You got about forty guys in there, or so the thermals say. No telling how many of them are fighters though."

"Best assume all of them." Kalas swore. "Any sign of the hardware?" The seed stock would be chilled, but there was no telling how well shielded the crate might be. Sen would have had to pack it *pretty* well to smuggle it out of the research park. It could have been in a sub-basement for all Kalas knew.

"No shine, boss."

Kalas swore again.

At that moment, a shadow passed over the stars, and Kalas ducked, pulled by some primordial reflex, as if he were some brush-dwelling rodent shrinking from a hawk in the night. Or an owl. He heard *something*. A high-pitched, thrumming *whine*. Drive cores. Repulsors. A ship overhead. He didn't see the tell-tale blue-white glow, nor the flashing green and blue of wing lights.

Pressing the comms patch against the skin of his throat, he said, "You hear that?"

"Sounds like a ship, but I don't see anything on the scope." Gant's words came across slow and considering, as if he was thinking hard.

The old hunter overrode him, "Bugger the scope, man! Use your eyes." It was thermal emissions a ship would try the hardest to hide. "Look for a shadow." He had a sinking feeling that Vela's buyer had arrived. He'd known time was short, had known it since Director Yin had ordered him and Gant to recover the contraband. Kalas knew he must be cursed. He must have had the worst luck in the whole damned Imperial universe and beyond. Couldn't they have come an hour later? Or two? Two would have been better.

He was getting too old for this sort of thing.

"I still don't see . . ." Gant's voice trailed off, and Kalas imagined him squinting over the railing, peering down over the stinking fisheries and Narayan building and the lower structures around. "No, there it is!" He sounded like he was pointing. "Right on top of the building, hanging off the south side. I don't recognize the make, though."

Kalas peered up at top of the building, but there was nothing to see. Some sort of active camouflage? That did not bode well. Abhanri didn't restrict flight, didn't have a customs office. Who would cloak themselves in such a place? Who would need to? "I'd better move fast," Kalas grumbled, more to himself than to his companion. He gauged the jump one last time, aimed for the ladder, and leaped.

The factory codes had worked perfectly, and Kalas slunk through the hissing airlock into a dimly lit hall. Only the odd glow panel still shone in the ceiling. Only the odd door stood open. Kalas moved slowly, careful not to make a sound as he moved down the hall. Not for the first time, Kalas understood the attraction of the sensory implants common out here beyond the borders of the Empire. He could never quite bring himself to get them, citizen of the Empire that he was. The mingling of man and machine was forbidden by the Holy Terran Chantry, and fear of such machines and loathing ran deep in Kalas, whatever his more freethinking tendencies. He might have had his eyes genetically augmented, but at home such augmentations were reserved, awarded for exemplary service by the great lords and ladies of the Empire. It felt wrong to Kalas to bypass the cultural order. Call him old-fashioned.

The hallways were precisely as Kalas expected them, the standard office unit made available by the

Consortium. If he turned left, towards the center of the building—yes, there were the lifts. He didn't like his chances with those lifts, not with a guest arriving on the rooftop. There should have been service stairs . . . he turned right, glad not to have been seen, and moved along a side hall, past a graffitied mural of a naked woman defaced by rude words in angry, block letters and a busted drinking fountain. A man emerged from the bathroom ahead. Kalas fired his phase disruptor without breaking stride, caught the man full in the side of his face with a stun blast. He spasmed, slumped against the door. He'd barely made a sound.

"I hope you're making progress with the cameras," Kalas mumbled, tidying the stunned man into the bathroom whence he'd come. He didn't envy the man. Taking a stunner shot at all was unpleasant, but to the face? Crouching, Kalas checked to make sure the man was still breathing. Even on its stun setting, a phase disruptor might disrupt the vagus nerve, stop a man breathing. He was alive, if quite unconscious. He'd wake up with a monstrous headache, and his face would be slow to recover its full motion. But at least that was one of the tower's occupants out of commission for the foreseeable future. Kalas studied him: thick neck, shaved head. He was only missing the tattoos to complete the stereotype image of the lowlife gangster. He even wore the nondescript button-down shirt and gold jewelry one expected, and a plasma burner at his belt. Kalas took the burner and cracked the compressor unit with the spiked cap on the butt of his phase disruptor, just in case this one woke up with a fury.

The stairs.

The stairs were right where Kalas expected them, right where they'd been in a thousand identical buildings. He pushed the metal door with its peeling white paint open and stepped out onto iron and concrete steps that switch-backed up and down just inside the outer wall of the building.

Up or down?

"Gant, any sign of contraband?"

"I'm not sure, I—"

"On the roof, man," Kalas cut into him. "With the ship."

Kalas could practically hear Gant shaking his head, as he looked for signs of the supercooled cargo, "No. No. About twenty guys, though."

This wasn't going to work. They hadn't counted on a ship arriving while they were just scouting things out. They'd been banking on a couple hours recon, easy, find the payload, get it out and into the flier. Things were starting to come undone. "Leave the scope up where you're at," Kalas said, "monitor the feed from the flier."

"What about cover?" Gant said, "I thought you wanted me shooting out windows if things got hairy?" The other man had carried a heavy-gauge MAR up the stack with him. The magnetic rifle would put an iron slug clean through the building if they had a mind, and irritating as he was, Gant was not a bad shot.

"We gotta go fast," Kalas replied. "I just want you ready with the flier at a moment's notice. I don't like this, Gant. I don't like anything about this." He made his choice.

Down.

The next floor was identical to the one he'd entered on: walls scratched and badly graffitied, lights broken or fading. The same arrangement of rooms. That was the trouble. It was hard to find a central *anything* in such a place, where everything was duplicated. What they were looking for should not have been that hard to find: a refrigerated metal cube about a foot and a half to a side.

There was no one here.

There was nothing here.

"Gant, where are the other guards?" he asked when he reached the level immediately above the ground floor.

The response was a moment coming, "Five floors up—two past where you started—and on the front door. Rest are on the roof. Looks like they're waiting for—"

The comms line went dead mid-sentence.

Fearing an attack was imminent, Kalas pressed himself through a side door into what once had been a set of office cubicles. Still holding his phase disruptor in his right hand, he fiddled with his terminal. Access to the Kanthi datasphere was blocked, and even the device's more primitive radio functions were blocked. It was no use trying to reach the Consortium's private satellite net, either.

His instinct to hide saved him.

"Arno! Bass! You two still fucking up in here?" a voice called from the hall, "Boss wants us on the ground floor, make sure no one gets in."

Another voice floated down the hall, nearer at hand, "She said she wanted us covering the street from up here!"

"You heard me!" The first voice again.

"Yeah, and I also heard your mom sells tricks down portside for the price of a cigarette," came a third voice, higher and more nasal than the others. "And not one of them good cigarettes, neither. Heard she sells out for those T-free cigarettes what they sell to little girls in school trying to impress their friends."

"Fuck you, Arno!"

"Fuck you, Kees. It's fucking cold out there and some of us still got balls as might freeze off!" A pause. "Say, why're comms out?"

Kalas pressed himself against the wall near the door, trying to see down the hall. He could just make out a thin slice of a man standing at a door not far down. The first man—Kees, if he was keeping track.

Voice suddenly hushed, Kees said, "The buyer. Boss agreed to let him jam up comms until he had everything he came for." That made Kalas sigh with relief. They hadn't been discovered, then. Everyone was jammed. "I'm going back up to eight. If you assholes won't do your job, don't come crying to me when the boss slaps you good."

"Fuck you, Kees!" said both men in unison.

From his vantage point, Kalas watched what little of Kees he could see turn, moving back up the hall. The old hunter gave the man two—three paces to get away from the door he'd been standing at before he leaned out into the hall and fired his phase disruptor. The shot spat silently down the grimy hall, caught the man between the shoulder blades. He fell with a solid thud—the stunner bolt had hit right over his spine. Not wasting time, Kalas slid towards the door, barely pausing to note much about the two men who sat by the big arc of window overlooking the street below and the bulk of the heated fishery drums rising into the cold night air. He fired, dropping both of them without ceremony.

If the comms really *were* down all over the building, he hardly needed to hide the stunned men. It might be minutes before someone came looking for Kees and his loudmouthed compatriots, and when they did they'd have to come running up the stairs.

The old-fashioned way.

Kalas clenched his teeth. He almost grinned.

He was from the Empire. He *was* the old-fashioned way.

Two men stood flanking a door on the eighth floor, plasma burners strapped to their thighs, hands ready, waiting. Kalas felt certain there had to be more guards inside, and felt even more certain that he was in the right place. None of the other rooms had been guarded. He stayed hidden around the corner. Gant could have told him how many hostiles were in that next room. Gant could have told him many things. He could—for example—have told him about the lift carriage that had just arrived from the rooftop, about the woman and her guest that had just stepped out into the lobby near at hand.

He heard their footsteps first, coming from the other end of the hall, beyond the guards. There was something *wrong* about them. Too heavy. Too metallic. A little bit too far apart. And Kalas knew then that Adri had been right all along, knew that sometimes the rumors were true—and the childhood legends also.

A woman came into view, tall and with the native copper complexion, dressed in a gown of simple black, and beside her . . . beside her walked a monster.

The Extrasolarian stood nearly seven feet tall on legs bent backwards like the legs of dog. His hands—where they emerged from voluminous black sleeves, looked more like the anatomical sketch of a pair of hands than hands themselves, with tendons and tissue of black carbon like pencil lead. The feet were like cloven hooves shod with titanium, and his face . . . Kalas had seen less pallor on a corpse. He might have been an albino, so pale was he and hairless, his scalp glistening, studded with mechanical implants behind his ears and along the column of his spine.

"My captain, Lady Marishka, is most grateful that you have found what we required on such short notice, M. Vela," the Extrasolarian said, and from his hiding place Kalas felt certain that the man's lips did not move, that his sepulchral voice came instead from somewhere in his chest.

The native woman, Vela, replied, "It was no trouble, M. Giacomo. Thank you for thinking of us."

The impossibly deep voice again: "Hardly, madam. Your reputation precedes you, and what you've gotten for us will go a long way to ensuring that the *Parliament of Owls* will go on sailing for another four thousand years."

Sailing.

Kalas paused, watching the mismatched couple come to a stop at the door with the two guards. *Sailing.* It was a ship. The *Parliament of Owls* was a ship, one of the nightmare vessels that plied the Dark between the stars.

It was the type of ship his old gran had told stories about when Kalas was a boy. He gripped his disruptor tighter, watching as the Extrasolarian and the woman passed within. It was now or never, and so Kalas stepped out into the hall, raised his arm.

And someone else fired.

The stunner bolt took him in the side, and he lurched into the wall. His arm still worked, and in desperation Kalas aimed his stunner at the guards on the door. Where had the shot come from? He fired, caught one man in the face before he could turn. He crumpled even as the other man leaped back, pounding on the door.

A second stunner bolt caught Kalas in the shoulder, and he fell.

Everything had gone wrong. Everything.

They should have pulled out the moment the ship arrived. Cut their losses. Lied to Director Yin and the local board. Kalas's last thought before he lost consciousness was that he was going to miss his date with Adri after all, and that he'd lied to her. Then a sound like rushing water filled his ears, and everything went black.

Red pain lanced across his face, went black as a thunderclap. Someone winced. Was it him? He could move his arms. Good. Legs? Good. But someone had tied him to a chair. Less good. His neck felt tacky where someone had peeled the subvocalizing patch off, which meant that even if the comms started working again, Gant was out of the picture.

"I said 'Who are you?'" A woman's voice. Adri? No, that was a native accent.

Kalas looked up with blurry eyes, saw the woman in the black dress standing over him. Vela. He would have touched his forehead in salute, murmured instead. "Ma'am."

She slapped him again, less hard. She wasn't strong, but it was enough to snap Kalas's head back. Dimly, he was aware of the pale devil watching him. That Extrasolarian with his satyr legs and black hands. Up close, Kalas could see his eyes were all white, like the eyes of a statue. "Who are you?"

"Who do you think?" he said, words bitter. There was no point in denying it. "Consortium repo man."

Vela smiled, teeth almost as white as Gant's. "Is that all? Are you all they sent?"

He was ready for the next slap, and rolled with it. The woman had an arm, but she was nothing next to the rebel on Janeiro who'd beaten the young Triaster Kalas of Maglona nearly to death when he refused to talk. "Didn't find anyone else, did you?" Kalas asked, shrugging as if to say *Doesn't that answer your question?*

The woman smiled. "Those corporate sods *are* cheap."

A smile flickered over Kalas's bruised face. She was sloppy. At least now he knew Gant was in the clear.

"I assume this is what you're after," she said, slapping a heavy, white plastic crate a little more than a cubit to a side. She leaned against the edge of the desk. "Did you kill Sen?" Kalas didn't answer. His silence was loud enough. "Seems like a lot of trouble to go to for a stack of human embryos."

"Ten thousand of them," Kalas said, glancing over his shoulder at the monstrous figure with his white eyes. "You could have just bought them."

The Extrasolarian stepped forward—Kalas could hear the servos whining in his legs. "No need."

Kalas looked up into that dead, white face. He could see lights blinking in the black metal implants behind the creature's right ear; still more shone from beneath the papery white skin. "What do you need them for?" Kalas asked, looking to the crate. "The children, I mean." Silence from the woman and the machine man. "What?" he asked. "Won't tell a dead man?"

"You're not a dead man." Cold ceramic fingers stroked Kalas's cheek, and he flinched away. "You're coming with me. We need more men. You will serve nicely."

"I will not," Kalas swore.

"You will." Giacomo patted Kalas on the cheek with one cold hand. He moved to stand in front of Kalas, between the old hunter and the woman at her desk. He crouched on his satyr's legs and smiling, said, "You see, we're a bit short-handed at the moment. We need good men . . . but they're so hard to find." His teeth were the same white as his eyes, and those eyes seemed to turn—how Kalas knew he couldn't say—to look at the crate on the desk, "So much easier to make, mm?"

Kalas was still enough the Imperial soldier to recoil. He thought of all the embryos frozen in that crate. They had been destined for some colonial world, to be raised by the few living colonists to inject genetic diversity into their growing population. They would grow up slaves instead, transfigured into something less than human to serve this pirate and his horrid captain. Looking at the man, Kalas could see why the Empire forbade such machinery. Giacomo was a monster.

"You understand, don't you?" Giacomo said, "Children are the future. But we cannot go on as we are." He knocked on his metal chest to indicate his problem. "We need a next generation. New blood."

He found suddenly that he had nothing to say. Kalas had never been a great talker, but surely he ought to have said *something*. But there was nothing. He strained against his bonds, but nothing came. It was bad enough that someone would choose to destroy his own body the way this man had done—but to force such an existence on a hundred hundred lives?

"What did you mean, *no need?*" Vela asked, interposing herself once more.

It took Kalas's muddied brain a moment to catch up. *No need.* He'd asked why the Extrasolarian hadn't just bought the embryos from the Consortium directly . . . it was all too much. Kalas started laughing. Not loud, but softly to himself, shaking where he sat restrained by plastic ties. "He's not going to pay you, you idiot," he smiled up at her.

Vela rounded on Giacomo, but the Extrasolarian was faster. One of his ceramic hands lashed out, catching Vela across the face even as he lanced out with one hoof—catching the seat of Kalas's chair just between his knees—and kicked. Kalas went skidding back against the wall with a crash as Vela hit the edge of her desk and fell. Giacomo moved smoothly, reaching out of a hand to take the crate.

Bang!

Something hit Giacomo in the shoulder, shattering his arm. Bits of ceramic armor scattered on the air, carbon fiber tendons unraveling as the heavy machinery fell apart from the shoulder. A red alarm began to sound, indicating that the building's air integrity was compromised.

Bang!

A second shot took Giacomo in the thigh, but succeeded there in only bending his leg out of shape. A second later Kalas saw the tell-tale glimmer of a shield's energy curtain snap into being around the awful hybrid. A moment after that Kalas realized what was happening.

Gant.

The peacock had done it! He must have gone back to his vantage point after the communications went dead. Earth and Emperor! But he had dramatic timing! He must have been waiting, watching to see what happened, and seized his chance when he saw things start to fall apart. A third shot from the man's magnetic acceleration rifle caromed clean off Giacomo's body-shield and buried itself in an inner wall.

"Untie me!" Kalas yelled, hoping to reach Vela where she still slumped shell-shocked at the foot of her desk. The Extrasolarian paid them no mind, but seized the crate with his one remaining hand and turned to go, limping badly on his bent leg. He looked at Kalas a moment—only a moment—and reached the door just as Vela's guards were coming in, drawn by the sounds of scuffle. Giacomo kicked one square in the chest with his good leg, staggering as his damaged limb took his weight. The fellow hit the far wall of the corridor with such force that Kalas heard his skull crunch. The second man got a shot off, but the bullet shattered when it hit the Extrasolarian's shield. Kalas didn't see how he died.

"Untie me!" he snarled. "Cut me loose, damn it!"

Vela was slow to find her feet. She glared at him, hair falling across her face. She seemed almost not to comprehend him, but when she did at last, she clambered to her feet, stumbled towards him. "What are you going to do?" she asked.

"Just get me out."

He'd known, of course. Known what it was they were retrieving, what Dr. Sen had stolen, and what this woman had sold—or tried to sell—to the Extrasolarians. Growing new colonists was big business, and it wasn't the first time a stock had gone missing in the Consortium's long history. Ten thousand souls. Ten thousand lives yet unlived. Unless Kalas got free, they would be ten thousand slaves, twisted as Giacomo was twisted.

Vela cut him loose, and Kalas stood, lurching as his muscles struggled to remember their proper function. He was still numb in places from the stunner fire, but his hands worked. Reminded by the alarm, he fished his nose-tubes out of the osmosis pack at his belt and threaded them into his nose, sucking deep breaths of oxygen. He stopped in the doorway. Were the lifts left or right? Belatedly, he realized he was unarmed, and stooped to examine the bodies of the dead men. One of them had a simple pistol, which Kalas discarded. Giacomo was shielded. Bullets were useless. But the other had a plasma burner, a heavy piece: gloss-black and threatening as the Extrasolarian himself. Its range was limited, but against a shielded opponent it was better than nothing.

"I set you free!" Vela called after him. "You owe me!"

Kalas looked back a moment. He ought to have shot

her. Killed her. Had she been a man, he might have done just that. But it didn't feel right shooting a woman, even a woman willing to sell human embryos to the Extras. Still, he raised the plasma burner to make his point. She froze.

He walked away, hurried after the injured chimera. There were deep gouges in the hard plastic floor where Giacomo's injured hoof cut in, and three bodies between Kalas and the lifts. It only took a moment for one of the lift carriages to arrive, and Kalas punched the button for the roof.

When he'd been a soldier, he'd fancied himself a knight. The sort of paladin they sang about in the old songs, the sort of hero who gave himself to the people—who safeguarded the helpless and protected those who could not protect themselves. The more time he spent in the Imperial service, the more Kalas realized that real knights were no such men. They were *men,* the same as all the rest, and he was only a man himself. A killer now. But he'd realized, too, just how much the world needed *real* knights. Real heroes. Or needed to believe in them.

He needed to believe in them.

As he checked the charge in his plasma burner—checked the heat sink and the gas reserve—Kalas fancied himself a knight once more. It wasn't exactly a princess he was saving, but there was a tower with a dragon at its top. Maybe he was only a hired dog, but it seemed to him that there were lives on the line. Ten thousand lives unlived. And if he didn't act the knight, who would?

The doors opened.

The lift had played the role of airlock, and Kalas wasted no time. Dead ahead, the Extrasolarian was limping across twenty yards of open space, his one remaining hand still clasping the storage crate. Directly opposite, a ramp seemed to disappear into nothingness, rising from the far edge of the rooftop into the night. Kalas could almost see the shimmer of the cloaked Extrasolarian ship. How it hid itself he couldn't speculate, and he didn't care.

He was close enough.

He raised both hands and aimed, the plasma burner in one, Dr. Sen's antique autorevolver in the other. The hammer back, it was an easy thing to fire the old-fashioned pistol. The handgun jumped in his hand, and the bullet caught Giacomo between the shoulder blades. It caromed off his shield, but the shot surprised the chimera, and he turned, snarling, teeth and eyes so white they were almost blue in the night light. They glowed violet as the plasma burned forth, chasing magnetic lines in a great arc like the blades of chainsaw, shooting out and curling back again from the plasma burner's mouth like the bow of a solar flare. Blue and violet, half as bright as Kanthi's pale sun.

Kalas had aimed for the creature's face, for the parts of him that were still flesh—still human. The energy shield could absorb the kinetic energy of impact, but the air plasma burned hot as the surface of a dwarf star, and that heat at least would radiate across a shield's curtain and cook the pirate like lobster in his shell. But when the glow died down, Kalas saw Giacomo still standing. His pale face had vanished, was lost beneath a caul of white ceramic that shut over his face like a giant eyelid.

"You nearly got me, boy," the Extrasolarian said,

"that's promising." The visor retracted, folding back up over Giacomo's face and forehead. "You're not bad, you know? You'd make a fine addition to our crew!"

"Why would I want to do that?" Kalas asked, both weapons still pointed directly at the Extrasolarian. Where was Gant? If he was still watching, the other hunter should have seen what was going on. He should have gone for the flier.

"Eternal life!"

"Like you?" Kalas asked, taking in the dented horror of the man's metal body. "No thanks."

"Very well!" The Extrasolarian let the crate with its stock of human lives slide to the ground, arm lengthening to deposit its cargo. "Suit yourself!" He leaped forward, faster than Kalas could have believed on his damaged leg. The old hunter threw himself backwards, firing the old-fashioned handgun on reflex. The bullets all shattered against Giacomo's shield, filling the air between them with shrapnel.

What had he been thinking? The man was more than half machine. Stronger, faster, more resilient than any mortal man. What chance did an old soldier from Maglona have against such a one?

A knight, indeed.

The handgun clicked—empty—and desperate Kalas threw it at the chimera. It pinged off Giacomo's head, but the man kept coming, reaching out with his one remaining hand. Hard fingers seized Kalas by the shirt front, lifted him bodily into the air. For a moment, Kalas feared to lose his nose-tubes, but he had bigger problems. He pounded uselessly against Giacomo's armored torso as the man pivoted, hurling Kalas across the plastic rooftop. He tried to get a bead on the Extrasolarian and right himself at the same time. No good. The chimera was too fast, despite his injuries. He seized Kalas again, by the throat this time, iron fingers implacable as the crush of tectonic plates. He raised Kalas up before him, and Kalas could sense the man's smile even through that blank white plane he called a face.

"You could have been so much more, little man," he said, squeezing. "I don't think you get it. There's no place for us out here, not like we are. Look at you. Can't even breathe in the world you call home. We're the future humanity needs. Not the Empire, not *you!* We're the ones who can survive what's out there!"

Though he could hardly breathe, Kalas managed to croak one word, one single word, "Doubt . . ." And on that note he jammed the muzzle of his plasma burner through the man's shield and into the ragged hole in his chassis left by the ragged ruin of his shattered arm.

And fired.

The plasma chewed through Giacomo's innards, melting wires and sending ugly tongues of black smoke curling out through slits in his pale torso. Kalas winced as he felt the skin on his hand sear from radiated heat. He tried to cry out—to scream—but the pressure on his throat stopped his voice with his breath. Until it didn't. Giacomo released him, and with a cry more of surprise now than pain, Kalas fell to the ground at the Extrasolarian's feet. Giacomo took a step backwards before keeling over.

Silent.

Dead?

Kalas found his knees, his feet. He'd dropped the plasma burner, and clutched his burned hand to his chest, cradling it delicately so the oozing flesh didn't touch anything. The mere touch of the air was agony, and he grit his teeth. There was the plasma burner, not three paces from where he'd fallen. He stooped and collected it.

The crate wasn't far—was right where Giacomo had left it, just near the base of the ramp to his unseen ship. With his left hand fouled up, Kalas shoved the weapon into the pocket of his coat and picked the crate up with his good hand. It must have weighed forty pounds. Maybe fifty. He stopped a moment, breathing deeply. He forgot to breathe in through his nose a moment, and felt suddenly lightheaded.

He needed to go.

"Gant!" he said, and remembered—too late—that his comms patch and earpiece had been taken away when he was stunned. He sighed. The lifts then. He turned to go.

The whine of a flier's repulsors filled the night, and a bright light came streaking down from the heavens above. Kalas whirled, helpless with his weapon in his coat pocket. Gant's flier barreled down out of the darkness, flying low and fast. Kalas had a brief impression of a white-armored figure leaping towards him, one hand outstretched.

Giacomo.

The Extrasolarian wasn't dead after all, but lumbering towards him across the open rooftop. Gant's flier collided with the chimera at full speed, knocking the Extrasolarian off his course. Giacomo tumbled through the air, soaring like a payload dropped out of the back of a shuttle in the moments before the parachutes engage.

He didn't fly far.

Something broke inside the machine-man's chest. Some containment field or fuel cell. A moment later Giacomo exploded, the white-armored man transformed into a ball of white light. The sound of it crushed Kalas's eardrums, the force of it blew him from his feet, and he flew—and Gant's flier flew with him—back over the edge of the building.

He was a long time falling. The crate was still in his hand. A cool, detached piece of himself nodded in approval. It wouldn't matter anyway. He felt certain that he wouldn't live to collect the reward. No matter. He had lived a lived a life of violence. And violent lives should end violently. At least Gant would be all right. At least they'd won in the end.

Kalas hit the ground a moment after and sank through it. The shock of impact knocked the wind from him and made him release the handle to the refrigerated crate. Something was wrong. Or right. He wasn't dead, but he couldn't breathe either. There were hard pincers on his throat again, strong as the hands of the Extra had been.

Water.

He had landed in one of the great fishery vats that stood open beneath the Narayan building.

He was underwater.

Something brushed past him in the deep, green darkness. Another.

He tried to breathe through his nose-tubes, but nothing came. Which way was the surface? Which way was up? Another something swam past him. It touched his wounded arm, and the pain sharpened his vision.

Green light and red filtered up towards him past his boots. Up? No. Down. He'd fallen in head first. And the payload? It must have sunk to the bottom. The bottom?

Another something—something silver—flickered past his eyes.

A fish. Of course it was a fish.

He might have laughed. He found fish on Kanthi after all.

And soon enough someone would have to come fishing for him.

QUIETUS

by Ross Rocklynne

Explorers will take their hometowns with them in their head; they won't be able to help it. Which could lead to misunderstandings, even tragic ones, when they forget that they're not back on the block and misinterpret a situation, whether on another continent or another planet, and act accordingly—and wrongly. Which will likely be just as true if the explorers are not human . . .

★🜨★

THE CREATURES from Alcon saw from the first that Earth, as a planet, was practically dead; dead in the sense that it had given birth to life, and was responsible, indirectly, for its almost complete extinction.

"This type of planet is the most distressing," said Tark, absently smoothing down the brilliantly colored feathers of his left wing. "I can stand the dark, barren worlds which never have, and probably never will, hold life. But these that have been killed by some celestial catastrophe! Think of what great things might have come from their inhabitants."

As he spoke thus to his mate, Vascar, he was marking down in a book the position of this planet, its general appearance from space, and the number and kind of satellites it supported.

Vascar, sitting at the controls, both her claws and her vestigial hands at work, guided the spherical ship at slowly decreasing speed toward the planet Earth. A thousand miles above it, she set the craft into an orbital motion, and then proceeded to study the planet, Tark setting the account into his book, for later insertion into the Astronomical Archives of Alcon.

"Evidently," mused Vascar, her brilliant, unblinking eyes looking at the planet through a transparent section above the control board, "some large meteor, or an errant asteroid—that seems most likely—must have struck this specimen a terrible blow. Look at those great, gaping cracks that run from pole to pole, Tark. It looks as if volcanic eruptions are still taking place, too. At any rate, the whole planet seems entirely denuded—except for that single, short strip of green we saw as we came in."

Tark nodded. He was truly a bird, for in the evolutionary race on his planet, distant uncounted light-years away, his stock had won out over the others. His wings were short, true, and in another thousand years would be too short for flight, save in a dense atmosphere; but his head was large, and his eyes, red, small, set close together, showed intelligence and a kind benevolence. He and Vascar had left Alcon, their planet, a good many years ago; but they were on their way back now. Their outward-bound trip had taken them many light-years north of the Solar System; but on the way back, they had decided to make it one of the stop-off points in their zigzag course. Probably their greatest interest in all this long cruise was in the discovery of planets—they were indeed few. And that pleasure might even be secondary to the discovery of life. To find a planet that had almost entirely died was, conversely, distressing. Their interest in the planet Earth was, because of this, a wistful one.

The ship made the slow circuit of Earth—the planet was a hodge-podge of tumbled, churned mountains; of abysmal, frightfully long cracks exuding unholy vapors; of volcanoes that threw their fires and hot liquid rocks far into the sky; of vast oceans disturbed from the ocean bed by cataclysmic eruptions. And of life they saw nothing save a single strip of green perhaps a thousand miles long, a hundred wide, in the Western Hemisphere.

"I don't think we'll find intelligent life," Tark said pessimistically. "This planet was given a terrific blow—I wouldn't be surprised if her rotation period was cut down considerably in a single instant. Such a change would be unsupportable. Whole cities would literally be snapped away from their foundations—churned, ground to dust. The intelligent creatures who built them would die by the millions—the billions—in that holocaust; and whatever destruction was left incomplete would be finished up by the appearance of volcanoes and faults in the crust of the planet."

Vascar reminded him, "Remember, where there's

vegetation, even as little as evidenced by that single strip down there, there must be some kind of animal life."

Tark ruffled his wings in a shrug. "I doubt it. The plants would get all the carbon dioxide they needed from volcanoes—animal life wouldn't have to exist. Still, let's take a look. Don't worry, I'm hoping there's intelligent life, too. If there is, it will doubtless need some help if it is to survive. Which ties in with our aims, for that is our principal purpose on this expedition—to discover intelligent life, and, wherever possible, to give it what help we can, if it needs help."

Vascar's vestigial hands worked the controls, and the ship dropped leisurely downward toward the green strip.

A rabbit darted out of the underbrush—Tommy leaped at it with the speed and dexterity of a thoroughly wild animal. His powerful hands wrapped around the creature—its struggles ceased as its vertebra was snapped. Tommy squatted, tore the skin off the creature, and proceeded to eat great mouthfuls of the still warm flesh.

Blacky cawed harshly, squawked, and his untidy form came flashing down through the air to land precariously on Tommy's shoulder. Tommy went on eating, while the crow fluttered its wings, smoothed them out, and settled down to a restless somnolence. The quiet of the scrub forest, save for the cries and sounds of movement of birds and small animals moving through the forest, settled down about Tommy as he ate. "Tommy" was what he called himself. A long time ago, he remembered, there used to be a great many people in the world—perhaps a hundred—many of whom, and particularly two people whom he had called Mom and Pop, had called him by that name. They were gone now, and the others with them. Exactly where they went, Tommy did not know. But the world had rocked one night—it was the night Tommy ran away from home, with Blacky riding on his shoulder—and when Tommy came out of the cave where he had been sleeping, all was in flames, and the city on the horizon had fallen so that it was nothing but a huge pile of dust—but in the end it had not mattered to Tommy. Of course, he was lonesome, terrified, at first, but he got over that. He continued to live, eating, drinking, sleeping, walking endlessly; and Blacky, his talking crow, was good company. Blacky was smart. He could speak every word that Tommy knew, and a good many others that he didn't. Tommy was not Blacky's first owner.

But though he had been happy, the last year had brought the recurrence of a strange feeling that had plagued him off and on, but never so strongly as now. A strange, terrible hunger was settling on him. Hunger? He knew this sensation. He had forthwith slain a wild dog, and eaten of the meat. He saw then that it was not a hunger of the belly. It was a hunger of the mind, and it was all the worse because he could not know what it was. He had come to his feet, restless, looking into the tangled depths of the second growth forest.

"Hungry," he had said, and his shoulders shook and tears coursed out of his eyes, and he sat down on the ground and sobbed without trying to stop himself, for he had never been told that to weep was unmanly. What was it he wanted?

He had everything there was all to himself. Southward

in winter, northward in summer, eating of berries and small animals as he went, and Blacky to talk to and Blacky to talk the same words back at him. This was the natural life—he had lived it ever since the world went bang. But still he cried, and felt a panic growing in his stomach, and he didn't know what it was he was afraid of, or longed for, whichever it was. He was twenty-one years old. Tears were natural to him, to be indulged in whenever he felt like it. Before the world went bang—there were some things he remembered—the creature whom he called Mom generally put her arms around him and merely said, "It's all right, Tommy, it's all right."

So on that occasion, he arose from the ground and said, "It's all right, Tommy, it's all right."

Blacky, he with the split tongue, said harshly, as was his wont, "It's all right, Tommy, it's all right! I tell you, the price of wheat is going down!"

Blacky, the smartest crow anybody had—why did he say that? There wasn't anybody else, and there weren't any more crows—helped a lot. He not only knew all the words and sentences that Tommy knew, but he knew others that Tommy could never understand because he didn't know where they came from, or what they referred to. And in addition to all that, Blacky had the ability to anticipate what Tommy said, and frequently took whole words and sentences right out of Tommy's mouth.

Tommy finished eating the rabbit, and threw the skin aside, and sat quite still, a peculiarly blank look in his eyes. The strange hunger was on him again. He looked off across the lush plain of grasses that stretched away, searching into the distance, toward where the Sun was setting. He looked to left and right. He drew himself softly to his feet, and peered into the shadows of the forest behind him. His heavily bearded lips began to tremble, and the tears started from his eyes again. He turned and stumbled from the forest, blinded.

Blacky clutched at Tommy's broad shoulder, and rode him, and a split second before Tommy said, "It's all right, Tommy, it's all right."

Tommy said the words angrily to himself, and blinked the tears away.

He was a little bit tired. The Sun was setting, and night would soon come. But it wasn't that that made him tired. It was a weariness of the mind, a feeling of futility, for, whatever it was he wanted, he could never, never find it, because he would not know where he should look for it.

His bare foot trampled on something wet—he stopped and looked at the ground. He stooped and picked up the skin of a recently killed rabbit. He turned it over and over in his hands, frowning. This was not an animal he had killed, certainly—the skin had been taken off in a different way. Someone else—no! But his shoulders began to shake with a wild excitement. Someone else? No, it couldn't be! There was no one—there could be no one—could there? The skin dropped from his nerveless fingers as he saw a single footprint not far ahead of him. He stooped over it, examining, and knew again that he had not done this, either. And certainly it could be no other animal than a man!

It was a small footprint at which he stared, as if a child, or an under-sized man, might have stepped in the soft humus. Suddenly he raised his head. He had definitely heard the crackling of a twig, not more than forty feet away, certainly. His eyes stared ahead through the gathering dusk. Something looking back at him? Yes! Something there in the bushes that was not an animal!

"No noise, Blacky," he whispered, and forgot Blacky's general response to that command.

"No noise, Blacky!" the big, ugly bird blasted out. "No noise, Blacky! Well, fer cryin' out loud!"

Blacky uttered a scared squawk as Tommy leaped ahead, a snarl contorting his features, and flapping from his master's shoulder. For several minutes Tommy ran after the vanishing figure, with all the strength and agility of his singularly powerful legs. But whoever—or whatever—it was that fled him, outdistanced him easily, and Tommy had to stop at last, panting. Then he stooped, and picked up a handful of pebbles and hurled them at the squawking bird. A single tail feather fell to earth as Blacky swooped away.

"Told you not to make noise," Tommy snarled, and the tears started to run again. The hunger was starting up in his mind again, too! He sat down on a log, and put his chin in his palms, while his tears flowed. Blacky came flapping through the air, almost like a shadow—it was getting dark. The bird tentatively settled on his shoulder, cautiously flapped away again and then came back.

Tommy turned his head and looked at it bitterly, and then turned away, and groaned.

"It's all your fault, Blacky!"

"It's all your fault," the bird said. "Oh, Tommy, I could spank you! I get so exasperated!"

Sitting there, Tommy tried to learn exactly what he had seen. He had been sure it was a human figure, just like himself, only different. Different! It had been smaller, had seemed to possess a slender grace—it was impossible! Every time he thought of it, the hunger in his mind raged!

He jumped to his feet, his fists clenched. This hunger had been in him too long! He must find out what caused it—he must find her—why did the word *her* come to his mind? Suddenly, he was flooded with a host of childhood remembrances.

"It was a girl!" he gasped. "Oh, Tommy must want a girl!"

The thought was so utterly new that it left him stunned; but the thought grew. He must find her, if it took him all the rest of his life! His chest deepened, his muscles swelled, and a new light came into his blue eyes. Southward in winter, northward in summer—eating—sleeping—truly, there was nothing in such a life. Now he felt the strength of a purpose swelling up in him. He threw himself to the ground and slept; and Blacky flapped to the limb of a tree, inserted his head beneath a wing, and slept also. Perhaps, in the last ten or fifteen years, he also had wanted a mate, but probably he had long ago given up hope—for, it seemed, there were no more crows left in the world. Anyway, Blacky was very old, perhaps twice as old as Tommy; he was merely content to live.

Tark and Vascar sent their spherical ship lightly plummeting above the green strip—it proved to be vegetation, just as they had supposed. Either one or the other kept constant watch of the ground below—they discovered nothing that might conceivably be classed as intelligent life. Insects they found, and decided that they worked entirely by instinct; small animals, rabbits, squirrels, rats, raccoons, otters, opossums, and large animals, deer, horses, sheep, cattle, pigs, dogs, they found to be just that—animals, and nothing more.

"Looks as if it was all killed off, Vascar," said Tark, "and not so long ago at that, judging by the fact that this forest must have grown entirely in the last few years."

Vascar agreed; she suggested they put the ship down for a few days and rest.

"It would be wonderful if we could find intelligent life after all," she said wistfully. "Think what a great triumph it would be if we were the ones to start the last members of that race on the upward trail again. Anyway," she added, "I think this atmosphere is dense enough for us to fly in."

He laughed—a trilling sound. "You've been looking for such an atmosphere for years. But I think you're right about this one. Put the ship down there, Vascar—looks like a good spot."

For five days Tommy followed the trail of the girl with a grim determination. He knew now that it was a woman; perhaps—indeed, very probably—the only one left alive. He had only the vaguest of ideas of why he wanted her— he thought it was for human companionship, that alone. At any rate, he felt that this terrible hunger in him—he could give it no other word—would be allayed when he caught up with her.

She was fleeing him, and staying just near enough to

him to make him continue the chase, and he knew that with a fierce exultation. And somehow her actions seemed right and proper. Twice he had seen her, once on the crest of a ridge, once as she swam a river. Both times she had easily outdistanced him. But by cross-hatching, he picked up her trail again—a bent twig or weed, a footprint, the skin of a dead rabbit.

Once, at night, he had the impression that she crept up close, and looked at him curiously, perhaps with the same great longing that he felt. He could not be sure. But he knew that very soon now she would be his—and perhaps she would be glad of it.

Once he heard a terrible moaning, high up in the air. He looked upward. Blacky uttered a surprised squawk. A large, spherical thing was darting overhead.

"I wonder what that is," Blacky squawked.

"I wonder what that is," said Tommy, feeling a faint fear. "There ain't nothin' like that in the yard."

He watched as the spaceship disappeared from sight. Then, with the unquestioning attitude of the savage, he dismissed the matter from his mind, and took up his tantalizing trail again.

"Better watch out, Tommy," the bird cawed.

"Better watch out, Tommy," Tommy muttered to himself. He only vaguely heard Blacky—Blacky always anticipated what Tommy was going to say, because he had known Tommy so long.

The river was wide, swirling, muddy, primeval in its surge of resistless strength. Tommy stood on the bank, and looked out over the waters—suddenly his breath soughed from his lungs.

"It's her!" he gasped. "It's her, Blacky! She's drownin'!"

No time to waste in thought—a figure truly struggled against the push of the treacherous waters, seemingly went under. Tommy dived cleanly, and Blacky spread his wings at the last instant and escaped a bath. He saw his master disappear beneath the swirling waters, saw him emerge, strike out with singularly powerful arms, slightly upstream, fighting every inch of the way. Blacky hovered over the waters, cawing frantically, and screaming.

"Tommy, I could spank you! I could spank you! I get so exasperated! You wait till your father comes home!"

A log was coming downstream. Tommy saw it coming, but knew he'd escape it. He struck out, paid no more attention to it. The log came down with a rush, and would have missed him had it not suddenly swung broadside on. It clipped the swimming man on the side of the head. Tommy went under, threshing feebly, barely conscious, his limbs like leaden bars. That seemed to go on for a very long time. He seemed to be breathing water. Then something grabbed hold of his long black hair—

When he awoke, he was lying on his back, and he was staring into her eyes. Something in Tommy's stomach fell out—perhaps the hunger was going. He came to his feet, staring at her, his eyes blazing. She stood only about twenty feet away from him. There was something pleasing about her, the slimness of her arms, the roundness of her hips, the strangeness of her body, her large, startled, timid eyes, the mass of ebon hair that fell below her hips. He started toward her. She gazed at him as if in a trance.

Blacky came flapping mournfully across the river. He

was making no sound, but the girl must have been frightened as he landed on Tommy's shoulder. She tensed, and was away like a rabbit. Tommy went after her in long, loping bounds, but his foot caught in a tangle of dead grass, and he plummeted head foremost to the ground.

The other vanished over a rise of ground.

He arose again, and knew no disappointment that he had again lost her. He knew now that it was only her timidity, the timidity of a wild creature, that made her flee him. He started off again, for now that he knew what the hunger was, it seemed worse than ever.

The air of this planet was deliciously breathable, and was the nearest thing to their own atmosphere that Tark and Vascar had encountered.

Vascar ruffled her brilliant plumage, and spread her wings, flapping them. Tark watched her, as she laughed at him in her own way, and then made a few short, running jumps and took off. She spiraled, called down to him.

"Come on up. The air's fine, Tark."

Tark considered. "All right," he conceded, "but wait until I get a couple of guns."

"I can't imagine why," Vascar called down; but nevertheless, as they rose higher and higher above the second growth forest, each had a belt strapped loosely around the neck, carrying a weapon similar to a pistol.

"I can't help but hope we run into some kind of intelligent life," said Vascar. "This is really a lovely planet. In time the volcanoes will die down, and vegetation will spread all over. It's a shame that the planet has to go to waste."

"We could stay and colonize it," Tark suggested rakishly.

"Oh, not I. I like Alcon too well for that, and the sooner we get back there, the better—Look! Tark! Down there!"

Tark looked, caught sight of a medium large animal moving through the underbrush. He dropped a little lower. And then rose again.

"It's nothing," he said. "An animal, somewhat larger than the majority we've seen, probably the last of its kind. From the looks of it, I'd say it wasn't particularly pleasant on the eyes. Its skin shows—Oh, now I see what you mean, Vascar!"

This time he was really interested as he dropped lower, and a strange excitement throbbed through his veins. Could it be that they were going to discover intelligent life after all—perhaps the last of its kind?

It was indeed an exciting sight the two bird-creatures from another planet saw. They flapped slowly above and a number of yards behind the unsuspecting upright beast, that moved swiftly through the forest, a black creature not unlike themselves in general structure riding its shoulder.

"It must mean intelligence!" Vascar whispered excitedly, her brilliant red eyes glowing with interest. "One of the first requisites of intelligent creatures it to put animals lower in the scale of evolution to work as beasts of burden and transportation."

"Wait awhile," cautioned Tark, "before you make any irrational conclusions. After all, there are creatures of different species which live together in friendship. Perhaps the creature which looks so much like us keeps the other's skin and hair free of vermin. And perhaps the other way around, too."

"I don't think so," insisted his mate. "Tark, the bird-creature is riding the shoulder of the beast. Perhaps that means its race is so old, and has used this means of transportation so long, that its wings have atrophied. That would almost certainly mean intelligence. It's talking now—you can hear it. It's probably telling its beast to stop—there, it has stopped!"

"Its voice is not so melodious," said Tark dryly.

She looked at him reprovingly; the tips of their flapping wings were almost touching.

"That isn't like you, Tark. You know very well that one of our rules is not to place intelligence on creatures who seem like ourselves, and neglect others while we do so. Its harsh voice proves nothing—to one of its race, if there are any left, its voice may be pleasing in the extreme. At any rate, it ordered the large beast of burden to stop—you saw that."

"Well, perhaps," conceded Tark.

They continued to wing their slow way after the perplexing duo, following slightly behind, skimming the tops of trees. They saw the white beast stop, and place its paws on its hips. Vascar, listening very closely, because she was anxious to gain proof of her contention, heard the bird-creature say,

"Now what, Blacky?" and also the featherless beast repeat the same words: "Now what, Blacky?"

"There's your proof," said Vascar excitedly. "Evidently the white beast is highly imitative. Did you hear it repeat what its master said?"

Tark said uneasily, "I wouldn't jump to conclusions, just from a hasty survey like this. I admit that, so far, all the proof points to the bird. It seems truly intelligent; or at least more intelligent than the other. But you must bear in mind that we are naturally prejudiced in favor of the bird—it may not be intelligent at all. As I said, they may merely be friends in the sense that animals of different species are friends."

Vascar made a scornful sound.

"Well, let's get goin', Blacky," she heard the bird say; and heard the white, upright beast repeat the strange, alien words. The white beast started off again, traveling very stealthily, making not the least amount of noise. Again Vascar called this quality to the attention of her skeptical mate—such stealth was the mark of the animal, certainly not of the intelligent creature.

"We should be certain of it now," she insisted. "I think we ought to get in touch with the bird. Remember, Tark, that our primary purpose on this expedition is to give what help we can to the intelligent races of the planets we visit. What creature could be more in need of help than the bird-creature down there? It is evidently the last of its kind. At least, we could make the effort of saving it from a life of sheer boredom; it would probably leap at the chance to hold converse with intelligent creatures. Certainly it gets no pleasure from the company of dumb beasts."

But Tark shook his handsome, red-plumed head worriedly.

"I would prefer," he said uneasily, "first to investigate the creature you are so sure is a beast of burden. There is a chance—though, I admit, a farfetched one—that it is the intelligent creature, and not the other."

But Vascar did not hear him. All her feminine instincts had gone out in pity to the seemingly intelligent bird that rode Tommy's broad shoulder. And so intent were she and Tark on the duo, that they did not see, less than a hundred yards ahead, that another creature, smaller in form, more graceful, but indubitably the same species as the white-skinner, unfeathered beast, was slinking softly through the underbrush, now and anon casting indecisive glances behind her toward him who pursued her. He was out of sight, but she could hear—

Tommy slunk ahead, his breath coming fast; for the trail was very strong, and his keen ears picked up the sounds of footsteps ahead. The chase was surely over—his terrible hunger about to end! He felt wildly exhilarated. Instincts were telling him much that his experience could not. He and this girl were the last of mankind. Something told him that now mankind could rise again—yet he did not know why. He slunk ahead, Blacky on his shoulder, all unaware of the two brilliantly colored denizens of another planet who followed above and behind him. But Blacky was not so easy of mind. His neck feathers were standing erect. Nervousness made him raise his wings up from his body—perhaps he heard the soft swish of large-winged creatures, beating the air behind, and though all birds of prey had been dead these last fifteen years, the old fear rose up.

Tommy glued himself to a tree, on the edge of a

clearing. His breath escaped from his lungs as he caught a glimpse of a white, unclothed figure. It was she! She was looking back at him. She was tired of running. She was ready, glad to give up. Tommy experienced a dizzy elation. He stepped forth into the clearing, and slowly, very slowly, holding her large, dark eyes with his, started toward her. The slightest swift motion, the slightest untoward sound, and she would be gone. Her whole body was poised on the balls of her feet. She was not at all sure whether she should be afraid of him or not.

Behind him, the two feathered creatures from another planet settled slowly into a tree, and watched. Blacky certainly did not hear them come to rest—what he must have noticed was that the beat of wings, nagging at the back of his mind, had disappeared. It was enough.

"No noise, Blacky!" the bird screamed affrightedly, and flung himself into the air and forward, a bundle of ebon feathers with tattered wings outspread, as it darted across the clearing. For the third time, it was Blacky who scared her, for again she was gone, and had lost herself to sight even before Tommy could move.

"Come back!" Tommy shouted ragingly. "I ain't gonna hurt you!" He ran after her full speed, tears streaming down his face, tears of rage and heartbreak at the same time. But already he knew it was useless! He stopped suddenly, on the edge of the clearing, and sobbing to himself, caught sight of Blacky, high above the ground, cawing piercingly, warningly. Tommy stooped and picked up a handful of pebbles. With deadly, murderous intent he threw them at the bird. It soared and swooped in the air—twice it was hit glancingly.

"It's all your fault, Blacky!" Tommy raged. He picked up a rock the size of his fist. He started to throw it, but did not. A tiny, sharp sound bit through the air. Tommy pitched forward. He did not make the slightest twitching motion to show that he had bridged the gap between life and death. He did not know that Blacky swooped down and landed on his chest; and then flung himself upward, crying, "Oh, Tommy, I could spank you!" He did not see the girl come into the clearing and stoop over him; and did not see the tears that began to gush from her eyes, or hear the sobs that racked her body. But Tark saw.

Tark wrested the weapon from Vascar with a trill of rage.

"Why did you do that?" he cried. He threw the weapon from him as far as it would go. "You've done a terrible thing, Vascar!"

Vascar looked at him in amazement. "It was only a beast, Tark," she protested. "It was trying to kill its master! Surely, you saw it. It was trying to kill the intelligent bird-creature, the last of its kind on the planet."

But Tark pointed with horror at the two unfeathered beasts, one bent over the body of the other. "But they were mates! You have killed their species! The female is grieving for its mate, Vascar. You have done a terrible thing!"

But Vascar shook her head crossly. "I'm sorry I did it then," she said acidly. "I suppose it was perfectly in keeping with our aim on this expedition to let the dumb beast kill its master! That isn't like you at all, Tark! Come, let us see if the intelligent creature will not make friends with us."

And she flapped away toward the cawing crow. When Blacky saw Vascar coming toward him, he wheeled and darted away.

Tark took one last look at the female bending over the male. He saw her raise her head, and saw the tears in her eyes, and heard the sobs that shook her. Then, in a rising, inchoate series of bewildering emotions, he turned his eyes away, and hurriedly flapped after Vascar. And all that day they pursued Blacky. They circled him, they cornered him; and Vascar tried to speak to him in friendly tones, all to no avail. It only cawed, and darted away, and spoke volumes of disappointingly incomprehensible words.

When dark came, Vascar alighted in a tree beside the strangely quiet Tark.

"I suppose it's no use," she said sadly. "Either it is terribly afraid of us, or it is not as intelligent as we supposed it was, or else it has become mentally deranged in these last years of loneliness. I guess we might as well leave now, Tark; let the poor creature have its planet to itself. Shall we stop by and see if we can help the female beast whose mate we shot?"

Tark slowly looked at her, his red eyes luminous in the gathering dusk. "No," he said briefly. "Let us go, Vascar."

The spaceship of the creatures from Alcon left the dead planet Earth. It darted out into space. Tark sat at the controls. The ship went faster and faster. And still faster. Fled at ever-increasing speed beyond the Solar System and into the wastes of interstellar space. And still farther, until the star that gave heat to Earth was not even visible.

Yet even this terrible velocity was not enough for Tark. Vascar looked at him strangely.

"We're not in that much of a hurry to get home, are we, Tark?"

"No," Tark said in a low, terrible voice; but still he urged the ship to greater and greater speed, though he knew it was useless. He could run away from the thing that had happened on the planet Earth; but he could never, never outrun his mind, though he passionately wished he could.

MEN AGAINST THE STARS

by Manly Wade Wellman

Though nowadays, Manly Wade Wellman is best known for his fantasy, in the pulp era of the Thirties and Forties he was a prolific producer of science fiction adventure yarns, and "Men Against the Stars" is one of the best of his sf stories. Unusually for the time, in which paper spaceships crewed by fearless heroes, or even just one such specimen, roared off into the unknown with nary a malfunction, not even needing a spare fuse or two, this story paints the conquest of space as taking a terrible human toll when a technical problem in the void strikes without warning, all hands lost. Yet, the ships keep flying out, showing courage and determination that I wish I could believe are still present in the modern day world.

IN SHIP NUMBER FIFTY-ONE, halfway from Moon to Mars, four stubbled faces turned to a common, grinning regard as the pounding roar of the rockets died away at last. The skipper, the rocketman, the navigator, the spacehand.

"So far so good," said the skipper grimly. "We've reached speed. But the fuel may decide to go any minute. And that'll be—that."

Even as he spoke, the fuel—frightful unstable solution of atomic hydrogen—went. Four men—the flimsy metal shell—the hopes, determination and courage that sought to conquer the stars—all were gone. For an instant, a warm, ruby glow, sprinkled with stars of incandescent metal, blossomed in space. The men did not mind. They did not know.

Tallentyre watched Major DeWitt step through the door. DeWitt closed the door. Immediately, he slumped back against it, his body drained of some stiffening thing that had held him up. But for support of the doorframe, he would have fallen.

"They won't go," DeWitt said hoarsely.

Tallentyre looked at him with a wooden, unmoving face. If he moved his face, if he moved himself in the slightest, he felt he would shatter to dust, like a scratched Prince Rupert's Drop. Gray, bloodshot eyes in his lean, high-boned face watched his superior motionlessly. The leathery skin of his face did not move.

"They won't go." DeWitt looked up at him, his blotched face working. Tallentyre noticed it was hideous. The unshielded sunlight of space here on Luna tanned human skin black in irregular spots. The untanned spots on DeWitt's face were white as paper and they wiggled.

Tallentyre sighed sharply, and moved. His gray eyes were cold as fractured steel as he watched DeWitt.

"They won't go—and I won't send them!" DeWitt straightened against the doorframe and glared at Tallentyre, daring him to challenge the statement. "I can't—I won't let them!" His voice rose to a hoarse, grating scream.

Major John Tallentyre faced him stonily. Outside lay the rock-and-pumice-paved Luna Spaceport, black and silver under shifting sunlight and shadow. Above, the star-spattered jet of the Eternal Night. The red eye of Mars was low in the east. Tallentyre looked at it for a moment, quietly and thoughtfully. He was cold and icy as the spaceways out there. He, too, was burned to the patchy blackness of space-sun exposure. His gray eyes were startlingly light in that sun-scorched face.

"Keep your voice down, DeWitt. Those mutineers will hear you. You won't build up their morale by shouting that yours is shot. Straighten up."

DeWitt shook his head groggily. Tallentyre was his junior here. For a moment, the slap of Tallentyre's words shot an anger into him that half-roused him, as had been intended. But it faded.

"I," he grated, "don't care anymore. I *want* them to hear me. I won't send—I won't *let*—any more human beings go into *that*." His arm gestured weakly toward the starred blackness beyond, his face working. "Fifty-One's gone. You just saw it blow. Those—mutineers—just saw it blow. The men in Fifty-One though—they didn't see it.

"Sixty ships, Tallentyre. Sixty of 'em—and two

hundred and forty-two men started from Earth. Fifty-six ships, and two hundred and twenty-two men reached Luna Port. Eighteen men lost on that little hop. Four ships blew their tubes—and that bloody six-man experiment first of all.

"But fifty-six ships landed, and we warped 'em off to Mars. And how many of these fifty-six got through?" His grating scream roared in the cubbyhole office and pounded through its flimsy metal door. Tallentyre's eyes moved toward the door.

DeWitt's roar dropped to a whisper as the man leaned abruptly forward, close to Tallentyre's moveless, sun-blackened face. "*Four.* Four got to Mars, my friend. The rest were pretty red firecrackers in space."

He straightened slowly from the table, hunching his baggy, greasy uniform back over his shoulders. "I'm in command of this altar of human sacrifices they call Luna Port. And there aren't going to *be* any more sacrifices!"

Tallentyre's eyes stared into his steadily. "You knew men were going to die when you swore to take this duty, DeWitt," Tallentyre said steadily. "And you swore to uphold your trust. Keep your voice down, please. We'll reason with those mutineers."

DeWitt shook his head. His eyes were blazing now with a new determination; the gray-and-black mottling of his face had given way to red-and-black, as willess despair gave way to a different fanaticism. "No!" he roared. "We'll send 'em—but we'll send 'em back to Earth, where men belong. Duty? Duty! I'm not, and will not be, high priest of human sacrifice. *Those ships don't go.*

"And the spineless slugs back on Earth that tell 'em to

do things that can't be done can come and try it if they want. I'm going to tell those men right now . . ."

DeWitt swung round and started toward the thin metal door with fanatic stretch of stride. Tallentyre leaped to his feet and gripped DeWitt's arm.

"Wait," said Tallentyre.

"Wait for what?" DeWitt sneered, and threw back his head to laugh harshly.

For an instant, Tallentyre watched him. Then his fist moved in an invisible blur. DeWitt slumped easily, tiredly, to the floor under Luna's light pull.

Tallentyre stood for an instant above his fallen superior, the same wooden, moveless set to his lean, leathery face. Then abruptly, he trembled, and fell awkwardly beside the fallen man to listen for an instant to his strongly beating heart.

Shuddering, he rose to his feet and looked desperately about the room. A relaxation, from without and within, flooded over him. His eyelids fluttered; he had to bite his lip to keep it from twitching. He slumped back into the desk chair and let his arms hang limply down beside him, staring at the fallen man.

Finally, he spoke, very softly, to himself. His eyes were fixed out beyond the double-glass window of the tiny office. Beyond, where the space-black-and-silver of the spaceport blended with the black of space and the silver of stars. Mars, a ruby on jet velvet, lay over the horizon— the cruel, jagged horizon of Luna. "Thanks, DeWitt. You—you made me hold together.

"Altar of human sacrifice? So was Nevada Port once. But they reached the Moon. Before that—for centuries before that—the air was the altar of sacrifice. But those men that died in the air weren't seeking air. They sought the stars beyond. They didn't die on the way to the Moon. They died on the way to the stars. They weren't dying now to reach Mars; again they're seeking the stars beyond. Someone's always had to—"

He looked up abruptly. The door on the other side of the office creaked softly. The frightened young face of Noel Crispin, the blond girl who kept the office files, looked in. Her eyes changed as she looked at Tallentyre and then at DeWitt.

"Take care of Major DeWitt," ordered Tallentyre. He slipped something from the desk drawer into his pocket and rose. "I've got to persuade the boys in the vestibule." He crossed the office in three long strides. His steadiness was back entirely when he turned the knob; he stepped into the outer room with an air, almost, of insouciance.

Four men dressed in the rubberized canvas of spacehands stood together in the middle of the vestibule floor. No doubt they had heard most, if not all, of what had passed in the office. Tallentyre looked at them. Two were huge and burly, tough, hard-shelled men who'd try anything once. Two were of a different breed; two who would do anything, at any risk, for some things, things in which they believed. The biggest, the toughest, wore a golden comet. The skipper.

He wasn't afraid now. He'd simply determined the odds were bad, and he wasn't having any. The other burly figure looked up to him; what the skipper said was right with him.

The two leaner, wiry men were white-faced. Nerve-shock release was their trouble. Like plane-pilots who'd lived through a crash, they were afraid of their fire-ships. The psychology of the things preyed on them. Nobody had ever been injured in a rocket accident. Nobody, ever. They landed sound—or simply weren't.

They'd landed. They couldn't, now, face the thing again. But, like the plane-pilot who'd survived a crash, once started again they'd be all right.

"In six minutes," said Tallentyre, "Sixty-One takes off to Mars."

"We're not going," said the skipper. "We told DeWitt that."

"You volunteered," reminded Tallentyre.

"We didn't know what we were tackling. Only ten ships had tried then, and two had gotten through. Now we do know. The trip from Earth to this hole—not three hundred thousand miles—was enough. It wasn't carelessness that snapped those other ships. We know. It was rotten tubes and rotten fuel. I drove a nitro-wagon in the oil country and felt safe. But not on this buggy. Nitro's baby's milk to this stuff. Atomic hydrogen!

"Hu-uh. We don't go." He looked at Tallentyre coldly. He meant what he said, and meant to stick with it.

"I suppose there's no use," said Tallentyre woodenly, "to say anything about guts and keeping a promise and how much you men mean to this thing. If you don't go, you know, others won't."

"Guff," grunted the skipper. "It isn't any use."

"I call this mutiny," Tallentyre informed him.

"Call it whatever you damn well like," growled the

skipper. He looked down at the slighter figure of the Spaceport official challengingly. "We don't blast. And there's no sense chucking your rank around, either. There's four of us. And just what in hell do you call it when you klunk out your chief, eh?"

Tallentyre's right hand rested easily in the pocket of his tunic. The cold, gray eyes watched the big spaceman steadily. "You think you could get away with violence?"

The big man took a step forward with a hamlike fist clenched before him. "Think, brother? Hu-uh. I *know* I can," he said softly. "You tried it yourself inside there." Without turning his head, he spoke to the men behind him. "Come on, boys. Grab this guy. And one of you tail for the ship and that gun."

Without relaxing his moveless, wooden face, Tallentyre drew his hand from his tunic pocket. Space volunteers have to have a queer, reckless courage. With a bull roar, the giant captain dove forward with outstretched hands, his face twisted with sudden hate.

Tallentyre shot him between the eyes. The big body fell with exaggerated slowness under Lunar pull.

The roar of the heavy weapon drowned the sudden, soft cries of the other three. Tallentyre eyed them coldly, his face unchanged. The other burly man looked confused and bewildered, his eyes fixed muddledly on the fallen leader. He looked around toward the lean, white-faced youth with red hair and startling blue eyes. The other spacehand was looking at him, too, for encouragement and decision. He swallowed raggedly.

A new, terrific tension had built up. It reduplicated, somehow, the tension that had made bearable that trip from Earth. The redhead shrugged, and a wry smile twisted his lips. "I guess I'll go, sir."

Tallentyre's wooden face relaxed. "Good. She's your ship then. You're the skipper. Your name? Joe? All right, you go in five minutes. This man was your rocket expert, I think? You won't need him, or a replacement. You have a navigator, and a couple of hands. Go to it."

Five minutes later, Tallentyre watched Joe seat himself in the pressure chair in Number Sixty-One's central cabin. He waved once, with a white-faced grin that made it seem he liked but feared this command of his. Then the metal shutters came up over the rocketship's tough windows. A smooth, metal shape screamed soundless fire into the vacuum that wrapped Luna. The rushing, ruddy gas-streams scoured the pumice of the spaceport field. Number Sixty-One shot out toward Mars.

Tallentyre sat motionless in his office, his face somehow disconnected from his mind, betraying no hint of what went on behind it. Number Sixty-One. It might get there. Four had, already.

But if it didn't? None of the great of rocketry had gotten where they had hoped to land. That other Joe, that great Joseph—Joseph Moessner. He'd sought the rocket fuel that would take him above the stratosphere. He'd recognized the inadequacy of hydrogen-oxygen. It was too heavy. The hydrogen was light enough as fuel. But for every two pounds of hydrogen, sixteen pounds of oxygen had to be used. If only hydrogen would burn alone . . .

It would; Moessner had known that, and he'd done it. Hydrogen gas is H_2—two atoms combined. Monatomic hydrogen—atomic hydrogen, so-called—would burn with itself to produce diatomic hydrogen gas, and enormous heat.

Old Moessner had been right, and he'd seen the way; stabilize the monatomic form in some solvent. He'd even found the solvent. But he never found the top of the stratosphere. For the solvent didn't stabilize the frightful stuff sufficiently. He and his two assistants—when they'd made nearly twenty pounds of the saturated fuel— became particles almost as fine as hydrogen atoms themselves.

No rocketman had ever reached the goal he sought, himself. But others took hold where Moessner so decisively left off. Less disastrous experiments showed that the combustible, oil-like solvent Moessner had used could be modified just a trifle, and made more stable. The saturated stuff generated power eleven times greater, weight for weight, than did the oxy-hydrogen fuel. They had *moessnerol*. The rest was trial and error—and death.

The first passenger-carrying rocketship to pass the stratosphere exploded fifty miles above Earth's surface. The trouble, investigation showed, was in the metal of the tubes. In 1961, Moessner's younger brother set out for the Moon. He didn't reach his goal, but astronomers saw the red flash of his explosion a scant one hundred miles from the Lunar peaks. None of the great of rocketry ever quite got there.

Others, in better craft, survived later landings. At first they didn't come back, though. Then the World League, having settled decisively the question of international peace and trade, took interest in rocketry.

Money, now, and Moontrips became regular and generally successful. The new Rocket Service prepared to accept the challenge that must be answered—Mars. The Moon, with one-sixth Earth's surface gravity and less than one-eightieth Earth's mass, was obviously the stepping stone and refueling station for Mars.

In 1996, Luna Spaceport was constructed. In 1997, Major DeWitt was placed in charge—and Tallentyre had been second then.

Twenty-eight ships that year. All that were left of the thirty that set out from Earth to Moon. Two landed on Mars. Horror crept down the tubes of the telescopes that watched from the airless Moon. Red firecrackers in space, two—three—five had gone. Then one landed. Then another! Then—but it missed. The rockets blasted in a long, circling trail as the radio signals faded away. The control mechanism was gone. Frantic voices that became thin and died.

Firecrackers and dancing mice with long red tails. And no sense of direction.

It was 1998 now. There were to be thirty-five ships this year. Two ships had landed of the first thirty. DeWitt had stood that, silent and moody as ship after ship flashed bright red and vanished or danced its brief, whirling waltz of death. There were fewer dancers now; in that year they'd done a lot with control mechanism. In the last twelve ships, there'd been no wanderers. But they cracked for some reason no man could say. Tubes or fuel? Only the wreckage might have told, and that . . .

That was shining droplets spattered through space.

The rebellion this day had finished DeWitt. It had

nearly finished Tallentyre; only DeWitt's failure had forced him to defense. Tallentyre took over.

He made entries on the log as the dwindling ruby of Number Sixty-One vanished outward in space.

"What a cinch to run that Luna Port!"

Five days out in space, Mars bound, the crew of Number Fifty-Nine was exercising the age-old privilege of able workmen to belittle superior officers.

"DeWitt! Tallentyre!" growled the engineer. "Who are they but a couple of straw-stuffed uniforms in a soft job they got by a hefty pull? They sit back there with their feet on desks, while we're gunnin' out here, out where the danger and the work is." He spat into the waste container.

"Oh, I don't know," temporized a spacehand with an ambition to be an executive. "They've probably got worries of their own."

"Worries of their own?" echoed the engineer. "On that button-pusher's work? Say, if either of them ever worried a day of his life, I hope this ship blows apart right now . . ."

Number Fifty-Nine was rose-red flame and sparklets of incandescent metal in that instant.

Number Fifty-Nine was one of Tallentyre's worries.

Consciousness returned slowly to Major DeWitt after Tallentyre's blow. He found himself dragged into the record room, and Noel Crispin ministering to him, as Tallentyre had ordered. He sat up, pondered blackly for several minutes, then went into the office. Without addressing his colleague, he sat before the radio, tuned in

Earth, and told the secretary of the Rocket Service Board that he was resigning, to take effect immediately. After some time there came back a tentative acceptance, with the additional information that a ship would arrive to carry him away. In the same message, Tallentyre was ordered to take command at Luna Port.

DeWitt went to his quarters and locked himself in.

Tallentyre called a pair of men from the machine shop, consigned the body of the dead rocket-skipper to them, with directions that it go back to Earth when the ship arrived for DeWitt. Returning to the administration office, he sat down before the screen that recorded telescopic views. After some correction of angles and focus, he picked up a clear rectangle of black, starry sky. In the center hung a cartridge-shaped hull—the last ship to leave the port.

Small in the sky beyond, a lesser capsule of metal was visible.

"A ship heading back?" muttered Tallentyre to himself. "More mutiny?"

Wearily, he decided to deal with the case as it matured. His present attention must be concentrated on the craft so recently launched.

Leaning back in his chair, he fumbled the radio into operation. "Hello, hello," he said. "Ship ahoy, Sixty-One!"

"Hello, sir," same back a voice he knew—Joe, whom he had appointed captain.

"What goes on, Joe?"

"All well, sir. I'll drop you a picture postcard from Mars."

"See if there are gondolas on the canals."

Laughter from the radio—healthy laughter. "This isn't as bad as I thought it'd be, sir." Then, in sudden alarm, "Hey! Something's going bad! Looks like . . ."

The view on the screen suddenly flashed into white fire, blinding the observer. At the same instant something roared in the radio, then broke off. Silence, while Tallentyre clasped his hands to his tortured eyes. The flare ebbed from them, and his vision returned. The screen showed only sky and stars. The ship was gone.

"Boom!" said Noel Crispin behind him. "Just like the Fourth of July." Her voice grew harsh, mocking. "Are you quite satisfied, Major Tallentyre?"

He turned around and got to his feet. For months he and the girl had been "Nollie" and "Talley" to each other. But that had changed now. Her set face matched the fierce formality of her greeting.

"Do you feel that you've served your gods, whatever they are?" she demanded. "Will that last burnt offering be sweet in their nostrils?"

Tallentyre gazed at her dumbfounded. "What's all this?" he asked.

She laughed, bitterly and humorlessly. "I suppose that you couldn't help knocking Major DeWitt down—in fact, it brought him to his senses and showed him that he must clear out. As for shooting that captain, I saw through the open door all that led up to it. He had threatened you, and shooting's a clean death, anyway. He can sleep in a grave, back home on Earth. But those other three fellows!"

She lashed Tallentyre with her contemptuous gaze. He cleared his throat uncomfortably. On a desk at hand lay a pack of well-thumbed playing cards. He scowled at them as though they were a new and perplexing mechanism. Automatically, he went to the desk, seated himself at it, and picked up the cards. Still automatically, he began to lay them out for a game of patience.

"Is all this death necessary?" asked Noel Crispin, her voice trembling as if with passionate hatred of him. "Isn't Earth big enough for humanity? Isn't it?"

Tallentyre shook his head without looking up from the cards. "No," he replied, "it isn't. Earth never was big enough for humanity, not since the first of our ancestors lifted his eyes to heaven. You understood that once, Nollie."

"Don't call me pet names, if you please, Major Tallentyre."

"If you didn't understand," he went on, "why did you volunteer for this service?"

"Because I loved you, that's why."

Tallentyre seemed ready to fall backward, chair and all. His lips moved soundlessly, his face grew pale. "But I—I never dreamed—"

"Wait a moment. Please don't misunderstand me. I don't love you anymore, and that's why I can talk about it as if it had happened to somebody else. But once—oh, I worshipped you as a hero. I thought you were brilliant, brave. I thought you were handsome, in that neat, tight uniform. I signed up so as to be near you. But now!"

Tallentyre stared at the cards in his hand. "I may as well remind you," he said, "that every man in every ship is a volunteer. Nobody is obliged to go."

"You got the answer to that from the captain in the vestibule, just before you shot him. Men don't realize what they're in for when they offer to make the trip. How many do you think would volunteer a second time?" Again she laughed. "If there ever is a second time for any of them, if a single man survives!" She leveled a finger at him, as though it were the muzzle of a gun. "If you're so full of fervor for this murderous business, why don't you volunteer to go to Mars yourself?"

"I've done so, half a dozen times." The statement surprised Noel, and she let him continue. "The Board says that I'm needed here, in an administrative position. But when I leave here, it won't be for home." He glanced at the window, whence Mars was discernible. "My home will be out there."

She shot him one final glare of almost white heat, whirled around and fled from the room. Tallentyre resumed his game of patience. After a few moments, a slight, stooped figure came through the door. It was Ernie, a white-haired old mechanic.

"Something wrong with the radio?" he inquired gently.
"Seems that way. Let me have a look. I thought I heard it blow out."

"It was tuned in on a ship that exploded," Tallentyre informed him.

The slender old man shook his head sadly. "Too bad. Too bad." He poked into the radio mechanism. "Oh, this isn't serious. I'll have everything fixed in a jiffy."

"Everything?" echoed Tallentyre.

Spacehand O'Hara, who should have been watching the jet-gauges of Number Forty-Two scribbled final words on the scrap of grubby paper he held on his knee. Then he surveyed his creation.

Lost beyond power to follow or seek,
Slain for their gallant defi—
Their spirits were strong but their pinions were weak,
The birds that were lost in the sky.

Why should the eyes of a man turn aloft?
The voices of warning chant loudly and oft,
The fireside is cozy, the armchair is soft,
Yet danger spells dare to the bold.
To search after doom as a knight for the Grail,
With death as a crewmate, abhorrent and pale,
To perish as small, glowing sparks on the trail—
Wee stars in the black, empty cold—

Out of dead darkness and into clear light,
Marking a pathway on high,
See how they soar on a happier flight,
The birds that were lost in the sky.

O'Hara put his pencil to the second line and substituted "steadfast" for "gallant."

"It tells something," he assured himself. "Perhaps some editor would—"

His eyes came by chance to the jet-gauge. He had barely time to cry out at what he saw, before the explosion tore him and his poem and all the ship into small, glowing sparks on the trail.

Something like twenty hours after DeWitt's resignation by radio, a short-shot rocket came from

Earth, made a fairly good landing at Luna Port, and bore away the somber DeWitt, as well as the corpse of the captain. Twenty hours and a few minutes passed before a second craft dropped down on the field, aided by fall-breaking jets of gas directed against its bottom. From it emerged two sturdy men in drab, who came at once to the office.

"Major Tallentyre?" said the oldest of the pair, a tallish man whose harsh eyes were not happy with what he was about to do. "I'm Inspector Barnes and this is Constable Dunlap. We've got a warrant for you."

"Warrant?" Tallentyre rose from his chair. "What kind of a warrant?"

The harsh-eyed Baynes had opened his tunic and was drawing out a paper. "We're from the World League Police. The warrant's charging you with the murder of"—he broke off to read—"of Captain Sturgis Riser, whom you killed on the . . ."

"But I had to," protested Tallentyre. "He was mutinous and threatening. I acted according to my duty, and in self-defense." He turned toward the door of the record room. "Miss Crispin!"

Noel appeared. Her level eyes regarded the two officers as though she had been expecting them.

"You saw the shooting," said Tallentyre. "Tell these men what happened."

She still kept her eyes upon Baynes and Dunlap, and she spoke quietly, without expression, "Major Tallentyre shot and killed him."

"He's admitted that," said Baynes. "What were the circumstances?"

Noel Crispin shook her blond head.

"Nollie!" cried Tallentyre. "You aren't telling the whole truth. You saw him defy and threaten me." He broke off, for at last she looked at him, in hard and merciless triumph.

Constable Dunlap took a step forward, as though to lay hands on Tallentyre. But the port commander faced him so fiercely as to freeze him to the metal floor.

"Hold on," snapped Tallentyre. "You haven't authority, here on the Moon. I'll resist arrest."

"Right, Major!" piped a clear old voice from the direction of the hall. White-haired Ernie, pausing on some errand, had stepped into the office. Both policemen stared truculently at him.

"Who's this?" grumbled Inspector Baynes to Noel.

"He's Ernie. Rocket mechanic, second class. What's your last name, Ernie?"

"Moessner," said the old fellow. "Major Tallentyre, stand your ground. You can't let them take you—not when you're needed here so badly."

Noel was looking at Ernie with widened eyes. "You're—you say your name's Moessner?"

"That's right."

Tallentyre and the officers were also watching the aged mechanic. "Hm-m-m," said Baynes, "that's the name of the guy who invented *moessnerol.*"

"He was my father."

The silence that fell was as effective as though it had come at the high point of a stage drama. Ernie Moessner, who had brought about that silence, broke it again.

"I'm the last Moessner, folks. I'm getting old—so old

that I was supposed to retire—but I hope I can die with my boots on like the rest of my family."

His old eyes met Noel's, and they glowed as palely as the heart of a rocket-blast. He laughed shortly. "You're breaking down under the bloodshed, aren't you, lady? How'd you feel if these men who kept dying were your own flesh and blood? Answer me that."

Her lips trembled open. "I never knew—"

"But I did!" cried the mechanic, tossing back the white locks from his burning eyes. "I know how they died, and why. Listen!"

Everyone was listening.

"I'm seventy-six years old. My first memory was when my dad held me up on his shoulder, so that I could see a parade. The air was all snowy with paper confetti, and sitting on the folded-back top of the mayor's car was a tall young fellow without a hat. That was Charles Lindbergh, in 1927, and my dad said, 'This is only the beginning, son.'

"You all know how he studied atomic hydrogen for a fuel, and how he was killed by it when he perfected it. His kid brother, my uncle, died flying the first rocket to the Moon. I was in the second, the successful flight—though why I was spared when better men were taken, I don't know."

Baynes and Dunlap were gazing, rapt and abashed. Noel again attempted to speak. "But Ernie, others are dying and—"

"I'm coming to that. Remember when Major Tallentyre here killed this mutinous captain, and made over the command to a chap named Joe? Like me, he got along without folks worrying about his last name. Well, it was the same as mine. Moessner."

"Your son!" cried Noel.

"My son. My only son. He almost backed out, I guess. But he went, and I'm glad he went. The old prophet was wrong—a living dog isn't better than a dead lion. I'm glad, too, that I sneaked out of retirement to do plain greasy labor here. And one thing more; everything else can crack, but the rockets will keep going to Mars if Major Tallentyre and I are the only ones to shove them along!"

Noel spun around. "Talley," she began, "I want to say something that I didn't think I—"

But Tallentyre was gone.

In the midst of the old man's speech he had backed out into the vestibule and turned down the hallway to an airlock. There hung space-armor, into which he fairly plunged, making its metal-mounted fabric airtight with a single tug of the seal-zipper. On went metal-shod sandals, the heavy girdle that supported oxygen tank and breathing apparatus, and the helmet, a transparent globe clouded against the pitiless sunrays of space.

Up the hall rose a clamor of voices, a fall of excited feet. Tallentyre was in the airlock, through it, clanging across the metal face of the landing field. He meant to flee, but only for a while. Perhaps the officers would follow. Then he could slip back into the unguarded port building, organize his defense. He would make the Rocket Service Board listen to him over the radio, exonerate him. Meanwhile, which way lay sanctuary?

Deeper and deeper into the blackness walked

Tallentyre, half-groping, half-trusting to his memories of many journeys along the trail to the crag.

Funny to feel so heavy on the Moon, where gravity is only one-sixth that of Earth. Surely it wasn't because of Noel—he, Tallentyre, had never thought of her as a lover until she had admitted her own secret. Now she had turned into an enemy, one who would keep silent when a single truthful word would clear him of the murder charge. Better put her out of mind.

Lights danced in the gloom behind him—those who hunted him. He made some degree of speed, gained the foot of the rock. Three thousand feet upward it soared, but he, even in armor, would weigh less than forty pounds against Moon's feathery pull. Up the hewn trail he scrambled, scarcely pausing for breath until he gained the topmost shelf. There he felt safe in turning on his head-lamp. Far below he saw the landing field, its lights undiluted and unrefracted. It was a gold coin on tarry blackness. He turned away and entered the observatory building.

His glow-lamp revealed the inside of the dome—a metal-lined compartment, pierced above with a starry slit into which sloped the tube of the telescope like a gun at an embrasure. At its lower end the sensitized screen—even on the Moon, this new device had replaced the old reflection mirror—displayed a segment of the heavens. A blob of light showed in the center. Mars, of course. Tallentyre switched off his lamp again, in order to see more clearly.

The image was not of Mars. That egg-shape could be but one thing: a spaceship. To judge by the direction of the rocket-blasts, it was heading Moonward. The same craft, Tallentyre made no doubt, that he had observed earlier as doubled about and returning along its track. Now it was very close indeed. He judged that it would make port within an hour—within minutes, perhaps—

A new glow was creeping into the observatory.

Spinning on his metal-shod heel, Tallentyre stared. A human silhouette paused on the threshold, a figure made bulky and mysterious by space-overall and helmet.

This meant capture. The newcomer bore a gun in a holster at one side, and he, Tallentyre, was unarmed. But the gauntleted right hand did not reach for the weapon. Instead it beckoned to Tallentyre, then pointed outward and downward.

"Go back to the port," said the gesture.

Tallentyre lifted his own arms in token of surrender, but his heart was far from concurring. He walked across the floor, made to push past the other and step outside. Then he spun and sprang. His two hands clutched like lightning. His right caught and imprisoned his discoverer's right wrist. His left found and captured the automatic pistol. A moment later he pressed the muzzle into the midst of the stranger's inflated jumper. Tallentyre's helmet-front grated against the glass that covered the other's face. He could see dimly—features that he recognized.

Noel Crispin.

Plainly, she expected him to shoot. He grinned scornfully, and tossed the gun away. It sailed out into darkness, over the hidden ledge and into the abyss. Tallentyre gave her a little shove across the doorsill. She moved away, stooping dejectedly in her clumsy armor, and her glowing lamp showed her the direction of the down trail. Another moment, and she was lowering herself out of sight.

Alone again, Tallentyre gazed into the stars. That bright new gleam would be the incoming ship. It meant to land here. Then what? He, the port commander, could play hide-and-seek no longer. He must be on hand to receive those mutineers, to pass judgment upon them. He sighed as though in exhaustion, and said, "Damn!" all to himself, in the little bubble of air that was confined about him in this immensity of void.

Minutes later, he turned on his own lamp and began the descent.

As he scrambled, alone in the empty dark, he thought glumly about Noel, then about women in general. Womankind must be considered in this whole great Martian adventure. It couldn't be all a stag party. Sooner or later, the feminine angle would have to be introduced, made room for. What then? Would women help or hinder, simplify or complicate? Would women even trust themselves in those danger-ridden rocketships?

Engineer Dague of Number Forty-Five stared blankly at the stowaway whom the spacehands had just dragged from hiding. "You, Ethel!"

"Me," she replied ungrammatically, and smiled her sauciest. "I told you that I'd follow you. It's Mars or bust, right beside you, darling."

"You know that it's more than an even chance of bust."

"Then we'll bust together!"

As if in acceptance of that proposition, the ship exploded around them like a shell. Poppy fire bloomed briefly in requiem.

Nobody challenged the port commander as he strode across the landing field and let himself through the lock-panel. He paused in the hall to unship his helmet. At once he heard a hub-bub of voices. Noel Crispin's troubled soprano dominated them for an instant.

"I found him, by a hunch—he was up at the observatory. I tried to signal to him that everything was all right, and to come back, but for a moment I thought he'd kill me. Then he almost pushed me down the rock."

"He thought you were hunting him," rejoined the growl of Inspector Baynes. "I say once more, you ought to have spoken up and cleared him when he asked you to."

"Never mind scolding her, Inspector," chimed in Ernie Moessner, as authoritatively as though he were the chairman of the World League instead of a simple mechanic. "She's a woman, and women have a way of changing their minds. The thing is to find Major Tallentyre before something happens to him."

"I'm here," called the man they were seeking, and walked into the office. The four searchers crowded around him, but he silenced their questions with a quick gesture.

"A ship's coming into port," he announced crisply. "From Mars. Prepare to help it to land."

They all gasped at that, and their surprised exclamations overlapped each other.

"A ship . . . From Mars . . . Coming back!" Tallentyre's pose of official sternness forsook him.

"The fools," he groaned. "Oh, the utter fools! To turn around in space and come back here—mutiny! I'll have to put them under arrest, send them to Earth, maybe kill some of them if they resist. And all the time maybe they're only showing good sense in not fighting nature."

Noel's strong little fingers dug into his shoulder, as though she was holding together his crumbling resolve. His own big hand went up to close upon hers. Then, once more the commander, he spoke into the house microphone.

"Attention, machine shop!" he rasped. "Stand by to help approaching craft into port." To Dunlap and Baynes he said. "There's something for you to do. Arrest the crew as soon as it disembarks."

The two policemen nodded. They were good men of their trade, hardened to arresting and subduing law-breakers. Zipping tight their loosened space-overalls and once more donning their helmets, they tramped out. Moessner followed.

Tallentyre and Noel gazed through the window. The craft was settling down outside. Tallentyre could not make out its number, for it seemed to be mended and patched all over in a way he did not remember, as he checked over the ships in his mind. From many tiny nozzles in the metal face of the landing field came the strong gush of steamy vapor. High-pressure gas jets, to break the descent of the ship. It paused, danced overhead like a ball on a fountain spray, then came gently to rest. A moment later the lock-panel opened and two space-overalled figures emerged. The officers were hurrying toward them, hands on weapons. The four men came together, formed a single party, and passed slantwise across the field, out of range of the window.

Tallentyre sighed. Noel patted his shoulder. After a moment, metal shoes rang flatly in the vestibule. The door opened. Four men came in, tugging at their helmets.

A pudgy man disclosed his face first. He was ruddy and bearded, his sun-mottled face grinning. "Major Tallentyre, sir," he boomed, "I don't know whether you remember me or not. I'm Waddell, spacehand, first-class. Acting skipper of . . ."

"You're neither," interrupted Tallentyre. "I put you under arrest, Waddell. Why didn't you go on to Mars?"

Waddell looked blank. Then the grin reappeared and widened. "Because I'd been there once, sir."

Tallentyre felt himself stumble. Noel's hands helped him to a chair and to sit down. He listened, comprehending by degrees.

"Yes, sir. Number Six, that ship was. There's a colony there now, getting ready to gather up the last bunch that came through. You remember the orders—orbital speed, and land on Diemos. Photograph maps of Mars made from there. It worked perfectly. With the help of telephoto lenses we had regular air-maps of the planet.

"There aren't any canals, sir. But there is vegetation, lots of it. Spiny growths like cacti, and tougher'n rubber. But the pith of some of 'em makes a flour we can eat.

"Most important, they throw off oxygen. There's damn little air on Mars, but what there is is mostly oxygen. No trick at all to blow it into the ships—into the dome we set up from hull plates. And—there's oil there, Major! Fuel!

"Now with that there," Waddell's face split in a broad grin, "and a gang of men that were all hard-boiled technicians, it wasn't much of a trick to set up some of the auxiliary-power Diesels for power."

He stopped for a while, and looked at Tallentyre's seamed face. "Been a damned tough life you've had here, hasn't it? Sending men out in those firecrackers.

"Well, that's gone too." His hand dipped into his tunic pocket to come out with a nodule of blue-silvery metal. He tossed it to Tallentyre. "That's the answer. That's why our ships went through—and the others blew their tubes. We had something to work on that you birds didn't. Tubes that had been *proven*. The metal changes in the tubes, under the long, heavy firing. The alloy shifts. If it crystallizes that way—you land. There's another modification though. If it crystallizes that other way—you blow. That other way is catalytic on the hydrogen, that's the trouble. The fuel's all right. It's the metal. If those cockeyed crystals form—they catalyze the burning. It doesn't burn then, it blows. You get a flash-back, a sort of special explosion wave that sets off the whole tank.

"We found out how to make those crystals every time, controlled. Old Six's tubes were torn out, and the new ones put in. She rode back to Luna here as smooth as an engineer's theory. Somebody had to come through. We need more men out there. Grayson's trying to set a station on Deimos. His figures look right, and he thinks he can make Callisto."

"Callisto!" Noel's hand left Tallentyre's shoulder, crept around him. Her arm hugged his body. Still sitting, he leaned against her as though to find rest.

This, he knew in his heart, was the beginning of the triumph. Men could go—men had gone—to Mars and back. The labors and the sorrows had not been in vain. Hadn't Waddell brought back the secret—the secret men on Earth couldn't learn—that made fleets possible? Wasn't Grayson, there on Mars, already looking on, beyond the asteroids to Jupiter . . .?

The officers had taken off their helmets again. Tallentyre turned and smiled at them. "Sorry, gentlemen," he said. "It's a dry haul for you this time. Why don't you go back to Earth—take Waddell here with you to make his report to the Board—and . . ."

"Hey," Waddell interrupted, "nothing doing. That ship out there is O.K. right now for the trip back home—Mars, I mean. Gimme some *moessnerol* and we'll hop that hole like a frog-puddle. I'm going back there.

"And I wouldn't ride in one of those ships just out from Earth now. That's the only ship in the System I'd trust to ride anyway. Give him the metal samples, and the books and notes Grayson and Hudson fixed up. They said it's all there. I'm no metallurgist—just a spacehand, first-class."

Tallentyre shook his head. A tight little grin tucked in the corners of his mouth. "I'm ordering you to Earth, Waddell. You make that report in person for three reasons; they need to see a man that's been to Mars and back. It will give them courage again. We'll fix the tubes on the ship that takes you back. And—you'll be taking my resignation."

"But the ship!" Waddell protested. "If it doesn't go today, sir, Mars'll get away from us for nearly two years!"

Tallentyre rose from his chair. He looked smug. "Oh, the ship will start today. But I'll command. *I'm* going to Mars for a change. And perhaps . . ."

He broke off and looked at Noel. Her face became radiant. She whirled about as tears brimmed her eyes, but her words were a song.

"I'll start packing," she said. "This can't be a stag party forever!"

OVER THE TOP

by Lester del Rey

Some of the stories in this compilation have the early steps of the exploration of space as it might have happened, but didn't. Though his one still might happen, at least as far as how the first man sent to Mars was selected, and why. Of course, a female short person would be even lighter . . .

★☄★

THE SKY WAS LOUSY with stars—nasty little pinpoints of cold hostility that had neither the remoteness of space nor the friendly warmth of Earth. They didn't twinkle honestly, but tittered and snickered down. And there wasn't even one moon. Dave Mannen knew better, but his eyes looked for the low scudding forms of Deimos and Phobos because of all the romanticists who'd written of them. They were up there all right, but only cold rocks, too small to see.

Rocks in the sky, and rocks in his head—not to

mention the lump on the back of his skull. He ran tense fingers over his wiry black hair until he found the swelling, and winced. With better luck, he'd have had every inch of his three-foot body mashed to jelly, instead of that, though. Blast Mars!

He flipped the searchlight on and looked out, but the view hadn't improved any. It was nothing but a drab plain of tarnished reddish sand, chucked about in ridiculous potholes, running out beyond the light without change. The stringy ropes of plantlike stuff had decided to clump into balls during the night, but their bilious green still had a clabbered appearance, like the result of a three days' binge. There was a thin rime of frost over them, catching the light in little wicked sparks. That was probably significant data; it would prove that there was more water in the air than the scientists had figured, even with revised calculations from the twenty-four-inch lunar refractor.

But that was normal enough. The bright boys got together with their hundred-ton electronic slipsticks and brought forth all manner of results; after that, they had to send someone out to die here and there before they found why the sticks had slipped. Like Dave. Sure, the refractory tube linings were good for twenty-four hours of continual blast—tested under the most rigorous lab conditions, even tried on a couple of Moon hops.

So naturally, with Unitech's billionaire backer and new power-handling methods giving them the idea of beating the Services to Mars—no need to stop on the Moon even, they were that good—they didn't include spare linings. They'd have had to leave out some of their fancy radar junk and wait for results until the rocket returned.

Well, the tubes had been good. It was only after three hours of blasting, total, when he was braking down for Mars, that they began pitting. Then they'd held up after a fashion until there was only forty feet of free fall—about the same as fifteen on Earth. The ship hadn't been damaged, had even landed on her tripod legs, and the radar stuff had come through fine. The only trouble was that Dave had no return ticket. There was food for six months, water for more by condensing and reusing; but the clicking of the air machine wouldn't let him forget his supply of breathing material was being emptied, a trickle at a time. And there was only enough there for three weeks, at the outside. After that, curtains.

Of course, if the bright boys' plans had worked, he could live on compressed air drawn from outside by the airlock pumps. Too bad the landing had sprung them just enough so they could barely hold their own and keep him from losing air if he decided to go outside. A lot of things were too bad.

But at least the radar was working fine. He couldn't breathe it or take off with it, but the crystal amplifiers would have taken even a free fall all the way from mid-space. He cut the power on, fiddling until he found the Lunar broadcast from Earth. It had a squiggly sound, but most of the words come through on the begacycle band. There was something about a fool kid who'd sneaked into a plane and got off the ground somehow, leaving a hundred honest pilots trying to kill themselves in getting him down. People could kill each other by the millions, but they'd go all out to save one spectacular useless life, as usual.

Then it came: "No word from the United Technical Foundation rocket, now fourteen hours overdue in reporting. Foundation men have given up hope, and feel that Mannen must have died in space from unknown causes, leaving the rocket to coast past Mars unmanned. Any violent crash would have tripped automatic signalers, and there was no word of trouble from Mannen—"

There was more, though less than on the kid. One rocket had been tried two years before, and gone wide because the tubes blew before reversal; the world had heard the clicking of Morse code right to the end, then. This failure was only a secondhand novelty, without anything new to gush over. Well, let them wonder. If they wanted to know what had happened, let 'em come and find out. There'd be no pretty last words from him.

Dave listened a moment longer, as the announcer picked up the latest rift in the supposedly refurbished United Nations, then cut off in disgust. The Atlantic Nations were as determined as Russia, and both had bombs now. If they wanted to blast themselves out of existence, maybe it was a good thing. Mars was a stinking world, but at least it had died quietly, instead of raising all that fuss.

Why worry about them? They'd never done him any favors. He'd been gypped all along. With a grade-A brain and a matinee idol's face, he'd been given a three-foot body and the brilliant future of a circus freak—the kind the crowd laughed at, rather than looked at in awe. His only chance had come when Unitech was building the ship, before they knew how much power they had, and figured on saving weight by designing it for a midget and a consequently smaller supply of air, water, and food. Even then, after he'd seen the ad, he'd had to fight his way into position through days of grueling tests. They hadn't tossed anything in his lap.

It had looked like the big chance, then. Fame and statues they could keep, but the book and endorsement rights would have put him where he could look down and laugh at the six-footers. And the guys with the electronic brains had cheated him out of it.

Let them whistle for their radar signals. Let them blow themselves to bits playing soldier. It was none of his worry now.

He clumped down from the observatory tip into his tiny quarters, swallowed a couple of barbiturates, and crawled into his sleeping cushions. Three weeks to go, and not even a bottle of whiskey on the ship. He cursed in disgust, turned over, and let sleep creep up on him.

It was inevitable that he'd go outside, of course. Three days of nothing but sitting, standing up, and sleeping was too much. Dave let the pumps suck at the air in the lock, zipping down his helmet over the soft rubber seal, tested his equipment, and waited until the pressure stood about even, outside and in. Then he opened the outer lock, tossed down the plastic ramp, and stepped out. He'd got used to the low gravity while still aboard, and paid no attention to it.

The tripod had dug into the sand, but the platform feet had kept the tubes open, and Dave swore at them softly. They looked good—except where part of one lining hung out in shreds. And with lining replacements, they'd be good—the blast had been cut off before the tubes themselves were harmed. He turned his back on the ship finally and faced out to the shockingly near horizon.

This, according to the stories, was supposed to be man's high moment—the first living human to touch the soil outside his own world and its useless satellite. The lock opened, and out stepped the hero—dying in pride with man's triumph and conquest of space! Dave pushed the rubbery flap of his helmet back against his lips, opened the orifice, and spat on the ground. If this was an experience, so was last year's stale beer.

There wasn't even a "canal" within fifty miles of him. He regretted that, in a way, since finding out what made the streaks would have killed time. He'd seen them as he approached, and there was no illusion to them—as the lunar scope had proved before. But they definitely weren't water ditches, anyhow. There'd been no chance to pick his landing site, and he'd have to get along without them.

It didn't leave much to explore. The ropes of vegetation were stretched out now, holding up loops of green fuzz to the sun, but there seemed to be no variation of species to break up the pattern. Probably a grove of trees on Earth would look the same to a mythical Martian. Possibly they represented six million and seven varieties. But Dave couldn't see it. The only point of interest was the way they wiggled their fuzz back and forth, and that soon grew monotonous.

Then his foot squeaked up at him, winding up in a gurgle. He jumped a good six feet up in surprise, and the squeak came again in the middle of his leap, making him stumble as he landed. But his eyes focused finally on a dull brownish lump fastened to his boot. It looked something like a circular cluster of a dozen pine cones, with fuzz all over, but there were little leglike members coming out of it—a dozen of them that went into rapid motion as he looked.

"Queeklrle," the thing repeated, sending the sound up through the denser air in his suit. It scrambled up briskly, coming to a stop over his supply kit and fumbling hurriedly. "Queeklrle!"

Oddly, there was no menace in it, probably because it was anything but a bug-eyed monster; there were no signs of any sensory organs. Dave blinked. It reminded him of a kitten he'd once had, somehow, before his usual luck found him and killed the little creature with some cat disease. He reacted automatically.

"Queekle yourself!" His fingers slipped into the kit and came out with a chocolate square, unpeeling the cellophane quickly. "It'll probably make you sick or kill you—but if that's what you're after, take it."

Queekle was after it, obviously. The creature took the square in its pseudopods, tucked it under its body, and relaxed, making faint gobbling sounds. For a second, it was silent, but then it squeaked again, sharper this time. "Queeklrle!"

Dave fed it two more of the squares before the creature seemed satisfied, and began climbing back down, leaving the nuts in the chocolate neatly piled on the ground behind it. Then Queekle went scooting off into the vegetation. Dave grimaced; its gratitude was practically human.

"Nuts to you, too," he muttered, kicking the pile of peanuts aside. But it proved at least that men had never been there before—humans were almost as fond of exterminating other life as they were of killing off their own kind.

He shrugged, and swung off toward the horizon at random in a loose, loping stride. After the cramped quarters of the ship, running felt good. He went on without purpose for an hour or more, until his muscles began protesting. Then he dug out his water bottle, pushed the tube through the helmet orifice, and drank briefly. Everything around him was the same as it had been near the ship, except for a small cluster of the plants that had dull red fuzz instead of green; he'd noticed them before, but couldn't tell whether they were one stage of the same plant or a different species. He didn't really care.

In any event, going farther was purposeless. He'd been looking for another Queekle casually, but had seen none. And on the return trip, he studied the ground under the fuzz plants more carefully, but there was nothing to see. There wasn't even a wind to break up the monotony, and he clumped up to the ramp of the ship as bored as he had left it. Maybe it was just as well his air supply was low, if this was all Mars had to offer.

Dave pulled up the ramp and spun the outer lock closed, blinking in the gloom, until the lights snapped on as the airlock sealed. He watched the pressure gauge rise to ten pounds, normal for the ship, and reached for the inner lock. Then he jerked back, staring at the floor.

Queekle was there, and had brought along part of Mars. Now its squeaks came out in a steady stream as the inner seal opened. And in front of it, fifteen or twenty of the plant things went into abrupt motion, moving aside to form a narrow lane through which the creature went rapidly on into the ship. Dave followed, shaking his head. Apparently, there was no way of being sure about anything here. Plants that stood steady on their roots outside could move about at will, it seemed—and to what was evidently a command.

The fool beast! Apparently the warmth of the ship had looked good to it, and it was all set to take up housekeeping—in an atmosphere that was at least a hundred times too dense for it. Dave started up the narrow steps to his quarters, hesitated, and cursed. It still reminded him of the kitten, moving around in exploratory circles. He came back down and made a dive for it.

Queekle let out a series of squeals as Dave tossed it back into the airlock and closed the inner seal. Its squeaks died down as the pressure was pumped back and the outer seal opened, though, and were inaudible by the time he moved back up the ladder. He grumbled to himself half-heartedly. That's what came of feeding the thing—it decided to move in and own him.

But he felt better as he downed what passed for supper. The lift lasted for an hour or so afterward—and then left him feeling more cramped and disgusted than ever as he sat staring at the walls of his tiny room. There wasn't even a book to read, aside from the typed manual for general care of the ship, and he'd read that often enough already.

Finally, he gave up in disgust and went up to the observatory tip and cut on the radar. Maybe his death notices would be more interesting tonight.

They weren't. They were carrying speculations about

what had happened to him—none of which included any hint that the bright boys could have made an error. They'd even figured out whether Mars might have captured the ship as a satellite and decided against it. But the news was losing interest, obviously, and he could tell where it had been padded out from the general broadcast to give the Lunar men more coverage—apparently on the theory that anyone as far out as the Moon would be more interested in the subject. They'd added one new touch, though!

"It seems obvious that further study of space conditions beyond the gravitic or magnetic field of Earth is needed. The Navy announced that its new rocket, designed to reach Mars next year, will be changed for use as a deep-space laboratory on tentative exploratory trips before going further. United Technical Foundation has abandoned all further plans for interplanetary research, at least for the moment."

And that was that. They turned the microphone over to international affairs then, and Dave frowned. Even to him, it was obvious that the amount of words used had no relation to the facts covered. Already they were beginning to clamp down the lid, and that meant things were heading toward a crisis again. The sudden outbreak of the new and violent plague in China four years before had brought an end to the former crisis, as all nations pitched in through altruism or sheer self-interest, and were forced to work together. But that hadn't lasted; they'd found a cure after nearly two million deaths, and there had been nothing to hold the suddenly created cooperation of the powers. Maybe if they had new channels for their energies, such as the planets—

But it wouldn't wash. The Atlantic Nations would have taken over Mars on the strength of his landing and return, and they were in the lead if another ship should be sent. They'd gobble up the planets as they had taken the Moon, and the other powers would simply have more fuel to feed their resentments and bring things to a head.

Dave frowned more deeply as the announcer went on. There were the usual planted hints from officials that everything was fine for the Atlantic Powers—but they weren't usual. They actually sounded super-confident— arrogantly so. And there was one brief mention of a conference in Washington, but it was the key. Two of the names were evidence in full. Someone had actually found a way to make the lithium bomb work, and—

Dave cut off the radar as it hit him. It was all the human race needed—a chance to use what could turn into a self-sustaining chain reaction. Man had finally discovered a way to blow up his planet.

He looked up toward the speck that was Earth, with the tiny spot showing the Moon beside it. Behind him, the air machine clicked busily, metering out oxygen. Two and a half weeks. Dave looked down at that, then. Well, it might be long enough, though it probably wouldn't. But he had that much time for certain. He wondered if the really bright boys expected as much for themselves. Or was it only because he wasn't in the thick of a complacent humanity, and had time for thinking, that he could realize what was coming?

He slapped the air machine dully, and looked up at the Earth again. The fools! They'd asked for it; let them take their medicine now. They liked war better than eugenics, nuclear physics better than the science that could have found his trouble and set his glands straight to give him the body he should have had. Let them stew in their own juice.

He found the bottle of sleeping tablets and shook it. But only specks of powder fell out. That was gone, too. They couldn't get anything right. No whiskey, no cigarettes that might use up the precious air, no more amytal. Earth was reaching out for him, denying him the distraction of a sedative, just as she was denying herself a safe and impersonal contest for her clash of wills.

He threw the bottle onto the floor and went down to the airlock. Queekle was there—the faint sounds of scratching proved that. And it came in as soon as the inner seal opened, squeaking contentedly, with its plants moving slowly behind it. They'd added a new feature—a mess of rubbish curled up in the tendrils of the vines, mixed sand, and dead plant forms.

"Make yourself at home," Dave told the creature needlessly. "It's all yours, and when I run down to the gasping point, I'll leave the locks open and the power on for the fluorescents. Somebody might as well get some good out of the human race. And don't worry about using up my air—I'll be better off without it, probably."

"Queeklrle." It wasn't a very brilliant conversation, but it had to do.

Dave watched Queekle assemble the plants on top of the converter shield. The bright boys had done fine, there—they'd learned to chain radiation and neutrons with a thin wall of metal and an intangible linkage of forces. The result made an excellent field for the vines, and Queekle scooted about, making sure the loads of dirt were spread out and its charges arranged comfortably, to suit it. It looked intelligent—but so would the behavior of ants. If the pressure inside the ship bothered the creature, there was no sign of it.

"Queeklrle," it announced finally, and turned toward Dave. He let it follow him up the steps, found some chocolate, and offered it to the pseudopods. But Queekle wasn't hungry. Nor would the thing accept water, beyond touching it and brushing a drop over its fuzzy surface.

It squatted on the floor until Dave flopped down on the cushions, then tried to climb up beside him. He reached down, surprised to feel the fuzz give way instantly to a hard surface underneath, and lifted it up beside him. Queekle was neither cold nor warm; probably all Martian life had developed excellent insulation, and perhaps the ability to suck water out of the almost dehydrated atmosphere and then retain it.

For a second, Dave remembered the old tales of vampire beasts, but he rejected them at once. When you come down to it, most of the animal life wasn't too bad— not nearly as bad as man had pictured it to justify his own superiority. And Queekle seemed content to lie there, making soft monotonous little squeaks and letting it go at that.

Surprisingly, sleep came easily.

Dave stayed away from the ship most of the next two days, moving aimlessly, but working his energy out in pure muscular exertion. It helped, enough to keep him away from the radar. He found tongs and stripped the lining from the tubes, and that helped more, because it occupied his mind as well as his muscles. But it was only a temporary expedient, and not good enough for even the two remaining weeks. He started out the next day, went a few miles, and came back. For a while then, he watched the plants that were thriving unbelievably on the converter shield.

Queekle was busy among them, nipping off something here and there and pushing it underneath where its mouth was. Dave tasted one of the buds, gagged, and spat it out; the thing smelled almost like an Earth plant, but combined all the quintessence of sour and bitter with something that was outside his experience. Queekle, he'd found, didn't care for chocolate—only the sugar in it; the rest was ejected later in a hard lump.

And then there was nothing to do. Queekle finished its work and they squatted side by side, but with entirely different reactions; the Martian creature seemed satisfied.

Three hours later, Dave stood in the observatory again, listening to the radar. There was some music coming through at this hour—but the squiggly reception ruined that. And the news was exactly what he'd expected—a lot of detail about national things, a few quick words on some conference at the United Nations, and more on the celebration of Israel over the anniversary of beginning as an independent nation. Dave's own memories of that were dim, but some came back as he listened. The old United Nations had done a lot of wrangling over that, but it had been good for them, in a way—neither side had felt the issue offered enough chance for any direct gain to threaten war, but it kept the professional diplomats from getting quite so deeply into more dangerous grounds.

But that, like the Chinese plague, wouldn't come up again.

He cut off the radar, finally, only vaguely conscious of the fact that the rocket hadn't been mentioned. He could no longer even work up a feeling of disgust. Nothing mattered beyond his own sheer boredom, and when the air machine—

Then it hit him. There were no clicks. There had been none while he was in the tip. He jerked to the controls, saw that the meter indicated the same as it had when he was last here, and threw open the cover. Everything looked fine. There was a spark from the switch, and the motor went on when he depressed the starting button. When he released it, it went off instantly. He tried switching manually to other tanks, but while the valve moved, the machine remained silent.

The air smelled fresh, though—fresher than it had since the first day out from Earth, though a trifle drier than he'd have liked.

"Queekle!" Dave looked at the creature, watched it move nearer at his voice, as it had been doing lately. Apparently, it knew its name now, and answered with the usual squeak and gurgle.

It was the answer, of course. No wonder its plants had been thriving. They'd had all the carbon dioxide and water vapor they could use, for a change. No Earth plants could have kept the air fresh in such a limited amount of space, but Mars had taught her children efficiency through sheer necessity. And now he had six months, rather than two weeks!

Yeah, six months to do nothing but sit and wait and

watch for the blowup that might come, to tell him he was the last of his kind. Six months with nothing but a squeaking burble for conversation, except for the radar news.

He flipped it on again with an impatient slap of his hand, then reached to cut it off. But words were already coming out:

". . . Foundation will dedicate a plaque today to young Dave Mannen, the little man with more courage than most big men can hold. Andrew Buller, backer of the ill-fated Mars rocket, will be on hand to pay tribute—"

Dave kicked the slush off with his foot. They would bother with plaques at a time like this, when all he'd ever wanted was the right number of marks on United States currency. He snapped at the dials, twisting them, and grabbed for the automatic key as more circuits coupled in.

"Tell Andrew Buller and the whole Foundation to go—"

Nobody'd hear his Morse at this late stage, but at least it felt good. He tried it again, this time with some Anglo-Saxon adjectives thrown in. Queekle came over to investigate the new sounds and squeaked doubtfully. Dave dropped the key.

"Just human nonsense, Queekle. We also kick chairs when we bump into—"

"Mannen!" The radar barked it out at him. "Thank God, you got your radar fixed. This is Buller—been waiting here a week and more now. Never did believe all that folderol about it being impossible for it to be the radar at fault. *Oof,* your message still coming in and I'm getting the typescript. Good thing there's no FCC out there. Know just how you feel, though. Darned fools here. Always said they should have another rocket ready. Look, if your set is bad, don't waste it, just tell me how long you can hold out, and by Harry, we'll get another ship built and up there. How are you, what—"

He went on, his words piling up on each other as Dave went through a mixture of reactions that shouldn't have fitted any human situation. But he knew better than to build up hope. Even six months wasn't long enough—it took time to finish and test a rocket—more than he had. Air was fine, but men needed food, as well.

He hit the key again. "Two weeks' air in tanks. Staying with Martian farmer of doubtful intelligence, but his air too thin, pumps no good." The last he let fade out, ending with an abrupt cutoff of power. There was no sense in their sending out fools in half-built ships to try to rescue him. He wasn't a kid in an airplane, crying at the mess he was in, and he didn't intend to act like one. That farmer business would give them enough to chew on; they had their money's worth, and that was that.

He wasn't quite prepared for the news that came over the radar later—particularly for the things he'd been quoted as saying. For the first time it occurred to him that the other pilot, sailing off beyond Mars to die, might have said things a little different from the clicks of Morse they had broadcast. Dave tried to figure the original version of "Don't give up the ship" as a sailor might give it, and chuckled.

And at least the speculation over their official version of his Martian farmer helped to kill the boredom. In another week at the most, there'd be an end to that, too, and he'd be back out of the news. Then there'd be more long days and nights to fill somehow, before his time ran out. But for the moment, he could enjoy the antics of nearly three billion people who got more excited over one man in trouble on Mars than they would have out of half the population starving to death.

He set the radar back on the Foundation wavelength, but there was nothing there; Buller had finally run down, and not yet got his breath back. Finally, he turned back to the general broadcast on the Lunar signal. It was remarkable how man's progress had leaped ahead by decades, along with his pomposity, just because an insignificant midget was still alive on Mars. They couldn't have discovered a prettier set of half-truths about anybody than they had from the crumbs of facts he hadn't even known existed concerning his life.

Then he sobered. That was the man on the street's reaction. But the diplomats, like the tides, waited on no man. And his life made no difference to a lithium bomb. He was still going through a counterreaction when Queekle insisted it was bedtime and persuaded him to leave the radar.

After all, not a single thing had been accomplished by his fool message.

But he snapped back to the message as a new voice came on: "And here's a late flash from the United Nations headquarters. Russia has just volunteered the use of a completed rocketship for the rescue of David Mannen on Mars, and we've accepted the offer. The Russian delegation is still being cheered on the floor! Here are the details we have now. This will be a one-way trip, radar-guided by a new bomb control method—no, here's more news! It will be guided by radar and an automatic searching head that will put it down within a mile of Mannen's ship. Unmanned, it can take tremendous acceleration, and reach Mannen before another week is out! United Technical Foundation is even now trying to contact Mannen through a hookup to the big government high-frequency labs where a new type of receiver—"

It was almost eight minutes before Buller's voice came in, evidently while the man was still getting Dave's hurried message off the tape. "Mannen, you're coming in fine. Okay, those refractories—they'll be on the way to Moscow in six hours, some new type the scientists here worked out after you left. We'll send two sets this time to be sure, but they test almost twenty times as good as the others. We're still in contact with Moscow, and some details are still being worked on, but we're equipping their ship with the same type refractories. Most of the other supplies will come straight from them—"

Dave nodded. And there'd be a lot of things he'd need—he'd see to that. Things that would be supplied straight from them. Right now, everything was milk and honey, and all nations were being the fool pilots rescuing the kid in the plane, suddenly bowled over by interplanetary success. But they'd need plenty later to keep their diplomats busy—something to wrangle over and blow off steam that would be vented on important things, otherwise.

Well, the planets wouldn't be important to any nation for a long time, but they were spectacular enough. And just how was a planet claimed, if the man who landed was taken off in a ship that was a mixture of the work of two countries?

Maybe his theories were all wet, but there was no harm in the gamble. And even if the worst happened, all this might hold off the trouble long enough for colonies. Mars was still a stinking world, but it could support life if it had to.

"Queekle," he said slowly, "you're going to be the first Martian ambassador to Earth. But first, how about a little side trip to Venus on the way back, instead of going direct? That ought to drive them crazy and tangle up their interplanetary rights a little more. Well? On to Venus, or direct home to Earth?"

"Queeklrle," the Martian creature answered. It wasn't too clear, but it was obviously a lot more like a two-syllable word.

Dave nodded. "Right! Venus."

The sky was still filled with the nasty little stars he'd seen the first night on Mars, but he grinned now as he looked up, before reaching for the key again. He wouldn't have to laugh at big men, after all. He could look up at the sky and laugh at every star in it. It shouldn't be long before those snickering stars had a surprise coming to them.

KYRIE

by Poul Anderson

Two Poul Anderson stories constitutes an embarrassment of riches, but at my age, I'm hard to embarrass. This one is deservedly well-known, was nominated for the Nebula Award (and should have won, imho) and has been anthologized several times—but not lately, so if you missed it before, now's your chance! Set much farther in the future than "Third Stage," it nonetheless pointedly reminds us that things can still go wrong, and the cold, uncaring universe may require a human sacrifice—or an inhuman sacrifice.

ON A HIGH PEAK in the Lunar Carpathians stands a convent of St. Martha of Bethany. The walls are native rock; they lift dark and cragged as the mountainside itself, into a sky that is always black. As you approach from Northpole, flitting low to keep the force screens along Route Plato between you and the meteoroidal rain, you see the cross which surmounts the tower, stark athwart Earth's blue disc. No bells resound from there—not in airlessness. You may hear them inside at the canonical hours, and throughout the crypts below where machines toil to maintain a semblance of terrestrial environment. If you linger a while you will also hear them calling to requiem mass. For it has become a tradition that prayers be offered at St. Martha's for those who have perished in space; and they are more with every passing year.

This is not the work of the sisters. They minister to the sick, the needy, the crippled, the insane, all whom space has broken and cast back. Luna is full of such exiles because they can no longer endure Earth's pull or because it is feared they may be incubating a plague from some unknown planet or because men are so busy with their frontiers that they have no time to spare for the failures. The sisters wear spacesuits as often as habits, are as likely to hold a medikit as a rosary.

But they are granted some time for contemplation. At night, when for half a month the sun's glare has departed, the chapel is unshuttered and stars look down through the glaze-dome to the candles. They do not wink and their light is winter cold. One of the nuns in particular is there as often as may be, praying for her own dead. And the abbess sees to it that she can be present when the yearly mass, that she endowed before she took her vows, is sung.

Requiem aeternam dona eis, Domine, et lux
perpetua luceat eis.
Kyrie eleison, Christe eleison, Kyrie eleison.

The Supernova Sagittarii expedition comprised fifty human beings and a flame. It went the long way around from Earth orbit, stopping at Epsilon Lyrae to pick up its last member. Thence it approached its destination by stages.

This is the paradox: time and space are aspects of each other. The explosion was more than a hundred years past when noted by men on Lasthope. They were part of a generations-long effort to fathom the civilization of creatures altogether unlike us; but one night they looked up and saw a light so brilliant it cast shadows.

That wavefront would reach Earth several centuries hence. By then it would be so tenuous that nothing but another bright point would appear in the sky. Meanwhile, though, a ship overleaping the space through which light must creep could track the great star's death across time.

Suitably far off, instruments recorded what had been before the outburst: incandescence collapsing upon itself after the last nuclear fuel was burned out. A jump, and they saw what happened a century ago: convulsion, storm of quanta and neutrinos, a radiation equal to the massed hundred billion suns of this galaxy.

It faded, leaving an emptiness in heaven, and the *Raven* moved closer. Fifty light-years—fifty years—inward, she studied a shrinking fieriness in the midst of a fog which shone like lightning.

Twenty-five years later the central globe had dwindled more, the nebula had expanded and dimmed. But because the distance was now so much less, everything seemed larger and brighter. The naked eye saw a dazzle too fierce to look straight at, making the constellations

pale by contrast. Telescopes showed a blue-white spark
in the heart of an opalescent cloud delicately filamented
at the edges.

The *Raven* made ready for her final jump, to the
immediate neighborhood of the supernova.

Captain Teodor Szili went on a last-minute inspection
tour. The ship murmured around him, running at one
gravity of acceleration to reach the desired intrinsic
velocity. Power droned, regulators whickered, ventilation
systems rustled. He felt the energies quiver in his bones.
But metal surrounded him, blank and comfortless.
Viewports gave on a dragon's hoard of stars, the ghostly
arch of the Milky Way: on vacuum, cosmic rays, cold not
far above absolute zero, distance beyond imagination to
the nearest human hearthfire. He was about to take his
people where none had ever been before, into conditions
none was sure about, and that was a heavy burden on him.

He found Eloise Waggoner at her post, a cubbyhole
with intercom connections directly to the command
bridge. Music drew him, a triumphant serenity he did not
recognize. Stopping in the doorway, he saw her seated
with a small tape machine on the desk.

"What's this?" he demanded.

"Oh!" The woman (he could not think of her as a girl
though she was barely out of her teens) started. "I . . . I
was waiting for the jump."

"You were to wait at the alert."

"What have I to do?" she answered less timidly than
was her wont. "I mean, I'm not a crewman or a scientist."

"You are in the crew. Special communications
technician."

"With Lucifer. And he likes the music. He says we come closer to oneness with it than in anything else he knows about us."

Szili arched his brows. "Oneness?"

A blush went up Eloise's thin cheeks. She stared at the deck and her hands twisted together. "Maybe that isn't the right word. Peace, harmony, unity . . . God? . . . I sense what he means, but we haven't any word that fits."

"Hm. Well, you are supposed to keep him happy." The skipper regarded her with a return of the distaste he had tried to suppress. She was a decent sort, he supposed, in her gauche and inhibited way; but her looks! Scrawny, big-footed, big-nosed, pop eyes, and stringy dust-colored hair—and, to be sure, telepaths always made him uncomfortable. She said she could only read Lucifer's mind, but was that true?

No. Don't think such things. Loneliness and otherness can come near breaking you out here, without adding suspicion of your fellows.

If Eloise Waggoner was really human. She must be some kind of mutant at the very least. Whoever could communicate thought to thought with a living vortex had to be.

"What are you playing, anyhow?" Szili asked.

"Bach. The Third Brandenburg Concerto. He, Lucifer, he doesn't care for the modem stuff. I don't either."

You wouldn't, Szili decided. Aloud: "Listen, we jump in half an hour. No telling what we'll emerge in. This is the first time anyone's been close to a recent supernova. We can only be certain of so much hard radiation that we'll be dead if the screenfields give way. Otherwise we've nothing to go on except theory. And a collapsing stellar core is so unlike anything anywhere else in the universe that I'm skeptical about how good the theory is. We can't sit daydreaming. We have to prepare."

"Yes, sir." Whispering, her voice lost its usual harshness.

He stared past her, past the ophidian eyes of meters and controls, as if he could penetrate the steel beyond and look straight into space. There, he knew, floated Lucifer.

The image grew in him: a fireball twenty meters across, shimmering white, red, gold, royal blue, flames dancing like Medusa locks, cometary tail burning for a hundred meters behind, a shiningness, a glory, a piece of hell. Not the least of what troubled him was the thought of that which paced his ship.

He hugged scientific explanations to his breast, though they were little better than guesses. In the multiple star system of Epsilon Aurigae, in the gas and energy pervading the space around, things took place which no laboratory could imitate. Ball lightning on a planet was perhaps analogous, as the formation of simple organic compounds in a primordial ocean is analogous to the life which finally evolves. In Epsilon Aurigae, magnetohydrodynamics had done what chemistry did on Earth. Stable plasma vortices had appeared, had grown, had added complexity, until after millions of years they became something you must needs call an organism. It was a form of ions, nuclei and forcefields. It metabolized electrons, nucleons, X-rays; it maintained its configuration for a long lifetime; it reproduced; it thought.

But what did it think? The few telepaths who could communicate with the Aurigeans, who had first made humankind aware that the Aurigeans existed, never explained clearly. They were a queer lot themselves.

Wherefore Captain Szili said, "I want you to pass this on to him."

"Yes, sir." Eloise turned down the volume on her taper. Her eyes unfocused. Through her ears went words, and her brain (how efficient a transducer was it?) passed the meanings on out to him who loped alongside *Raven* on his own reaction drive.

"Listen, Lucifer. You have heard this often before, I know, but I want to be positive you understand in full. Your psychology must be very foreign to ours. Why did you agree to come with us? I don't know. Technician Waggoner said you were curious and adventurous. Is that the whole truth?

"No matter. In half an hour we jump. We'll come within five hundred million kilometers of the supernova. That's where your work begins. You can go where we dare not, observe what we can't, tell us more than our instruments would ever hint at. But first we have to verify we can stay in orbit around the star. This concerns you too. Dead men can't transport you home again.

"So. In order to enclose you within the jumpfield, without disrupting your body, we have to switch off the shield screens. We'll emerge in a lethal radiation zone. You must promptly retreat from the ship, because we'll start the screen generator up sixty seconds after transit. Then you must investigate the vicinity. The hazards to look for—" Szili listed them. "Those are only what we can foresee. Perhaps we'll hit other garbage we haven't predicted. If anything seems like a menace, return at once, warn us, and prepare for a jump back to here. Do you have that? Repeat."

Words jerked from Eloise. They were a correct recital; but how much was she leaving out?

"Very good." Szili hesitated. "Proceed with your concert if you like. But break it off at zero minus ten minutes and stand by."

"Yes, sir." She didn't look at him. She didn't appear to be looking anywhere in particular.

His footsteps clacked down the corridor and were lost.

—Why did he say the same things over? asked Lucifer.

"He is afraid," Eloise said.

—?—

"I guess you don't know about fear," she said.

—Can you show me? . . . No, do not. I sense it is hurtful. You must not be hurt.

"I can't be afraid anyway, when your mind is holding mine."

(Warmth filled her. Merriment was there, playing like little flames over the surface of Father-leading-her-by-the-hand-when-she-was-just-a-child-and-they-went-out-one-summer's-day-to-pick-wildflowers; over strength and gentleness and Bach and God.) Lucifer swept around the hull in an exuberant curve. Sparks danced in his wake.

—Think flowers again. Please.

She tried.

—They are like (image, as nearly as a human brain could grasp, of fountains blossoming with gamma-ray colors in the middle of light, everywhere light). But so tiny. So brief a sweetness.

"I don't understand how you can understand," she whispered.

—You understand for me. I did not have that kind of thing to love, before you came.

"But you have so much else. I try to share it, but I'm not made to realize what a star is."

—Nor I for planets. Yet ourselves may touch.

Her cheeks burned anew. The thought rolled on, interweaving its counterpoint to the marching music.

—That is why I came, do you know? For you. I am fire and air. I had not tasted the coolness of water, the patience of earth, until you showed me. You are moonlight on an ocean.

"No, don't," she said. "Please."

Puzzlement:—Why not? Does joy hurt? Are you not used to it?

"I, I guess that's right." She flung her head back. "No! Be damned if I'll feel sorry for myself!"

—Why should you? Have we not all reality to be in, and is it not full of suns and songs?

"Yes. To you. Teach me."

—If you in turn will teach me—The thought broke off. A contact remained, unspeaking, such as she imagined must often prevail among lovers.

She glowered at Motilal Mazundar's chocolate face, where the physicist stood in the doorway. "What do you want?"

He was surprised. "Only to see if everything is well with you, Miss Waggoner."

She bit her lip. He had tried harder than most aboard to be kind to her. "I'm sorry," she said. "I didn't mean to bark at you. Nerves."

"We are everyone on edge." He smiled. "Exciting though this venture is, it will be good to come home, correct?"

Home, she thought: four walls of an apartment above a banging city street. Books and television. She might present a paper at the next scientific meeting, but no one would invite her to the parties afterward.

Am I that horrible? she wondered. *I know I'm not anything to look at, but I try to be nice and interesting. Maybe I try too hard.*

—You do not with me, Lucifer said.

"You're different," she told him.

Mazundar blinked. "Beg pardon?"

"Nothing," she said in haste.

"I have wondered about an item," Mazundar said in an effort at conversation. "Presumably Lucifer will go quite near the supernova. Can you still maintain contact with him? The time dilation effect, will that not change the frequency of his thoughts too much?"

"What time dilation?" She forced a chuckle. "I'm no physicist. Only a little librarian who turned out to have a wild talent."

"You were not told? Why, I assumed everybody was. An intense gravitational field affects time just as a high velocity does. Roughly speaking, processes take place more slowly than they do in clear space. That is why light from a massive star is somewhat reddened. And our supernova core retains almost three solar masses. Furthermore, it has acquired such a density that its attraction at the surface is, ah, incredibly high. Thus, by our clocks it will take infinite time to shrink to the Schwarzschild radius; but an observer on the star itself would experience this whole shrinkage in a fairly short period."

"Schwarzschild radius? Be so good as to explain." Eloise realized that Lucifer had spoken through her.

"If I can without mathematics. You see, this mass we are to study is so great and so concentrated that no force exceeds the gravitational. Nothing can counterbalance. Therefore, the process will continue until no energy can escape. The star will have vanished out of the universe. In fact, theoretically the contraction will proceed to zero volume. Of course, as I said, that will take forever as far as we are concerned. And the theory neglects quantum-mechanical considerations which come into play toward the end. Those are still not very well understood. I hope, from this expedition, to acquire more knowledge." Mazundar shrugged. "At any rate, Miss Waggoner, I was wondering if the frequency shift involved would not prevent our friend from communicating with us when he is near the star."

"I doubt that." Still Lucifer spoke, she was his instrument and never had she known had good it was to be used by one who cared. "Telepathy is not a wave phenomenon. Since it transmits instantaneously, it cannot be. Nor does it appear limited by distance. Rather, it is a resonance. Being attuned, we two may well be able to continue thus across the entire breadth of the cosmos; and I am not aware of any material phenomenon which could interfere."

"I see." Mazundar gave her a long look. "Thank you,"

he said uncomfortably. "Ah . . . I must get to my own station. Good luck." He bustled off without stopping for an answer.

Eloise didn't notice. Her mind was become a torch and a song. "Lucifer!" she cried aloud. "Is that true?"

—I believe so. My entire people are telepaths, hence we have more knowledge of such matters than yours do. Our experience leads us to think there is no limit.

"You can always be with me? You always will?"

—If you so wish, I am gladdened.

The comet body curvetted and danced, the brain of fire laughed low.—Yes, Eloise, I would like very much to remain with you. No one else has ever—Joy. Joy. Joy.

They named you better than they knew, Lucifer, she wanted to say, and perhaps she did. *They thought it was a joke; they thought by calling you after the devil they could make you safely small like themselves. But Lucifer isn't the devil's real name. It means only Light Bearer. One Latin prayer even addresses Christ as Lucifer. Forgive me, God, I can't help remembering that. Do You mind? He isn't Christian, but I think he doesn't need to be, I think he must never have felt sin, Lucifer, Lucifer.*

She sent the music soaring for as long as she was permitted.

The ship jumped. In one shift of world line parameters she crossed twenty-five light-years to destruction.

Each knew it in his own way, save for Eloise who also lived it with Lucifer.

She felt the shock and heard the outraged metal scream, she smelled the ozone and scorch and tumbled through the infinite falling that is weightlessness. Dazed, she fumbled at the intercom. Words crackled through: ". . . unit blown . . . back EMF surge . . . how should I know how to fix the blasted thing? . . . stand by, stand by . . ." Over all hooted the emergency siren.

Terror rose in her, until she gripped the crucifix around her neck and the mind of Lucifer. Then she laughed in the pride of his might.

He had whipped clear of the ship immediately on arrival. Now he floated in the same orbit. Everywhere around, the nebula filled space with unrestful rainbows. To him, *Raven* was not the metal cylinder which human eyes would have seen, but a lambence, the shield screen reflecting a whole spectrum. Ahead lay the supernova core, tiny at this remove but alight, alight.

—Have no fears (he caressed her). I comprehend. Turbulence is extensive, so soon after the detonation. We emerged in a region where the plasma is especially dense. Unprotected for the moment before the guardian field was reestablished, your main generator outside the hull was short-circuited. But you are safe. You can make repairs. And I, I am in an ocean of energy. Never was I so alive. Come, swim these tides with me.

Captain Szili's voice yanked her back. "Waggoner! Tell that Aurigean to get busy. We've spotted a radiation source on an intercept orbit, and it may be too much for our screen." He specified coordinates. "What *is* it?"

For the first time, Eloise felt alarm in Lucifer. He curved about and streaked from the ship.

Presently, his thought came to her, no less vivid. She lacked words for the terrible splendor she viewed with him: a million-kilometer ball of ionized gas where luminance blazed and electric discharges leaped, booming through the haze around the star's exposed heart. The thing could not have made any sound, for space here was still almost a vacuum by Earth's parochial standards; but she heard it thunder and felt the fury that spat from it.

She said for him: "A mass of expelled material. It must have lost radial velocity to friction and static gradients, been drawn into a cometary orbit, held together for a while by internal potentials. As if this sun were trying yet to bring planets to birth—"

"It'll strike us before we're in shape to accelerate," Szili said, "and overload our shield. If you know any prayers, use them."

"Lucifer!" she called; for she did not want to die, when he must remain.

—I think I can deflect it enough, he told her with a grimness she had not hitherto met in him.—My own fields, to mesh with its; and free energy to drink; and an unstable configuration; yes, perhaps I can help you. But help me, Eloise. Fight by my side.

His brightness moved toward the juggernaut shape.

She felt how its chaotic electromagnetism clawed at his. She felt him tossed and torn. The pain was hers. He battled to keep his own cohesion, and the combat was hers. They locked together, Aurigean and gas cloud. The forces that shaped him grappled as arms might; he poured power from his core, hauling that vast tenuous mass with him down the magnetic torrent which streamed from the sun; he gulped atoms and thrust them backward until the jet splashed across heaven.

She sat in her cubicle, lending him what will to live and prevail she could, and beat her fists bloody on the desk.

The hours brawled past.

In the end, she could scarcely catch the message that flickered out of his exhaustion:—Victory.

"Yours," she wept.

—Ours.

Through instruments, men saw the luminous death pass them by. A cheer lifted.

"Come back," Eloise begged.

—I cannot. I am too spent. We are merged, the cloud and I, and are tumbling in toward the star. (Like a hurt hand reaching forth to comfort her:) Do not be afraid for me. As we get closer, I will draw fresh strength from its glow, fresh substance from the nebula. I will need a while to spiral out against that pull. But how can I fail to come back to you, Eloise? Wait for me. Rest. Sleep.

Her shipmates led her to sickbay. Lucifer sent her dreams of fire flowers and mirth and the suns that were his home.

But she woke at last, screaming. The medic had to put her under heavy sedation.

He had not really understood what it would mean to confront something so violent that space and time themselves were twisted thereby.

His speed increased appallingly. That was in his own measure; from *Raven* they saw him fall through several days.

The properties of matter were changed. He could not push hard enough or fast enough to escape.

Radiation, stripped nuclei, particles born and destroyed and born again, sleeted and shouted through him. His substance was peeled away, layer by layer. The supernova core was a white delirium before him. It shrank as he approached, ever smaller, denser, so brilliant that brilliance ceased to have meaning. Finally, the gravitational forces laid their full grip upon him.

—Eloise! he shrieked in the agony of his disintegration.—Oh, Eloise, help me!

The star swallowed him up. He was stretched infinitely long, compressed infinitely thin, and vanished with it from existence.

The ship prowled the farther reaches. Much might yet be learned.

Captain Szili visited Eloise in sickbay. Physically she was recovering.

"I'd call him a man," he declared through the machine mumble, "except that's not praise enough. We weren't even his kin, and he died to save us."

She regarded him from eyes more dry than seemed natural. He could just make out her answer. "He is a man. Doesn't he have an immortal soul too?"

"Well, uh, yes, if you believe in souls, yes, I'd agree."

She shook her head. "But why can't he go to his rest?"

He glanced about for the medic and found they were alone in the narrow metal room. "What do you mean?" He made himself pat her hand. "I know, he was a good friend of yours. Still, his must have been a merciful death. Quick, clean; I wouldn't mind going out like that."

"For him . . . yes, I suppose so. It has to be. But—"

She could not continue. Suddenly she covered her ears. "Stop! Please!"

Szili made soothing noises and left. In the corridor, he encountered Mazundar. "How is she?" the physicist asked.

The captain scowled. "Not good. I hope she doesn't crack entirely before we can get her to a psychiatrist."

"Why, what is wrong?"

"She thinks she can hear him."

Mazundar smote fist into palm. "I hoped otherwise," he breathed.

Szili braced himself and waited.

"She does," Mazundar said. "Obviously she does."

"But that's impossible! He's dead!"

"Remember the time dilation," Mazundar replied. "He fell from the sky and perished swiftly, yes. But in supernova time. Not the same as ours. To us, the final stellar collapse takes an infinite number of years. And telepathy has no distance limits." The physicist started walking fast away from that cabin. "He will always be with her."

AUTHORS' BIOGRAPHIES

Poul Anderson (1926-2001) was one of the most prolific and popular writers in science fiction. He won the Hugo Award seven times and the Nebula Award three times, as well as many other awards, notably including the Grand Master Award of the Science Fiction Writers of America for a lifetime of distinguished achievement. With a degree in physics, and a wide knowledge of other fields of science, he was noted for building stories on a solid foundation of real science, as well as for being one of the most skilled creators of fast-paced adventure stories. He was author of more than a hundred science fiction and fantasy novels and story collections, and several hundred short stories, as well as historical novels, mysteries and non-fiction books. He wrote several series, notably the Technic Civilization novels and stories, the Psychotechnic League series, the *Harvest of Stars* novels, and his Time Patrol series, In my not-all-that-humble opinion all novels and stories in his gigantic opus are worth seeking out, but then, they were written by Poul Anderson, so that really goes without saying. Which is why this story leads off the book, and another, much less obscure Anderson gem closes it.

★ ★ ★

Fredric Brown (1906-1972) was a writer with towering reputations in both the science fiction and mystery fields. After writing many short stories for the mystery pulps of the 1940s, he won the Edgar Award of the Mystery Writers of America for his first mystery novel, *The Fabulous Clipjoint* in 1947. He also wrote many stories for the SF magazines of the 1940s, and was a fixture of *Astounding Science-Fiction*'s "Golden Age." He was a master craftsman in both fields, with a wide range of solid characterization, a lean hard-boiled style, and a sneaky touch of humor. In particular, he was the unchallenged master of the short-short story, a story so short it would take up only one or two pages, yet would have a tightly controlled plot, and usually a surprise ending—often not a happy one for the characters. His sardonic sense of humor was also displayed at greater length in such darkly humorous SF novels as *What Mad Universe* and *Martians, Go Home*, but he also wrote deadly serious novels such as *The Lights in the Sky Are Stars* and *The Mind Thing*. His short story, "Arena," was adapted into one of *Star Trek*'s first season episodes (though there was an episode of *The Outer Limits* a couple of years earlier which had a suspicious resemblance to the same story, yet gave no credit to Brown). He inserted into "Knock," a story of more usual length a story which has become known as the shortest horror story ever told: "The last man on Earth sat in a room. There was a knock on the door." While the pair of short-short stories which follow are not *that* brief (though they certainly are far pithier than this biography), each has its own sharp concluding punch.

★ ★ ★

Tony Daniel is the author of seven science fiction and fantasy books, the latest of which are the first two novels in the Wulf Saga, *The Dragon Hammer* and *The Amber Arrow*. The total includes the award-winning short story collection, *The Robot's Twilight Companion*. He also collaborated with David Drake on the novels *The Heretic*, and its sequel, *The Savior*, new novels in the popular military science fiction series, *The General*. His story "Life on the Moon," was a Hugo finalist and also won the *Asimov's* Reader's Choice Award. Daniel's short fiction has been much anthologized and has been collected in multiple year's best anthologies. He has also co-written screenplays for SyFy Channel horror movies, and during the early 2000s was the writer and director of numerous audio dramas for the critically-acclaimed SCIFI.COM's Seeing Ear Theater. Born in Alabama, Daniel has lived in St. Louis, Los Angeles, Seattle, Prague, and New York City. He is now an editor at Baen Books and lives in Wake Forest, North Carolina with his wife and two children.

★ ★ ★

Lester del Rey (1915-1993) was a science fiction Grand Master (the Science Fiction Writers of America made him one officially) and a man of multiple talents—a writer, not just of SF and fantasy, but of many other forms of more mundane fiction, as well as many nonfiction books. He was editor of many SF magazines, from the early 1950s to the late 1960s, an authors' agent, a book reviewer, and probably most influentially, an editor, with his wife, Judy-Lynn del Rey, for over two decades at Del Rey Books. (Incidentally, Del Rey Books, one of the strongest SF lines in the late 20th century, was named for the lady, not Lester.) He was also a sheet metal worker during WWII, but I can't say what influence that may have had on his writing. In person, he was a superb, if contentious, speaker, an energetic debater, and if he didn't have the entire history of SF and fantasy stored in his head, anything left out was probably unimportant. He also wrote either the third or fourth SF novel I ever read, while I was in the third grade: *Marooned on Mars*, helping to seal my fate as an SF addict. That you're reading this book is at least partly his fault—and in more ways than one. That novel was one of the early titles in the celebrated Winston line of hardcover SF juveniles, a trail-blazing publishing program at a time when established publishers were afraid to take a chance on that crazy Buck Rogers stuff, and which Mr. del Rey had much more to do with than did the two prestigious editors listed on the books' jacket flaps.) The man was diminutive in physical stature, but a titan in his influence on SF and fantasy, and I wonder how much of a self-portrait he made of the hero in the story which appeared here.

★ ★ ★

David Drake, author of the best-selling *Hammer's*

Slammers future mercenary series, is often referred to as the Dean of military science fiction, but is much more versatile than that label might suggest, as shown by his epic fantasy series that began with *Lord of the Isles* (Tor), and his equally popular Republic of Cinnabar Navy series of space operas (Baen) starring the indefatigable team of Leary and Mundy, whose latest exploit, starring a new added character, is *Though Hell Should Bar the Way*. His latest novel is *The Spark* (Baen), and its sequel *The Storm*, will be a 2019 release. He lives near Chapel Hill, NC, with his family.

★ ★ ★

James E. Gunn (b. 1923) is a man of many hats: science fiction and fantasy writer (of course), academic, editor, and a Grand Master of Science Fiction, pronounced so by the Science Fiction and Fantasy Writers of America in 2007, the title making him a member of a small select club that includes other names you may have come across, such as Robert A. Heinlein, Arthur C. Clarke, and Isaac Asimov, to name three Grand Masters. A native Kansan from a family of editors and publishers, he served three years in the U.S. Navy during WWII, then took a B.S. at the University of Kansas, then an M.A. in English at Northwestern in 1951, and he may be the only person who had his Master's thesis, which was a critical appraisal of sf, published in a science fiction pulp as an article. Selling his first stories in 1948 under the pseudonym of "Edwin James" (his middle initial stands for "Edwin"), he has subsequently published nearly 100 stories, as well as writing 28 books, fiction and nonfiction, and editing 10 more. His novels began with *Star Bridge* (in collaboration with Jack Williamson) and *This Fortress World*, followed by *The Joy Makers*, *The Immortals* (which became a TV movie and series, *The Immortal*), *The Listeners*, and more. His *Alternate Worlds: The Illustrated History of Science Fiction* received a special award from the 1976 World SF Convention, and a 1976 *Locus* Award. A later nonfiction book, *Isaac Asimov: The Foundations of Science Fiction* won the 1983 Hugo for Best Non-Fiction Book. His series of anthologies, *The Road to Science Fiction*, originally six volumes, now expanded to eight, which combines classic stories (going back to Gilgamesh, the original pulp hero) with a running history of the field, and is still in print 41 years after the first volume's publication. He is a past president of the Science Fiction and Fantasy Writers of America and of the Science Fiction Research Association, as well as being a professor emeritus at the University of Kansas, where he is Director of the Center for the Study of Science Fiction. In 2015, he was inducted into the Science Fiction and Fantasy Hall of Fame.

With all that, it's surprising that he has had time for an impressive career writing science fiction, but he has.

★ ★ ★

Edmond Hamilton (1904-1977) was one of the most prolific contributors to *Weird Tales*, which published 79 of his stories between 1926 and 1948. Unusually for a *WT* mainstay, most of his work was science fiction (or, as the magazine tagged it initially, "weird-scientific stories") rather than fantasy, dark or otherwise He was also prolific outside the pages of *WT*, with stories in many other pulps, sometimes under pseudonyms. In the late 1940s, as interest in rip-roaring adventure SF waned, Hamilton developed a more serious style, with deeper characterizations, notably in "What's It Like Out There?" included herein, and his 1960 novel, *The Haunted Stars*.

During the 1950s, he was also a prolific writer for such D.C. comic books as *The Legion of Super-Heroes*. He continued writing into the 1970s, with stories in the SF magazines and new novels in paperback. He was a writer's writer, with a gift for exciting tales of adventure. Some critics may have felt that such tales were insignificant, but that was and is their loss. Readers should be grateful for such a good and prolific writer.

★ ★ ★

Robert A. Heinlein began his career with a competently-told, but not very striking story, "Lifeline," which gave no clue that it was the first installment of the grandest saga in the history of science fiction, his "Future History" series, but soon, more substantial and vitamin-packed landmark yarns followed in those magical years when new Heinlein stories were regularly appearing in John W. Campbell, Jr.'s *Astounding*, making it known to all what untapped potential the SF field was capable of reaching. Sometimes, there would even be more than one Heinlein story in an issue, though the originator of some of those masterpieces would be concealed under pseudonym such as Anson MacDonald and John Riverside. (True, John Riverside's byline appeared only once, in Campbell's other classic pulp, *Unknown Worlds*, rather than *Astounding*, but as long as Heinlein and Campbell were remaking the shape of science fiction, fantasy had it coming, too.)

Alas, it was much too soon to take a long pause, but, thanks to Hitler, Mussolini, and the Japanese warlords, it was utterly necessary. Heinlein's incandescent writing career had to cool down while Heinlein and several million others around the globe pitched in to put Hitler and his pals out of business. Of course, Heinlein's career resumed after the war for a bit more than four decades, bringing the classic juvenile novels, the sales to high-paying "slick" magazines, the trailblazing movie, *Destination Moon*, the *New York Times* best-sellers, and more. But "Delilah and the Space-Rigger" came early in that glorious resumption of the Future History series, with yarns such as the one which follows.

This is, of course, an inadequate introduction to a Heinlein yarn; but, then, aren't they all?

★ ★ ★

Sarah A. Hoyt won the Prometheus Award for her novel *Darkship Thieves*, published by Baen, and has also authored *Darkship Renegades* (nominated for the following year's Prometheus Award) and *A Few Good Men*, as well as *Through Fire* and *Darkship Revenge*, novels set in the same universe, as was "Angel in Flight," a story in the Baen anthology, *A Cosmic Christmas*. She has written numerous short stories and novels in science fiction, fantasy, mystery, historical novels and genre-straddling historical mysteries, many under a number of pseudonyms, and has been published—among other places—in *Analog*, *Asimov's* and *Amazing Stories*. For Baen, she has also written three books in her popular shape-shifter fantasy series, *Draw One in the Dark*, *Gentleman Takes a Chance*, and *Noah's Boy*.

Her *According to Hoyt* is one of the most outspoken and fascinating blogs on the internet, as is her FaceBook group, *Sarah's Diner*. Originally from Portugal, she lives in Colorado with her husband, two sons and "the surfeit of cats necessary to a die-hard Heinlein fan."

★ ★ ★

While many sci-fi authors write short stories and novels about space travel and space settlement, **Jeff Greason** is taking another path: opening the space frontier as an aerospace engineer, space entrepreneur and commercial space consultant. Inspired by *Star Trek*, Robert Heinlein, and Gerard O'Neill, Jeff has dedicated more than 20 years of his career to space technology development and making space travel available to civilians. He leapt from engineering next-generation computer processors at Intel to rocket engine development at Rotary Rocket. At the turn of the century, he co-founded and led XCOR Aerospace, an early commercial space transportation firm that made history with dozens of manned rocket airplane flights. He helped Congress develop regulations to govern and foster the U.S. commercial human spaceflight industry and co-founded the

Commercial Space Federation trade association. Jeff can currently be found innovating wireless-power technology and beamed-power propulsion at Electric Sky, and promoting smart investment in propulsion and energy technologies for solar system and interstellar flight as chairman of Tau Zero Foundation. Jeff is a popular speaker on space policy and commercial markets for space, and a TIME Inventor of the Year. To add that this CalTech alumnus holds 25 U.S. patents is almost anti-climactic, but there is nothing anti-climactic about the story included herein.

★ ★ ★

William F. Jenkins (1986-1975) was a prolific and successful writer, selling stories to magazines of all sorts, from pulps like *Argosy* to the higher-paying slicks such as *Collier's* and *The Saturday Evening Post*, writing stories ranging from westerns, to mysteries, to science fiction. However, for SF he usually used the pen name of **Murray Leinster**, and he used it often. Even though SF was a less lucrative field than other categories of fiction, he enjoyed writing it (fortunately for SF readers everywhere) and wrote a great deal of it, including such classics as "Sidewise in Time," "First Contact," and "A Logic Named Joe," the last being a story you should keep in mind the next time someone repeats the canard that SF never predicted the home computer or the internet. Leinster did it (though under his real name, this time) in *Astounding Science-Fiction* in 1946! His first SF story was "The Runaway Skyscraper," published in 1919, and his last was the third of three novelizations of the *Land of the Giants* TV show in 1969.

For the length of his career, his prolificity, and his introduction of original concepts into SF, fans in the 1940s began calling him the Dean of Science Fiction, a title he richly deserved.

★ ★ ★

Larry Niven is renowned for his ingenious science fiction stories solidly based on authentic science, often of the cutting-edge variety. His *Known Space* series is one of the most popular "future history" sagas in sf and includes the epic novel *Ringworld*, one of the few novels to have won both the Hugo and Nebula awards, as well as the *Locus* and Ditmar awards, and which is recognized as a milestone in modern science fiction. Four of his shorter works have also won Hugos. Most recently, the Science Fiction and Fantasy Writers of America have presented him with the Damon Knight Memorial Grand Master Award, given for Lifetime Achievement in the field. Lest this all sounds too serious, it should be remembered that one of his most memorable short works is "Man of Steel, Woman of Kleenex," a not-quite serious essay on Superman and the problems of his having a sex life. Niven has also demonstrated a talent for creating memorable aliens, beginning with his first novel, *World of Ptaavs*, in 1966. A reason for this, Niven writes, is that, "I grew up with dogs. I live with a cat, and borrow dogs to hike with. I have passing acquaintance with raccoons and ferrets. Associating with nonhumans has certainly gained me insight into alien intelligences." While no aliens are present in this highly original story of the first expedition to a Venus realistically drawn up to Astronomers' specs, it shows Niven's talent for creating very realistic human characters is not lacking, either.

★ ★ ★

Jerry E. Pournelle (1933-2017) was the first writer to use a computer to write a novel . . . a published novel, I should add, and while that might be a historical curiosity, the novels and short stories that poured forth, not to mention ones written prior to 1977 on stone age typewriter tech. The future history series, usually known as the Falkenberg's Legion series (and one of the best is only a few pages away) alone would be a memorable reading experience (*King David's Spaceship* and *The Mercenary* are particularly recommended), but he also wrote such non-Falkenberg stories as *Exiles to Glory* and *Janissaries*, the latter novel being currently under development to be a movie, cross fingers. And his collaborations with Larry Niven—*Lucifer's Hammer*, *Footfall*, and *Fallen Angels*, to mention three—have been runaway bestsellers.

He also wrote columns and articles on the uses of home computers, particularly to write on, beginning when many in the pre-Internet era would say, "Why would I want a computer? To play games on?" And that remark about games alone sounds touchingly naïve nowadays.

James Blish once complained that sf writers would write stories about galactic empires, and didn't even know the name of their local town council rep. Not Dr. Pournelle, who has been an advisor to Sam Yorty (Democrat), Newt Gingrich (Rep-, oh you knew that) and the Reagan administration (you knew that, too). His string of degrees in psychology and political science were obviously put to good use. Closer to home, he has served as President of the Science Fiction Writers of America, and director of aNewDomain Media.

Among the awards he received were the Bronze Medal of the American Security Council, the John W. Campbell Award for Best New Writer (1973), the Prometheus Award for *Fallen Angels* (shared with collaborators Larry Niven and Michael Flynn), and that novel also won the Seiun Award for Best Foreign Novel in its Japanese translation, the Heinlein Society Award (again shared with Larry Niven and Michael Flynn), and the National Space Society Robert A. Heinlein Memorial Award for lifetime achievement in promoting the goal of a free, spacefaring civilization.

It's sad to think that no more well-constructed, controversial novels or stories will be coming from his pen, pardon me, his PC, but you only need to read the story included here for a stellar sample of why he is going to be missed.

★ ★ ★

Ross Louis Rocklin (1913-1988) who wrote most often under the semi-pseudonym of **Ross Rocklynne** was a prolific contributor to the science fiction magazines from the 1930s, where he was mainstay of *Astounding* during its "Golden Age," into the 1950s, when he frequently appeared in the newer, but equally prestigious magazine, *Galaxy*—stopped writing for a decade, then made a return to sf, even having a story, "Ching Witch," in Harlan Ellison's landmark anthology, *Again, Dangerous Visions*. And yet, his name is unknown to readers nowadays, possibly because he wrote short fiction rather than novels. (Two novels which he did write appeared complete in one issue of the pulp, *Startling Stories*, and may actually be novellas, and, in any case, never achieved book publication.) Or it might just be the fickleness of the reading public. Mothers, don't let your chillun grow up to be science fiction writers.

Bio information about Mr. Rocklin is also sparse, though I did find he was born in Ohio, and was a professional guest at the first World Science Fiction Convention in 1939. Also, he was a founder of the National Fantasy Fan Federation (the N3F), but we all make mistakes. . . .

Nearly all of Rocklynne's work must be in public domain by now, and maybe the Internet will rescue his reputation and expose the sf audience to some of his stories, which were often very good, such as "The Men and the Mirror," "Time Wants a Skeleton" (which took the cover of the issue of *Astounding* in which it appeared), "The Last Outpost," and many more.

★ ★ ★

Christopher Ruocchio is the author of The Sun Eater, a space opera fantasy series from DAW Books, as well as the

Assistant Editor at Baen Books, where he has co-edited two anthologies. He is a graduate of North Carolina State University, where a penchant for self-destructive decision-making caused him to pursue a bachelor's in English Rhetoric with a minor in Classics. An avid student of history, philosophy, and religion, Christopher has been writing since he was eight years old and sold his first book — *Empire of Silence*— at twenty-two.

Christopher lives in Raleigh, North Carolina, where he spends most of his time hunched over a keyboard writing. He may be found on both Facebook and Twitter at @TheRuocchio.

★ ★ ★

Clifford D. Simak (1904-1988) published his first SF story, "The World of the Red Sun" in 1931, and went on to become one of *Astounding's* star writers during John W. Campbell's Golden Age of Science Fiction in the 1940s, notably in the series of stories which he eventually combined into his classic novel, *City*. Other standout novels include *Time and Again, Ring Around the Sun, Time is the Simplest Thing,* and the Hugo-winning *Way Station.* Altogether, Simak won the International Fantasy Award (for *City*), three Hugo Awards, a Nebula Award, and was the third recipient of the Grand Master Award of the Science Fiction Writers of America for lifetime achievement. He also received the Bram Stoker Award for lifetime achievement from the Horror Writers Association. He was noted for stories written with a warm, pastoral feeling, though he could also turn out a chilling horror story, such as "Good Night, Mr. James," which was made into an episode of the original *Outer Limits*. His day job was newspaperman, joining the staff of the Minneapolis Star and Tribune in 1939, becoming its news editor in 1949, retiring in 1976. He once wrote that "My favorite recreation is fishing (the lazy way, lying in a boat and letting them come to me)."

★ ★ ★

Theodore Sturgeon (1918-1985) was one of the great writers of science fiction's "golden age" in the 1940s, and by the 1950s was renowned for his three-dimensional characters and highly individual style. His early works were elegantly constructed, fast-paced stories told by a wisecracking narrator, but he soon developed a fluent prose poetry of style. Another notable prose poet, Ray Bradbury, admitted the strong influence Sturgeon's writing had on his own work in the introduction he wrote for *Without Sorcery*, Sturgeon's first story collection. His now-classic novel, *More Than Human*, won the International Fantasy Award, the first of several awards (though there should have been many more). The distinguished editor and reviewer Groff Conklin once wrote, "You don't read [Sturgeon's] stories. They happen to you." (Nailed it, Mr. Conklin!) Two *Star Trek* episodes were scripted by him, and one of them, "Amok Time," was a high point of that program. He wrote over 400 short stories, all of which have now been collected in thirteen volumes published by North Atlantic Books. (Many thanks to the late Paul Williams and Noel Sturgeon for bringing this miracle to pass.) He was also the author of many unforgettable horror stories, such as "It!," "The Professor's Teddy Bear," "Farewell to Eden," and, of course, "Bianca's Hands." Not to mention the dreamlike story included here, except that it's too far ahead of nearly all sf to be *following*. Lead on, Mr. Sturgeon . . .

★ ★ ★

Manly Wade Wellman (1903-1986) was a writer's writer, selling stories to the pulps (*Weird Tales*, *Unknown*, *Startling*, *Astounding* among others), to the "slick" magazines, and to the prestigious *Magazine of Fantasy and Science Fiction*, He wrote numerous books, both fiction and nonfiction. One of the former is his time travel classic, *Twice in Time*. In the latter category are *Rebel Boast*, which was nominated for a Pulitzer Prize, and *Giant in Grey*, an acclaimed biography of his namesake, Confederate General Wade Hampton. He also wrote mysteries, westerns, historical novels, and, late in his life, still more fantasy, including new stories and novels of his two most popular characters, both named John.

One, John Thunstone, is an occult investigator and champion against supernatural evil, aided by his sword cane, whose silver blade was forged by Saint Dunstan, the patron Saint of Silversmiths.

The other, identified in the stories only as "John," though sometimes referred to as "Silver John," is another valiant champion against supernatural threats, and is probably Wellman's most enduring creation. He wanders the Appalachian hills with his silver-stringed guitar, defending the folk there against danger from both the "natural" world and the realm beyond it.

Wellman received the World Fantasy Award for his story collection *Worse Things Waiting*, and later received the World Fantasy Award for lifetime achievement. Karl Edward Wagner called him the Dean of fantasy writers.